LAST TRAIN TO Istanbul

AYŞE KULIN

Translated by John W. Baker

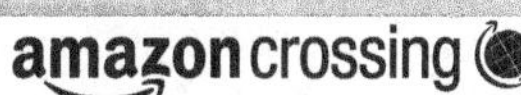

The characters and events portrayed in this book are fictitious. Any similarity to real persons, living or dead, is coincidental and not intended by the author.

Printed in the United States of America.

Last Train to Istanbul was first published in 2002 as *Nefes Nefese.* Translated from Turkish by John W. Baker. First published in English in 2006 by Everest Yayınları. Published by Amazon Crossing in 2013.

Published by Amazon Crossing
PO Box 400818
Las Vegas, NV 89140

ISBN-13: 9781477807613
ISBN-10: 1477807616
Library of Congress Control Number: 2013904883

LAST TRAIN TO Istanbul

ANKARA 1941

Even though, when leaving that morning, Macit had warned Sabiha that he would be late coming home, his good manners made him uneasy when he realized it was already past eight o'clock. He excused himself from the meeting room, went to his office, and dialed home on the black telephone with its noisy dial.

"We're having a meeting again this evening. Please don't wait for me for dinner," he said.

"Not again," said his wife exasperatedly. "For nearly three weeks, we haven't been able to have dinner together. Really, darling, hasn't anyone there got a wife or children waiting at home?"

"For God's sake, what are you going on about? The Bulgarian army is on our doorstep and you are talking about dinner!"

"How typical of women!" he said, putting the phone down.

His wife was just like his mother. The running of the house, the children's eating and bedtime, the whole family gathering around for dinner—these things were top priority for organized housewives. Atatürk's attempt to turn them into women of the world was in vain, Macit thought. Obviously, our women are only good at being mothers or housewives. And he was even beginning to have second thoughts about that. Hadn't Sabiha abandoned her motherly duties and left their daughter's upbringing to a nanny? Deep down, Macit was certainly beginning to find his wife's behavior odd.

At first he was angry, thinking maybe her distant attitude was a silent protest against his endless meetings that lasted into the early hours. What right did she have to get angry about his long hours? After all, was *he* responsible for the war? Was *he* to blame for these late nights? What if Turkey actually found itself fighting in the war? If that were to happen, which woman in their circle would even catch a glimpse of her husband's face?

But Macit knew in his heart Sabiha's attitude wasn't due to selfishness alone. She seemed on the verge of a nervous breakdown. For some time this young woman who liked going on picnics, watching horse races when the weather was fine, and playing cards on rainy days didn't seem to enjoy anything anymore. He often found his wife in bed, fast asleep, when he got home. If, when he got into bed, he put his arms around her, she would turn away. On the rare occasion they managed to go to bed at the same time, she always had an excuse to go to sleep immediately. It was obvious that she had a problem, but she had chosen the wrong time to have a nervous breakdown. How on earth could he find the time to care for her when he was inundated with work? Even if his meetings finished after midnight, Macit would still have to be back at the ministry by seven the next morning.

They were living in very unsettled times. Turkey had found herself between a rock and a hard place. On the one hand, there was Britain, who had only her own interests at heart, insisting that Turkey should be her ally; on the other, there was Germany's threatening attitude. As if that weren't enough, Russia extended an iron hand in a velvet glove to Turkey. Their interest in Kars, Ardahan, the Bosphorus, and the Dardanelles hung over them like the sword of Damocles. If Turkey chose the losing side, Russia would make her pay dearly where the Bosphorus and the Dardanelles were concerned. This nightmare had been ongoing for two years.

The First World War had taught President Inönü the cost of choosing the wrong side, and he had learned his lesson well. There was nothing he wouldn't give to know which side would be victorious this time, but no fortune-teller could possibly predict the outcome. It was up to the foreign ministry and general staff to make this prediction. Every possible contingency had been discussed, considered, and recorded during those endless meetings that dragged on into the night.

Macit was proud to be a member of the general staff. At the same time, ever since the Italians had attacked Greece, the ring of fire had been tightening, and government employees and their families were getting nervous.

The capital, Ankara, was preparing for a hot summer again. In Turkey the winters were extremely cold and snowy, and the summers were unbearably hot. It was already obvious that the approaching summer months would be hotter than hell.

About a week before, the German ambassador, Franz von Papen, had brought a personal message from Hitler to the prime minister, and the officials had waited with bated breath for the meeting to end. Macit guessed correctly the contents of Hitler's message: on the surface the letter was full of good wishes and intentions. It offered Turkey every kind of armament and help strengthening control of the Bosphorus and Dardanelles, and it promised not to put German soldiers on Turkish soil. However, if read between the lines, the letter implied that now was the time for Turkey to make up her mind, and if she didn't side with Germany she would have to suffer the consequences when the war was over and decisions were made about her waterways.

After the long meeting, Inönü said, "The Germans are telling us not to try their patience, and at any time, they could make a deal with Russia behind our backs." He went on to say, "Britain is fighting in Greece, and they've had a disaster in Libya; she is in no position to come to our aid. This is why we shouldn't risk angering the Germans. Gentlemen, we must find a way to hedge our bets."

What they were looking for was a way to play for time without saying yes or no to either side—a way of stroking their backs without aggravating them.

The morning after that long night, the prime minister invited the British ambassador to the ministry to explain Turkey's predicament. She was heading toward the most fearful days she had encountered during this Second World War. The war was like a forest fire, spreading in all directions, and both sides had expectations of Turkey.

In his office, Macit lit a cigarette, took two puffs, and stubbed it out in the crystal ashtray before returning to the meeting room. The foreign minister and the secretary general were no longer there. His assistant said, "Macit, the president has asked to see today's assessments. I have prepared the reports for you. He is waiting in his office."

Macit hurried back to his office, in the section allocated to the foreign ministry of the presidential mansion. For some months now, they had been working there so that they could instantly report to and receive instructions from Inönü. Macit took files of notes that he had updated a few hours ago from his drawer, glanced through them, and dashed off.

Inönü was sitting in a club chair behind a huge table. He looked naive—smaller and more irritated than usual—leafing through the papers his private secretary took from Macit. Looking at the pages, it was as if he were listening to the voices of foxes in his mind, but he didn't say anything. The other men sitting around the table were silent too.

Suddenly, he asked, "Have you listened to the radio today?"

"Yes, sir. Our colleagues have been listening to all the European stations. I gave our report to the secretary general a short while ago.

They haven't had a moment's rest, sir, yet they continue to listen to Bulgaria and are preparing reports every half hour."

"Our agents in Bulgaria are keeping us informed on a daily basis. However, it's still unknown if Hitler is going to move south, or move north to attack the Russians, sir," another young official said.

The young men left the room, and Macit stayed behind.

"Thanks to you," the foreign minister said, "we have been able to take every precaution to make sure the fire doesn't spread to us. Rest assured you can now go to Yalova with a clear conscience. We'll keep you informed of developments every minute."

Macit heard Inönü mutter, "I wish I knew what direction the Germans will go. Ah! If only I knew."

The Germans had reached an agreement with Bulgaria, so the Germans had become Turkey's neighbors. Inönü was terrified, not knowing Hitler's next move. Hitler's modern armaments and powerful army were just across the border. He might want to move in on Egypt through Turkey. Or he could move toward the Caucasus. No one, not even his immediate staff, knew what the next target was, so Turkey had to be prepared for every eventuality. The worst scenario would be for the Germans to reach an agreement with Russia. That would spell disaster for Turkey.

Macit waited for the men to finish reading the reports and then returned to the meeting room with the secretary general. There was another long meeting, with more reports to be read, assessed, and put together before they could be presented to Inönü. Hours later, as he was walking home alone, Macit worried. The government was paying a high price in order to avoid this fire spreading throughout the world.

At home all the women, as if in a chorus, were complaining about the high price of everything. If civil servants and their families in Ankara were distressed, who knew how the poor people of

Anatolia felt? In an effort to protect civil servants, the state was selling state products—textiles, shoes, and sugar—at considerably reduced prices. Furthermore, to prevent the black market and hoarding, it applied a rationing system, which meant that everybody's identity card was covered in stamps. Despite these precautions the black market thrived. Unscrupulous people looking for a big chance became wealthy selling goods off the back of a truck. Most people were angry but resigned; they couldn't find or afford basic supplies, and had only bread and cereal to eat. The president thought his prime concern—a matter of life and death—was to prevent his country from going to war. Approaching him with the people's complaints was pointless. For a man like him, who had already personally experienced the hell of war, anything besides this was of secondary importance.

Macit was exhausted. It was almost certain that Inönü would go to Yalova the following day, which meant that possibly, probably, there would be no late meetings next week. He might be able to go home earlier, and thus temporarily avoid Sabiha's reproaches.

❧

"One spade."

"Two diamonds."

"Pass."

"Pass…Sorry, sorry. Four spades."

The young women looked up from their cards across the table at Sabiha. She blushed, looking thin and delicate in her pale-mauve suit.

"You are very absentminded today," said Hümeyra. "What's wrong with you, dear?"

"Nothing. I couldn't sleep last night. I can't concentrate. Couldn't Nesrin take my place?"

"Absolutely not! Let's have some tea. That will sort you out."

"Hümeyra, I have to leave before five today anyway."

"Why?"

"I've got to pick Hülya up from Marga at her ballet class."

"Doesn't the nanny do that?"

"She has something else to do today."

"Oh, for God's sake, what else does a nanny have to do?"

"She wants to do some shopping before she goes back to England at the end of the month."

"I didn't know she was leaving, Sabiha! Why?"

"Well, Hülya has grown up; she is a big girl now. She no longer needs a nanny to fuss over her."

"But I thought she was teaching Hülya English too."

"She has learned enough. Her father wants her to be able to stand on her own two feet now and be more independent."

The ladies all put down their cards and got up from the card table. Sabiha walked toward the room where tea was being served. She wanted neither tea nor any of the pastries on the table. She only wished she could go outside for a breath of fresh air, but she took a cup of tea and sipped it, hoping to avoid further questions. The other women followed Sabiha to the tea table, swaying rhythmically to the music on the radio. Suddenly the music stopped and an announcer's urgent voice was heard.

"Ladies and gentlemen, we interrupt this program to bring you some important information regarding this morning's state committee meeting with the prime minister."

The ladies immediately changed direction, from the tea table to the radio.

"Shh! Shh! Listen!" said Belkıs.

Sabiha too walked toward the radio, her cup and saucer in her hand. Her hands shook as she listened to the grim news. The troops had retreated in Thrace behind the Çatalca line and were apparently digging in. The government was ordering all civilians in Istanbul to build shelters in their basements. Furthermore, those who had homes in Anatolia were being offered free transport there, and could bring up to fifty kilos of luggage per family.

"My God, what somber news. For God's sake, Hümeyra, turn that radio off," said Nesrin.

"No, please don't, there may be news about France," Sabiha said. "I wonder what—"

Nesrin interrupted. "So what about France? Who cares?"

Sabiha looked at her in dismay, putting her cup and saucer on the table.

"You should have some fruitcake; you like that," offered Hümeyra.

Sabiha declined her offer, saying, "I must have caught a chill at the races last weekend. I feel nauseous, darling. I have no appetite at all."

"Did you hear that they are evacuating Edirne?" Belkıs continued. "In other words, war is on our doorstep!"

"My husband will be totally unbearable," said Necla bluntly. "He barely answers yes or no these days as it is. Can you imagine what he'll be like if we go to war?"

Sabiha felt completely suffocated by her friends' conversation. While they were occupied with their tea and cake, she made her apologies to Hümeyra and quickly left the house.

The heady scent of lilac and wisteria filled the Ankara air. The beautiful wisteria tumbling over the garden walls, hanging like bunches of grapes, seemed almost to accentuate her gloomy mood. Her pale-mauve suit was the only thing that harmonized with the surroundings. A thousand and one things were going through her mind as she walked home to Kavaklıdere. She bumped into an old man, and as she was apologizing, she tripped on a stone and almost fell over. Sabiha was very unhappy. She was unable to devote any attention to either her daughter or her husband, and everything was beginning to fall apart. She was gradually distancing herself from those around her. From the beginning, her daughter had been a disappointment, as she had expected a son; her husband was only interested in his work; her parents were perpetually ill; and she had begun to have less and less in common with her friends. It was almost as if she were breaking away from life itself.

Macit was so busy that it seemed—to her, at least—that he didn't even notice the change in his wife. This made it easier for her to keep to herself. As for her friends, lately she had started making up excuses so as not to attend their various get-togethers. The nanny wasn't doing any shopping today and she didn't have to collect Hülya from Madame Marga's Ballet School. What was true was that the nanny was indeed returning to England. Macit wanted it that way. He believed Hülya no longer needed a nanny now that she was going to school, and that Sabiha should devote more time to their daughter herself.

Sabiha was aware that she hadn't been in control of her life for some time now. This damned war was running her life! What's more, it wasn't even in her own country. Nothing could be found in the shops, and no one could travel; war was the only topic of conversation. Macit was like a prisoner of war; it was as if he were a soldier himself! They had been such a happy couple, had had so much fun together once upon a time—before her sister went away, before the war. Sabiha missed those long-gone days. On the other hand, she couldn't help thanking her lucky stars whenever she read the newspapers or listened to the radio. At least in Ankara their lives were secure. No policeman or soldier was knocking on their door at some ungodly hour. There weren't people around wearing yellow badges on their chests like branded asses. Branded asses! Whose words were those? Necla was the only one who would make such crude remarks. Suddenly Sabiha remembered: two weeks ago during a bridge party, Necla, in one of her callous moods, had said, "The poor Jews have been made to wear yellow badges on their clothes, just like branded asses!"

"What on earth are you saying?" Sabiha screamed. "How can you possibly compare people to asses? You call yourself a diplomat's wife. I wonder if you can actually hear yourself!"

Necla, almost in tears, had asked her friends, "What's got into her? Why is she screaming at me like that?"

"This war has got to all us girls," their hostess had said, trying to defuse the situation. "These days the slightest spark causes an explosion. Come on, let's get on with the game. Whose turn was it?"

Sabiha now felt embarrassed remembering her outburst. She certainly was in a terrible mood. It was the same thing every day when she read the news in the papers. The Nazis storming over Europe…The fleeing emigrants…France…Ooooh! Sabiha reached out to touch one of the wisteria blooms on a wall, but just as she was about to pick it, she withdrew her hand. She couldn't bring herself to snap off the flower. Suddenly she felt a lump in her throat, and as she turned toward the street, tears streamed down her face. As night descended she gasped for breath. The sad day would turn into yet another sad night.

Macit was probably going to come home late. Hülya would have her endless whens, whys, and wheres throughout the meal. The nanny would sit across the table, undoubtedly talking about the war. Ankara, which was so full of happy memories, only represented sadness now. Not just sadness, but monotony, dreariness as well. Life was just gray!

❧

Macit opened the front door as quietly as possible; he didn't want to disturb his wife if she was sleeping. He tiptoed into the bedroom, and could see by the pale, pink light of the bedside lamp that she was awake. She lay with her hair spread across the pillow, looking at her husband through puffy red eyes.

"What's wrong? Why have you been crying?" asked Macit.

Sabiha sat bolt upright in bed. "I'm on edge. This letter arrived by the evening delivery; the postman left it on the doormat. I found it as I was taking out the garbage. Here, read it."

"Who's it from? Your mother? Is your father ill again?"

"It's not from Istanbul, Macit. The letter is from Selva."

"Really?"

"Macit, I am scared. We've got to do something. We *must* get her here. This cannot go on. Sooner or later, my mother will hear what's happening in France, and I swear it will give her a heart attack."

Macit took the letter and tried to read it by the dim light.

"Selva would never agree to come here, leaving Rafo behind," he said. "Rafo wouldn't agree to come back."

"But this can't go on. Selva has got to consider our mother. I have asked the telephone exchange to connect me to her. God knows how long it will take. Maybe by the morning or sometime tomorrow…"

"You've done what, Sabiha? How many times have I told you not to call Selva from the house?"

"Well, I certainly couldn't go to someone else's house at this hour of the night. I have to speak to my sister; I have to persuade her before it is too late."

"I'm going to cancel the call," said Macit, rushing to the telephone.

"How can you do that? She's my sister. Don't you understand?"

Macit returned to the room. "Sabiha, I am working for the foreign ministry, the Germans are at our borders, war is on our doorstep, and you are booking a call to a Jew in France. You're asking for trouble!"

"I'm fed up with your foreign ministry. I'm really fed up. I'm always imagining that I am being followed by spies."

"It's almost the school holidays. Then you and Hülya can go to your parents in Istanbul. I just wonder if your father will be as understanding as I am on the subject of your sister."

Sabiha heard her husband walk to the end of the hall, dial the operator, cancel the call, and then go to the living room. Sabiha started to cry again, very quietly.

Macit went out onto the balcony. He lit a cigarette and looked at the midnight-blue horizon far, far away. Macit was happy with the cool Ankara nights, but tonight, for the first time, he felt cold and uncomfortable. He tried to warm his arms by rubbing them with his hands. It wasn't just the weather that made him feel cold. They were living through days that—for those who understood what was going on—were dangerous enough to make one's hair stand on end. Neither the man in the street nor his capricious wife whimpering indoors was aware just how close they were to the brink. They simply switched on the radio, listened to the news, then complained about the black market and how expensive everything was before pulling up a blanket and drifting off to sleep. They weren't aware of anything. No one knew the extent of the disaster Turkey would face if she was dragged into the war by either side. How could anyone know the knife edge that Inönü and his colleagues trod? The government was trying its best not to alarm the public or cause a panic. Macit wondered whether it was better to disclose the truth so everybody could face the facts, or take on the role of a protective father, shielding the children from bad news.

Not long ago, just a few months in fact, the country had been sucked into the whirlpool of war. War...It was worse than that, it was a cesspit, a filthy cesspit! Macit threw his cigarette butt in anger. It fell somewhere in the pitch-darkness without a glimmer of light. He remembered the stories his war-hero father told about this darkness and the cigarette lights at night—one, two, three lights, five lights, ten lights—bodies without arms or legs, corpses without heads. People miserable, hungry, covered in lice, like wounded, skinny animals. Starving, abandoned children. Women who'd lost their humanity; men who had no money, no home, and no hope. He vaguely remembered his father in that state appearing at the garden gate, all skin and bones, covered in lice, his uniform in rags. He had staggered toward the edge of the pool and collapsed. This was a memory imprinted in Macit's mind, but he wasn't sure if he had actually witnessed it or was told about it later. What he did remember was that the gardener hadn't recognized his master, and thought he was a beggar. It took some time before they realized who the man was. The tall, strong, sociable Ruhi had become a cadaver, a spiritless skeleton dragging one leg, without the usual gleam in his eye. Such was war! Macit was certain that victory was to be won around the table, not on the battlefield. He was working so hard to save the people of his nation from that dreadful fate again, but how could he explain that to his sobbing wife?

Slumping into a straw armchair and drifting into his memories, he realized he had gotten used to the coolness on the balcony. Macit had contributed a lot toward the signing of the agreement with England and France in 1939. According to that agreement, the French and the British would provide the Turkish army with its vital needs. In return, Turkey was to sell the chrome she produced to France throughout the war. The Turkish foreign minister himself had traveled to France with Macit to sign the agreement. They had gone to Paris with great expectations, but, unfortunately, the end result didn't meet their hopes. France desperately needed the money they'd make selling the Turkish chrome, but despite Menemencioğlu's insistence on supplying the chrome for the duration of the war, France would only sign for two years. Then Britain drastically reduced the quantity of arms, tanks, and antiaircraft guns it was willing to supply to Turkey.

The Turkish army needed 11 million bullets and 6,500 machine guns. The British were only prepared to supply two million bullets and 200 machine guns. With these pitiful supplies, how on earth could Turkey be expected to stop the Germans in the Balkans? One could understand a person fighting with his bare hands to save his own country, but to fight for the British, who had stirred up the Arabs against the Turks in the First World War when they had their eyes set on Musul and Kerkük, was too much to expect. At the same time, other European countries, for their own reasons, had supported various Middle Eastern tribes who were seeking independence.

Had it been left to Macit, he would not have lifted a finger for any of them. Let the Europeans go at each other's throats. Wasn't it enough that they were dragging each other into this war? Macit had no doubt that if, for some reason, Turkey was eventually forced to join the war, she would have to foot the bill for the ambitions of the great powers.

During a meal on the train on the way back from Paris, Macit learned that the foreign minister was concerned about another thing. He addressed the delegation. "Gentlemen, as I see it, the British haven't got enough weapons and the French have none. They aren't able to deliver the goods because they have bad intentions. It is simply impossible. I became fully aware of this situation during our talks in Paris. There are all sorts of questions in my mind. I have doubts about their eventual victory. I wonder if we are backing the wrong horse, signing these agreements that will make us their allies." After a year of endless discussions—who would win the war? Which side should Turkey support?—it had been decided that Turkey should support the French and British. Now, in Paris, they had found out about France's lack of weapons. Gradually they had begun to realize that they may have chosen the wrong partner. Although they didn't return to Ankara empty-handed, they were very disappointed that less than half their expectations had been met.

At the end of the talks, on the evening of their last day in Paris, Macit had managed to keep a promise he had made to Sabiha to meet up with Selva. He had told his friends that he had to see a relative who lived in Paris, and they were courteous enough not to ask questions.

Macit chose to meet Selva at the Café de Flore, because it was tucked away out of sight. Selva arrived with an armful of gifts for her mother, sister, and niece. She hugged Macit tightly and kissed him on both cheeks. It was obvious how happy she was to see someone from home. She asked about everyone in great detail: Was Sabiha still tying Hülya's hair with huge satin ribbons? Had they been inviting the same old friends to their Friday soirees? Who was Sabiha's bridge partner? Did her mother close down the summer house at the end of the season, or when it got cooler? She even asked about her father, who was so disappointed in her.

Macit looked at all the presents his sister-in-law had piled on a chair. With an embarrassed look on his face, he said, "I really can't take all this back with me, Selva. I only have a small suitcase."

"Please, Macit, don't deny me the pleasure of sending a few things to my family. I might not get another opportunity. I can duck out and get another little bag from Lafayette."

"No, for God's sake, don't! What will my colleagues think? We are here on official business. They'll say I have done so much shopping for myself and my family that I had to buy an additional suitcase to carry everything."

"At least take the lavender perfumes I got for my mother and sister. There are also some chocolates for Hülya…"

"I wish you hadn't gone to all this trouble; you must have spent quite a bit of money. What a shame."

After exchanging news, suddenly there was a lull in the conversation. It was only then that Macit noticed the dark circles under Selva's eyes. In the evening sun, he realized how pale and haggard she looked. She was still wearing the green raincoat that Macit knew so well—which indicated that she couldn't afford a new one here in Paris. This was Fazıl Reşat Paşa's daughter, who had been born with a silver spoon in her mouth! The things one does for love! Macit couldn't help wonder if Sabiha would have had the courage to act the same way if her parents hadn't approved of him. Macit wasn't sure that he wanted to know the answer. Sabiha might not have chosen to endure hardship for the sake of love. Would she have married him had he been of another religion, been Armenian, for instance? No! Not in a million years. No doubt his coming from an old respected Istanbul family, well educated and with a good career, contributed considerably to her choice. But why should he feel disappointed? Hadn't he made similar choices? Wasn't Sabiha a beautiful, intelligent, educated girl, well brought up in a respected family, and well adjusted to boot? He remembered the sensible advice Sabiha had given to her sister in those days when Selva was head over heels in love. It had not had much effect, but that was beside the point.

"Love is like a flame; it burns itself out eventually," Sabiha had told Selva. "What will you do then? When you finally come to your senses, if you repent and wish to divorce Rafo, it won't be the same as divorcing someone else. No one will want to marry you after that. I swear you'll end up an old maid."

"Because I'll be considered the leftover of a Jewish husband—is that it? Don't you worry, dear sister, I am sure that if the flame burns out, as you say, our friendship will survive. We will be lovers and best friends."

"What if, God forbid, something should happen to Rafo? Will you come home as the Jewish Madame Alfandari?"

"I certainly won't do that. I won't return to the house of our father, who has rejected me, simply because I have fallen in love with a man who is not a Muslim. Who knows, by then anyway I may have children of my own, or even grandchildren."

When Sabiha realized she was getting nowhere with Selva, she tried talking to their father.

"Times have changed, Father. These sorts of differences don't matter anymore. Please don't do anything you'll regret later. I beg of you, Father, please be sensible. Look at Sami Paşa's daughter-in-law—she's Greek, isn't she? Then there is Vecdi's wife, who is German. What about them? Plus, you were educated in Europe. You're supposed to be more open-minded."

"If she marries that man, she will no longer be a daughter of mine. She'll have to forget she was ever my daughter."

"But, Father, how can she possibly forget she is your daughter!"

Fazıl Paşa looked far away, out the window.

"You mean 'was.'"

This dreadful situation had turned the family upside down and lasted not just a few days, weeks, or months, but years. Fazıl Paşa's unsuccessful attempt at shooting himself hadn't stopped Selva; she simply waited until he was well again and then went to her lover. Then it was their mother's turn to cause havoc. She took to her bed, seriously ill, and needed constant care and attention. Fazıl Paşa refused to leave the house. The family was so ashamed; they couldn't look any of their friends directly in the eye. The incident hadn't done the family any good, but at least now they knew who their real friends were. Now, even friends they had considered close were gossiping behind their backs, blaming Paşa because he had educated his daughters in Christian schools, as indeed many of them had.

Sabiha and Selva, like most of their friends' children, were sent to the American school in Gedik Paşa for their primary education, then to the French school for their secondary education, and finally to the American college. Both sisters grew up speaking English and French fluently.

Macit remembered how impressed he was, many years ago, when he first saw his fiancée reading poems by Baudelaire and Byron. Even his mother, God rest her soul, had been impressed. "Just the sort of wife who would be right for a diplomat," she had commented.

Selva's voice brought him back to reality from where he had been lost in his thoughts. "Will Turkey join the war then?"

"No, she won't."

"Are you sure?"

"We are doing our best to see to it that she doesn't. We certainly can't afford another war, Selva."

"Macit…There is something I need to ask."

"Please do."

"My father? Will he—will he ever forgive me?"

"Frankly I don't know, Selva. Your sister and I have closed this subject. We no longer talk about it."

"Really?"

"Yes, what else is there to say?"

"You really think so, Macit?"

Macit took a sip of coffee before replying. "What I think is neither here nor there. You have done what you wanted. Aren't you happy, at least? Was it worth the upheaval you caused?"

"I resent your attitude, I must say. You are talking as if you had never met Rafo yourself."

"I don't see why you should resent my telling the truth. You simply refused to listen to anyone. You went ahead and burned your bridges. You hurt your father, your mother, and Sabiha. I only hope that it was worth it. We all hope you'll have no regrets."

"I love Rafo very much, Macit. I have no regrets, but I am very unhappy…"

Tears were streaming down her face. Macit took her trembling hands in his. "Come on, Selva, you shouldn't be unhappy if you love him so much. Think of all you have endured to be together. You are a very strong person; you have always known what you wanted and had the courage to stick to your guns. I'm sure your father is aware of this too. He may not have forgiven you yet, but I am sure that deep down inside he still loves you dearly."

"I miss everybody…so much."

"Time is a great healer. Give this a little more time."

"I wonder how much more time," Selva said anxiously.

Was there any? Macit thought. Time was so very precious these days—particularly the past few months—as precious as gold. Wasn't it time that the Turkish delegation had come to Paris for? President Inönü was seeking time more than anything else: time to think, time to distract, time to avoid war. In fact, Inönü kept answering questions regarding the war by saying, "Time will tell."

Macit now gave the same answer to his sister-in-law. "I don't know, Selva. Time will tell!"

He realized he was now using diplomatic tactics in his personal life. He had always thought that things could change in the blink of an eye, bringing unforeseen results. But in the present circumstances, Europe could find no solace in predictions or hope.

Before leaving Selva, Macit held her hands tightly and looked into her eyes. "Everything can change, Selva, and change rapidly. Should anything happen that puts your life in danger, you must return home immediately."

"I can't return without Rafo, Macit."

"I think you should. He's a man; he can look after himself."

"We've vowed to stick together throughout our lives. He wouldn't want to go back. You know all he went through, all those insults. And I just couldn't leave him."

"Think carefully. We only have one life to live. We alone are responsible for it."

"Macit, try to understand. I am not only responsible for my own life."

"Exactly. Even at sea women and children abandon ship first."

"You don't understand; I'm not talking about Rafo."

Macit, who had stood up to leave, sat down again. "No! You don't mean…"

"Yes, I do."

"When?"

"Early next year."

"Why didn't you tell me before?"

"I had hoped you'd notice."

Looking at her more closely, Macit could indeed see that she had put on weight around the waist and that her breasts were fuller than he remembered. On the other hand, her face was drawn. He thought she must be mad to get pregnant in wartime. Rather reluctantly, Macit wished her well.

"Do you want me to tell Sabiha?" he asked.

"I have already written her, but she may not have received my letter yet. If you are going back tomorrow, you may as well spread the news, but I'd rather she hear it from me first."

"Of course."

"I have also written my mother."

"Think very carefully, Selva. You now have one more reason to return to Istanbul."

"I can't raise my child without its father. Don't worry, Macit. Rafo also believes that staying here is dangerous. He is following up a few work possibilities outside Paris, somewhere in the countryside. We may be leaving Paris within a month."

Rafo and Selva did eventually manage to leave Paris and move to Marseilles, but to what use? The Nazis had cast their shadow even down there. In order to save the southern part of the country from being invaded, Marshal Pétain's newly formed government sacrificed the French Jews in order to cope with Hitler. Gradually, the French Jews, who had thought they might be able to go unnoticed by living in remote areas, began to realize they were wrong. The Germans penetrated everywhere, just like smoke. It became impossible to get away from them.

Rafo had started working in Marseilles with a friend of his who was a chemist. Selva's mother had sold a diamond ring at auction and managed to send the money to her younger daughter without the knowledge of her husband. Rafo invested the money in a partnership with his friend the chemist. He and Selva lived in an attic apartment right across the street from the shop. Selva gave English and piano lessons to three young girls who were neighbors. They had managed to make a few friends, but Selva's best friend was still her sister. She wrote to Sabiha every day, giving her details of their life. Her pregnancy was going fine. No morning sickness. No financial problems, but they were living hand-to-mouth. Their only luxury was the telephone they'd installed so that the sisters could keep in touch. Nevertheless, Rafo and Selva were well aware of the net closing around them. Selva had even heard atrocious reports of men being stopped by the police and asked to drop their pants in order to check if they had been circumcised. Luckily, Rafo hadn't been subjected to this humiliation. All of their friends looked upon them as Turkish, since they always spoke Turkish to each other. Back in March, Selva had even fasted for Ramadan and had made sure everyone knew she was fasting.

Despite all their efforts, she feared that sooner or later the truth would come out.

Macit knew his wife constantly worried about her sister, but there was nothing much he could do about it. These days personal dramas were a drop in the ocean compared to those that confronted the nation. He went indoors after finishing a second cigarette. He was shivering as he walked toward the bedroom. He stopped outside and heard his wife breathing heavily; Sabiha had managed to fall asleep. He crept into the bathroom and undressed there so as not to disturb her. Then Macit got into the warm bed, but he couldn't sleep. He tossed and turned until he heard the telephone ringing.

My God! he thought. They probably forgot to cancel the call.

He rushed out of bed and, without even pausing to put on slippers, ran down the hall, reaching the phone and answering it breathlessly.

"Hello."

"I'm sorry, sir. I knew I'd wake you, but…"

"Hello…hello…who's that?"

"It's me…Tarık…Tarık Arıca."

"Oh, Tarık." Macit took a deep breath. "What's happened?"

"I'm sorry for calling at this late hour. I hope I haven't woken the rest of the family."

"Tell me, what's the matter?"

"Bad news, I'm afraid. I'm on duty at the office, and, well, half an hour ago the Germans attacked Rhodes."

Macit slumped into the armchair. "I can't believe it," he mumbled.

"I'm afraid so. The secretary general, the minister, and the chief of staff are to meet in about twenty minutes. The president has been informed."

"I understand," said Macit. "I'm on my way. Thank you."

He crept toward the bedroom again. Sabiha was still sound asleep. He went into the bathroom and dressed in the same clothes he had taken off earlier.

When Sabiha heard Macit close the door, she sat up in bed and waited for a while in the dark. She turned on the lamp on her bedside table. Tears were running down her face onto her pink nightdress.

She held up her arms to pray. "Please, God, protect my darling Selva. Save my sister from that hell. I beg of you, God."

She clasped her hands to her face and rocked in despair. "Forgive me, my little sister," she whispered. "Forgive me, Selva."

ISTANBUL 1933

Selva was drying her long blonde hair in the sun, combing it with an ivory comb and at the same time shaking it, scattering a myriad of tiny drops that looked like little balls of crystal. Sabiha looked on enviously and snapped, "Don't dry your hair over here; you'll stain my dress."

"You must be joking! Whoever heard of water leaving stains?"

"I assure you that water stains silk."

Selva walked away from the window and sat cross-legged on her bed, continuing to dry her hair.

"You could take me with you, you know!"

"But I don't want to."

"Why?"

"Because you're too young, that's why. Maybe next year."

"But I'm taller than you."

Sabiha looked at her sister angrily. She was going to respond, but bit her lip for a while.

Knowing how proud Selva was of her long hair, Sabiha couldn't resist saying, "You know, I think it's about time you cut your hair. You'll be sweeping the floor with it soon."

"Father won't let me cut it."

"You're lying. You just don't want to. That's all there is to it!"

"Maybe so…"

"It's so old-fashioned, Selva; it's almost down to your ankles! It's difficult to wash and difficult to dry too. For years now you have had that huge knot on top of your head. Two plaited strands of hair tied into a topknot. Aren't you tired of it, for God's sake?"

"Nope."

"Well, that's fine by me, but if you want to go to tea parties with me, you'll have to do something different with your hair. I can't have you walking beside me looking like Queen Victoria. I hope you understand that."

"I do, Sabiha."

Sabiha wasn't surprised by her sister's answer. She was one of those people who never contradicted anybody, but somehow always managed to get her own way. It was impossible to argue with her, so Sabiha changed the subject. Trying necklaces on in front of the mirror, she asked her sister, "Which one do you think?"

"That one!" Selva suggested.

"No, I think this one is better. This will do. Can you help me with the hook, please?"

She pulled up her hair and knelt down for her sister to fasten it.

Selva admired her sister's choice. "You were right, it is perfect. You'll be the most beautiful girl at the party."

Sabiha looked at herself in the mirror; the three strands of pearls complemented her light-green silk dress. Very elegant, she thought. She touched up her hair, tucking the sides behind her ears. She certainly looked good; she smiled at her reflection in the mirror.

Just then her mother opened the bedroom door. "Your friends are here, dear. Hurry up, and for God's sake, don't be home late. You must be back before your father or there'll be trouble!"

Sabiha blew her sister a kiss and followed her mother out of the room. Moments later she rushed back, hugged Selva, and said, "I promise to take you with me next time," and rushed out again.

Selva listened to their footsteps down the hall, got up from the bed, plaited her hair, and walked toward the mirror, fixing her hairpins. "I'll never forgive you, my Lord; no, no, never. I shall never forgive you, Lord Seymour. I trusted you with all my heart. You may now leave me," she said, pointing to the door.

Hearing her daughter, her mother returned to the bedroom, asking, "What on earth are you doing, my child?"

"Oh, Mother! I didn't hear you come in," she said with a laugh. "I am rehearsing the end-of-term play. I am playing Elizabeth the First..."

"Who's the king?"

"There is no king, Mother. When Henry the Eighth died, all hell broke loose. The play is about the rivalry between two women fighting over the throne of England. Mualla is playing Mary Stuart and Rafo is playing Lord Seymour. Of course, there are other parts too, priests and lords, et cetera. Please, Mother, can I invite the cast for tea next week? Please don't say no."

"You can invite just the girls."

"Really, Mother, how can we rehearse with just the girls? Who's going to play the boys' parts?"

"Oh dear! What will I do with your father again? You know how he feels about these things. You know what I went through to persuade him to let you go to parties."

"What do you mean? You never let me go to parties."

"But, darling, you're not even eighteen yet."

"Don't fret, Mother. I won't want to go to parties even when I am eighteen. I only say I want to go to tease my sister."

"And why on earth won't you want to go?"

"Don't you think I know why girls go to parties? They go because they want to find themselves a husband!"

"And where does all this come from?"

"I hear Sabiha talking to her friends about it. It seems that they are all after the same thing, they all have one thing on their mind."

"And what's wrong with that, may I ask? Of course, suitable young men with good educations are invited to those parties. They all speak several languages and behave impeccably. Besides, these parties are always held at home, where their elders can keep an eye on things."

"I know, and that's exactly what annoys me. The mothers arrange these parties so they can choose a suitable husband for their daughters."

"So, what's wrong with that? What's wrong with a mother wanting her daughter to have a good marriage?"

"Well, I certainly don't want that!"

"That's all right by me then; your father and I won't help. You can rely on the old-fashioned method, like I did. Let's see how you react when the matchmaker comes knocking on our door!"

"God forbid—that's not what I meant at all!"

"I can hardly imagine you being happy with that."

"Never. Over my dead body!"

"I didn't think so…so what are you carrying on about?"

"I don't really know. I just find it odd for eligible young men and sweet little girls to be herded together to try to…Oh…I give up…I can't explain."

"Perhaps you can explain exactly how you will find the appropriate young man to be your husband. Are they to be found in the marketplace, by any chance?"

"All I know is that I will find my own husband myself. I would hate to find someone through a competition organized by keen mothers."

"That's just great; you have spoken just like the child you are. What would someone of your age know about choosing a husband? Enough of this; you had better get on with your rehearsal."

Just as her mother left the room, Selva called after her, "Mother, wait! What about next week's rehearsal here? Would you at least allow me to ask just one, I mean, just one boy who has the lead?"

"Who is this star, then?"

"Rafo. Rafael Alfandari."

"Alfandari? Is he the famous doctor's son?"

"Grandson."

"Well, what can I say? I suppose you can. I believe your father knows the family. He might not be against it."

Leman Hanım left the room and Selva continued to practice her lines in front of the mirror.

Later that evening Selva was studying when her mother rushed into her room in a flurry. "Selva, it's half past five and your sister isn't back yet."

"It can't be that time already. I haven't heard the clock chime yet."

Just as she said it, the cuckoo called once from the clock in the hallway, as it did every half hour.

"There you are," said Leman Hanım.

"Don't panic, Mother, she'll be here any minute."

"I just hope she comes home before your father."

Selva walked to the window and looked outside, "Here she is—she's coming now."

Mother and daughter squeezed together in the bay window and saw Sabiha running toward the house, her cloak and dress billowing around her.

"Stop, don't run; you'll fall over," shouted her mother, as if Sabiha could hear her.

Kalfa, the manservant, had already opened the door before Selva got downstairs. Sabiha looked radiant. Her eyes sparkled and her face was glowing.

Leman Hanım called over the banister, "How did it go? Was it fun? Were there interesting people?"

"What Mother means is, were there any eligible young men?"

Leman Hanım was angered by Selva's remark. "That's enough, Selva, you've had your say and now it's becoming boring."

Selva realized that she had overstepped the mark. "Sorry, Mother."

Sabiha gave her cloak to Kalfa and rushed straight upstairs to her room. She threw herself on her bed, clasped her hands under her chin, and gazed starry-eyed into the distance.

Her mother followed her into the room. "My God, you'll ruin your pretty dress. You shouldn't be lying around in that lovely silk dress. Come on, don't keep us in suspense. Who was there? How was it?"

"Oh, Mother, it was wonderful. There was someone called Macit. Apparently he is Necmiye Hanım's nephew. He was educated in Paris and has joined our Ministry of Foreign Affairs. He was great—I mean, very handsome."

"And?"

"Well, it is difficult to say. He danced with Necla but he spent most of the time talking to me. He seemed very interested in me."

Selva interrupted, "Didn't I tell you that you'd be the prettiest one there?"

"The other girls were very pretty too, but he spent most of his time with me."

"What about the others? Who else was there?"

"Let me see, there was Necla's brother, Burhan, for instance."

"What about him? What does he do?"

"Who?"

"This Burhan."

"Oh! I really don't know. He did tell me but I can't remember."

"I see. It seems you are keen on this Macit. I'd better find out more about him before it goes any further."

"There's nothing to find out. I told you, Mother."

"You'd better take off that dress before you ruin it completely. Your father should be home shortly," Leman Hanım said as she left the room.

Selva watched Sabiha undress. She couldn't help admiring her sister as she removed her clothes, examining herself in the mirror.

"Have you actually fallen in love, Sabiha?"

"I don't think so. Can one fall in love in one day? But he really was very attractive!"

"I have asked Mother if I can invite some school friends over next week. Why don't we ask him too?"

"With all those girls? You must be joking. He'd be bored to death." She wasn't keen for Macit to meet Selva. After all, she was taller, if not more beautiful, than Sabiha.

"I'll invite Rafo as well."

"You mean the Jewish guy?"

"Yes, the Jewish guy," said Selva, imitating her sister.

"Don't get uppity. Am I lying? He is Jewish, isn't he?"

"Yes, he is, but he is different from the others. He's much more intelligent, he's got good manners, and he is very mature—"

"Don't bother going on. Save your breath. Whatever he may be, it is an impossible situation."

"Impossible? Can one only be friends with an eye to marriage? Is that it?"

"Life is too short, Selva. How often has Father told us about the value of time? Time is not to be wasted."

"If life is too short, isn't that more reason to make the most of what we've got? To live the way we want to?"

"Does that mean Rafo is what you want?"

Selva didn't reply.

"Rafo…" Sabiha continued. "He's certainly a gentleman, I won't deny that. On the other hand, if you're to remain just friends, why not?"

"If he is a gentleman, why shouldn't one marry him?"

"Don't be silly; you know that's impossible."

"Why? Didn't we form the Turkish republic to do away with such ridiculous prejudices?"

"Now stop right there, Selva. Did you or I form the republic? Stop giving me all that 'we' business! Furthermore, those who did form it didn't have the marriage of Turkish girls to non-Muslims in mind, that's for sure. Anyway, this is a typical Selva argument. I don't know why you continue with these loony ideas. You're being childish again and that's that."

Selva decided not to continue the argument and Sabiha's mind went off on a tangent. If her sister was occupied with this Rafo, it would prevent any rivalry between them over Macit. Why was it that men always paid so much attention to girls like Selva who didn't make themselves attractive or dress well or even flirt? As far as Sabiha was concerned, Selva's only redeeming features were her long hair and swanlike neck. She was polite and sincere, and those qualities appealed to some guys. Still waters run deep, she thought. Sabiha felt a pang of jealousy.

It was her paternal grandmother who had first planted the seeds of jealousy in her heart; she always made such a thing about being tall. Sabiha still remembered how her grandmother would check their height against the bedroom door almost daily, and what a fuss she had made when Selva, two years younger than Sabiha, had reached the same height. She believed that she and Sabiha, with their opalescent green eyes, were cut from the same cloth, and longed for her granddaughter to be tall and slender. As she marked off her height with a pencil, she would scold Sabiha: "You're not drinking enough milk. Look at Selva—she's getting taller and taller. You'll stay a midget if you're not careful." Sabiha even heard her grandmother telling Leman Hanım off when her mother tried to erase the pencil marks on the bedroom door with soap and water. She overheard her mother saying, "Please don't do this. You're subjecting poor Sabiha to unnecessary pressure."

"I am doing it deliberately in order to encourage her to have more dairy products."

"Dearest Mother, it isn't quite as simple as that. Genes are genes. Selva has taken after my grandfather; Sabiha hasn't. It is as simple as that and very little can be done about it."

"Oh God! Dear God! How can you say that? Do you want your daughter to remain a midget?"

"She isn't a midget at all; she is quite normal for her age. It's the other one who is like a beanpole."

"Height is a wonderful thing. It suits both men and women. I just love it."

"I don't think it suits women. Women should be tiny. After all, don't they say good things come in small packages?"

Sabiha was too young to appreciate the wisdom of the proverb and returned to her bedroom. She was her father's beautiful daughter, and Selva was his intelligent one. No matter how Fazıl Reşat tried to cover up his weakness for his younger daughter, he couldn't hide it. His admiration was obvious to anyone who saw the affectionate look in his eyes. He wasn't impressed by Sabiha's beautiful green eyes framed by very long eyelashes that were just like her mother's. Sabiha knew only too well that her father was far more impressed by brains than beauty. She was used to that, but now this height business too. Small package indeed! She was what she was, a small package. She had the more beautiful face, but that didn't count. She was still a shorty compared to her sister, a full handbreadth shorter, a small package. Sabiha buried her face in her pillow and cried.

Selva sat innocently admiring her sister, not knowing of Sabiha's guilty feelings because she was scheming to avoid potential rivalry.

"Rafo is indeed a gentleman," Sabiha said, "and what's more, he's very handsome. I don't suppose it would do any harm to flirt a little."

"Do you really mean that?"

"Yes, why not? Why don't you invite him to the end-of-term ball?"

"You must be joking—they would never allow it."

"I could come with you."

Selva threw herself into her sister's arms and nearly drowned her with kisses.

"I didn't realize how much you thought of Rafo. Why didn't you say something before?"

"Well, I have now, so there."

Selva looked at her sister with her big brown eyes. Why this sudden change of heart? she thought.

Sabiha was thinking too. How would Macit react to her younger sister dating a Jew? Would he mind? Somehow she didn't think so. After all, a young man educated in France must have more worldly ideas. Why should he care if her sister was flirting with a guy who had a different religion? Better she was flirting with him than no one at all. But then, if that was the case, maybe Macit would be interested in Selva, being taller and doe-eyed, and with bold ideas.

"Come on, then, let's invite them both to tea. You can concentrate on Rafo and I'll look after Macit."

Selva clapped her hands with joy.

A week later, they were all enjoying a lovely tea party. Selva's classmates rehearsed their play, and then wound up the gramophone to dance the fox-trot to their 78s.

The following day Leman Hanım couldn't help asking her eldest daughter about Rafo. "Did you see how Selva kept looking at that Jewish boy? She was almost devouring him every time he spoke."

"He's a polite young man. As far as I am concerned, he is more of a gentleman than those Turkish guys who are so full of themselves."

"The Alfandaris are an old, established family. They come from a line of palace doctors. They have savoir faire, but all the same, our girl is...well, you know what she is like. She is unpredictable and stubborn. She has a mind of her own."

"Yes, Mother, but Rafael wouldn't dare take things further with Selva. Please don't worry. Besides, don't forget that I am around, and if I notice anything untoward, I'll tell you."

Sabiha's promise relaxed Leman Hanım a little. After that first tea party, the same group went to several concerts and picnics together, and each time, Leman Hanım sent Kalfa along as a guardian.

Sabiha and Macit became engaged to marry soon but, according to tradition, Leman Hanım insisted that Selva accompany the couple whenever they went out together. Sabiha turned this to her advantage. The three of them left the house together and went off to a prearranged point, where Rafo would be waiting. From there the two couples went their separate ways until it was time to return home. By the time Sabiha realized how wrong this was, it was too late.

Eighteen months later Sabiha and Macit were married. After a splendid wedding, they moved to Ankara so Macit could take up his position in the foreign ministry.

Selva started university, studying literature, while Rafo decided to follow in his family's footsteps and study chemistry. Rafo often picked up Selva from her classes or, if he had time, even attended her lectures, just so he could be near her. Some of the other students took exception to this and sometimes picked fights with him because he was daring to court a Muslim girl. One of them remonstrated with Selva: "Can't you find someone of your own religion in the whole of Istanbul?" Another student from the East said, "If you were back home, we'd shoot you for this!"

"Are you really proud of those primitive thoughts?" asked Selva. "How does shooting a person reconcile with being a Muslim, I wonder?"

The situation escalated with continual abuse and harassment toward them until, finally, two years into his studies, Rafo had to leave the university. Selva was distraught; Rafo had had to leave because of her. She began to skip lectures and by the end of the year had left the university altogether too. She found it very difficult to explain all this to her father.

Gossip about the love between the son of the Alfandaris and the younger daughter of Fazıl Reşat Paşa gradually spread to the family. When it got back to Leman Hanım's ears, she took action to try to keep it from her husband. Rafo was banned from visiting the house and Selva wasn't allowed to go out alone. She spent her time playing the piano, reading books, and corresponding with her sister in Ankara. The only people she saw were either close family friends or relatives.

Fazıl Reşat Paşa wasn't very happy with his wife's strict attitude toward Selva. He thought that Leman Hanım was devoting too much energy trying to control Selva now that Sabiha was living away from home. He suggested that Selva should be sent to stay with Sabiha on the pretext of helping her with the new baby. Leman Hanım liked the idea and hoped that her younger daughter might meet a suitable young man.

Having received many letters from her mother on this subject, Sabiha set about introducing Selva to as many of their friends as possible. She organized parties at home and took Selva along whenever they were invited out. Through Macit she introduced Selva to every eligible bachelor in the Foreign Office. Many of the young men took a shine to Selva, but none really interested her. She left them all in Ankara and returned home.

Then Leman Hanım insisted that Selva should spend some time with her uncle in Cyprus. The poor woman hoped that if her daughter went away, the flame inside her would burn out, and that would put an end to the gossip. All of these frantic efforts came to nothing. Selva kept that flame alive through her correspondence with Rafo wherever she was.

It was inevitable that Fazıl Reşat Paşa would hear about it, and when he did, he was furious. The paşa confronted his daughter.

"Is what I hear true? Please tell me that these are false accusations spread by nasty-minded people. Tell me that it's malicious gossip," he said.

"I wish I could, Father, but I love Rafael Alfandari with all my heart, and if you should grant us permission, I will marry him."

"Never! Over my dead body! Do you really expect me to permit such a thing? Doing that would destroy all of our family values and make a mockery of us all. Is this how you repay me for taking such care of you and sending you to foreign schools?"

"I had thought that my education was meant to expand my horizons, that you wanted me to be an equal, Father."

"I had you and your sister well educated hoping that one day you would present me with grandchildren, not so you'd rebel against me."

"Rebelling against you is the last thing on my mind, Father; all I ask is that I choose my own life's partner. I am not asking you to accept an immoral, worthless person as a son-in-law. The only thing you can object to is that he is not a Muslim. Haven't you told us on countless occasions that people should be free to worship exactly how they wish and that every belief was holy?"

The gravity of the situation brought about a rage that could not be associated with the sort of gentleman Fazıl Reşat Paşa was.

He managed to control his actions around his daughter, but the moment he dismissed her he set about breaking every single crystal vase and mirror in the room.

Sabiha was asked to come from Ankara at once to try to help calm her father down and to persuade Selva to give up her obsession. Both she and Leman Hanım spent days on end trying to bring Selva to her senses.

Leman Hanım was beside herself. She couldn't sleep at night and spent hours walking from room to room tearing at her hair. *How on earth did we come to this? Why the hell did I allow that snake to slither into my house? Why didn't I see this coming?*

Seeing her mother's despair made Sabiha feel very guilty, but she didn't have the strength to tell her mother the truth. If she had only been able to say, "It's not your fault, Mother, it was me, I used Rafo to get Selva out of my way." Just these few words would clear her conscience a little. She had even wished that she were a Catholic. If she were, it would simply be a matter of confession, accepting whatever penance was meted out by the priest. At least she would have been able to rid herself of this burden. Realizing that Selva was a lost cause, Sabiha turned her attention to her father. He felt that Sabiha had made a good choice and found an ideal husband, but she couldn't even rejoice in that, knowing how she had gone about it.

Fazıl Reşat Paşa felt completely betrayed. He had brought up his daughters to be part of the modern world—exactly the same as if they'd been sons—as was expected by the new republic. They had had good educations, spoke several languages, and were fit to play active roles in society. But he was beginning to have second thoughts now. What exactly had he achieved, having such great ambitions for them? Hadn't his eldest daughter married before she was nineteen, just like in the old days? As for the younger one—that wise, clever, quiet girl with personality to spare—hadn't she betrayed him in the cruelest way? This all seemed to be a terrible nightmare. What made it even worse was that Selva had used all the advice he had ever given her against him.

Fazıl Reşat Paşa realized he had been wrong; the only honorable thing an officer and gentleman could do was to pay with his own life. He felt sure that if Selva saw him dead she would realize how foolish she had been. Maybe she would change her mind if she saw that his only peace lay in his grave.

Selva wrote a note to her father saying that, as the family didn't approve, she would not marry Rafo, but that she would not give him up. Fazıl Reşat Paşa went ahead with his suicide attempt, but it was foiled by Kalfa, who wrestled the gun from him, causing him to shoot himself in the shoulder.

This emotional blackmail annoyed Selva more than it frightened her. "It has become impossible to live in this city," she told her sister. "We are going to live in France. His family is against our marriage too. We have no alternative under these circumstances."

Leman Hanım swallowed her pride and sent word to Rafo, asking him to reconsider this move. The only real problem was his religion. Maybe he could convert to Islam. If he were to do that, then maybe they could persuade Fazıl Reşat Paşa to accept him into the family.

Selva didn't give Rafo a chance to respond to this preposterous suggestion, telling her sister, "I'd rather give him up than ask him to change his religion for me. What sort of people are you? Can you imagine if the boot were on the other foot? How would you all feel if he asked me to change my religion to please his family?"

Macit was then asked to try to intervene. Maybe the young rebel would listen to her brother-in-law, because she loved him very much.

"Macit, I am sure you know about the Jewish way of life. They believe that the children should follow the mother's religion.

Can you imagine what it would mean to them to have a daughter-in-law of a different religion? Oh, Macit, why is there all this fuss? Something that should bring joy has turned our lives into a nightmare."

"Listen, Selva, we can talk about religion till the cows come home, but let's first of all try to solve this problem. To begin with, why are you being so stubborn about asking Rafo to convert to Islam?"

"It's a matter of principle, Macit; we fell in love knowing exactly where we came from. Everyone has the right to their own beliefs. Had he asked me to convert, I would have been hurt and angry myself. No! Rafo will never change his religion! Please give my apologies to my father."

"You should apologize yourself. Give it another try. Speak to him."

"He refuses to see me."

In despair, Leman Hanım, caught between a stubborn husband and an equally stubborn daughter, broke down and sobbed. "Let her marry the Jew! God forbid we should have to bear the shame of our daughter living as someone's mistress."

Selva and Rafo were married that September at the Beyoğlu registry office in Istanbul, in the presence of two witnesses and a handful of friends. After the ceremony the small group dined at the Pera Palace Hotel, where the young couple spent the night before leaving for Paris by train the next morning. None of Rafo's family was at the station, but Leman Hanım and Sabiha were there on the platform to say good-bye. Leman Hanım chose to ignore Rafo but waved to Selva as the train pulled away. Selva returned their waves. Her outward calm covered her inner turmoil. The three women continued waving to each other until the train was out of sight.

On the way home, Sabiha felt a sudden sharp pain, as if she were being stabbed by a knife. The sister she had been jealous of for all those years had disappeared in the black smoke of the train. No more rivalry, no more sharing their parents' affections, no more sharing her husband's admiration. They were all hers, now that Selva would be hundreds of miles away. Strangely, instead of feeling relieved, Sabiha felt inconsolably sad.

About a month later, Sabiha was again called back to Istanbul. Leman Hanım had had an acute attack of asthma as well as uncontrollably high blood pressure. Both parents had been continuously ill—one after the other—since Selva's departure. They seemed to be falling apart at the seams. If it wasn't blood pressure, it was chest pains; if it wasn't chest pains, it was rheumatism; one thing after another. Each time there was a problem, Sabiha came from Ankara on the night train and remained until her parents had recovered.

When she returned to Ankara, Sabiha took off her nurse's hat and put on that of a diplomat's wife, carrying out her duties. The cocktail parties, dinners, and receptions she once enjoyed dressing up for now became a chore. She continued to attend them, but she no longer enjoyed being part of the crowd. She was permanently miserable, guilty at having been the culprit; yes, she was the devil that had imposed all the pain and turmoil on her family for her own ends. Time and again, she tried to discuss the matter with Macit, but he would only say that she wasn't to blame; her bullheaded sister would never change her mind, whatever they said. It was obvious that he was bored of the subject. What had happened had happened. What was the use of opening up old wounds?

ANKARA

Sabiha had made a few friends in Ankara, especially among the mothers at her daughter's school. There were also the wives of her husband's colleagues, most of whom had been raised in Istanbul too. These ladies would often get together to play bezique or bridge. In fact, Sabiha had her own bridge group. But since Selva had married and left for Paris, more often than not she preferred to stay at home and read a book or play the piano. She was almost scared that if she went along, the inevitable gossip session would turn to Selva, and she didn't want to face their questions.

Leman Hanım, despite her various ailments, was better at dealing with the gossipmongers. Whenever the subject was raised in her presence, she would simply say, "Our daughter went ahead with her own life, although we obviously didn't approve. We may be apart but we certainly include her in our prayers. There is nothing more to say on the subject."

Sabiha would react to this by thinking, That's OK for you, Mother. You have no reason to have a guilty conscience.

Sabiha's best and most trusted friend in Ankara was one of Macit's young clerks, Tarık Arıca.

Tarık was born in Malatya in eastern Anatolia; he went to primary school there, then secondary school and then the lycée in Sivas, all of which gave him a good grounding for the Istanbul School of Political Sciences, where his excellent results enabled him to join the ministry. He was very bright, eager to learn, and gained rapid promotions. The only problem was his lack of languages, but he was determined to put this right. He took weekend classes in French and studied very hard. Having heard from Macit that Sabiha spoke very good French, he asked if she could help him and she gladly agreed. If he hadn't any commitments in the evening, he would visit the house and sit and talk to Sabiha in French until dinnertime. Selva would send French magazines to her sister and she in turn would pass them on to Tarık and help him solve the French crosswords. Sabiha grew to love this bright, calm, honest young man; he hadn't an ounce of prejudice or malice in him. In a way Sabiha felt that Tarık and Selva were very similar in character. One day she plucked up enough courage to tell Tarık about Selva's scandal. What a relief to be able to tell someone; what a weight off her mind. Maybe her depression was caused from trying to hide the truth. If only Macit wouldn't stop her talking about it. Macit had behaved this way in order to stop his wife from getting upset. What he hadn't realized was that she needed to open the floodgates; she needed to cry, stamp, and kick to release all her pent-up tension. Now that she had such a good, trusted listener as Tarık, she was relieved. He had read between the lines and he understood the problem entirely. He hadn't asked painful questions; he had just listened. Tarık never spoke to Macit on this subject. This was between Sabiha and Tarık alone.

AN OVERSEAS POSTING

Macit entered the ground-floor meeting room at the foreign ministry to find his colleagues chatting around the table. The foreign minister soon joined them and the meeting began officially.

For some time now, Britain had been urging Turkey to declare war on Italy and form a front line with Yugoslavia and Greece. President Inönü had continually dragged his feet to avoid getting involved in this conflict. Now Britain had sent another communiqué. The British requested that Turkey declare publicly that, if the Germans invaded Bulgaria, Turkey would consider that as an attack on herself. Furthermore, Britain asked Turkey to send troops to some of the Greek islands in order to stop the Germans from attacking them.

After reading the note, those around the table began offering their opinions.

"Our president doesn't agree with any of it," said the foreign minister, "and I totally agree with him. Taking such actions—albeit with good intentions—may be interpreted wrongly."

"But sir, we wouldn't be sending our troops to invade the islands, we'd be providing protection from the Germans," one of the delegates said.

"I know the president doesn't want to have the slightest confrontation with the Greeks," interrupted the minister. "We may have the best of intentions, but the Greeks may misunderstand this. We shouldn't risk any possibility of conflict with our neighbors in these heated times. When Hitler attacked the Balkans, Turkey and Greece began the most amicable relationship in their history. This relationship shouldn't be jeopardized under any circumstances."

"There is another thing we should consider," said Macit. "If we send troops to Greece, Hitler will attack us immediately. How are we to defend ourselves then? The Allies haven't even provided us with the arms they promised."

"And I have doubts they ever will," said the foreign minister.

Britain had signed an agreement with Greece pledging to defend her if she was attacked, but when the Italians did attack, all the British did was send two aircraft squadrons.

"We signed an agreement with them in Paris, but, as Macit has just pointed out, so far nothing has come of it," said the prime minister. "They haven't been able to deliver any of the promised arms."

"That, despite the fact that you pointed out the importance of having a well-equipped army in Turkey to dissuade attacks on the Balkans, sir," said Macit, turning to the foreign minister.

"They didn't keep to the agreement—not because they didn't want to, but because they couldn't," the foreign minister said. "Maybe this is a blessing in disguise. Since they haven't delivered the goods, we don't have to abide by our side of the agreement either."

Macit didn't find it necessary to hide his joy at this; neither, it appeared, did the rest of the gathered assembly. "What is it that they say? Every cloud has a silver lining."

Inönü now had the perfect excuse for not joining the war. It was as though luck were on his side. If the Italians invaded Greece, then they would be on Turkey's doorstep. Since Turkey didn't have the arms to defend herself, what would be the good of siding with Britain?

After hours of discussion, the minister was able to draft a response to the British. Macit took the draft. He opened the door for the minister to leave.

"I will bring it to you as soon as it is ready," he said respectfully.

"I'll be in my office," the minister said to the general secretary. "We must remember that there are other important matters to deal with too, including the posting to Paris. You know they are desperate for more staff there. We mustn't let them down."

Macit got home in the early hours of the morning. He undressed in the sitting room and lay down on the sofa, so as not to disturb Sabiha. He was absolutely exhausted and fell into a deep sleep, not even missing his bed. He was dead tired, but nightmares kept invading his mind. It was as though those long meetings were coming back to haunt him. He dreamed that the Germans had attacked Ankara and were dragging his wife and child toward a train bound for a labor camp. He ran desperately to the train, trying to get on it himself to be with them.

The next morning at the office, Macit saw Tarık. They were both still really tired. "Have you got any plans for the weekend?" Macit asked.

"I have my French lesson between nine and twelve on Sunday, as you know, but nothing else after that."

"Don't make any plans. I'll ask Halit to join us if he is free and we can all have lunch together at Çiftlik open-air restaurant if the weather is fine. Then we can play bridge at home. How does that sound?"

"Sounds good to me," said Tarık. "How is Sabiha Hanım?"

"Fine, fine. Well, neither good nor bad, really. I've never been able to understand what makes women tick...Well, enough of that," he said. "Don't forget Sunday. I am sure Sabiha will be thrilled if you join us."

Macit was on his way to another of his long meetings. He collected the files from his office, tucked them under his arm, and rushed out. The telephone rang, and Tarık picked it up. "Hello... yes, sir...yes...yes...of course I can...I'll be there right away, sir." Buttoning his jacket, Tarık told the secretary that the secretary general wanted to see him, adding, "If anybody rings, tell them—hell, never mind, I'll be back shortly."

"I hope it's nothing serious," she said as Tarık left the room. Why would the chief want to see Tarık and not Macit? she wondered.

Tarık returned to his office half an hour later with the same look of surprise he'd had when he left. When Macit returned about an hour later, he found Tarık emptying his desk, piling everything on top.

"When you have finished tidying up, maybe we can grab some lunch," Macit said. "There are some interesting developments we need to discuss."

Tarık hurriedly replaced the files in the drawer. "I've got things to tell you too," he said.

"Really?"

"I'd like to thank you for the kind reference you wrote for my file."

"What's this all about?"

"I heard about your reference today."

"Those are supposed to be strictly confidential."

"Yes, of course. I only got the gist of it, but I know that you wrote some very positive things."

"Who told you so?"

"The secretary general."

"Unbelievable!"

"Macit, I'll tell you all about it over lunch. However, I'd like to tell you right away that you will have to find someone to replace me for bridge on Sunday."

"What on earth are you talking about, Tarık?"

"I won't be in Ankara on Sunday."

"I do hope that it is nothing serious. *İnşallah*, there is no death or sickness in the family?"

"No, no, thank God."

"Sabiha will be most disappointed."

Walking downstairs, the two colleagues continued their conversation.

"When Sabiha Hanım finds out where I'll be, she will be very happy for me."

Macit stopped suddenly and looked directly into Tarık's face. "Are you telling me that you are getting married, by any chance?"

"I'm talking about an overseas position, Macit. I've just been appointed second secretary in Paris."

"Oh, that!"

"You knew, then?"

"I knew it was under discussion. There was no question that you could cope with the job, but there was the language problem. This foreign minister asked me about your progress with French. I told him about your weekend lessons and the conversation practice with Sabiha."

"Yes, he told me that too. He told me everything was fine and that I could improve my French when I got there."

"I agree. You're one of the ministry's brightest young men, my friend. I am very happy for you, but the occupied area is dangerous."

"Yes, of course. That's why they prefer someone who is single."

Macit put his hand on Tarık's shoulder. "Congratulations," he said. "I'm sure you'll be very successful. Sabiha will be pleased, and sorry too. You know how she values your friendship. When are you off?"

"Apparently I'm to leave immediately. I had intended to visit my family in Malatya over the holiday, but it isn't to be. I wonder when I'll see them again. Needless to say, I must come and say good-bye to Sabiha Hanım. There may be a few things she would like me to take to her sister."

Macit tried to conceal his surprise that Sabiha had told Tarık a secret she'd kept from everyone else in Ankara. "Come on. I am taking you to my favorite restaurant, Karpiç, for a farewell lunch."

"Thank you, Macit," said Tarık. The look of surprise on his face was beginning to turn to anxiety about the future, with a hint of pride.

Sabiha indeed had mixed feelings about Tarık's posting. On the one hand, she was losing her close, trusted friend; on the other, she hoped that Tarık being in Paris would be advantageous for Selva. Should there be the need, Selva and her child could at least seek refuge in the embassy. Tarık would also be able to help Rafo too, if necessary. When they spoke about this during their good-byes, Macit was quick to point out that Tarık was going to Paris and Selva and her family were in Marseilles.

"Don't worry about that," Tarık said. "I am sure I will be able to communicate with them. I'll telephone them as soon as I arrive in Paris."

When Sabiha went into the kitchen to fetch the tea, Macit turned to Tarık with a word of warning. "Be careful, Tarık, this is very sensitive. Don't get yourself into any trouble. You are a Turkish diplomat and your duties come first. You shouldn't jeopardize your own position because of Selva and Rafo."

Sabiha was in tears when Tarık left. "I'll miss you, Tarık. I'm losing a very dear friend," she said, her voice trembling.

"You're not losing me at all. *Inşallah*, we'll see each other again after my posting is over. If I can manage to speak French at all, it is thanks to you, Sabiha Hanım."

He gently kissed Sabiha's hand, just as Macit and Numan did on such occasions, stopping himself from touching his forehead with his hand as they did back home. How could anyone know that this was the first time that he had kissed a lady's hand without touching it to his forehead? What he really wanted was to press Sabiha's hand tightly in his. He wished he could put his arms around her slender figure, and breathe in the scent of her long blonde hair. The woman of his dreams, the woman he would one day marry, must resemble Sabiha. Walking down the long hallway on his way out, what he'd never wanted to admit before suddenly dawned on him. Wherever he went he'd never forget Sabiha's fair complexion, or her sad green eyes. She would always have a special place in his heart.

❧

After Tarık left, Sabiha went straight to her room and lay motionless on her bed with her eyes closed. Macit entered the room. "There is something I want to propose to you," he said.

"About the fourth for bridge tomorrow?"

"No, darling. It's just that I have been thinking. You spend a lot of time on your own…" Sabiha opened her eyes, looking at her husband as he continued. "It looks like we are going to be extremely busy at the office over the next few days. I won't have any spare time to spend with you. We seem to be facing a new crisis every day. I was wondering…"

"What were you wondering?"

"Why don't we invite your parents here? Now that Istanbul is being evacuated, they could stay with us for a while. It would be a change for them and you won't have to worry."

Sabiha sat up on her bed. "That's an excellent idea!"

"Yes, I think so," Macit said, continuing with a certain reproach in his voice, "since you no longer have anyone to share your secret with."

"What? What do you mean by that?"

"I find it very interesting that you'd tell no one here about Selva, and yet Tarık seems to be fully aware of it."

"Macit, he listened to me."

"Did you try to tell anyone else who would listen, Sabiha?"

"To whom would I turn?"

"How do I know? Birsen, Necla, Hümeyra? You see them at least once a week. Don't you have any other friends? Why are you so obsessed with talking about Selva? Honestly, I don't understand why you continue to torture yourself about her."

"You'll never understand," Sabiha replied reproachfully, feeling a little proud. After all, wasn't there the hint of jealousy in Macit's remark?

FROM ISTANBUL TO PARIS

Tarık put the letter he had written to his mother, together with a few banknotes, in an envelope and sealed it carefully. He was sad that he wouldn't be able to visit his family for the holiday, and the thought of not knowing when he would see them again really depressed him. What bothered him most was that his father hadn't lived long enough to see his promotion. He would have dearly loved to visit his grave, say a prayer, and thank him. "Dear Father, your sacrifices haven't been in vain. May you rest in peace, safe in the knowledge that I'll conduct my life in the honorable way that you would want me to." Luckily, his apartment mates in Ankara returned the deposit he had paid for his room, and it was this money that he was able to send to his mother. He hoped he would be able to save money in Paris so he could continue to support her.

He had not been able to go to his family, nor had he had time to have a haircut before leaving! As soon as he was notified about his posting, he managed to duck out of the office, buy a suitcase, and book his ticket to Istanbul on the overnight train. His friends had advised him to do his shopping in Istanbul, and Macit gave him the names of several stores, insisting that he at least buy himself a good coat.

Tarık meticulously packed his gray suit and three white shirts. Between the shirts, he placed the letter and the small gift Sabiha had given him. He hoped that she hadn't put any money in her letter, but he hadn't the heart to open it and check. Yet friends who had been abroad had warned him that the Germans regularly rummaged through suitcases.

Tarık got everything ready for the overnight train to Istanbul next evening. He hung his new, freshly pressed, dark-blue suit in the wardrobe; he placed his passport, wallet, and train ticket on his bureau, beside the pocket watch he kept as a reminder of his father. From the frame of the mirror, he removed a photograph and looked at it for a moment. It was a picture taken of a group at the races. The half dozen or so faces were tiny. Yet Sabiha, with her long blonde hair, stood out distinctly. He put the photograph in his wallet.

He was about to embark on an adventure he could never have dreamed of back in the lycée in Sivas, and a cold shiver went down his spine. He switched off the bare overhead light and turned on his bedside lamp, holding his French book in his hand.

"*Moi, je m'appelle Tarık Arıca,*" he said to himself. "My name is Tarık Arıca. *Je viens d'Ankara. Je suis le consul général de Turquie*...I come from Ankara. I am the consul general of Turkey...My God, surely not!"

No, that wasn't right at all. He would merely be the second secretary; there was a long way to go before he became the consul or even the deputy consul!

"Mr. Consul," he murmured, closing his eyes tightly, "or how about Mr. Ambassador? Yes, Mr. Ambassador, His Excellency, Tarık."

He tried to picture himself in a top hat and tails, with a white scarf around his neck, holding a silver-topped cane, but the only vision that came to mind was that of a blonde woman. She was bent over a desk covered with books, sweeping back her blonde hair with her long fingers as it fell across her face. He only imagined it, but her green eyes were so clear. Perhaps her daughter was called Hülya (meaning "illusion") after her mother's dreamy eyes. Still in his dream, the same slender woman approached him and spoke to him in French, asking a question and then looking directly into his eyes. Tarık's hands began to sweat; what would this beautiful woman think of him if he was to answer in his funny accent? Such a vision…such a beauty…he tried to clear his throat before speaking.

Oui, je voudrais beaucoup…er…*avoir*…er…"Yes, I would very much like…to have…"

"Please don't be nervous, Tarık," said the vision. "Keep calm, think of what you want to say first."

"My accent is dreadful. I feel embarrassed."

"Nonsense, you shouldn't worry about your accent. Everyone speaking a foreign language has an accent. French isn't your mother tongue. Macit has an accent; so do I."

"No, not you. You don't."

"Perhaps it's because we had a French nanny when we were young, but rest assured, no foreigner can speak a new language without an accent. Don't feel embarrassed, Tarık. Repeat what you said, and I will correct you if you make a mistake."

Tarık felt the agony in his dream. He was deliriously happy, yet his palms were sweating and his heart fluttering like a bird's wings. He was scared not only of making a mistake but also, and more importantly, that he was falling in love.

Tarık got out of bed and paced the room. No, this wasn't love; perhaps it was a kind of idealization, he thought. Did he simply desire what was unattainable? To an Anatolian from the east of Turkey, Sabiha was the ideal woman—blonde, beautiful, well educated, and with all the social graces. She could speak several languages and was able to mix with all sorts of people, from all walks of life. He had never met such a woman before. On top of all this, she was his boss's wife, his friend's wife. Wasn't it Macit who had written that excellent report about him, who was so instrumental in his promotion? Should he eventually marry, Tarık knew that Sabiha was everything he wanted in a wife. That's it! This wasn't love; it was admiration!

Back in bed, Tarık wanted to fall asleep, but this time his excitement for the day ahead kept him awake. He was returning to Istanbul for the first time since his university days, and he was looking forward to being back in the city of domes and plane trees. He thought of the days when just walking down Pera Street in Beyoğlu was considered an adventure! And now he was returning to that enchanted city as a diplomat. A busy time lay ahead. Macit had recommended shopping at Karlman Arcade followed by dinner at Rejans, the Russian restaurant, where he should have chicken kiev washed down with yellow vodka to the strains of the balalaika orchestra. Another of Macit's "musts" was a visit to the Garden Bar at Tepebaşı or to the Park Hotel for a nightcap. Tarık wasn't one for drinking on his own, but he thought that he should make the most of his couple of days in Istanbul. They might be a sampler of the sophisticated times ahead for him. He didn't really care for the company of the boring snobs who frequented the bars and restaurants of Istanbul, but at least they spoke his language.

And then what?

What would become of him once he boarded that train and mixed with the other passengers? They probably wouldn't be speaking Turkish. He was headed for an occupied country. Europe was in the grip of war, and what if that war spread to Turkey? What if he never returned to his country again? He had only enough money to last him a couple of weeks, and he spoke a little bit of French. What if he got stuck in that turmoil? The few French words he'd uttered a short while ago came back to him. With fear in his voice, he said to himself, *Je suis le deuxième secrétaire à l'ambassade de Turquie.* He repeated this in his head, and then another sentence came to mind: "Please, God, help me!"

It was almost five in the morning before he fell asleep.

❧

That year spring had arrived in Istanbul hand in hand with sorrow. The dark lines of anxiety under everyone's eyes didn't go unnoticed by Tarık. The fear of war burdened everyone, young and old, men and women, rich and poor—no one was spared. By radio and newspaper, the government had issued the instructions for everyone to build bunkers or shelters. If an apartment building was more than three floors high, its ground floor had to be converted to a shelter with windows covered by sandbags. As a result, the city looked like one giant construction site. In spite of all this, Beyoğlu was still as buzzing, as colorful and joyful as Tarık remembered.

When Tarık left the Haydar Paşa Station on the Asian side of Istanbul, he could smell the salty sea air. He took the ferry over to Karaköy on the European side. Even though he was cold, he deliberately sat on the outside deck so he could watch the white, frothy waves on the sea. Once at Karaköy, he hailed a taxi and sat next to the driver, giving him the slip of paper with the address of his hotel.

The taxi driver drove through Yüksek Kaldırım to Pera and stopped in front of the Londra Hotel. There were sandbags piled in front of it, just as Tarık had seen in front of other buildings on the short drive.

"Look at all this," the driver said, pointing to the sacks. "It gets on people's nerves. We are not at war, but just look at this mess. We can hardly drive through the streets."

"It is always better to be cautious," said Tarık. "God forbid there should be a sudden air raid. Where would people find shelter?"

"It's fate, sir," said the driver. "Who knows when their number's up?"

The driver's words sent a chill down Tarık's spine, and yet, how typically fatalistic of a Turk. Tarık had thought that abandoning oneself to fate was a trait of people from the East, but here this Istanbul driver thought along the same lines. He got out of the taxi, and even before paying his fare he stood gazing at the view spread out before him. The silhouettes of the mosques, the domed cupolas, the plane trees on the hills, and the minarets pointing into the sky—it was indeed a breathtaking view. On the hillside, the red buds of Judas trees were just beginning to bloom. Istanbul looked like a watercolor: bright purple, blue, and green all mixed together with dashes of black India ink. In three days he would be leaving this extraordinary city to go to a war zone.

He paid the driver and collected his luggage. He couldn't help imitating the driver's tone of voice as he mumbled to himself, "It's fate, sir. Who knows when their number's up?" Walking up the hotel steps, he came face-to-face with the commissionaire dressed like a palace guard. He put down his suitcase as the commissionaire, full of his own importance, summoned the bellboy.

Just as the bellboy was putting the suitcase on the trolley, there was a frightful bang and Tarık fell flat on his face. Suddenly all hell let loose. There was the crashing of broken windows and people shrieking for help all around. Tarık lifted his head and saw the bellboy lying next to him.

"Are you all right?" he asked.

The boy turned his head and looked with a dazed expression. The mucus on his upper lip looked like a greasy mustache.

"Where the hell are we? Are we dead or alive?"

"We're not dead, my boy. We're lying at the entrance to the hotel."

"I don't believe it, sir!"

"A bomb exploded nearby," Tarık explained, struggling to stand up. He had hurt his knees very badly and had difficulty straightening up. The whole area was enveloped in a cloud of smoke and dust. Others around them who had been caught up in the explosion were coming out from under stairs or doorways and stretching. A short period of silence, broken by the agonized howling of a dog, ended with the din of Judgment Day: children started to cry, men and women called for help, police and guards blew their whistles, and cars sounded their horns. Tarık finally stood up; there was glass in his hair and his clothes were filthy. The bellboy was still lying facedown on the ground.

Tarık tried to lift him up. "Come on, my boy, you'd better try to stand up."

The young boy sat up but was still visibly shaken. When Tarık realized he couldn't get him up, he knelt down beside him and slapped him across the face. The boy started to cry.

By now people were pouring out through the hotel lobby in panic. Tarık looked around for his suitcase and saw the overturned trolley across the street. Tarık made his way through the panic-stricken crowds toward his suitcase. People were running in all directions trying to find out what had happened; sirens were sounding everywhere.

When Tarık returned with the trolley and his suitcase, the bellboy was on his feet but looking around in shock.

"Are you OK now? Look, I've got your trolley. Come on then, back to work."

"Was it a bomb, sir?"

"Yes, I'm afraid it was."

"Where?"

"I really don't know, but we'll soon find out. It must have been very near."

"Is anybody dead?"

"I don't know that either."

Tarık led the boy into the lobby, both of them trying to avoid stepping on the shattered glass. There they found total chaos and no receptionist. Several guests were attending to their wounds using their pristine white handkerchiefs. Tarık looked around. What was he to do now? It was then that he noticed that his pants were torn at the knees. "Damn it!" he mumbled. His new suit was ruined.

He decided to go upstairs and just find a vacant room. He went along the corridor trying one door after another. The first three were locked; the fourth opened but there were some belongings scattered around and the beds weren't made up. He tried another door on the opposite side; luckily this one was vacant. The beds were made and the cupboards empty. Tarık closed the door, opened his suitcase on the bed, and took out his old gray suit. In the bathroom, he took all the glass out of his hair and freshened up. A little while later, he went back down to the lobby wearing his gray suit. The receptionist was there, talking in an agitated manner to the guests.

"You weren't here when I arrived, so I was obliged to find myself a room. Here's the key," Tarık said. "I'm Tarık Arıca from Ankara. I believe the foreign ministry has reserved my room."

The receptionist looked confused. He stared briefly at Tarık and took the key without saying a word; it was obvious that he was still in shock.

"Have you been able to find out what happened?" Tarık asked.

"Apparently a bomb exploded at the Pera Palace Hotel nearby. Six people are dead and there are many wounded," replied the receptionist.

"Dead?"

"I understand the British ambassador to Sofia is on a visit to Istanbul. They say he has come to see Inönü. I wonder if there is a connection. Maybe it was an attempt to kill him."

"You mean Mr. Rendel?"

"Oh, you know him, do you?" asked the receptionist in amazement.

"No, I don't, but I know of him. Is he dead?"

The man knocked on wood. "Those working behind the reception desk were killed, but apparently the ambassador had just walked into the bar a few minutes before and he's safe and sound."

Tarık walked out of the hotel and down the street toward the Pera Palace Hotel. Policemen were trying to disperse the crowd in front of the hotel while nurses and doctors, stumbling over uprooted paving stones and twisted tram lines, carried the wounded to waiting ambulances. Squeezing through the crowd, Tarık approached a group of young men. He assumed they were journalists, as they were busy taking photographs.

He asked one of the men how it had happened.

"It seems the bomb was placed in a suitcase in the lobby."

Who was the bomb meant for? Tarık wondered. He thought probably the British ambassadors, Rendel and Hugessen, the ambassador to Turkey.

Tarık couldn't help feeling sorry for the poor souls who had been behind the reception desk, not to mention the innocent commuters who had just been going about their daily business. The taxi driver's words came back to him: "Who knows when their number's up?"

MARSEILLES 1940–41

Selva poured herself a cup of hot coffee, breathing in the aroma, thinking how interesting it was that human nature adapts itself to all sorts of situations. When she and Rafo had first settled in France, she hated this bitter coffee served in these huge cups. Fortunately, Sabiha, or rather, Macit had managed to bring her many packages of tea, plus six dainty Turkish tea glasses. Macit had visited France quite often in those days. It was such a joy to drink that Turkish tea at breakfast with Rafo.

After the birth of their son, Selva got used to this bitter coffee. She drank it to keep herself awake until the baby's last feeding at night. What had begun as a way of keeping herself awake had turned into an addiction. Rafo couldn't understand how she could drink "this poison." In fact, there were a number of things Rafo couldn't get used to here in France.

"For goodness' sake, don't criticize things in front of other people," she'd said when he first expressed his lack of enthusiasm. "They'll think you are a peasant. Fancy not enjoying the best cuisine in the world."

"I don't care what they think. The best cuisine in the world is Turkish. What do I care if they are ignorant?" Rafo insisted. "I will never understand how on earth French food has this great reputation. Those heavy sauces play havoc with your digestion, and just the thought of swallowing snails makes me want to throw up. And as for that cheese that smells like sweaty feet..."

Selva tried to get him to stop, but he wouldn't give up.

"Is there anything to beat the flavor of fresh vegetables cooked in olive oil, for instance? Can you tell me how they justify ruining the flavor of beautiful fish by smothering it in all those sauces?"

"Why on earth have we come here, then, if you hate the food so much?"

"Because their wines are absolutely magnificent."

"That may be, but we can't afford them, can we?" Selva reminded him.

"We will, my darling, we will. Trust me. Be a little patient. Look how well we have budgeted this month. If we can stick to this for a few more months, we will be able to afford all the best wines in the country."

If Rafo hadn't been able to fulfill that promise, Selva would not have been very upset, but as it happened just as Rafo had achieved his aim, everything turned upside down. Selva was sitting at the dining table helping their neighbor's daughter Yvonne with her English homework when suddenly they heard a commotion outside. Both rushed to the window. Yvonne, who was only nine, was so excited to see all the policemen on their motorcycles that she started to clap. Sitting stiff-backed on the motorcycles, they looked like statues. Selva immediately felt as though a desperate bird were fluttering in her heart. She put her hand on her huge tummy and prayed, "Please, God, protect our child."

As soon as Yvonne left, Selva rushed across the street to the pharmacy where Rafo worked, and when she saw his pale face, she felt she might miscarry. But she didn't, and the baby was born one month later, two weeks prematurely, a tiny son. They called the boy

Fazıl, after her father. Not that she hadn't worried about her father's objections to a Jew's son having his name. Even though she was still angry with him, she put those worries to the back of her mind because she still loved and missed him so much.

They had decided that should the baby be a boy, they would have him circumcised after seven days according to Jewish tradition. However, because of the ominous Nazi presence, they decided against it. The day Rafo made this decision, he hadn't been able to sleep all night.

Selva would sip her coffee and go through the accounts in her notebook. They were in a mess. By the time the Germans occupied the north of France and Paris, Selva and Rafo had already left for Marseilles; they had hoped they would be safe there, but events had taken an unexpected turn.

Marshal Pétain, who had taken over the Vichy government and declared himself president, had decided to cooperate with the Germans in order to prevent the rest of the country from being occupied. In his effort not to step on the Germans' toes, he had begun to accede to their every demand. The Vichy police even started to hunt down the Jews. De Gaulle, who had opposed any collaboration, had fled to Britain to form his Free French Forces. Unfortunately, neither the underground resistance nor de Gaulle in Britain could do much to help the Jews.

Selva lost two of her students when their Jewish parents decided to leave the area, but that turned out to be a blessing in disguise. Other parents who were planning to escape to America wanted Selva to teach their children. So she immediately had three new students and had to turn others away. She was happy to have more students, but Rafo warned her to be cautious.

"For God's sake, Selva, be careful. The Fascists are all over the place. They are bound to notice these youngsters coming and going."

"What's wrong with teaching English, Rafo? Is it forbidden to teach?"

"No, but it is forbidden to be Jewish."

Selva became more and more frustrated each day. She hadn't been able to forgive her father, because he looked down on people who were of a different faith. He, in turn, hadn't forgiven his daughter for his own reasons, probably mainly because his daughter had rebelled against his wishes. Selva had never wanted to believe that her father had opposed her marriage solely on religious grounds. She couldn't believe that the man she respected and loved so much was a religious bigot. What was all this fuss about religion? Surely, she thought, religion should be practiced without thought of race or color, with all its ceremonies carried out in mosques, churches, and synagogues. God was worshiped in these communities, and people reached out to him and found peace in their souls. Selva recalled the joy of Ramadan back home: the excitement of preparing the evening meals before breaking the fast; the special care not to miss prayers; the serenity of the older members of the household in their white headscarves before they prayed; the aura of mystery surrounding the muezzin's call. All these were exciting. Yes, religion was a many-splendored thing; surely it should be part of life and not used to separate people. Couldn't people from different religions love one another? Oh, dearest Father, she thought, is religion worth sacrificing your daughter? Is it worth rejecting your son-in-law, just because he prays in a synagogue?

Selva could well remember the debates she'd had with her father on the subject. In those days, Fazıl Reşat Paşa had no idea of what was to come. He too enjoyed having philosophical discussions with his daughter—that clever girl who willingly read every book he suggested. Later, they discussed them in detail for hours on end. The paşa had often pointed out that the more people became interested in science, the pursuit of knowledge, and culture, the less importance they placed on religion. He often told his daughter that most bigots or fanatics came from poor, ignorant backgrounds. Even during the time when Selva was falling madly in love with Rafo, she had discussed these issues with her father in depth. Respect for other religions? Of course! It is one of the conditions of being contemporary.

What about being enlightened by other religions?

Why, after all, was Fazıl Reşat Paşa giving Selva books to read about Far Eastern religions? Wasn't it because he wanted his daughter to understand not everybody was alike? There were those who didn't think the same. It was up to her to draw her own conclusions.

She had hoped to use her father's own views to defend herself regarding Rafo. She would remind him of his every word. But, sadly, when he learned of the romance, he put up a brick wall, simply saying, "Over my dead body. You cannot marry him. I won't give my permission."

At first Selva kept asking why. Even though her father was an open-minded person, he opposed a marriage that would go against his customs, his traditions. Dismayed, she soon found out that he had provided his daughters with a good education for his own reason. It wasn't to broaden their horizons, but so they'd raise good Muslim grandchildren for him.

Finally, she had to compromise. "Fine, if that's the way it must be. I certainly won't marry anyone else. Not one of Macit's friends at the ministry or the son of some paşa. It will have to be Rafael or no one."

Rafo seemed resigned to his fate. He was more concerned about the problems they might encounter than Selva was herself. What would be the reaction of his friends and family? How would he provide for this girl who was used to nothing but the best? Those were responsibilities he would have to shoulder.

Selva wrote to Rafo during the time she spent with her sister in Ankara—not love letters, but those of a friend. While she was there, Selva took the opportunity to observe those around her. Those in her sister's circle were mostly people who had made good marriages. What she'd learned from this experience was that if people chose to marry partners from a similar background, they stood a better chance that the relationship would last after their early passion waned. Especially after their children were born.

When she returned to Istanbul, Selva realized that none of the young men she'd been introduced to were of interest. She felt nothing for any of the young diplomats she had met through her brother-in-law. She wasn't just being stubborn; she simply had nothing in common with these young men. In her opinion, they were only interested in themselves, and, dictated by their mothers, they were looking for suitable wealthy debutantes to marry. None of them made her smile, much less roamed the streets with her, happily and aimlessly. They only wanted to take her dancing at the Ankara Palace after the receptions. Putting their arms around her waist, they waltzed in their squeaky, patent-leather shoes. Some tried to kiss her, merely touching her lips with their own, and she felt nothing. She was bored. Back at Sabiha's house, she lay on her bed in her young niece's bedroom. She looked up at the shadows thrown onto the ceiling by the streetlights outside.

She had only one life to live: Did they expect her to waste it? Her father was behaving totally against his nature, and, in so doing, poisoning her life. She would not be able to marry, or to be happy, or to know the love of a child. In short, she wouldn't be able to live her life. Why? Because Fazıl Reşat Paşa said so! Because of what their relatives, friends, and neighbors would say! Was what people thought more important than her happiness? No! With these thoughts she decided to send word to Rafo and ask if he still wanted her.

Rafo certainly did want her, but at the same time he was reluctant to disrupt her life. He was scared of not being able to offer her the life to which she was accustomed. Since his own family would renounce him too, they would have to live on what he could earn. Was Selva ready for this? He urged her to wait and think carefully about her decision. He didn't want her to have regrets later.

Selva had thought about all of this when she was sent to stay with her uncle in Cyprus and decided she was willing to take the risk. She was willing to face the problems ahead, to live in a foreign country far from her family, even to make do with little money. She had thought about everything, and had answers for every question. She hadn't discussed it with Rafo because she was sure that she knew his answer. She knew Rafo wanted her just as much as she wanted him.

After she spent that difficult year in Cyprus, Selva's mind was made up, and she informed Rafo of her decision. She was, however, taken aback to find out that Sabiha, who had been her confidante and staunch supporter, had changed her tune. Hadn't she initially encouraged her relationship with Rafo? Now she spent hours—until early in the morning—trying to make her change her mind, as if she hadn't been instrumental in helping Selva's clandestine meetings with Rafo.

"How could I have known that you'd be crazy enough to let things go so far?" Sabiha kept saying. "How could I have known that you would fall in love, let alone want to marry him? Never! It never entered my mind!"

And what of her father, her father she had loved and respected above all others her entire life? He had even attempted suicide, hoping that she would change her mind. In fact, as far as Selva was concerned, that was the point of no return.

"Let's run away from here as soon as possible, Rafo," she said. "Let's go somewhere with different values that aren't so extreme. Let's run away from our families' emotional blackmail."

Finally they left. But now the torment they had endured in Istanbul seemed nothing in comparison to the humiliation and suffering the Germans inflicted on the Jews. The Germans, with their steely eyes and hard expressions, were putting the Jews in France through hell. Selva loathed them, and she wondered how Rafo felt deep down inside.

Just as Selva was checking the additions in her accounts book she heard the footsteps of the postman. He delivered a couple of bills and a letter from Sabiha!

She closed the accounts book and poured herself a fresh cup of coffee. Sitting in the armchair in front of the window, stretching her legs on the footstool, she tore open the letter. The best minutes of her day were about to begin. Before young Fazıl woke up, she would have about an hour to devour the letter's every word and dream of the old country.

Her sister wrote about someone called Tarık. She vaguely remembered that name—yes, that's right, Sabiha had mentioned him once before. Tarık had now been posted to France and was due to arrive very soon. Apparently she'd sent some money with him, and she gave instructions that Selva should call him if she ran into trouble.

Selva wondered, for goodness' sake, am I supposed to call this Tarık for the smallest problems? What if we need to escape? What is she going on about? Escape, run away, to where? Haven't we already run away? Haven't we escaped from all our friends' anger and gossip? Our neighbors', even our butcher's nasty looks? Where on earth are we supposed to run to this time? Are we never going to find peace? It's as if those that didn't allow us to finish university have donned Nazi uniforms and followed us here.

Anyway…Hülya did very well at school. Mother, Father, and Sabiha attended the end-of-term ceremony, although Macit was again too busy at the ministry to attend. It appears the change of air has really improved Father's health; he is much more relaxed in Ankara.

Relaxed! thought Selva. Of course. No one knows him in Ankara. Nobody points him out as "the man whose daughter ran off with a Jew."

Mother too has benefited from the dry Ankara air—she has no more asthma attacks, for one thing. Since Father is more relaxed, he helps her as well. The poor woman carries a photograph of little Fazıl with her wherever she goes.

Well, Selva decided, at least Father has not objected to my calling my son after him. Who knows? Maybe one day…

Suddenly there were loud noises outside in the street. Selva jumped up to the window to see what was going on, knocking her coffee cup to the floor with a crash. Young Fazıl woke up and started to cry. Two people were running after a man, overturning everything in their way. A woman was screaming at the top of her voice. Selva wiped up the spilled coffee and put the letter away before going in to check on Fazıl.

"Don't cry, my baby," she said. "I know your father doesn't like us going out, but we both need some fresh air."

Selva seldom left the apartment. Rafo tried to protect her from all the dreadful things that were happening in the streets, and he continually created all sorts of pretexts to keep her indoors. He even came home for lunch to stop his wife from coming to him. He was adamant that she should be safe, adapting to their new life in France and bringing up a new baby. The streets of Marseilles were getting more alarming, more depressing.

It hadn't been easy for them to sever themselves from the easy-going, comfortable lives they had led with their families in Istanbul. But they had both chosen to change their lives to be together. They were both trying hard to adjust; it had almost been like changing their identities.

Selva was no longer Fazıl Reşat Paşa's spoiled little girl who lived in a mansion during the winter and a villa by the sea in the summer. She was no longer the rich girl who wore couture dresses and was admired by all; she was now simply the wife of a Jewish apprentice chemist. Rafo hadn't been able to get his French citizenship, and was therefore unable to register his partnership at the pharmacy legally. He had completed the papers, but due to the collaborationist Vichy regime, Rafo decided with his business partner to postpone the idea of citizenship for the time being.

Rafo was the middle son of the Alfandari family, highly respected not only in their own community but also in the wider Istanbul medical community. Four generations of the Alfandaris had served as palace physicians. Rafo's mother's greatest wish was that he should follow the family tradition and become a chemist. Giving up his studies for Selva had shattered her dream. Not only was Rafael Alfandari no longer a Turkish Jew, he wasn't even a French one. Furthermore, his decision not to circumcise his son had put his Jewishness in doubt. Rafo had ended up without identity, country, or religion.

Yes, undoubtedly, he loved Selva, but he had never foreseen burning all his bridges. Neither he nor Selva had actually wanted this, and he wondered how on earth they had found themselves in this position.

When he met Selva, Rafo would still have been considered a youth. He was a student, wearing a school uniform. The tall girl who had joined his class was very different from all the other girls, had drawn his attention, and they had become friends.

One day he had been invited for tea at the girl's mansion. Oh, how proud and excited his mother was. She starched his shirt and pressed his pants herself. Her son certainly couldn't go to tea empty-handed. Should he take chocolates or flowers? When he came home, she bombarded him with questions. Was the inside as opulent as the outside? Were the paşa and his wife at home? Had Rafo met them? How many guests were there? What did they have for tea? Were the pastries from Lebon or were they homemade? Did they have tea or soft drinks? Who had actually served the tea?

Later, Rafo was invited to the grand mansion again, and then to other places. He had started to follow Selva like a shadow. Selva, the girl with the blonde plaits on top of her head; Selva, the calm girl with the big brown eyes, who always looked a little perplexed, but whose whole face lit up when she laughed, the girl who not only had a lot to say for herself but could also listen attentively.

Selva's relationship with Sabiha changed the summer that her sister got engaged. They would leave the summer villa on one of the Princes' Islands in the Sea of Marmara and take the ferry to the European side of Istanbul. There Sabiha and Selva would go to a café in Pera to meet Macit. Rafo would join them a little later. Rafo and Selva would leave the engaged couple and venture off into the side streets. On one occasion they even hopped on a tram and crossed the Karaköy Bridge over the Golden Horn, going on to Eyüp to visit the Eyüp Sultan Mosque. Once there, they wandered around the cemetery reading interesting verses on the tombstones. Another time they walked along the Golden Horn as far as the Feshane Pier. They had really enjoyed exploring the Greek quarter at Fener. Rafo had also taken Selva to Tatavla, where all the Greek tavernas were. Selva felt as if she had discovered a fascinating new world, with all its colors and cultures, existing beyond her own narrow world. She became eager to learn more.

One September afternoon, after leaving Sabiha and Macit at the Marquise Café, Rafo at last took Selva to his home. His parents were away at their summerhouse in Tarabya by the Bosphorus. The furniture in the drawing room was covered with dust sheets; the carpets were rolled up neatly against the walls; the crystal chandeliers were wrapped in newspaper. It was all rather dark. Selva sat on the edge of the covered sofa next to Rafo. He gently turned Selva's face toward him and kissed her.

"Do you want to make love to me?" Selva asked, much to Rafo's surprise. "Rafo, I asked you a question."

"No, I don't know what you mean. Yes. No. I mean, what sort of a question is that?"

"I think that it was very clear. Yes or no?"

"You know I do, but I shouldn't. Of course…I mean, I didn't have that in mind when I kissed you."

"I didn't ask about your intention. I asked if you *wanted* to."

"Selva, darling, you know I wouldn't do anything to hurt you."

"You're not answering my question."

Rafo looked at her intensely, trying to figure out what she meant. Selva was waiting for an answer, her eyes wide open.

"Yes, I do want to make love to you, very much."

"Why?"

"Because I love you, of course."

"Do you really love me?"

"Don't you know that?"

"You've never told me so."

"Maybe because I haven't dared to."

"Why's that?"

"I didn't want to make you angry."

"How could I possibly be angry that you love me?"

"Well, I thought that you might think I was being audacious."

"Fine, let's consider it said then, and as you can see I'm not angry."

Rafo lowered his head and kissed her again.

"Just imagine, Rafo, that even though you love me, you might end up getting married to someone else and making love to her. The same goes for me too, of course."

"It isn't possible to change your destiny, Selva."

"Isn't it?"

As Rafo lowered his head to kiss Selva for the third time, he suddenly realized that he was passing the reins of their fate into Selva's hands. They spent the rest of the day in that dark room until it was time to rejoin Sabiha. He hadn't managed to pluck up the courage to kiss her again. Selva had neither encouraged nor discouraged him. For his part, he couldn't decide whether or not his advances might have a negative effect. His mind and his feelings were in turmoil. He had had the desire to let her long blonde hair flow down her slender body, which he presumed was as smooth as velvet and as white as snow. But in the end he had to make do with continuing their conversation, which was led by Selva.

When the clock struck six, announcing it was time to leave, she got up, swayed toward the door, and left the room without exchanging another kiss. They walked hand in hand down the marble steps of the house and onto the narrow streets of Pera. They took the metro from Tünel to Karaköy, where they met Sabiha at the pier before the two sisters took the boat back to the Princes' Islands.

"So what have you been doing today?" Sabiha asked.

Rafo was about to answer, but Selva interrupted him.

"We went to Rafo's home," she replied.

"What? Was there anybody there?" she asked, sounding surprised.

"No."

"So what were you up to then?"

"What do you do sitting at home? We talked."

"Goodness gracious, you two never stop talking. You could have gone to the cinema."

"We never run out of things to talk about," Selva said before turning to Rafo and kissing him good-bye on the cheek. Rafo was thrilled, as if a shock went straight from his cheek to his heart.

It was something totally different from what he had felt when he kissed Selva on the lips. It was as though she was taking care of him; she was publicly acknowledging their relationship. Rafo felt an inexplicable warmth toward her as he walked to the bus stop for Tarabya. He felt proud! Good Lord, she loves me! he thought to himself. Mother, Mother, Selva loves me!

Rafo's mother, Rakela, was no longer as enthusiastic as she had been when Rafo first told her that he had been invited to Fazıl Reşat Paşa's house. At the time, she had felt very proud that one of her sons had befriended the daughter of one of the most prominent Turkish families. Her mother-in-law had been less excited. "What's so special about that? Don't forget that your husband is an Alfandari!"

Rakela would never have known what was going on if one of her friends hadn't told her about the gossip concerning her son. She had been having endless arguments with Rafael herself already. She believed him to be her most intelligent son. Later, his decision to leave the university came as a great shock. Rafael was unlike his brothers. He always had a mind of his own. He was the one who criticized his family for speaking Spanish Hebrew—Ladino—and not Turkish at home. He didn't see any sense in speaking the language of a country that had tortured and banished his people many years ago. Rakela presumed that her son's decision to leave university had something to do with that. But maybe he had gotten too emotional about an incident there, and turned it into a matter of pride and honor. She'd noticed that her son had had bouts of depression ever since his father died. Did he feel guilty that he hadn't been able to help his father? No one in the family had realized how bad Salvador Alfandari's heart was until the night he had that fatal heart attack.

Rakela badgered her son with questions. Why was he studying chemistry if he found it so difficult? Why didn't he choose another subject at least? Why couldn't he take a sabbatical and continue with his studies the following year?

When Rakela's friend Rosa visited her one evening, what she had to relate was typical of the gossip at the time. The story, of course, bore no resemblance to the facts. Rosa told Rakela that it was Fazıl Reşat Paşa who had had Rafael removed from the university, because Rafo had the audacity to pester his daughter.

That was the first time in her life that Rakela had cursed the Turks. The following day she sought the assistance of all the family elders whom Rafael loved and respected. She asked them to intervene and give him advice.

She blamed herself for not having foreseen this catastrophe. Her darling son had abandoned his studies because of this despicable blonde devil in disguise! All those hopes and dreams she had had for her son. He was supposed to launch a range of lavender-based perfumes—she had discussed this project with a nephew in France, and he'd been preparing to market the products for them. Who knew? Maybe one day Rafael would become the owner of his very own perfumery. Even names had been discussed—Les Nuits du Bosphore or Essence d'Orient for the ladies' range, or Raff for the men's products.

When she finally confronted her son about Selva, she received yet another blow. Rafo had gone as far as discussing the possibility of marrying her. Rakela's dismay at Rafo's academic underachievement was nothing in comparison to the thought that he was considering marrying a Muslim girl.

That year the Passover meant nothing to Rakela. She hadn't bothered to bring down and wash her precious piñatas from the attic. She couldn't bring herself to prepare the special celebration meal of *pescado con huevos y limones*. She didn't even supervise the making of the matzo.

The rest of the family didn't feel much better. Every single person had tried to dissuade Rafo from taking this step. Each had either chastised him or tried to advise him, some even resorting to emotional blackmail. Rafo began to think that he was lucky that his father had died two years previously. He shuddered to think how he would have reacted. The only person to adopt a totally different approach was his uncle Jack.

"Every cloud has a silver lining," he said to his elder sister Rakela. "Just think of the advantages should your son become Fazıl Reşat Paşa's son-in-law. Instead of wishing that your son would leave this girl, you should be praying that he is accepted into such a family."

Rafo had not been accepted by the paşa, and Selva had not changed her mind.

And yet, Rafo had not been able to express his fears for their future. Was what they were about to do madness? At first he thought that the fire inside him would cool, or that Selva would be persuaded to change her mind. But Selva had no such intention; she wasn't giving him up. Nor did he have the nerve to stop himself. He was proud to be so loved by this girl he admired so much, and there was also the excitement of tasting forbidden fruit. Many of his friends looked upon him with envy, as if he were the hero in a fairy tale. Unfortunately, his relatives—particularly his mother—did not share this view.

Rakela did not give up. "One would think you were Aladdin in love with the sultan's daughter," she said, crying her eyes out. "Can't you see they don't even deign to speak to us? All we hear about is how angry and disappointed the paşa and his wife are. What about me, what about my family, for God's sake? One would think that we are enamored of that beanpole! How heartbroken and ashamed we are! Where is your dignity?"

Rafael did indeed have dignity, and that was precisely why he couldn't give Selva up.

Selva still believed that eventually both families would come around to accepting the situation, especially after they had children.

Rafael, on the other hand, knew very well that if their child was brought up as a Muslim, his family would never forgive him. Likewise, if the child was brought up as a Jew, Selva's family would never forgive her.

"Time will heal everything," Selva said. "They are bound to miss us when we live abroad. Surely they will mellow when they see how solid our relationship is. Leave it to time."

Rafo envisaged all sorts of scenarios in his mind. He knew they'd have financial problems, as well as difficulties adapting to a foreign country. He knew that they would be lonely too, at times. But he'd never imagined the hell they were suffering these days. It was all beyond his worst dreams.

Here he was, in Marseilles, without a valid passport, an apprentice, even though he had paid to become a partner. He was truly pitiful: afraid to have his son circumcised and in a position where at any time he might be dragged away from his wife and child and sent to a labor camp. He was risking a death sentence even though he had committed no crime. He could be sent to the gallows without a trial. Yes, he had foreseen problems, but nothing of this magnitude.

These were the thoughts going through Rafo's mind as he perched among the cardboard boxes in the pharmacy storeroom. Waiting for the commotion outside to calm down, he couldn't help cursing his fate.

How long he awkwardly sat there in the dark waiting for the all clear he didn't know, but when he tried to get up, he realized he had strained his back.

"They're gone," said Benoit. "You can come out now; I don't think they're coming back. Why won't you go to the Turkish consulate? If I were you, I would have gone ages ago."

The light outside blinded Rafo, and he rubbed his eyes, squinting. "You're really obsessed with this idea," he said.

"I promise you, I have heard from various sources that those with Turkish passports can save their skins."

"Don't believe everything you hear," Rafo said, rubbing his back.

"I swear it's true. Why do you think the lines outside the consulate are getting longer every day?"

"Those are lines of people who left Turkey after the First World War. In fact, we have friends among them. My situation isn't the same."

"Rafo, most of them got their French nationality. They gave up their Turkish citizenship years ago. Now they are lining up for days on end for their Turkish passports again."

"Where did you learn all this from, Beno? You have your French nationality. Nobody knows that your mother was Jewish, so what's all this to you?"

"I've made inquiries on your behalf. One of the consulate employees is my aunt's tenant. The other day when I went to see her, he came to pay his rent. He's a very nice man. He speaks French. We had a cup of coffee together."

"So?"

"I mentioned you…Oh, for God's sake, don't get on your high horse. I didn't give him your name. I simply said that I had a friend from Istanbul with a residence permit who hasn't applied for citizenship yet. 'Let him come,' he said. 'Even if his Turkish passport has expired, we can immediately extend it.'"

"I don't believe this!"

"I swear that's what he said."

"You're joking."

"Rafo, I'm telling you the truth. If you have doubts, why not let your wife apply on your behalf?"

"I've told Selva to leave and go back to Istanbul, but she won't listen. She'll never go back on her word, so a Turkish passport won't solve our problem."

"It certainly will, Rafo. I'm telling you."

"How?"

"Well, I don't really know. Maybe the Turks have some sort of agreement with the Germans. Maybe they are their allies. How the hell do I know? I'm a chemist, not a diplomat."

"Nonsense," said Rafo. "The Turks would never take the Germans' side."

"Why not? Didn't they in the First World War?"

Rafo felt like saying, "They certainly did, but what a mistake that was." He kept quiet. He stretched to ease his back, trying to change the subject. "Let's get out of here. I've been stuck in this cramped place for hours."

"Just twenty-three minutes," Benoit replied.

"Twenty-three minutes, it feels like twenty-three hours."

They walked downstairs from the storeroom to the pharmacy, Rafo still rubbing his back. An old man entered the shop.

"Welcome," said Rafo.

The man didn't say a word.

"What can I do for you, monsieur?"

"I don't really know. Actually, there's nothing I wanted. I'll have an aspirin, please. Yes, just an aspirin."

"Monsieur, you're shaking. Are you all right? Would you like to sit down?"

Benoit offered the man a chair from behind the counter. "Sit over here, relax," he said.

The old man sat down, put his elbows on his knees, and cradled his head in his hands. He was shaking visibly.

"Epilepsy?" Rafo whispered to Benoit.

"No, he's crying."

The two friends looked at each other.

"Would you like some water?"

"Maybe a sedative?"

The old man shook his head and continued crying for a while before straightening up. "I want my dignity back, gentlemen," he said. "Nothing else, neither water nor medicine."

"These are hard days for everyone," Benoit said. "Life isn't easy for any of us."

"You know this decrepit old man, Pétain, the conspirator, the traitor. Once I used to admire him. I thought he was a hero. I even had a framed photograph of him on my desk. I wish I'd known then what I know now."

"Marshal Pétain believes he is protecting the French. If he hadn't cooperated, the invasion forces would have reached us here," Benoit said softly. "Would that be better?"

"My dear boy, two-faced Pétain isn't capable of stopping them coming south. Don't kid yourself. They'll be here soon enough. When that day dawns, we'll be doomed. You'll see. When that day comes, we'll lose everything. This Vichy government has taken over and we've lost everything anyway, including our dignity."

Benoit looked around anxiously. "You're distressed, monsieur. Don't talk this way. Someone might hear."

"Just now, they stopped a man walking two paces in front of me. They asked for his identity papers. Apparently, he didn't have them. They started to manhandle him and he resisted. Then they dragged him into their jeep. Can you guess what they did then? Do you by any chance know how they check if you are Jewish? Luckily, I am all skin and bone, so I was able to hide behind a big tree. I ran and ran all the way down the street, from tree to tree, to get away from them. I haven't run that way for at least fifteen years. I ducked into every street. I even pissed myself. Look. I didn't have my identity papers with me either. I had to run away, otherwise I would have had to show my penis to those bastards who call themselves policemen. I ran away. And why am I running away, son? I'm not a thief, I'm not a murderer, and I'm not guilty of anything. I'm eighty-two years old. I haven't got the strength anymore...I can't keep running away."

Rafo pretended not to notice the wet stain on the front of the man's pants.

"Give me some sleeping pills!"

"I can't sell those without a prescription," said Benoit. "You'd better get one from your doctor."

"I haven't got a doctor. He left. Those who were intelligent and young left. The trash stayed behind; we couldn't make it. Why don't you be a good boy and give me some sleeping pills?"

Rafo took two pills from a box and gave them to the man. "This will do you for tonight; you should get a good night's sleep," he said, refusing to accept payment.

The old man got up, put the two pills in his pocket, and staggered out. He came back immediately looking very confused.

"Gentlemen, where am I now? I don't think I recognize this district. I'm sure I visited a friend in a hospital in that square, but I don't know my way around. Is there a bus stop near here?"

Benoit went outside with the old man. "Let me show you the way."

When Benoit returned, Rafo was sulking. "We could have done without harboring that damned informer," he said.

"For heaven's sake, Rafo, do me a favor and stop talking like that. Even walls have ears nowadays. You could get us both into trouble if you carry on like that. That poor old man had nothing to lose. Didn't you see? He wouldn't have been so outspoken if he'd been fifteen years younger."

"Was he telling the truth, Beno? Is it possible the police have stooped that low?"

"I honestly don't know. I don't think so. He was probably exaggerating."

"I might go to the Turkish consulate after all. If I am going to be messed and shoved around, I can do that just as well back home."

"Come on, Rafo, you wouldn't be shoved around there. Many German Jews escaped to Turkey. There is a cousin of mine on my mother's side—Leon Arnt—and a very close family friend, Auerbach. Both managed to get away and are now teaching chemistry at the Istanbul University. Do it, Rafo. Get up and go before it's too late. Forget about your pride, you owe it to your wife and child."

"It isn't just a matter of pride. If that were the case, I wouldn't have come all the way here. Do you know what would be ahead for me? For a start, my son—will he be Jewish or Muslim? Whichever we choose will cause outrage. Our families and friends won't want to know us. It isn't as bad feeling lonely in a country where you don't know anyone. Can you imagine being ignored by everyone in a place where you have many friends and family? My father-in-law doesn't even want to know his daughter. As for my family, can you imagine, they no longer set my place for Passover? Why do you think we came all the way here?"

"Yes, I understand," said Beno. "It must be difficult, very difficult, but as I said before, no one's situation is easy these days. We all seem to live in some kind of hell or other."

Rafo didn't reply. He was standing in the doorway watching the bent old man stumbling down the street, still trembling visibly.

ANKARA 1941

As Macit walked home from the ministry, he was happy that he had things to relate to his father-in-law over their raki. He and the old man had been living under the same roof for some time now, and Macit had grown to like Fazıl Reşat Paşa. At first he was rather nervous of this elderly Ottoman gentleman who still dressed in the old style, but the paşa had adapted well to the new republic. Whether intentionally or not, he had gradually relaxed with Macit and begun to reveal his weaknesses. In spite of all his progressive ideas, the paşa hadn't been able to come to terms with the collapse of the empire and the fact that the sultan had been forced to run away. As far as he was concerned, the War of Liberation ought to have been fought under the sultan's banner. If a change was necessary, maybe the sultan ought to have been changed, but not the regime. People living on Ottoman soil weren't as cultured as the Europeans; they didn't have the know-how to govern themselves. They could only be governed by a leader like a sultan or *padishah* who also had religious authority. Whenever the old man spoke, he deliberately avoided mentioning the republic, preferring instead to use words like *Ottoman*, *Ottoman soil*, or *Ottoman administrators*. Like most of the Ottoman paşas, Fazıl Reşat was a well-educated man who hated fanatics. He believed that reactionaries were destroying his country. All the same, he was against being governed by those without religious authority; he was particularly against being "ruled by the people." Macit considered these ideas nonsensical but always listened quietly, respectfully, refraining from making comments. He could never understand how a cultured person, who had adapted so well to modern living, could go on and on about the importance of a sultan.

Although Fazıl Reşat Paşa was an advocate of a sultan, he was also a man who had an accurate understanding of most things and enjoyed life to the full. Every evening he would wait for Macit, sitting beside a small table with a selection of mezes that he had prepared himself. Together they would sit on their stools in the small hallway between the kitchen and dining room, chatting about the day's developments, sipping ice-cold raki, and nibbling on white cheese and roasted chickpeas. Macit was certain that the paşa chose this small corridor so that the ladies of the house couldn't join them. It was obvious that, after spending all day with his wife, daughter, and grandchild, listening to "woman talk," in the evening the poor man needed a change.

Fazıl Reşat Paşa always listened attentively to Macit and often made some unexpectedly incisive comments. For example, he was certain that getting involved with the Germans would have disastrous results. As far as he was concerned, it was the Germans who somehow always managed to stir up trouble in the world. Although he never mentioned Selva and Rafo, he was furious about the atrocities the Germans were inflicting on the Jews. He was sure that one day history would judge them and they would have to pay for their injustices. Macit couldn't understand how such a wise man was unable to find it in his heart to forgive his young daughter.

Today, the paşa had prepared their raki on the marble kitchen counter; they picked up their glasses and began to sip.

"A very important development took place today, sir," said Macit. "The British ambassador delivered a letter to President Inönü."

"Really! And what do they want?"

"They want two things. The first is, they definitely want us to sign an agreement with the Russians—"

"Surely not!"

"As a matter of fact, we have been putting that one on the back burner for some time. The other thing is something we've hoped for, even though it seems negative. Because, in the present circumstances, we are so isolated, both geographically and strategically, it appears that the British won't be able to come to our aid if we're attacked…"

"Well, well, just listen to them. We are expected to run to their rescue but they won't do the same for us. Doesn't still water run deep? They have certainly mastered the art of backstabbing."

"Actually we are rather happy about this, sir. They say that since they are in no position to help us, they'd consider it sensible if we should contact the Germans, making sure we at least eliminate the danger of an attack."

"You don't say! In other words our president, the deaf old fox, has solved the problem just by being patient."

Macit stifled a laugh.

"Inönü may have trouble hearing, sir, but he has a good brain. Now that Hitler has attacked Russia, he has finally relaxed a bit. Do you know that when they telephoned and woke him up in the early hours to tell him of Hitler invading Russia, he burst into laughter and couldn't stop? Can you believe the brilliance of Inönü's plan? Had we sided with the British, we'd now be face-to-face with Mr. Hitler. The way things are, we neither sided with the British nor the Germans, and we avoided becoming either's enemy. On top of that, the British are encouraging us to have good relations with the Germans."

"So, how did the British come to this brilliant decision?"

"It's the only way to stop the Germans invading Turkey. Of course there is another thing..."

"What's that?"

"We are to inform the British of the details of our negotiations in writing and act outside these parameters."

"Do you know, my son," said the paşa in a trembling voice, "I just can't stomach the fact that damned foreigners are dictating what we should do. Would the Great Ottoman have stooped to this?"

"But, sir, wasn't it the same before the republic? How on earth were we supposed to equip our forces when we inherited a crushing gold debt from the Ottomans? Didn't we need charity from the British?"

"I'm not defending the Ottomans, my son. I am aware of all of our mistakes, but it still hurts."

"They are not your mistakes, sir; they are mistakes that have accumulated over the centuries. Please, God, let us pave the way to a stronger and wealthier nation for our children."

"Yes, we have certainly made a mess of things. *Inşallah*, you will succeed," Fazıl Reşat Paşa said sadly.

"I do understand how you feel, sir, but believe me, Inönü is doing his best to protect our country's honor. I know because I deal with Hitler's correspondence. The Germans sent us a friendly letter back in February promising that their forces wouldn't come anywhere near the Turkish borders. But there was a restrictive amendment that said, 'as long as the Turkish government doesn't force us to change our attitude.'"

"And..."

"In his reply, Inönü thanked Hitler appropriately, but then he added a restriction using, more or less, Hitler's wording."

"What did he say?"

"He said, 'as long as the German government doesn't take measures that force Turkey to change *their* friendly attitude.' Tit for tat, in other words. Hitler has always addressed the weaker countries harshly. Perhaps Inönü's proud, almost haughty, manner baffled him a bit."

This conversation would have continued had it not been for Sabiha joining them. She was holding a letter and some photographs.

"Look, Macit, a letter sent ages ago has finally arrived today. Selva sent some pictures of little Fazıl." She glanced at her father. "The little boy must have grown since she sent this letter. Children change so quickly at this age. Have a look, darling…Isn't he cute? His eyes and nose are exactly like Selva's."

Macit looked at the photographs nonchalantly, avoiding eye contact with his father-in-law, and put them back in the envelope.

"Yes, very nice."

"Don't you agree that he looks like Selva, especially around the mouth?"

"Sabiha, I was in the middle of an important conversation with your father."

"You're always like that—whatever you're talking about is so important," she said angrily.

Sabiha laid the envelope with the photographs on the small table where her father could see it, and left. Fazıl Reşat Paşa didn't look. He poured himself a little more raki from the small carafe.

"Let me get some more ice for you," Macit said, going to the kitchen.

The so-called icebox was a small wooden cupboard lined with zinc. They would buy large blocks of ice from a restaurant, break them up, and put the ice in the box. Inside the icebox were some long brown bottles of Tekel beer. A carafe of water was crammed between the bottles. Leman Hanım had had the icebox brought by a porter from the summer villa to the Asian side of Istanbul and from there by rail to Ankara.

When the maid saw Macit trying to break off some ice, she tried to stop him.

"Please, sir, let me do that. I need to wash it as well after breaking it up."

Macit returned to where his father-in-law was sitting. He saw the old man looking through the photographs one by one, placing them back in the envelope with shaking hands. Macit went back to the kitchen on tiptoe so as not to disturb him.

MARSEILLES

Reading the newspaper, Selva saw the sickening headline.

According to the latest edict issued by the Vichy government, all Jews were required to register themselves and their belongings with the authorities. Those who didn't comply would be penalized and sent to concentration camps.

There was also a list published of those being sent to the camps because they hadn't obeyed the instructions, or were late doing so. Selva trembled as she read through the list. Luckily Rafo's name hadn't been registered on any of the pharmacy's legal papers. All the same the Vichy administration, with its spies and hunting dogs, was even more efficient at tracing Jews than the Nazis themselves. What if they found out that Benoit's mother was Jewish? She didn't even want to think about that now.

Many Turks, particularly from Istanbul, had migrated to France after the First World War, settling mainly in Paris, Lyon, and Marseilles. Later, the children of these families intermarried with the French and produced their own families. Benoit's mother was one such case. She had moved to France with her family from Istanbul and married a Frenchman who was not of the Jewish faith when she was twenty-one.

Benoit and his mother would go to Istanbul every year for their summer holiday. During these holidays they would spend some time with the Alfandaris in their Tarabya house. Who knew how many times they swam there in the dark-blue waters of the Bosphorus, played hide-and-seek in the groves on its hills, and fished along its shores?

Before the Germans occupied Paris, when Rafo was desperately seeking a safe base for his family somewhere, it was Benoit who had suggested that they go to Marseilles. He offered to make Rafo a partner in his pharmacy once he had sorted out his financial situation.

There were a few friends of Selva's family who had gone to France at this time. Selva read the lists in the newspaper with fear in her heart that she would come across any of their names. Doenyas, Alhadef, Eskenasy…Some names looked familiar. Eskenasy—wasn't that the surname of her grandmother's poker partner, Ester Hanım? Her now deceased grandmother, who had been so unhappy when they'd decided to move to Paris? Selva would ask Rafo when he came home for lunch. Surely he would know who was who. But what was the point? He would be so upset if he knew any of them.

Young Fazıl sat on his potty as she continued to read the newspaper. The baby started to scream at exactly the same time that the telephone started to ring. He must have some sort of built-in mechanism, she thought. "*Un moment, s'il vous plait,*" she answered, and rushed back to Fazıl. By then he had overturned the potty, and it took some time to empty the pot, clean up, and wipe him. My God, she said to herself, I forgot the telephone! She picked up the receiver, worried that the caller had hung up.

"Hello! Hello!"

A man's voice replied, "Selva Hanım, this is Tarık Arıca speaking. Your sister gave me your number. I'm the second secretary at the Turkish consulate in Paris."

"Oh, Tarık. Of course I know who you are. Sabiha has mentioned you in her letters so often."

"That's so nice of her. I'm sorry I seem to have called at an inopportune moment. I can call back at a more convenient time if you wish."

"No, no, Tarık, it's fine now. Please don't hang up. I was just changing Fazıl's…I mean my son's…I was just going to put him to bed…He's playing happily now. Oh! Tarık, I do miss home so much…especially talking to you right now. I've missed speaking my own language…it's perfectly all right to speak now."

"I promised your sister that I'd call you as soon as I got to Paris. Unfortunately, I've been extremely busy since I arrived. I couldn't call you sooner. Things here are rather hectic. Anyway, I bring you lots of love and regards. I also have a couple of things for you. I'll try to send them to you as soon as I can."

"There's no hurry. Perhaps you could give them to somebody who is coming down here. Please don't send them by post; I'm not sure I would get them."

"You're right. I know that we are sending a courier to our consulate in Marseilles next week. I'll send your things then."

"Did you have a good trip, Tarık? Did you get through without being harassed by the Germans?" Selva asked in an attempt to prolong the conversation.

Apart from the few occasions when she spoke to her mother or sister, and of course Rafo, she had no opportunity to speak Turkish to anyone. She hadn't admitted, even to herself, that she missed using her mother tongue. At this moment she was trying to satisfy her longing by speaking to a man she hardly knew. Listening to him was like breathing Istanbul air!

"My journey was very tiring. I couldn't get a direct train from Istanbul on the date I wanted. I had to travel to Edirne by bus, a very ramshackle old bus indeed, then a dreadful train from Edirne to Varna. From there, I took an equally dreadful steamboat to Köstence, where I boarded yet another train. The carriages were freezing and there was nothing to eat. The Germans often stopped the train for checks, but I must say they were all right with me. We kept changing trains. It was quite an adventure, but I am here now."

"Welcome," said Selva wholeheartedly. "In fact, I have been waiting for your call. From the way Sabiha has written about you, I feel I have a close friend in France, even if we are in different cities."

"Thank you, Selva Hanım. Is everything OK down there? Please don't hesitate to call me if you need anything."

"We're managing for the time being."

"I hope both you and your husband have your Turkish passports."

"We do, but we applied for our French citizenship, so Rafo didn't extend his."

"That's a big mistake! You should go immediately to our consulate in Marseilles and put all your papers in order. I urge you to do this. In fact I urge you to do this immediately, today!"

"Really? I'll tell Rafo when he gets home. We were a little embarrassed…I mean…anyway, I'll tell him when he comes in."

"Selva Hanım…"

"Please, call me Selva."

"Please give me a little time to call you this, Selva Hanım. I'll call our consulate in Marseilles today and give them your names. There's nothing to feel embarrassed about. You must ask for Nazım Kender; he's our consul there. I will put him in the know right away."

Selva became very quiet. She didn't know what to say to this man she hardly knew and yet who was so concerned about them.

"Selva Hanım, for God's sake, I'm telling you, do as I say without delay. If your Turkish papers are in order, they can't touch you."

"Thank you, Tarık," she said shakily. "Thank you for your concern. I feel as though my sister put you up to this, but…"

"I assure you this is serious. It has nothing to do with Sabiha Hanım. Look, Selva Hanım, I don't know if I should be telling you this, but according to a reliable source, the German army is to move south very soon. The occupation will spread. If you don't have your papers in order, you may be very sorry. You can't say I haven't warned you." He was very serious; his voice had changed entirely. He didn't prolong the conversation further, but wished her good day and hung up.

Selva went straight to the chest of drawers in their bedroom and found their passports. Since they had left Istanbul the day after they were married, she hadn't had time to change her surname. Her passport was still in her maiden name, Behice Selva Kırımlı. She had used this passport when she visited Italy with her parents a year before she and Rafo left Turkey. The holiday had been organized by Leman Hanım in an attempt to patch things up between her husband and daughter. She'd chosen Italy because she knew how Fazıl Reşat Paşa admired the country. She had imagined that the magnificent sights, delicious food, and wonderful wines would heal the rift. Unfortunately, she had been too optimistic, and her hopes hadn't materialized: the two remained distant and talked to each other only when necessary. They returned home after a week still feeling resentful toward one another. Italy's ornamental architecture, the ice-cold Frascati, and the various pasta dishes might have satisfied their senses, but had done nothing to warm their hearts.

Selva toyed with the passports. Little Fazıl had fallen asleep in his bed. She decided that she would leave him with his father when he woke up and go to the consulate herself. She would tell Rafo that she was taking his passport too, and if she managed to get his extended, then she'd tell him why. The staff at the consulate might choose not to extend it, she thought; after all, Rafo had committed an unforgivable crime—sacrilege, according to Sabiha. He had married a Muslim girl. Strangely enough, Turkish men who married

Greek, Armenian, or Jewish girls weren't subject to the same treatment as Rafo. Turkish men could marry whom they pleased, but it wasn't the same for Turkish girls. Feelings of injustice filled Selva's heart as she put the passports in her bag. Just then the telephone rang again.

"Hello!"

"Selva Hanım, this is Tarık Arıca from Paris again." She now recognized his voice well. "I got you an appointment to visit the consulate. You are expected at half past three today."

"You needn't have troubled, Tarık. I decided to go anyway."

"There's a long line at the gate. I didn't want you to have to go through all that, so I've given them your name. This way you can see the consul himself right away."

Selva was baffled as she put the phone down. Was this man crazy or what? Why had he taken it upon himself to make such a fuss?

The line outside the consulate really surprised Selva. To the right of the gate, there was a crowd of middle-aged men and women talking among themselves and jostling one another. Selva did as Tarık had instructed; she went straight to the gate and rang the bell. The man who answered the door told her off in French.

"You ought to have taken your line number from that man," he said pointing. Selva noticed an official standing on the other side of the gate.

"I've come to see the consul. I've got an appointment."

"What's your name?"

"Selva Kırımlı."

"Wait here."

The consulate doorman, a *kavass,* returned shortly. He was much more courteous this time.

"Please follow me, madame."

He led Selva up the stairs of the old building, and they stopped at a desk in a hall where a secretary was sitting.

"Please take a seat," said the elderly secretary with an Armenian accent. "The consul is engaged at the moment. I'll show you in as soon as he is free."

Selva sat on the edge of the chair in front of the desk and waited. Twenty minutes later the secretary announced that the consul was free. Selva stood up, straightened her skirt, ruffled her fringe, and strode down the long corridor to the consul's office. She waited a few seconds before knocking.

"Please come in," called a voice from the office.

She opened the door and walked in. The young man sitting behind the desk leaped to his feet. He walked around the desk and shook Selva's hand. She was most surprised to see a tall, handsome man standing in front of her. She had expected the consul to be stout and bald.

"Hello, won't you sit down…"

Selva sat in an armchair.

"I'm Nazım Kender. Your brother-in-law, Macit, is a colleague I admire a lot. Tarık, our friend in Paris, tells me you are Sabiha Hanım's sister. When he telephoned he told me to make this appointment for you. Why didn't you contact us yourself? I wish you had called and told me that you were Macit's sister-in-law. Had I known you were here, I would have called you myself long ago. We try to get together with the Turks here at least once a month. *Inşallah*, you are all right. What can I do for you?"

Selva wondered if the man sitting across the desk knew about Rafo—if he knew that her husband was Jewish.

"I'd offer you something, but I'm sure you'll understand that in the present circumstances supplies are short. We've even used up all the Turkish coffee that we had sent over last week."

"Thank you. I don't want anything to drink." Selva was sitting on the edge of the chair rather anxiously.

"Tarık told me that some documents need updating. I understand your passports need extending."

"Yes, that's right. It was very kind of Tarık to take the trouble to arrange this appointment. I had thought that it wasn't really necessary, but I realized why when I saw the line outside."

"The lines…yes, that's to do with the requirement that Turkish nationals have to register with the Turkish consulates. If they don't, they stand to lose their citizenship. Unfortunately it appears that many of our Jewish citizens took no notice of this requirement. Why should they when they already obtained their French citizenship? In fact, some of them did nothing, purely out of negligence. Now they are stateless. All they have are tattered old Ottoman passports written in Arabic. Now, because of the Vichy government's attitude, they are rushing to update them. What else can the poor souls do? The local authorities don't seem to be taking any circumstances into consideration, even one's age. They just gather people up, young and old, and send them to the camps. If they can show us anything to prove they were once Turkish citizens, we do our best to help them. Unfortunately it isn't always easy. Sometimes there's nothing we can do. Because the Germans are hoping that we might join their side in the war, they don't seem to want to aggravate us too much. Anyway, enough of that; your passports are republic passports, of course, and I don't suppose it's a question of renewing them, of just extending them."

"Well, yes. They're not written in Arabic, but…I mean…"

"We can extend them right away."

"My husband's passport is out of date. Would you be able to extend that too?"

"Of course."

"I think I must tell you that my husband is Rafael Alfandari."

"He is a Turkish national, isn't he?"

"Yes, he's Turkish."

"So why should there be a problem?"

Selva fidgeted in her seat. It was obvious from her manner that she felt very uncomfortable.

"I hope I shall have the honor of meeting him," said the handsome man. "You remember I told you that we organize get-togethers for the Turkish community from time to time. I sincerely hope you will accept our invitation to join us at our next gathering."

Selva's face brightened up. Hopefully the people she met here wouldn't be as condescending and hurtful as those she had considered her friends in Istanbul.

"Oh! Thank you very much; we'd love to, of course."

"May I have your passports, please?"

Selva took the passports out of her bag.

"I'm afraid our surnames aren't the same. Would you be able to correct that if I left my marriage license with you?" she asked.

Selva broke the silence that followed.

"We left Istanbul the day after our wedding and we didn't have time to change my name on my passport."

Selva placed the passports together with the marriage license on the desk.

The handsome consul looked through the pages of the license and appeared to be choosing his words carefully.

"Selva Hanım," he said. "Of course we can make the necessary changes, but since you have neglected to do this for so long, may I suggest you not do it just yet?"

"Why?" Selva said almost indignantly.

"Because it's difficult to know what the Germans will do next. I don't recommend you change your name from Kırımlı to Alfandari just yet. Let it stay the way it is. We are ready to help our Jewish citizens, I assure you, but as I said before, there are certainly times when our power doesn't go far enough. You have a young son, don't you?"

"How do you know that?"

"Tarık told me. I firmly believe that you owe it to your son not to change anything until the war is over. I will certainly add your son's name to your passport. What is it?"

"In other words, you expect me to save our skins and throw my husband to the devil. Is that it?"

"You're exaggerating, Selva Hanım. I'm ready to do anything you say. I'm merely suggesting caution. Maybe you should discuss this with your husband before deciding." He glanced at the names on the passports before adding, "I'm sure Mr. Alfandari will agree with my advice."

"Thank you, but the three of us are totally inseparable. Please make the appropriate changes. All three of us should have Alfandari on our passports!"

"Fine, as you wish. I sincerely congratulate you for your courage. Your husband is a very lucky man."

The handsome consul got up and showed Selva to the door.

"You can collect your updated passports in two days. Needless to say, if there is anything else I can do, don't hesitate to contact me."

"Thank you. Thank you very much, sir."

"Please convey my regards to Macit and that very lovely sister of yours—you are in touch with them, aren't you?"

"We try to correspond, but unfortunately it isn't so easy. It takes ages for our letters to arrive, but what can one do?" Selva offered her hand, thanked the consul sincerely again, and left the room. She hurried down the corridor. When she returned home, she would tell her husband that the Turkish consul in Marseilles was the best-looking man she had ever seen in her life.

PARIS

Tarık was banging the keys on his Remington typewriter with the intensity of a concert pianist. His body language reflected the words he was typing. He would raise one hand, nod, and strike a key, then raise the other hand, nod again, and so on, pausing from time to time to search for a particular letter. Tarık targeted the chosen letter before banging his finger down again, as if he was firing a gun, *rat-a-tat-tat.*

> *We, the Turkish Embassy, are honored to inform you of our Government's views concerning your Government's legal clause 2333, which was approved on 2/6/1941. According to this clause, Jewish people are required to register themselves and their possessions. This clause includes Jews of Turkish nationality. Turkey does not differentiate between its citizens on the grounds of race, color, or creed, and therefore is disturbed by this ruling from the French Government. The Turkish Government alone is responsible for protecting the rights of its citizens.*

The third secretary, Muhlis, sitting opposite Tarık, joked, "Why all this passion?"

"I'm using the kind of language these people understand."

"They only understand blasphemy."

"What a shame swear words aren't allowed in diplomacy."

"I think you are giving vent to your feelings on that poor machine."

"What do you expect? I've got to get it out of my system somehow. If only you knew what I went through last week…"

"Yes, I just heard! If I hadn't been away delivering the courier bag, I could have joined you. I understand you saved Rifka Mitrani, Yakop Barbut, and Eli Farhi from the hands of the Gestapo. I saw the thank-you notes they sent this morning, so I remember the names."

"It was really tragic. You should have heard Mitrani's daughter's voice on the phone…It was heartbreaking to hear her sobbing, yelling, and screaming that they'd taken her mother away."

"Where to?"

"They brought her from Lyon to Paris. They were going to send her to Drancy. Sometimes they send them to Berlin by train."

"Yes, and after that nobody knows what happens."

"That's right. I never knew civilized people could behave this way. Why this animosity? Why?"

"I wish I knew. If I ever meet Hitler one day, I'd like to ask him," said Muhlis.

"You never know. Maybe he was cuckolded by a Jewish beauty when he was young. Don't they say there's always a woman's finger behind everything? *Cherchez la femme!*"

Muhlis Edin was very new at the consulate. There had been an enormous increase in the number of passport queries after Tarık was posted to Paris, so he was given an assistant. Unlike Tarık, who was serious and hardworking, Muhlis didn't take life too seriously. He was frivolous and made light of everything. Tarık hadn't quite made up his mind whether or not he liked this young man. He had to admit, though, that in these dismal days Muhlis did manage to make him laugh and lightened the atmosphere a little. But Tarık wasn't quite sure how much he could trust him.

"My dear Muhlis, you'd better set these jokes aside. One day you may be faced with a similar situation and then what?"

"Right, I was just about to ask you. What exactly did you do after you got that call?"

"I called the German embassy in Paris immediately. I insisted that the person in question was Turkish. They in turn asked for her papers. It is always extremely important to have all the relevant documents in order. The girl sent her mother's birth certificate with her husband, and the young man traveled all night to bring it to me. He was totally exhausted when he got here. We were about to jump into my Citroën to go to the police station when there was another call. Apparently there were another two at the same station.

"Anyway, thank God we seem to get some respect from the Germans at the moment. You know they're buying chrome from us now. Anyhow, we got there. I don't know if you remember that I saved another two from a different police station last week. I think I'm getting good at this. You should have seen the joy, all the hugs and tears, when we crammed into the car later. The poor woman couldn't stop crying. She kept trying to hug and thank me while I was driving. No matter how many times I warned her not to distract me, she kept trying to give me sloppy kisses. She just didn't seem to understand. We could easily have had an accident.

"The others were similar. Yakop was in shock, so he could hardly talk and the other one kept praying in all the different languages he knew. Finally, tearfully, we got here. What I am trying to emphasize is that, if people have the necessary papers to prove they are Turkish, you shouldn't hesitate for a minute. After making your formal applications, you need to follow up personally, and with insistence. If necessary, you should also contact the Turkish embassy in Vichy for further pressure. If that doesn't work, you should also seek assistance from our embassy in Berlin."

"I understand," said Muhlis. "So then what happened?"

"Then we took all their old papers and replaced them with solid Turkish passports. They were so grateful. They thanked us a thousand times and left the office."

"Didn't you ask them why the hell they left Turkey to come here?"

"No! For God's sake, how can you ask those questions at such a time? Don't we wish we were Europeans at times? Don't we envy the Europeans' level of civilization, their knowledge, their order? Those poor souls must have felt the same way. Well, they got up and left. What a mistake!"

Just as Muhlis was going to answer, they were interrupted by a secretary.

"The consul is waiting for that letter, sir. He's asking if it is finished yet," the petite brunette said.

"I'll bring it over in ten minutes," said Tarık, and he went back to striking the keys. *Rat-a-tat-tat...*

MARSEILLES

Selva was thinking of the good news she had for Rafo on her way home. Before returning to their apartment, she went to the pharmacy to collect Fazıl. Rafo had put his son in his high chair behind the counter. He had given him a piece of paper and some colored pencils to amuse himself. As soon as he saw Selva, he lifted the boy up and handed him to his mother.

"Where have you been?" he asked in an irritated voice.

"Sorry, I only just made it. Why? Has anything happened?"

"For goodness' sake, don't ask silly questions. They took Rosa and her kid away. Benoit ran to the police station. I was waiting for you before I could join him."

Selva hugged her son tightly, and Rafo continued, "It seems they rounded them up just as they were getting on the bus today. They were carrying out an identity check. We received the news about twenty minutes after you left."

Rafo was already putting on his jacket.

"Come on, Selva. You'd better go home. I need to lock the door."

"Rafo, wait. I have to talk to you first."

"What's there to talk about? I can't leave Benoit alone. He was so sad, almost desperate."

"I understand, but maybe I could help him."

"Who? You?"

"Yes."

"Just who do you think you are? Being Fazıl Reşat Paşa's daughter won't get you very far in Marseilles."

"What you are saying, Rafo?"

"I'm sorry, Selva, I'm on edge right now, and you're making me late. I had to leave Benoit on his own because of you. If you hadn't left Fazıl, I would have been able to join him."

"Rafo, you've got to come home with me. You must tell me exactly where they took them and what time. I need their full names and addresses and—"

"And what will you do with these details, may I ask? Will you go to the police station and say 'Listen here, you. I am Madame Alfandari. You will regret your actions'?"

Finally Selva had to raise her voice.

"Shut up, Rafo! Shut up and listen!"

Rafo wasn't used to his wife speaking to him in that tone.

"Rafo, let's call the consul I saw today. I'm sure he can help."

"You're being ridiculous now." He led Selva by the arm out of the pharmacy, closed the door, pulled the shutters down, and locked up.

"Come on, darling, go home. I might be late for dinner, but I'll be back as soon as I can."

"Aren't you even going to ask what I did today?"

"We'll speak when I get back," said Rafo.

Selva crossed the street with her son cradled in her arms and went home.

"Now then, little one, please don't be difficult; play in there," she said, putting Fazıl in his playpen. "I need to make a call now and then I'll get you something to eat. OK? Will that be OK?"

The child looked as though he would resist at first, but seeing the determined look on his mother's face, he picked up his little red truck and began to play.

Selva looked through the notebooks by the telephone and found the piece of paper on which she'd written the consul's telephone number.

"Hello, is this the Turkish consulate? I'd like to speak to Nazım Kender, the consul, please. It's very urgent. Yes, very urgent indeed. This is Selva Kırımlı; I came to see him this afternoon. Would you tell him that…Yes, I'll wait. Thank you."

Selva put her fingers to her lips to indicate to her son that he should be quiet.

"Hello…yes, yes, it's me, Selva Kırımlı, Mr. Kender. I'm sorry to disturb you but apparently, as I was seeing you this afternoon, they took away someone very close to me, together with her son. Actually, she's my husband's business partner's cousin. Yes, on his mother's side. They're a family from Istanbul…"

Selva started sobbing, drowning her voice in her tears. "I don't really know where. I'll see if I can find out. Her name is Rosa, Rosa Hatem. Her child's name is Yako. Their address, their address is… My God, what was it now?…48 Rue Boissière…I'm sure that's right, yes, that's right. I understand that her husband is in the hospital. He had a gallbladder operation three days ago. I presume he knows nothing of this. Please help! I beg of you, Mr. Kender. Thank you. I can't thank you enough."

Selva put the phone down, went into the kitchen, and made sure that the door was closed so Fazıl wouldn't hear her crying.

LYON

Rifka was busily preparing pastries in the kitchen when the telephone started to ring. Rifka's family had originally emigrated from Toledo to Istanbul, and not even twenty-seven years in Paris had changed her taste in food or the customs surrounding it. Passover was approaching, and Rifka had already prepared a list of food she would be cooking for her small family, as well as the unleavened bread for the meal. What a pity, though, that she had left behind in Paris the special china she had for such a holy occasion. There were actually far more important things than plates that she had had to leave behind, but if she had them, she would be busy washing them now for the Seder feast.

Her first reaction was to ignore the telephone. It was probably for her daughter anyway, and she wasn't at home. However, when the ringing persisted, she hurried to the sitting room, wiping her hands on her apron.

"Hello," she said.

She listened to the voice on the end of the line for a while, slowly turning pale, and finally reached out for a nearby chair to sit on. She started rocking back and forth, hitting her knees with her fist. After replacing the receiver, she ran to the kitchen and picked up a sharp knife. She opened the front door and tried to prize off the mezuzah nailed to the top right-hand corner of the doorframe.

Rifka Mitrani had moved from Paris to Lyon. After the First World War, she and her husband had left Istanbul to live in Paris. Originally, her ancestors had migrated from Spain to Istanbul in 1492. That move was a direct result of the imperial declaration signed by the Spanish king, Don Ferdinand, and his queen, Donna Isabella, in March of that year. It commanded the Jews—who were considered to be heretics—to leave the country by July and never to return. Those who disobeyed this order and stayed, or even came back, would be executed no matter what their age or gender. Furthermore, they were to liquidate all their assets and leave behind all their money together with their gold, silver, and jewelry.

At the same time Beyazid II, the eighth sultan of the Ottoman Empire, issued an invitation to the 250,000 Jews banished by Spain to come to his country. Leaving everything behind, they boarded old, run-down ships for the dreadful journey to the only country offering them refuge. Some five hundred years later, Moris Karako, one of the descendants of those refugees, would write about the experience: "The Ottomans sincerely greeted us and gave us accommodation. We were free to practice our religion and to speak our own language. We were even protected from those who wanted to banish us yet again to foreign lands. Our honor and dignity were restored."

Beyazid II's statement at the time was: "It is said that Ferdinand is a wise king. However, the truth of the matter is that by getting rid of the Jews, he has made his country poorer and mine richer."

The refugees settled in their new country, becoming prosperous and happy. But their new homeland wasn't without its own problems. For centuries its inhabitants endured destitution and hardship. Toward the end of the nineteenth century, the five-hundred-year-old empire had started to fall apart, piece by piece.

As the Jews accumulated considerable fortunes through commerce, they started to spread to different areas and different countries. Many moved to glamorous France, particularly to its brightest star, Paris, which in those days was the center of civilization, art, and leisure.

Nesim Mitrani, Rifka's husband, established a financial company in Paris. By the time their first child, Maurice, was born, they'd not only become a well-to-do family, but they'd also obtained solid French passports. Rifka hadn't the heart to throw away the tatty old passports written in Arabic script, so she put them in the hatbox where she kept her old family photographs. She was as faithful to her religion as she was to the traditions passed on from her grandmothers, the Ladino language and the memorabilia that reminded her of her past. She kept everything with nostalgic significance, and this instinct was typical of people who are always on the move. "Our home isn't a home," her husband would say. "It's a flea market!"

From banking, their wealth accumulated over the years and Rifka continued to collect her knickknacks. By the time their daughter was born, they had become extremely rich. They would spend their summer holidays in the South of France and in the winter send the children skiing in the Alps. They lived in one of the most elegant districts in Paris, shopped at Faubourg St.-Honoré, and dined at the most expensive restaurants. By now, instead of knickknacks, Rifka was collecting antiques and rare objets d'art from auctions. But the good life came to an abrupt end in 1940, as though lightning had struck. The transfer of Mitrani's very own company to a French Catholic businessman took just three days.

Nesim Mitrani had thought that losing his company and fortune was the greatest disaster he would have to endure, but he was wrong. One day, while he was organizing his family's move to the South of France, away from the occupation, the Gestapo took him and his son and transported them to Drancy. They were never heard from again.

Rifka managed to escape to Lyon with her daughter, Constance. She hoped they would be able to start a new life there. Even though the French government appeared to be pro Hitler, she and Constance held French passports, after all. The days of wine and roses might be over. They found it hard to cope with the loss of their loved ones. But life had to go on.

Constance went to the university in Lyon, and there she met a young Frenchman and married him. Her husband was of Jewish descent, but he was not like her family. He was seventh-generation French. Because of his love for Constance, he had agreed to live with his mother-in-law, despite their different tastes in food and music. The young couple didn't have a lot of money, so they both had to work. When they came home tired in the evening, there was always a bowl of hot soup and something else that Rifka had prepared.

As a result of what had happened to her son and husband, Rifka had lost almost all interest in life herself. She was also suffering from a heart condition. She would go out shopping early in the morning, then cook food for the youngsters to come home to. In her free time she would visit the synagogue and pray for her loved ones. Her only joy was the rare occasion when she got news from old friends and relatives, most of whom had dispersed all over the world. Those who had the means had escaped to America; some had returned to Turkey and others had done as they had and moved to various cities in the South of France. It was true that Rifka had no friends in Lyon, but the monotony of her life gave her a certain peace.

She couldn't remove the mezuzah with the knife, so she looked for a screwdriver in the drawers. When Constance came home around lunchtime, Rifka was still struggling at the front door.

"For goodness' sake, Mother! What on earth are you doing?"

"Oh! Constance. I don't know how to tell you this…bad news, my dear. Rachel telephoned today from Marseilles."

"Which Rachel?"

"How many Rachels are there, Constance? Rosa's mother."

"Why did she phone?"

"Dear, dear Constance. Are we ever going to find peace on this earth?"

"What's happened? Tell me, Mother."

"The damned collaborators…The police took Rosa and her child to the police station."

"My God!"

Rifka began sobbing; it took her ages to tell Constance exactly what happened.

"In other words, the Turkish consul managed to save them, is that it?"

"That's right. Rachel thought she should tell me so we can be careful ourselves."

"Don't you have a Turkish passport, Mother? The way you hoard everything, I bet you still have it. Why don't you check?"

"Don't you remember the way we left Paris, my dear? I couldn't even take a spare pair of shoes, let alone the box where I kept that tattered old passport."

Constance noticed her mother still struggling with the screwdriver. "Stop it, Mother. You'll hurt yourself. Marcel can do that when he comes home this evening."

"I suppose I can always nail it on the top of my bedroom door," Rifka said, wiping her nose.

"You can put it where you like," replied Constance, shrugging her shoulders, "as long as you stay away from the synagogue area. I beg you, Mother, this is serious. Give me Auntie Rachel's phone number so I can call her. I bet they must have been petrified."

"They were lucky," said Rifka. "They were in one day and out the next."

Unfortunately, Rifka was not to be so lucky and was soon caught up in the web herself. Even though she had promised Constance that she wouldn't visit the synagogue, one day she couldn't resist going to pray. As she entered the synagogue, the Gestapo rounded her up together with the other Jews there. She struggled desperately, protesting strongly, saying she was Turkish. But no one listened. She was forced into a police car and taken to the police station, and from there in a bus to the train station and thence to Paris. The train was absolutely crammed full. Once in the Paris police station, she and many others were lined up against the wall in a hallway before being sent to Drancy.

A German officer called out her name: "Rifka Mitrani, take one step forward."

Rifka thought she was going to be shot. At last she could join her husband and son!...She took a step forward and followed the man to the end of the hallway.

A young man was sitting in a tiny room speaking to the police officers. He asked Rifka to sign some documents before taking her to his Citroën. There were already two men sitting in the back of the car.

"Where are you taking me, monsieur?" she asked.

"Where do you want to go, madame?"

"To my daughter."

"That's where I'm taking you."

"To Lyon?"

"No, madame. To the Turkish consulate, where your son-in-law is waiting."

When Rifka realized that she had been saved, she hugged and kissed this man driving the car. But she felt ashamed doing so—not because she was smothering a young man with kisses, but because she felt so happy to have been saved from death, and then she remembered her son and husband. She shuddered, thinking that she had faced death so bravely. It's interesting, she thought, that one isn't scared of death from a distance, but when it is staring you in the face it feels like a merciless enemy that you desperately want to avoid.

Back in Lyon another surprise awaited Rifka. Her daughter and son-in-law announced that in a few weeks they intended to cross the mountains into Spain. They would wait for the sunset, and then cross through the passes under cover of darkness. They were already preparing to put their plan into action.

"Listen, children, I can't scramble over the Pyrenees at my age. I'm bound to have a heart attack and die on the way," she said.

"But Mother, you'll die if you stay here too. The Nazis won't leave us alone. At least give yourself a chance," her daughter insisted.

"Constance, I promise you, I will not set one foot through this door. Please drop that idea."

"Mother, it's all right for you to say you won't go out, but what about us?"

"What about you? Surely you're not in as much danger as I am."

"And how!"

"But why? Nobody would know you're Jewish. You don't even have a Jewish accent."

"Mother, it's about time you knew…Marcel has been working for the Resistance. Some of those who were working in his cell have been caught already. It is impossible for us to stay here safely. We have to leave France as soon as possible."

Rifka listened in awe.

Marcel wanted to cross to Spain immediately, but his mother-in-law refused to return to the country that had caused her people indescribable pain and driven them away.

"All that happened centuries ago. What's the point of dwelling on it?" Marcel argued.

"You can go. I'll stay here. After all, what difference does it make whether I end up in the hands of the Germans or the Spaniards? As if that wasn't enough, you also expect me to scramble over the mountains like a goat. At my age and with my heart condition… What for? To end up being degraded? Never!"

"Mother, you're being ridiculous. Is this the way to behave because of something that happened in the fifteenth century? Don't you realize that you're putting us in danger? I already told you that they captured two men from Marcel's Resistance cell. If they are made to talk, it will be the end of us. Can't you see that? For God's sake, be sensible. We have to get away, and the sooner the better."

"You'd better go, then."

Constance firmly believed that her mother would change her mind, so she waited patiently for her to say yes. She and Marcel kept on the move. They stayed with friends for a couple of nights, and then moved on to others, constantly changing their abode. But Rifka had a plan. She wrote to the Turkish consul who had saved her from the Gestapo. She wondered if the consulate would be able to issue passports to her daughter and son-in-law as well. She pleaded with them in her letter. If necessary she was willing to relinquish hers in exchange for the two. Anything, as long as the Turkish consulate could spread its wings over her children.

ANKARA 1942

Leman Hanım untied the satin ribbon from around the dusty pink box. She took some photographs out of the box and spread them on her bed. Her entire life was spread out before her, captured in sepia-colored photographs glued to thick brown cards. She picked up one photo at random. There she was with her wavy hair held up by a huge bow and cascading across her shoulders and down onto her chest. She was leaning against her father's knees with a bouquet of flowers in her hand. Her childhood was staring back at her with wide-eyed innocence. Her father sat proudly in a carved armchair. In another photograph, taken at the famous Michailides studio, her hair was up in a bun with strands of bridal silver hanging from the top of her head to the floor. She appeared so fragile in her tiered lace dress; her waist was so tiny that she looked as if a puff of wind would blow her away. In another picture, she was wearing the same clothes, but this time her husband was standing beside her. He had a fine, twisted mustache and a fez that came down to the center of his forehead. He looked so tall, handsome, and wide-shouldered in his aide-de-camp uniform.

Leman Hanım took a deep breath, put the pictures down, and rummaged again through the box. The next photos she picked up had been taken at the Photo Sabah Studio. They were of her children, to her the most beautiful girls in the world. Every year without fail they would have their photographs taken on their birthdays. Even though the pictures were in black and white, one could immediately see the sparkle in Sabiha's eyes and the shine in her blonde hair. She was springlike, fresh and beautiful. Next to her was Selva, with her huge eyes and plaited hair. Although one could tell from some pictures that she was the younger of the two, in most she appeared to be looking down at her sister from above.

What was it that Sabiha had said that day at the studio? Leman Hanım smiled as she remembered: "Mother, I'd like to sit down for the photograph. Selva can stand beside me."

"That's not possible, my darling. If you sit and she stands, we can't get you both in the same frame," said Enver, the owner of the studio, not knowing how much that upset Sabiha. "*She* should sit down, and you stand beside her."

Sabiha immediately began to sulk. Where on earth had this complex about her height come from? It was ridiculous that a girl as beautiful as she was should worry so much about her height.

Leman Hanım continued to rummage through the photographs until she found what she was looking for: the last photo taken of Selva before she left. She was wearing a simple beige two-piece with her plaited hair up around her head as usual. Slender and elegant, Selva was sitting at the table in the registry office on her wedding day, signing the registry wearing her wedding ring. No other jewelry, no tiny diamond ring, no brooch on her lapel, no string of pearls around her neck, and she was supposed to be a bride! Leman Hanım felt tears running down her cheeks. Oh, my darling Selva, why, oh why did you do this? My stubborn little baby! What I would have given to see you in a long veil with strands of bridal silver, looking like a perfect bride! How I wish that I could have given you one of the family heirlooms to wear on your wedding day!

She kissed her daughter's photograph with longing and pressed it to her heart. She was sure that there were three or four other photographs taken that day. She looked through the box and found them. In one that Macit must have taken, the two sisters were standing side by side with that disgusting Rafo behind them. One wouldn't know that it was Rafo, because Leman Hanım had scratched his face off with a pin. In another—obviously taken by Rafo—Macit was standing between Selva and Sabiha. The last photograph of the wedding group must have been taken by someone at the registry office. How difficult it had been for Leman Hanım to hide these photographs from her husband. She had not put them in the family album, and took special care to hide them at the bottom of her box. As if Fazıl Reşat Paşa would bother to look for them! Anyway, she didn't want to take the chance. He might tear them up; they were, after all, the last photographs she had of her darling daughter, her tall, slender daughter, in her beige two-piece suit. The photographs might have faded, but her beloved daughter was always so vividly in her mind and heart.

When she heard the door open, she quickly slipped the photographs under the pillow.

"You're not looking at those photographs again, are you, Granny?" asked her granddaughter as she entered the room.

"Yes, I am, my darling. I am."

"Don't you get tired of looking at them over and over?"

"No, I don't. They're my whole life. They are my past..."

"You say that, Granny, but you don't look at all of them. I know which ones you're looking at."

"Really, and which ones are they?"

"Photos of my aunt. Do you miss her a lot?"

"A lot, yes. I miss her a lot."

"Why doesn't she visit us in the summer? Even if she's working, she could come for her summer holidays, couldn't she? I'd love to see little Fazıl. If only she'd bring him to us."

"There's war all around, my little darling. There's war where your auntie lives. They just can't come now! I'm sure they will, though—*inşallah*, when the war is over."

"Has Grandpa forgiven her then?"

"What sort of question is that?"

"Come on, Granny, I know. Apparently Grandpa was very angry because she married that man."

"Who told you that? Your mother?"

"No, Hacer."

Leman Hanım frowned. How tactless staff can be, she thought. Not only do they have an answer for everything, they also listen to *everything.* Those were the days when they were so devoted, when they were almost members of the family. Those were the days indeed!

"How inappropriate of her! There are things one doesn't discuss with children."

"Oh, don't say that, Granny. I'm not a child. I'll be nine next month."

"Don't exaggerate, child; you'll be eight. You're in such a hurry to get older, aren't you? Wait until you do get older and then it will be the reverse," Leman Hanım replied, handing the photographs to her grandchild. "Time just flies by," she said with a sigh. "It's almost five years since your auntie Selva left! Do you remember her, Hülya?"

"Yes, I do, Granny. She read fairy tales to me in the evenings and she often took me to Kızılay Park. I remember drinking mineral water out of huge glasses. Granny, could you show me the photograph of my auntie holding a bunch of daisies?"

Leman Hanım looked for the photograph of Selva wearing a white dress clinging to her figure, with layers and layers of petal-shaped chiffon hanging from the hips, the one in which she was holding a bunch of daisies. Daisies were Selva's favorite flowers. They are just like Selva, Leman Hanım thought. Maybe a little wild, but certainly down-to-earth. She remembered how the pollen from the daisies had stained the gorgeous dress. She eventually found the photograph and looked at it, trying to hold back floods of tears. Selva looked rather sad in the photograph. There was a kind of melancholy in her eyes…Of course! Leman Hanım thought. The picture was taken at the American college on her graduation day. She must have been thinking that it wouldn't be easy to continue seeing that wretched fellow Rafael!

"There you are, here it is. Isn't your auntie beautiful?"

Hülya took the picture and looked at it for a while. She gazed at Selva's sad face that looked as if it were carved out of marble. Then she looked at the other photos spread out on the bed and saw a picture of her mother as a teenager. Her oval face was framed by wavy hair as she pensively rested her chin on her hand.

"My mother is more beautiful, but you know, Granny, I wish I were my aunt's daughter."

"What do you mean? Why's that?"

"I think my aunt loved me more than my mother."

Leman Hanım froze on the spot. For a moment she was speechless.

"Really, Hülya! Where did that come from? Is it possible that your mother doesn't love you? You're her one and only daughter, for God's sake."

"Frankly, Granny, I think she's bored with me. She never seems to want to spend any time with me."

"Do you need to be entertained all the time? You know that because of your father's job, she needs to accompany him here, there, and everywhere. She has to go to dinners and cocktail parties whether she wants to or not, and she can't neglect herself when she has to go to those dos. There's the hairdresser, the seamstress…just you wait until you grow up…*inşallah*, if you should marry a diplomat like your father, you'll understand what I mean."

"I'll never marry a diplomat, that's for sure."

"Why, my darling? Don't tell me you're not proud of your father."

"I am, but…it's just that…well, I'd rather marry someone who can spend time with me."

Hülya's reply caused Leman Hanım's blood pressure to rise. Those words—those familiar words—that attitude. She prayed that destiny would not repeat itself.

"Sensible men have important jobs; they haven't got a lot of spare time to spend with their wives. Only idle men have time to spend at home with their families."

"But Grandpa always stays with us."

"Your grandfather is retired. He certainly didn't spend a lot of time with me when we were young. I hardly ever saw his face."

"What's retired, Grandma?"

"Old people retire when they get old. That's to say they don't work anymore. They stay at home, like Grandpa."

"Will my father spend time with us when he re…re…whatever it's called?"

"There's a long time to go yet, darling, but of course he'll always be at home then."

"I think it's better if he doesn't. Whenever he's at home there's a quarrel."

"I've never heard your parents quarrel," Leman Hanım said in a severe tone.

"That's true; they haven't, since you've been here. Oh! Granny, why don't you always stay with us? I wish you'd never leave. When you're not here, my mother is always ill. She keeps on sulking and crying."

Really! Out of the mouths of babes, thought Leman Hanım. Hülya was giving her grandmother some facts she hadn't known. She tried to elicit some more information without giving the impression that they were gossiping.

"Is Mummy ill often then?" she asked in a soft voice. "Sabiha suffers with bronchitis; it's possible that it gets worse in the winter."

"No, I don't think so. She hardly ever coughs. She spends a lot of time in bed and never allows me into her bedroom. What's more, she doesn't go to the hairdresser or whatever that often either."

"Well, I never! She hasn't been ill at all since we've been here."

"That's what I'm telling you, Granny. Please don't ever leave us. If you do, my mother will shut herself in her room and I'll be alone again."

Leman Hanım put the photographs back in the box, tied the silk ribbon, and pushed it to the back of the second chiffonier drawer, beneath her underwear. There were things going on that she obviously didn't know about. One thing was certain: her daughter was unhappy. She might not even realize it herself. Could Macit be involved with another woman?

"Let's go next door, my pet; let's see what Mummy's doing. Maybe if we ask her, she'll play us a Chopin nocturne on the piano."

Macit took the ciphered message from the administrative officer, put on his spectacles, and read it. It was a reply from the Vichy government in response to the Turkish government's note. In the message the Vichy government insisted that, as far as they were concerned, Jews were Jews no matter what their nationality.

"Our Government is honored to inform the Turkish Embassy that the persons in question are guests in France and as such are indirectly subject to this country's laws. Following this principle, the actions directed by us toward the Hebrew race include Jews of French and other nationalities."

Damn them! thought Macit. Damned thugs! For years, we have considered them the apostles of civilization and independence. We have envied them and taken great pains to emulate them. Just imagine this is the brave French nation that produced the best art, the best poetry, the best wine in the world! Brave! What bravery? They weren't able to last more than forty-six days under German pressure. They surrendered immediately! Now they expect others to die for them to save their skin. And if that weren't enough, they look down on us. Their arrogance is unbelievable! My name isn't Macit if we can't rub their noses in the fact that we fought against all odds and won our war of independence with only a makeshift army. Damned collaborators!

Macit pushed his chair back noisily, got up from his desk, and took the ciphered message out of his room. Walking down the corridor to the secretary general, he kept turning over in his mind how they should respond to this message. He believed that they should protest against the Vichy government's discrimination laws. Surely there was no other way for an honorable country to respond. Maybe, in order to be more effective protesting the sending of Jews to labor camps, they should form a consensus with other countries. How aggravating this was when he already had so much on his plate. The first thing was to prepare the response. He believed that Turkish Jews forced to go to labor camps should apply to the Turkish authorities for their papers and resist as long as possible.

"Macit! Macit!"

Macit turned around. Nihat was running down the corridor toward him. "Can I have a moment please, I need to tell—"

"Yes, yes, I already know. The Turkish-German negotiations are about to start. The minister has asked me to attend the preparatory meeting. I'll be there, but I need to see the secretary general for about twenty minutes to discuss our reply to this message. I'll be with you shortly."

Macit kept walking down the corridor.

"Macit, please wait…just a moment…"

Macit reluctantly stopped and turned around.

"Macit, there was a call for you, sir. It seems that your father-in-law has had a heart attack."

Macit entered his father-in-law's room at the same time as the doctor. Fazıl Reşat Paşa was lying on his back on the floor beside the bed. His face was as white as chalk. Sabiha was wiping the beads of perspiration from his forehead with her handkerchief. Leman Hanım was squatting next to her husband, looking desperately anxious.

Dr. Fahri asked the old man to sniff from a bottle he took from his bag; he unbuttoned the patient's shirt and, taking his pulse, asked Macit to call an ambulance. He also asked for some cologne.

Sabiha responded at once. Leman Hanım, with trembling hands, tried to place a pillow under her husband's head. Dr. Fahri told her not to, and she pulled away.

"We need something to calm you down. Do you have anything like Nevrol, for instance?" asked the doctor.

"No, no, don't give me anything," protested Leman Hanım. "I want to go before him," she added, starting to cry. "It's because of me that he had this attack. If he dies I'm to blame."

"You're in shock," said Macit, clasping her shoulders. "What on earth are you saying? Come on now; let's get you up on your feet and out of here." Macit supported her under the arms and tried to lift her up.

"I'm all right. I don't need any help. Don't feel sorry for me, Macit; he's the one to feel sorry for," she said pointing, to her husband. "I'm the one who caused this. Can't you see? I forgot those photographs under the pillow."

"Now, now, Mother, calm yourself down. What photographs?"

It was only then, right as he asked the question, that he noticed his father-in-law clasping some photographs to his chest. As he tried carefully to pry open Fazıl Reşat Paşa's fingers, the photographs fell to the floor. Macit bent down, picked up the pictures, and then realized they were the wedding photographs that he had taken of Selva and Rafo.

Macit was confused. "Where did these come from?" he asked.

"I wish I hadn't taken them out. How was I to know? It's all my fault, I'm telling you. It's all my fault!"

Dr. Fahri was totally confused.

Macit explained: "Years ago, my sister-in-law got married without her father's consent. These are wedding photographs taken at the registry office."

"Leman Hanım, rest assured, heart attacks aren't triggered by such things. Lots of other factors are involved. Don't punish yourself this way."

Dr. Fahri tried in vain to calm her, but she continued sobbing. Sabiha returned with a bottle of cologne, which the doctor proceeded to dab on Leman Hanım's forehead and arms. He was busy massaging her arms when the doorbell rang.

"Wouldn't you know, today of all days happens to be Hacer's day off," Sabiha said as she went to answer the door.

"Macit, my son, that must be Hülya. Don't let her in here," Leman Hanım said between sobs.

Loud footsteps and voices were heard in the hallway outside the room.

Sabiha was heard saying, "Don't go in there, my beauty…Stop, for God's sake!"

Hülya pushed her mother aside and dashed into the room. She threw herself on her grandfather lying on the floor and started to hug him, "Grandpa, dear Grandpa…Please don't go. What would I do without you? I couldn't bear being without you. Please don't leave me all alone."

❧

Macit walked to the hospital holding his little daughter's hand tightly and trying to work out how to approach the subject weighing on his mind.

"Now, my darling, Grandpa is much better, but you must remember not to tire him," he warned.

"I promise I won't, Daddy."

"He's still very fragile, so you mustn't clamber all over him, smothering him with kisses. We must be careful."

"Yes, I understand."

"I knew you would, my bright little star. Mummy is leaving Granny with Grandpa, so I thought I could take the two of you to Karpiç for lunch. How's that?"

"No thanks, Daddy."

"Why not?"

"I'd like to stay with Grandpa at the hospital. Besides, you must be very busy at work."

"Of course I am, but I asked my assistant to hold the fort for me today. I thought it's about time the three of us spent some time together."

"Well, you can have lunch with Mummy; I'll stay with Grandpa…with Grandpa and Granny."

"Don't you want to have lunch with us?"

"You know I haven't seen Grandpa for so many days. I've missed him."

"Hülya, on that day—the day your grandfather had the heart attack—do you remember what you said?"

"What did I say?"

"When you were crying and hugging him, you said that if he left you, you would feel all alone…"

"I thought he was dead. When I saw Mummy open the door crying, she told me he was very ill. She tried to stop me going into the room. I thought he'd died."

"Fine, but that's not what I'm asking you. What I mean is, even if your grandpa died, it's wrong for you to think you'd be alone. Surely there's me and Mummy, isn't there?" Hülya didn't answer but Macit felt the tension in his daughter's hand. "I'd love to know why you feel this way."

"I love Grandpa and Granny very much. They care for me. They love me very much. I don't want them to die."

"May Allah bless them. *Inşallah*, they have long lives ahead of them. But Mummy and I love you very much too. We love you dearly."

Hülya remained silent, and Macit persisted.

"Don't you know this, Hülya? Don't you know that we adore you? You're our one and only little girl."

"I do, Daddy."

"Didn't you see how what you said that day hurt your mother? Not only was she distraught because of her father's condition, she was also hurt by your behavior."

"I don't think she could be hurt by me. She doesn't worry about me."

"What do you mean?"

"Well...I mean...what I mean is that she has far too many worries of her own."

"What do you think she worries about?"

"About my auntie being away; she worries about not being able to see little Fazıl—things like that. I don't know exactly, but I do know she doesn't worry about me."

"How do you know?"

"I can hear her when she is talking."

"With whom for instance?"

"Well...with Granny for instance, with her various friends, even with Hacer. She never stops talking about Auntie Selva."

"Is that so unusual? Of course she misses her sister. That doesn't mean she doesn't care about you."

"But she has no time for me at all. Just like you, Daddy; you have no time for me either. You're always busy working. She's always worrying about one thing or another. It's just as well my grandparents are here now. Grandpa is all right, isn't he? He'll be coming home soon, won't he?"

This time it was Macit's turn to be silent. He didn't know when his father-in-law would be coming back home; what he did know was if Hitler occupied the South of France, it would be devastating for his family. The Germans had carried out attacks all over Europe and the occupations of Athens and Crete meant they were on Turkey's doorstep. As if that wasn't enough, now the Vichy government was rounding up Turkish Jews and sending them to camps. He was well aware of the significance of this for his family. Since Fazıl Reşat Paşa's heart attack, it was as if this damned war were actually encroaching on his little daughter's heart.

"I wasn't aware of how much we'd been neglecting you," he said affectionately.

The child didn't respond. She simply continued to walk along beside her father.

Macit decided not to insist on having lunch with his daughter. After all, it might be better to have lunch just with Sabiha. It would give him an opportunity he hadn't had for some time to chat with his wife in a different environment, away from his mother-in-law.

Anyway, since Hülya had been born, there hadn't been many opportunities for private conversation. If they were in the drawing room, there was always the possibility of being overheard by the maid or Hülya's nanny. It was just as well that the nanny had been sent packing when Hülya started school. But then Macit puzzled for a moment, realizing there hadn't been the need for private conversation since their marriage. By the time Fazıl Reşat Paşa and Leman Hanım came to stay with them, they had gotten out of the habit of using the drawing room unless they were entertaining at home. Sabiha would retire to her room to read while he either sat by the radio or went to his study to examine the files he'd brought home from work. It was almost as if they had forgotten how to speak to one another. Macit wondered how they would cope later over lunch at Karpiç.

The smell of disinfectant filled the air in the hospital as father and daughter climbed the two flights of stairs. They found Sabiha and her mother sitting along the corridor outside Fazıl Reşat Paşa's room. The morning sun shone through the window behind Sabiha and created a halo around her blonde hair. Hülya pulled her hand away from her father, ran toward her grandmother, and hugged her. Sabiha waited patiently for her turn, but it didn't come. Hülya only complained at having to wait outside the room.

"The nurses are giving your grandfather a sponge bath, so you will have to wait a minute," Sabiha said to her daughter. Sabiha looked pale from the sleepless nights, and Macit kissed her on both cheeks.

"How did it go last night?"

"Fine," said Sabiha.

"Well, you'll be able to have a good night's sleep tonight."

"I can't stop worrying when I'm not at his side. I couldn't sleep a wink last night," said Leman Hanım.

"So I gathered. You were up and out before Hülya and I woke up."

"Doesn't she have to go to school today?" Sabiha said, looking at her watch. "It isn't even her lunch break yet. Don't tell me she skipped school."

"I didn't send her to school today. We have both taken the day off. She will keep her grandpa company, and you, my dear, will join me for a lovely lunch at Karpiç."

Leman Hanım gave her son-in-law a disapproving look.

"You must be joking," said Sabiha. "Do you expect me to enjoy lunch when my father is in here fighting for his life?"

"Let's wait and see how he feels first. Besides, your mother is at his side and there are certain things that we need to talk about."

"What sort of things?"

Macit took her arm and tried to lead her away from his mother-in-law's prying eyes.

"We need to talk about Hülya, Sabiha. She seems depressed to me."

"She's only seven, Macit!"

"Eight..."

"Anyway, she's not at an age when one gets depressed."

"Maybe so, but she can't be considered happy."

"She's not the only one, Macit."

"Sabiha, we can't sort out our affairs without talking. Don't you understand?"

"So you think we can sort everything out over lunch at Karpiç. Is that it?"

Just as Macit was about to answer, Hülya came running up to them.

"It's OK now. Grandpa is ready. He's waiting for you." Then she ran back to her grandfather's room. Macit and Sabiha followed her, walking side by side.

Fazıl Reşat Paşa lay back in bed, propped up against a pile of pillows. He was unshaven and smiled at his son-in-law with an exhausted look.

"You look very well," Macit said, trying to hide his true feelings. The old man waved his hand as if to say, *don't bother*.

"He's fine, thank God. It seems we've overcome the worst; the rest is up to him," said Leman Hanım. "He has to stop smoking and even give up the raki you have together in the evenings."

"Can you believe that?" asked the old man shakily.

Just as Macit was about to answer, he stopped. He noticed one of the photographs—according to Leman Hanım, they were the cause of the heart attack—on the bedside table. It was resting against the water jug. Not one of Macit's photos, but the one of Selva signing the register, taken by a photographer at the registry office. Macit gulped and looked at his wife in amazement. Sabiha looked away and Macit did likewise; he pretended not to have seen the picture.

"So, if the doctors won't allow us to have raki, then we'll have to content ourselves with beer, won't we?" the old man said jokingly. "Macit, when am I supposed to come home? These women aren't telling me the truth. In fact, I thought we might go straight back to Istanbul from here. I'd hate to burden you any further."

Hülya took her grandfather's hand and kissed it.

"I won't hear of it," Macit said sincerely. "Our home is your home too. Having you stay with us isn't a burden, it's a pleasure."

"I'm sure Father doesn't mean that, he's just being coy," Sabiha said. "In any case Dr. Fahri gave strict instructions that he has to rest for at least a month."

"You can all go back to Istanbul when the schools…" Macit couldn't finish his sentence. A hospital attendant in white overalls was looking at everyone and then turned to Macit.

"You must be Macit."

"That's right."

"There's a call for you in the office."

"I wonder what's up," said Macit, hurriedly following the attendant out of the room and down the stairs.

As soon as Macit left the room, Sabiha turned to Hülya.

"Did you at least ask permission for the day off today?"

"Daddy phoned the head teacher."

"What did he say?"

"He said that Grandpa wanted to see me this morning and he asked for permission."

"You know, of course, that it's not right to skip lessons, don't you, Hülya? You could have visited your grandfather after school. Maybe you'll at least attend your afternoon lessons."

Hülya immediately became sulky and shrugged her shoulders.

"I wonder what this is all about," Leman Hanım inquired.

"Probably the ministry. One would think he was running Turkey single-handed. We don't have a moment's peace day or night. I'd love to know what they would do if he ever had an overseas posting. Probably fly him back at moments of crisis…"

Macit appeared at the door, looking very worried.

"What's up?" Fazıl Reşat Paşa asked in his fragile voice.

"I have to return to the ministry. It seems there are some new developments."

"What's the matter? What happened?"

"I'll find out the details. I'll let you know when I visit you this evening," he promised. Then he nodded to his wife to follow him.

"I thought we were going to Karpiç to sort out our affairs," she said mockingly.

"Sabiha, I didn't want to say this in front of your father. I didn't want to upset him but the situation is very serious. Hitler took over the rest of France this morning."

MARSEILLES 1942

For some time, Selva had been keeping an eye on the road from behind the net curtains. Then she summoned her husband.

"Rafo, the coast's clear. You can hurry across the road now. Don't hang around!"

Rafo planted a kiss on his wife's neck and walked to the door. "You worry too much, Selva. Nothing will happen today. Just you wait and see," he said reassuringly before closing the door behind him. Selva listened until the sound of his steps faded away down the stairs.

Rafo left the building, walked to the edge of the sidewalk, and waited for the policeman at the crossroads to stop the traffic. Selva heaved a sigh of relief after Rafo entered the pharmacy and closed the door. She drew the curtains aside, opened the window, and inhaled the cold damp air. She wouldn't be taking Fazıl to the park this morning; the black clouds were a sure sign of rain.

If only those black clouds would just remain in the sky; since the occupation had spread to the south, it was as if these clouds had invaded her home and her whole being. She had stopped giving lessons to her students, even though teaching was like a sunbeam in her monotonous, lonely life. No one had expected her to stop teaching, but since the beginning of the invasion on November 11, she had taken on a new role: to protect her husband as much as she could, her husband whom she'd persuaded to emigrate to France and unintentionally thrown into the lion's den.

Rafo, like all the other Jews, checked carefully before going out. Venturing out of doors while the SS were patrolling was asking for trouble. Thank God, Rafo's place of work was just across the street. The mission that Selva had set for herself began after her husband entered the pharmacy. Apart from the time she spent looking after Fazıl, she would spend the rest of the day sitting on a high stool in front of the window. The moment she heard the Gestapo on their motorcycles, or saw them patrolling the streets, she would telephone the pharmacy to tell Rafo to make himself scarce and hide in the storeroom.

"I hear the noises, my darling," Rafo kept saying. "I can assure you that I take precautions immediately. If you go on like this, you'll drive yourself crazy."

"But what if they creep up on you one day?"

"We need to let our lives take their natural course. After all, there is such a thing as kismet. I'm not a Muslim, but I certainly believe in destiny more than you do."

"And if they took you away, Rafo…"

"They wouldn't. Thanks to you, we finally have our Turkish passports."

"If the passports were enough to protect us, Tarık wouldn't be calling from Paris every other day to check that we are all right."

"For heaven's sake, darling, stop fretting. Remember how the consul managed to get Rosa out of their hands?"

"But you remember what he said? 'It's like Russian roulette. I was lucky, I managed it that time, but I may not be lucky again.'"

"If he managed to save one of us, he can probably save all of us!"

For some reason, Selva was unable to think like Rafo. Night after night she had a recurring nightmare of herself and her family being squashed into a trainload of screaming people and taken away. She would jump out of her bed and pace up and down the apartment. Selva now regretted having registered her son as Alfandari. Tarık had been angry with her too, for endangering her son's life, but Selva wouldn't swallow her pride and admit that she had changed her mind. God, she regretted taking after her father. This damned pride! She didn't approve of her own nature, but she just couldn't help it. It was as if there were someone else inside her telling her what to do.

Selva decided to take her surveillance duties one step further. The corner window of their apartment was in a good position to see when the SS were approaching. She could see them on the main road before they turned into the street. She telephoned the mothers of her former students in particular and, after introducing herself, offered to warn them of any approaching danger. But her neighbors were disturbed by this meddling Turkish woman whom they hardly knew, and Rafo scolded her for her intrusive behavior. Selva was taken aback; it appeared that no one understood her kindness.

Selva was feeding Fazıl some apple puree when there was a knock at the door. There was another hour before Rafo's lunch break, and since she had no students, she wondered who it could be. Before opening the door she asked who it was. A woman replied, "Madame Alfandari, I live in this area. My name is Afnaim, Camilla Afnaim."

Selva immediately opened the door to see a neatly dressed woman of about forty-five.

"Did you wish to speak to me, Madame Afnaim?"

"Yes, madame."

"Are you from Istanbul too, by any chance?"

"No."

"Perhaps somewhere else in Turkey?"

"My family is from Lebanon. We've never been in Turkey."

"Oh, in that case you must have come to inquire about lessons. I'm afraid I don't give lessons anymore."

"I've only come to talk to you."

Selva was surprised. The woman standing there wasn't even of her generation.

"About what, may I ask?"

"It's rather difficult to speak on the doorstep…"

"I do beg your pardon. Please come in."

Selva took the woman's coat and led her into the sitting room. Fazıl was sitting in his high chair, trying to eat his puree and spilling it everywhere.

"What a sweet child," said the woman.

"Won't you please sit down?" said Selva.

"Madame Alfandari, you don't know me, but I know quite a lot about you. I know, for instance, that your husband works in the pharmacy across the street, that you gave private lessons at home, and that, two weeks ago, you even kindly telephoned Lea's mother and offered to keep them informed about the goings-on outside. As I said, I live in this neighborhood as well."

"On this street?"

"No, two streets up from here."

Selva saw the woman looking at the tall stool by the window. "Yes, that's my observation tower," she said, nodding toward it. "I can see everything going on from the crossroads down our street and beyond. It's all spread out as if on a plate for me when I sit there. I was trying to help some of the families in this street, but none of them wanted to know."

"You shouldn't mind them; everybody is so scared these days."

"Yes, I didn't mind them. It's just that I have to keep watch for my husband's sake anyway…"

The woman didn't respond and Selva continued, "Was it in connection with this that you wanted to speak to me?"

"No, madame. True, I wanted to ask you a favor, but it wasn't that."

"How can I help you then?"

"You're Turkish, aren't you?"

"Yes."

"Apparently the Turkish consulate is being very helpful to the Jews."

"They're renewing the citizenship registrations of those who are of Turkish origin."

"Couldn't they do the same for someone who isn't Turkish?"

"I beg your pardon. How could that be possible? I don't really think so."

"Actually I'm not asking for myself or my husband. It's just that I have two brilliant young children..." The woman's voice was trembling. "I'm so worried about them. It was I who insisted that we come here, you see. I persuaded my husband to close down the business back home, and I dragged my family here."

The woman stopped talking and held her head in her hands for some time. Selva waited, heartbroken.

"When Lea's mother told me about your phone call, I realized what a helpful person you must be. Lea adores you."

"Lea is a very talented child; I'm sure she will eventually become a successful pianist."

"That is, of course, if she doesn't end up in a labor camp."

Selva bowed her head with sadness.

"If you happen to know someone at the consulate, madame. Maybe if, I mean..." The woman paused.

"I do know the consul."

"Couldn't you talk to him about my kids?"

"Frankly, I don't think talking to him will do any good."

"Maybe we could go together. If you introduced me, I could talk to him myself."

Selva didn't know what to say. "Would you like some coffee?" she offered.

The woman looked surprised.

"I'm sorry. It's customary in my country to offer tea or coffee to a guest."

"We have the same custom. Thank you. I'll have coffee, black, please. Can I offer you a cigarette?"

"No, thanks. I don't smoke. I quit when I was pregnant and I haven't gone back…yet."

Fazıl dropped his spoon and Selva rushed to pick it up. She lifted him out of his chair and took him into the kitchen while she made the coffee.

"I'd better keep an eye out for you," said the woman, sitting on the stool. "I must say you do have a clear view of the crossroads from here," she added.

A little while later Selva returned with two cups of coffee on a tray and Fazıl holding on to her skirt.

"Why on earth did you leave that beautiful country of yours to come here?" asked the woman. "Not that I have seen Istanbul myself, of course, but those that have go on and on about it."

"Neither Rafael's nor my family approved of our marriage. I am a Muslim, you see." Selva saw the woman raise her eyebrows in surprise. "Instead of living in the same city as our disapproving parents, we thought it would be better to live in another country."

"So you're a Muslim. I wouldn't have guessed it at all."

Placing a cup of coffee on a little table, Selva said, "Why's that? Can't a Muslim and a Jew love each other?"

"I'm sorry, that's not what I meant…"

"Why don't you sit over here? I can sit on my stool now."

"I can't believe you keep watch like this all day," said the woman, walking toward the sofa.

"Not all day, really," said Selva, "but once I've finished my housework I do sit here and listen to the radio, and knit or read the paper. At the same time, I manage to keep an eye on what's going on."

"But listen, madame," said the woman, pausing. "If you are a Turkish Muslim, that means your word would carry more weight at the consulate..."

"I can assure you, as far as our consulate is concerned, it doesn't matter what religion you are if you're Turkish," Selva said with pride in her voice. Out of courtesy, the woman didn't ask why, in case Selva had problems with her own family. Selva took a sip of coffee and glanced at the street.

"I can't promise anything, but I am willing to go to the consulate and ask if they can do anything on your behalf," Selva said.

"Oh, madame, Madame Alfandari, I don't know how to thank you."

"Don't thank me. I honestly have no hope at all."

The woman took a photograph from her bag and gave it to Selva.

"Please keep this picture. Maybe you could show it to the consul. It may soften his heart if he could just see the children's bright faces."

"I'm sure, madame, that the photograph won't make an ounce of difference. If the consul is in a position to help, he will, but you must agree that he can't abuse his authority in any way—"

"Maybe if you were to say that the children are close friends of yours, or even ask if there is a price for such a thing. I'm sure there must be a price."

Selva's face dropped. She vented her anger on Fazıl, who was carrying all of his toys from the bedroom into the sitting room.

"I want you to take those back where they belong immediately!" she shouted at her son. She got up and took the half-empty cup from the small table. "Well, I'm pleased to have met you. Now I have things to do."

It was obvious this woman hadn't expected such a reaction.

"I'm sorry if I offended you, madame," the woman said shakily.

"I'm not offended," Selva said.

"Can I possibly call on you again, in a week?"

"No, please don't come again."

"Can I telephone you?"

"No, don't."

"I can see I have offended you. I can assure you, I didn't mean to. I'm so desperate, please forgive me."

"There was no offense taken."

"Still, I'd better leave my telephone number in case you change your mind."

She took a pencil from her bag and wrote the number on the back of the children's photograph. Selva stood waiting by her side. Finally the woman got up and walked to the door. She and Fazıl followed, and stood by the door. The woman patted his head.

"You're a mother too," she said, almost in tears. "I have faith in you, only because of this…only because you are a mother."

Selva closed the door, picked up Fazıl, and, as she walked back to the sitting room, she muttered through her teeth, "Insolent woman!" She put Fazıl down, picked up her unfinished coffee, and glanced out of the window. There was a commotion at the crossroads. Opening the window, she heard the shouts. On their motorcycles, the Gestapo were gathering at the corner. She could see people running here and everywhere.

Selva leaned out of the window and called out, "Madame… Madame…Madame Afnaim."

The woman had just stepped out of the front door. When she heard Selva calling, she looked up.

"Come back," called Selva. "Come back upstairs immediately." She rushed to the telephone without even closing the window and dialed Rafo's number.

"Rafo? Rafo, is that you? Hide yourself. For God's sake, hide yourself immediately; don't dare come out of the storeroom until I call you again."

She put the telephone down and went to open the door.

"It's incredible; they sprang up from nowhere. They're harassing people at the crossroads. You'd better wait here until the coast is clear."

The woman was shaking in front of the door. "God bless you, my friend," she said, walking toward the corner window without even taking her coat off. "There are far too many Jews living in this neighborhood. That's why we haven't a moment's peace. Unfortunately, those who aren't Jewish have to contend with this too."

Selva and Camilla jostled one another to get into the narrow space at the corner window, and Fazıl started to cry because he wanted to sit on his mother's lap.

"Stop it!" she scolded. "This is no time to cry. Stop that at once, do you hear me?"

Fazıl heard the piercing sound of the sirens. He got frightened and stopped crying.

Selva knelt down beside her son. "Come on, why don't you go and play with your red truck in the bedroom, my darling."

"Madame Alfandari, look what they're doing! My God! No, no, surely that's too much!"

Selva stood up and tried to look out over the woman's shoulder. Two German soldiers were grasping the arms of a young man who was screaming at the top of his voice. A third German forcefully pulled his trousers down. With a burst of energy, the young man struggled to prevent them from pulling down his underpants, but to no avail. Selva shut her eyes tightly. When she opened them, they were dragging the young man, shoving him into an army vehicle.

"Look over there, on the left, they have lined up all the men. Do you see that? They're at it again!"

Selva changed places with the woman, and leaned slightly out the window. The woman was right. The men were being forcibly stripped and checked. A little boy was running down the street, hiding himself in the doorways.

"Have you got any binoculars?" asked the woman.

"What on earth for?"

"I can't recognize the men in the lineup from here. Maybe I could with binoculars. I'd like to know if there are any friends of mine."

"I don't have binoculars," said Selva. "Madame Afnaim—your surname is Afnaim, isn't it?—please keep away from the window. What good would it do even if you did know some of them?"

She closed the window and drew the curtain, but the woman continued watching the street.

"Look! Look, they're taking one more away; they're dragging him by force. My God! The poor man's pants are hanging around his ankles!"

Selva put her arm affectionately around the woman's shoulders. "Come on, madame, don't watch this brutality. Give me your coat and sit down over here."

"Please call me Camilla."

"Camilla, let me warm up the coffee you didn't finish before."

"Madame Alfandari..."

"Please call me Selva."

"Selva, don't you think we should do what you did before? Even though they refused your offer, I think we ought to call the people down your street to warn them. I can call those in my street and warn them not to go out."

"Excellent idea! You start calling your friends while I look for my telephone numbers."

As Selva went to the bedroom to find her notebook, Camilla had already dialed her first number.

"Menahim, this is Camilla. The Gestapo are at the crossroads and carrying out circumcision checks by force. Call the school and tell them that on no account should they send the boys home. Warn the Razons too, and tell them to warn those in their street; everyone should call one another. I'll call the Marcus family…"

ANKARA

Dr. Sahir Erhan tried to remember where he had met this handsome man who had insisted on a lunchtime appointment. He couldn't figure it out, and he looked again at the card in his hand.

Macit Devres
Ministry of Foreign Affairs
Political Department
Director

"I'm sorry," he said, "your face is so familiar to me, but I can't remember where we've met. Ankara's not a big city. Our paths must have crossed somewhere."

"Actually, you have an excellent memory. We played bridge at Dr. Celal's house about two years ago."

"Really!"

"But we weren't sitting at the same table."

"In that case, my memory is far from excellent. That's awful. I don't know how I could have forgotten."

"I probably wouldn't have remembered you either if Dr. Celal hadn't reminded me of that summer weekend when we played bridge. To tell you the truth, I couldn't picture you from his description, but I did recognize you as soon as I walked in."

"So, you play bridge too. You must play well if you have earned a place at Dr. Celal's house."

"I'm sure I'd get better if I had the opportunity to play more. Unfortunately, we are very busy at the office these days. I'm tied to my desk."

Eventually, Dr. Sahir put a stop to the niceties and got down to business.

"So, what can I do for you?" He handed a file he took from his drawer to Macit. "First of all, I'd appreciate it if you could complete this form for me. Obviously, there are some details I need."

Macit refused the file. "I'd rather not, Doctor. You see, I'm not here for myself."

"Oh!"

"I didn't want to tell your secretary. My wife has an appointment with you tomorrow, and I decided to come and have a preliminary chat with you beforehand."

Dr. Sahir was puzzled. Could this be a jealous husband? "Are you someone who doesn't believe in psychological treatment?"

"Not at all! Quite the opposite, in fact. You can't imagine what I went through to persuade my wife to see a psychiatrist. Dr. Celal is both our family doctor and a friend. It was he who persuaded Sabiha to come and see you."

"So what is it that you want to speak to me about?"

"Sabiha, my wife, is coming to see you at three tomorrow afternoon. I believe she's been going through a crisis for some time now. She can't sleep at night, and she's certainly unhappy; she's always on edge, and is becoming more and more withdrawn. But there's nothing in our lives to make her feel like this. It is true that, in view of the present circumstances, I'm not in a position to devote much time to her. Consequently, we've drifted apart a bit. But not to the extent that would cause a crisis."

"You are aware, of course, that there are many details that can affect one's life."

"I'm sure my wife will tell you all about her sister in France and her father's recent heart attack."

"I see!"

"That's all true, but it's not my reason for being here."

"I'm listening."

"I am actually here because I am concerned about my young daughter. Our dear Hülya; she's only eight, but I'm afraid my wife doesn't…let's just say that she doesn't seem very interested in her daughter. The child is very bright and is obviously aware of this. I believe she's reacting to the fact that her mother doesn't care about her. She needs affection. *Inşallah*, my wife will get over this problem, but my worry is the repercussions it will have on my daughter. How are we to sort out the damage done to the child?"

"If you don't mind, I think I ought to see my patient first."

"Of course, Doctor, I understand that, but I am sure Sabiha won't be talking to you about the situation with our daughter. That's why I took it upon myself to explain it to you. You might be able to get to the bottom of her indifference. It seems my daughter desperately seeks affection from her grandparents because her mother can't give her any. In my opinion, this is not at all healthy."

"Has it occurred to you that your wife's condition might be as a result of indifference too?"

"I beg your pardon. I don't understand."

"Lack of love damages older people just as much as it damages the young."

"Of course."

"You've told me that your wife is going through a crisis, and yet you are more concerned about your daughter than her. You told me that because the child is bright, she's aware of her mother's negligence and realizes that maybe her mother doesn't love her enough."

"True."

"Isn't it possible then that because your wife is bright and intelligent too, she might be aware of certain things that contribute toward her unhappiness?"

"I can assure you that I am entirely faithful to my wife and hold her in my highest esteem."

"Love and esteem are two entirely different things. From what you tell me, it is possible that you may be withholding love and affection from your wife, even though you hold her in high regard."

"Really!" Macit replied, feeling confused. He took his watch from his pocket and looked at the time. His lunch break was coming to an end. "It's true I may have been neglecting my wife because I am inundated with work lately, but then that's why we invited her parents to stay with us."

"I wish it were possible to assign deputies to deal with our loved ones; what a shame that mothers and fathers can't replace husbands and wives. Even you are exasperated because your daughter has more of an affinity with her grandparents than her own mother. There's a new therapy being practiced in Europe now. It's for family members who don't see eye to eye and it's called, simply, family therapy. It is not being used extensively yet, but I'm sure that very soon its value will be appreciated. The therapist gathers all the family together at the same time; he listens to their problems and tries to find a solution. Would you be interested in this method?"

"Frankly, I'd rather not get involved. I'm against my daughter seeing a psychiatrist at her age anyway. It's my wife who made the appointment to see you because of her stress. I merely wanted to give you the picture regarding my daughter."

"It's up to you; however, I'd rather you didn't see psychiatrists as some sort of bogeymen. We are here to help people of all ages."

"I can assure you I don't see you as bogeymen, of course not. As for that 'together therapy' or whatever it's called…I'm not for it."

"In that case, I'm very grateful that you took the time to inform me of these details. Let's hope that after I have spoken to your wife, I might be able to come up with some form of therapy to help all of you. Knowing your wife's attitude toward her daughter will be helpful; you've definitely helped me on that score." Dr. Sahir got up to show Macit to the door. "I'll ask Celal to organize a bridge party for us one evening when you are free," he added, shaking hands.

On his way out of the building, Macit muttered, "Yes, by all means let him organize a bridge party so I can really show you, you smart aleck!"

PARIS

Tarık Arıca had been living in a cheap hotel ever since he set foot in Paris. Sitting in a taxi with his two suitcases, on his way to his new apartment, he was very happy. Moving to rented accommodations meant that he no longer had to live in a cell-like room with just a bed, a bedside table, and a wardrobe. His new home had two bedrooms, a small sitting room, a kitchen large enough for a small breakfast table, and a big bathroom with a huge bathtub and a bidet. What was more, it was also fully furnished and close to both the Métro station and bus stops. It was almost perfect. As far as Tarık was concerned, his only problem was financial: because of the high rent, he would have to share the place with someone. That someone was Muhlis, his colleague at the consulate. When Tarık told Muhlis about the apartment he had seen, and mentioned it was too expensive, Muhlis, who was looking for a convenient apartment himself, immediately offered to share it with him. As there were two bedrooms, Tarık thought it was a good idea. Now, on the day they were to sign the contract, he suddenly wasn't so sure. Would he be able to share a place with someone he worked with day after day? Would he be able to cope with this person who never stopped talking, who was always telling jokes?

But the decision had already been made. They signed the contract and paid the deposit.

On the day they were due to move, Muhlis had to take some documents to the Turkish embassy in Vichy, so Tarık had to move his things on his own. After putting everything in the appropriate cupboards, he went out for a stroll. He sat in a café having some Pernod and enjoying a cigarette. He had planned to celebrate this day for a couple of reasons. More important than moving to a new apartment, Sabiha had telephoned!

It had been almost two years since he had heard Sabiha's voice. He was so surprised and excited that Muhlis, who was sitting at their desk, made signs to ask what was happening.

Sabiha was asking Tarık to protect her sister and her family who had moved south. Tarık wondered who could protect anyone from Hitler. Did she think he was God? Tarık explained that both Selva and her husband were in possession of perfectly valid documents and could therefore return to Turkey if they wished. Sabiha had also told Tarık about her father's heart attack. If anything should happen to Selva and her son, the old man's heart wouldn't be strong enough to stand it.

Tarık took in everything that Sabiha said, as if he were receiving news of his own family. It took him a considerable time to console Sabiha and convince her that Selva would be all right. He promised to let Selva know the timetable for trains from Paris to Istanbul. He would insist that she leave Marseilles. He would try to protect her and her family.

He had said all that on the telephone, but how he was to achieve it was a different matter. All he could do was contact Nazım Kender in Marseilles and ask him to keep an eye on her. Come to think of it, wouldn't Nazım Kender consider it odd that Tarık was asking him to protect a married woman?...No, he certainly couldn't do that.

As soon as he put the phone down, he felt obliged to at least check the trains going to Istanbul, because of his love for Sabiha. Train journeys through occupied countries were very dangerous. Because of the skirmishes en route, the timetables were haphazard. He couldn't force Selva to take such a journey, but while making inquiries he stumbled on something that gave him a glimmer of hope. He found out that Turkish diplomats were in the process of trying to gather all those Jews in Paris they had saved from the labor camps and send them by train to Istanbul, and then by sea to Palestine. It was the Turkish ambassador in Vichy who told Tarık of this scheme. It wouldn't be easy to accomplish. According to the plan, the Turkish government would hire a carriage and attach it to one of the trains going toward Edirne. Turkey was a neutral country, so she would exercise her right to take the train car under her protection. A lot of effort was being spent to bring this plan to fruition. This meant that he would actually be in a position to do something for Sabiha.

There was something else that pleased Tarık.

Sabiha told him on the phone that she had begun to see a psychiatrist. Apparently he had qualified in Austria and was a very unusual doctor, not one of those psychiatrists who simply treated their patients by prescribing sleeping pills and tranquilizers. On the contrary, he spent hours talking to them and as a result reached the root of their problems. Sabiha was going to see him twice a week and she was very pleased with him. He wasn't judgmental, he didn't apportion blame, he didn't even give her advice; he simply listened to her.

Sabiha had finally found someone she could talk to about her inner fears and doubts. Feeling a little jealous, Tarık had asked her what sort of man this specialist was—was he old, was he handsome? No, he wasn't old. Yes, he was handsome. "Really!" Tarık had responded. Sabiha's voice was like music to his ears. She reminded him that the psychiatrist was a doctor, after all, and he would never be able to take the place of a loyal friend. She missed Tarık's warm friendship.

Toward evening, Muhlis arrived at the new apartment loaded with shopping, which he took straight to the kitchen and put away on the various shelves.

"What on earth is all this? What on earth have you bought?" asked Tarık.

"These things make life worth living—various cheeses, wine, and bread."

"I thought that we might go out for dinner."

"These are not dinner, my dear friend, these are things from the delicatessen."

"Where did you find this cheese? I asked the grocer across the street as I was coming home but there was no Brie. He told me it's not easy to find these days…My God! Look at all this wine. Who's going to drink all this?"

"I can find anything," said Muhlis. "As for the wine, it's for us and our guests, of course."

"What guests?"

"Just you wait and see. Ferit and his wife will be here soon. Ferit is a friend from Galatasaray, my school in Istanbul. He was doing his master's here when the war broke out and he couldn't get back home, so now he's teaching at the university. I'm sure you'll like him. He's not cheeky like me. He's serious like you, and let me tell you he's also very talented. He was a track champion at school and also a very good actor in the school plays. I'll never forget the night he ecstatically danced a Kazakhstan dance! We were left speechless."

Tarık was upset. He'd hoped to listen to the radio or read a book after dinner on his first evening at home. He was looking forward to an early night, and even having the opportunity to think about that morning's telephone call. He would try to remember the conversation word for word and perhaps manage to read between the lines. He would try to analyze Sabiha's anxious, but happy, tone of voice with a clear head.

"I wish you'd asked me first," Tarık said.

"You can stay in your room if you don't want to join us. I thought it would be a good idea to celebrate our first day in our new home."

"It would be embarrassing if I stayed in my room, but I'd appreciate it if you would ask me before inviting guests again."

"You'd think we were still at school! Look, Tarık, you know that I always treat you with respect as my senior at work, but you have to understand that if we are to share this apartment, we have to have equal status, otherwise it won't work. Both of us should be in a position to come and go as we please. We've got to be free to ask whomever we want to come back home with us, whether it's female company or guests we want to entertain at home. Is that OK with you? After all, we're no longer kids anymore, are we?"

"If you don't mind, I'd like to think about this. If I don't agree, it might be better if we go our separate ways before we jeopardize our friendship," Tarık said, going to his room.

He sat in the armchair by the window, not switching on the light; he sat thinking by the light of the streetlamp. Was he being difficult? Muhlis's words had startled him—what was it that he had said? He said that they should be free to bring back whomever they wished—including female company. He was a young man himself too, but it had never occurred to him that he might want to bring a woman back, especially when someone was sleeping in the next room. This was the difference between someone raised in Anatolia, as opposed to Istanbul. Just the thought of it was enough to make someone who'd attended a lycée in Sivas blush, but it was perfectly normal for someone who went to the Galatasaray lycée in Istanbul.

Maybe it was time for Tarık to grow up, for him to realize that life didn't consist of just going back and forth to work, that love wasn't about being enamored with a woman who could never be his. Maybe meeting Muhlis was a godsend. Was Muhlis the mediator who could bring him out of his shell, introduce him to new friends and new places? Could he widen his horizons by introducing him to the Paris nightlife, where he could enjoy the company of women?

He left his room and went into the kitchen, where Muhlis was setting out various cheeses on a plate. Tarık put his hand on Muhlis's shoulder and spoke to him in his usual calm voice.

"You're right, my friend. We're not at school, we're in our apartment, our home. You must feel free to come and go just as you please, and of course you should be able to invite your friends whenever you wish. My only request is that you let me know when you're inviting people so I can make other arrangements if I don't want to join you. I can go to the cinema or whatever."

At the end of the evening, Tarık was pleased to have made the decision to join. Ferit and his wife were very pleasant indeed. They brought a bottle of wine with them and interesting conversation flowed easily. Far from Tarık's expectations, Ferit turned out to be a sensible and interesting man, not at all the frivolous guy he was expecting. He was exactly as Muhlis had described him. His wife, Evelyn, was a very nice French girl whom Ferit had met at the university; they had known each other for about six years and had finally gotten married six months ago. Evelyn could speak a little Turkish, but with difficulty. However, as the evening wore on and after a few bottles of wine, there was no language barrier. They all felt comfortable together and talked about everything under the sun. Inevitably, the conversation turned to the war that had engulfed Europe and the awful conditions they were living in.

Ferit shared their views on the cruel and inhuman attitude of the Germans toward the Jews. He himself had hidden several Turkish Jewish friends from the university in his apartment. Because they were afraid to go to the consulate themselves, he had gone on their behalf and filled out the application forms for them.

Tarık told them how he had also saved some Jews from the Gestapo's hands. Muhlis described how one old lady Tarık had saved kept trying to kiss him all the way to the consulate in the car, and they all burst into laughter.

Evelyn too had stories to tell. Apparently she had heard dreadful reports about what was going on in the labor camps, through the fiancé of a girlfriend. How had he found out? It seemed that because he had been pro-German, he had been allowed to carry provisions in a pickup truck into the camp. It was during his comings and goings that he chatted to those working at the camp and found out about the hair-raising atrocities being carried out there. Needless to say, that had been the end of his pro-German views.

Evelyn, Ferit, Muhlis, and Tarık stayed up talking until the early hours, their voices slightly slurred as a result of consuming wine. Their nerve-racking stories led all of them to agree these poor people needed support, and they promised each other to do everything they could to help.

"You're doing everything you can anyway," Ferit said, "but in our own little way we're doing our bit too!"

"Really, what do you mean? Some association, an organization, or what?"

"Not exactly," Ferit said, getting up from beside Tarık and switching on the radio, fiddling with the dial until he found a station playing music. The conversation came to an end. By the time Muhlis had another go at the radio and found some dance music, their mood had changed. When the guests had left, Tarık and Muhlis tidied up and retired to their respective rooms. Tarık lay down on his back with his hands behind his head; he was rather drunk but happy. His apartment mate who had verbal diarrhea had certainly managed to add some color to his life.

ANKARA

Sabiha was sitting in an armchair with her feet on a footstool in Dr. Sahir's consulting room, trying to relax.

"We'll wait until you are ready as usual," her doctor had said. "Please don't talk until you are ready. Just lie back and relax, allowing your thoughts to take over. I can even play some music for you if you wish. I know you like classical music. I've got the Brahms piano concerto right here. Would you like to listen to it?"

"Oh yes, please."

Dr. Sahir picked up the big black record, dusted it carefully, and put it on the gramophone. After the initial scratching noise, Sabiha heard the first few notes of the music. She closed her eyes and listened to the concerto she knew so well. It definitely helped her to relax, as if she were half-asleep. She could hear the doctor's voice but she wasn't sure where he was. He wasn't directly in front of her. Was he sitting behind her or pacing around the room? He would talk for a while, then listen, occasionally asking questions.

"Can you remember the day your sister was born?"

"Almost, as if in a dream…I was about two or two and a half. I can't say I remember clearly."

"Did you share the same bedroom?"

"No, Selva slept in our mother's room for about a year."

"You must have been angry about that."

"Yes, of course. She kept on taking things away that belonged to me."

"That's a very natural form of jealousy that most children go through when a sibling is born."

"I don't think so! It was a bit different with me. I remember times when I wanted to kill her."

"Come on now!"

"Well, maybe not actually wanted to kill her, but there were definitely times when I wanted her dead. When she had measles, for example, they sent me away because they didn't want me to catch them too."

"Where did they send you?"

"To my paternal grandmother, because when the measles got serious, my other grandmother came to stay with us to look after my sister. I remember being told to pray for Selva before going to bed. I did pray, but not for her to recover. I prayed for her to die."

"Did you feel abandoned?"

"And how! I was only six; I wanted to be with my family, even at the risk of catching measles."

"What happened next?"

"Next?…Next?…Then Selva's condition got really bad—when I was praying for her to die, that is. My grandmother was informed of the situation, and she took my grandfather and rushed away. They spent the whole night there. I was scared and cried all night long. Then I started praying continuously for my sister to get well."

"And she did."

"Yes, thank God, she did, but I must admit I felt remorse and pain for a long time after that. I have always felt guilty toward her for that."

"Were there other such occasions?"

"Not exactly like that. But as we were growing up, there must have been childish feelings, I suppose."

"Tell me about them."

"Sometimes I would get angry with my sister and wish awful things on her."

"Like what?"

"Oh, I don't know...once when she was offered the leading part in the school play, for instance, I felt the part should have been mine. I was older than her, after all. I felt it was my right."

"Why did they give her the part?"

"Because she was like a beanpole. It was a male part."

"So?"

"I wished she would get ill and miss the first performance. It was snowing that day, everywhere was covered in white. Wouldn't you know it? She fell and broke her arm!"

"Really! That's incredible! So what did you do then?"

"I was sorry; my conscience really bothered me. Of course I couldn't tell anyone. I wanted to clear my conscience, so I became her slave until she recovered."

"Did you reveal your feelings to her?"

"I wanted to, very much in fact, but I couldn't; she wouldn't have believed me anyway. She's very naive and always means well. She thinks I love her very much."

"But you do, don't you?"

"Yes, I do, very much. But I must have been jealous of her all my life."

"Listen, Sabiha Hanım, believe me, all firstborn children have similar feelings when the younger one gets more attention than they do. They feel jealous when they have to share their parents' love. Gradually, as they grow up, this feeling fades."

"That may be so, but I feel the traces are still there. I can't put my finger on it; it's like a guilty conscience. I feel I may have influenced my sister's life in some way by my senseless bouts of jealousy."

"None of us is powerful enough to influence other people's lives entirely."

"Not even extremely jealous firstborn children?"

"Absolutely not!…So, do you think *all* firstborn children are jealous?"

"Isn't that what you just said?"

"That's my point of view. I want to know yours."

"I agree with you. I actually believe that all firstborn kids are like the wrath of God!"

"Why?"

"Because they're cunning and capable of bad things. Trying to manipulate the lives of those who were born after them. They want all the toys, all the clothes, all the love for themselves."

"The firstborn *children*? Do you mean both boys and girls?"

"Well, I don't know about boys. Maybe they're different."

"Is that why you don't like firstborn girls? What do you think?"

"Just listen to that music, Doctor. Can you hear the excitement? *Da…daa da dada daa da…*What a magnificent concerto! I've always wanted to play the piano well. Do you by any chance have any of Beethoven's concertos?" Sabiha was moving her hands like an orchestra conductor.

"I promise to play Beethoven during our next session. How do you feel now? Do you feel more relaxed?"

"I certainly do. I can assure you that this is the first time I have admitted my feelings about Selva. I couldn't have done it with anyone else. But then, you're different. You understand, don't you? You're like a father confessor to me, Doctor. Once I'm in this chair, I start confessing everything. I relax."

"I'm very pleased to hear it."

"There used to be someone else I could confide in, a friend of mine; he was the only other person I could talk to about certain things, but not the way I do with you, of course."

"What happened to him?"

"He was posted to Paris."

"Were you sorry?"

"Very! He was my only friend in this city."

"So when he left, you turned to the sleeping pills, as if they were going out of fashion."

"That's right! But I think I might not need a handful of them to get to sleep anymore. At least that's how I feel."

"*İnşallah*."

"It's thanks to you, Doctor. Every time I visit you, I feel that you are getting closer to a malignant tumor in my head. I suspect that you'll eventually find the spot, lance it, the pus will ooze out, and I will recover."

"No, Sabiha Hanım, it won't be me doing it; it's you doing the work. We may have indeed gotten close to the tumor, as you call it—with your help—but I'm afraid that we haven't located the exact spot yet. You'll continue coming to see me, and when we do find it, we'll figure out together what caused it and then it will be up to you to lance it. We're not there just yet."

"Anything you say," said Sabiha. "So next week it's Beethoven; is that a promise?"

"Yes."

Sabiha got up slowly and yawned. She felt wobbly, as though she had returned from a boat trip.

Did Dr. Sahir hold on to her hand just a little too long as they said good-bye at the door, or did she imagine it?

When she left the building, the cold wind felt like a slap in the face. She didn't want to take a taxi, so she walked home. Dr. Sahir. Dr.…Sahir…What an extraordinary man! He could read her soul like an open book. Read…her soul…her soul…She went home as if she were sleepwalking.

Sitting at the family dinner table that evening, Sabiha was still daydreaming. Fazıl Reşat Paşa had returned from the hospital about ten days earlier and he was at last joining them for dinner.

"What's the matter with my darling daughter?" he asked. "You seem preoccupied."

"I'm very tired, Father. I walked a long way today."

"You shouldn't have walked in this weather, my dear; you'll catch cold," said Leman Hanım.

"It's good for me to walk, Mother. It makes me feel better."

"I think you need a holiday, Sabiha," Macit said enthusiastically. "I can't commit myself to anything at the moment, but I've put my name down for a break the next national holiday on April twenty-third. It falls between two weekends, so if my colleagues can manage without me, maybe we can get away for a few days, just the two of us. What do you think?"

"April's a long way off."

"I know, but I have to give them plenty of notice."

"Where do you suggest we go? There's war all over Europe."

"I wasn't thinking of Europe."

"So where?"

"I thought it might be nice to go to my aunt's farm in Gebze. It's marvelous there in the spring. We could have long walks together, assuming of course that nothing drastic happens at the ministry."

"I don't think I can do that. As you know, I have my sessions with my doctor."

"It's a hell of a long time to April. I'm sure your sessions will have finished by then."

"May I come with you too, Daddy?"

"There you are," Sabiha said. "You can take Hülya with you. The two of you can have a holiday together, and I'll carry on with my sessions here."

"My goodness! That's a lot of sessions," said Leman Hanım.

Sabiha looked daggers at her mother. "I can assure you they're doing me a lot of good. I'm already feeling better."

Macit looked at his wife in amazement. He remembered the endless efforts he had made to coax her into seeing this psychiatrist that Dr. Celal had recommended.

"Are you telling me that you don't want to take a vacation? Weren't you the one who was complaining you felt trapped in Ankara, and there was no opportunity for us to be together?"

"Macit, why do you always have to turn things into an argument?" Sabiha asked.

"I don't believe you said that! Did you say I pick arguments? Please, God, give me patience."

"Daddy, Daddy, please let us go. If Mummy doesn't want to go, we can go together, can't we? April twenty-third is the children's holiday—it's my holiday anyway!"

"You've got to consider school, my angel. You only get one day off; you can't be away longer than that. I arranged this for your mother; I thought the change of air would be good for her."

"But Daddy, because of the war, summer holidays are starting on April fourteenth this year—have you forgotten?"

"Oh dear! You're right, I had completely forgotten. I've been so preoccupied with where the Germans will strike next and what the Russians want from us that I totally forgot. I'm sorry, my angel. In that case we can all go on a vacation together. *Inşallah*, your grandfather will have recovered by then so he and Granny can come too. We'll all go as a family. We'll take the train," said Macit, looking into his wife's eyes for approval.

"Enough. You've gone on about this far too long, Macit," replied Sabiha. "In any case, there's plenty of time; we can think about it nearer the date."

When Sabiha's parents retired to their room, Leman Hanım started to criticize Macit. "I swear I don't understand that man. He used to complain about Sabiha not seeing a doctor, but now that our poor girl says that she is getting better, he insists that she stop the therapy and take a holiday in Gebze. Gebze, of all places! What sort of vacation can one have in Gebze among the cows and hens? Really!"

MARSEILLES

Selva deliberated by the telephone for some time before deciding it would be better to have this conversation face-to-face; she would take Fazıl with her and go to the consulate personally. She imagined that if there was the usual line, as a woman with a child she would be given priority over the others. In any case, Rafo didn't want Selva to leave Fazıl with him anymore because he had to keep on hiding in the storeroom. Selva did contemplate making an appointment with the Armenian secretary, but then she decided against it because if the secretary refused, she wouldn't be able to go at all. Having made this decision, she looked in her wardrobe for something suitable to wear. She knew that a well-dressed woman could open many doors, but she had nothing that helped her in that regard.

In the end, she decided to wear her green coat again and her Hermès silk scarf, and carry the crocodile bag Sabiha had insisted on giving her, which she pulled out from the bottom of the cupboard. She wrapped Fazıl up well, cradled him in her arms, and left the apartment. Before walking to the bus stop, she wondered whether she should tell Rafo where she was going, but she knew that he would try to put her off by telling her that the children of someone she hardly knew were none of her business. He would tell her that everyone had to fend for themselves these days; it was wrong of her to be asking favors for others when she might eventually have to ask for a favor herself. He would surely urge her not to exhaust their chances with the consulate.

The bus stop was usually crowded, but today it was almost empty. The people of Marseilles had taken to staying at home unless it was absolutely necessary to go out.

She found a seat near the front of the bus, put Fazıl next to the window, and sat beside him. As soon as the bus pulled away, the conductor came to her.

"One to the Avenue de Prado, please," said Selva.

"Two tickets."

"No, just one."

"You're occupying two seats, madame."

"But the bus is almost empty."

"All the same, you're occupying two seats."

Selva took Fazıl and put him on her lap. "There, now I'm occupying one seat."

"But you've already traveled this far occupying two seats."

"Is this a joke?"

"Do I look like I am joking? You fare-dodgers are all the same."

"What do you mean by that?"

"Forget it. Pay me for just one ticket and let's get on with it."

"You're behaving like this because I got on the bus in a Jewish area. I'll have you know that first of all I am neither Jewish nor French; that must be obvious from my accent. Secondly, I'm of German origin and not only that, I'm also—how shall I put it?—I have friends in high places, very close friends in the Gestapo. Believe me, I will make you pay for this. What's your name?"

"I'm not obliged to give you my name."

"It doesn't matter, I've memorized the number on your uniform, and I will take the route number when I get off the bus."

The conductor started to walk away, but Selva continued. "Wait, I haven't paid for my ticket yet."

"I'm not going to charge you for a ticket. Forget it."

"If you don't collect my fare, I'll have to report you to the administration office."

The conductor gave Selva a contemptuous look and issued a ticket, which she took and put in her pocket. When she reached her destination, she walked by the conductor.

"I really think you deserve all you are getting with this occupation, monsieur. God appears to be punishing you all for being so arrogant."

When she got off the bus, Selva's legs were shaking, so she sat on the bench at the bus stop to calm down. She reflected that it was just as well that Fazıl couldn't speak properly yet, and therefore he couldn't tell his father what had happened.

Carrying Fazıl had really tired Selva by the time she got to the consulate. There was the usual crowd gathered in front of the wooden building, so she decided to avoid it and walk straight to the gate and ring the bell. The same kavass, the consulate porter, answered the door, recognizing Selva and smiling at her son.

"I'd like to see Mr. Kender," she said.

"I presume you have an appointment."

"Would I come without one?"

"Please go upstairs to his secretary."

"Yes, I know the way. Thank you," said Selva, putting Fazıl down. Mother and son walked up the stairs hand in hand. The secretary was surprised to see Selva.

"What's the matter, madame? There isn't anything wrong with your papers, is there?" she asked.

"No, our papers are in perfect order. I've come to see Mr. Kender on a personal matter. I wonder if he has a few minutes to spare."

The secretary opened the diary in front of her and checked it. "I might be able to squeeze you in for ten minutes between two appointments, but you must be brief, I'm afraid."

"Yes, of course, very brief. I promise."

"This must be your son. Isn't he sweet? What's your name, young man?"

"Fafa...Fafa...Fa," gurgled Fazıl.

"Fazıl. We've named him after my father."

With Fazıl on her lap, Selva sat on the chair next to the secretary's desk, as she had done on her previous visits. She had no idea how long she'd waited, because she was still working out in her mind what shc would say, when suddenly she saw Nazım Kender standing, tall as he was, right in front of her. She leaped up. The consul appeared rather confused.

"Well, I never, Selva Hanım! I didn't know you had an appointment."

"Actually, I didn't...I was hoping you might be able to see me if you could spare a little time."

"I see you're here with your little son! Is something wrong?"

"Yes, there is."

Nazım Kender asked the secretary what time his next appointment was and turned to Selva.

"Luckily, the Italian consul is always late. Please come in, Selva Hanım, but I hope you understand that when my next guest arrives—"

"I will leave immediately," Selva interrupted. Turning to her son, she said, "Please wait here for Mummy, my little one." She ignored her son's grumbling. Nazım held his office door open for her, walked to his desk, and sat down, but Selva remained standing.

"I realize that we have very little time, so I'll get straight to the point: I want to help the children of a neighbor of mine. They are thirteen and fifteen years old. They're not Turkish—their parents are from Lebanon—but I believe that they have just as much right to live as my own son. Can you possibly provide them with papers too?"

"Selva Hanım! Do you realize that what you're asking me to do is illegal?"

"I do, but I am not asking you to do something inhumane. What's left in this world that's legal anymore? Even our right to live is at the mercy of the Gestapo."

Selva opened her bag, took out Camilla Afnaim's photograph, and put it on his desk.

"These are the children I'm asking you to save. I came here and risked being thrown out because I strongly believe they should live. Thank you, Mr. Kender, for not showing me out."

There was a knock on the door and the secretary looked in. "Your visitor is here, sir."

Selva put two identity cards with the names Sami Naim and Peri Naim beside the photograph on the desk.

"I'll call your secretary on Monday and come and collect them if you can't help. I promise I won't bother you again, Mr. Kender."

"Selva Hanım, you realize, don't you, that if anyone finds out during their transportation that these children aren't Turkish, they won't be the only ones to suffer the consequences. I'll be in very serious trouble indeed."

"No one will find out, I'm sure. I'll start teaching them Turkish today. They'll be able to learn enough to speak among themselves, I promise."

"I can't promise you anything at all."

Selva left the room. Fazıl was on the floor playing with pieces of paper he had emptied out of the wastebasket. She knelt down beside him, replaced all the paper, and thanked the secretary. Hand in hand, she and her son walked down the steps with great dignity.

Leaving the consulate, Selva could barely bring herself to look at the poor souls waiting hopefully outside.

My God, she thought, where on earth can I go to save my son from such suffering? Is there any corner of the vast world where people live without tormenting each other?

PARIS

Tarık felt rather pleased with himself as he was tying his new tie. Until he caught sight of himself in the mirror with pursed lips, he wasn't even aware that he was whistling—"Lili Marlene." He felt embarrassed and stopped, wondering what he was so happy about.

The woman was Hungarian, blonde with green eyes, just his type. Her French wasn't very good and she spoke with an accent, which pleased Tarık because although his French was improving, he was far from fluent and he liked to have the upper hand. What agitated Tarık most was the possibility of not finding enough to talk with Margot about during their time together. To this very day, the only woman outside his immediate family that he'd had the opportunity to be alone with or talk to for any length of time was Sabiha. He'd had no problems conversing with her, because she did most of the talking while he just listened and answered from time to time. Ever since he had invited Margot out for dinner, he'd wondered if this was why he was obsessed with Sabiha—because he never had a problem being alone or talking to her.

Muhlis had introduced him to Margot; she was a friend of his girlfriend, and they worked together in a pharmaceutical factory.

They had been out as a foursome to the cinema and the theater a few times and once for dinner.

About a week ago, Muhlis had asked him if he fancied Margot, and he had replied that he did.

"In that case, why don't you ask her out for dinner one evening?" asked Muhlis.

"Do you think she'd accept?"

"You won't know if you don't ask her."

So Tarık did ask, and she accepted. Muhlis chose the restaurant and made the reservation for him. Tarık wasn't too sure about this, but gradually he came to like the idea.

"How on earth do you speak all evening with someone you hardly know?" he asked Muhlis.

"Come on now, what do you mean you hardly know her? Haven't we all been out together a few times?"

"That was different, we weren't alone."

"Tell her about your homeland. Ask about her family. Tell her how beautiful she is. Don't tread on her toes if you dance together and kiss her before dropping her off at home."

"What!"

"Kiss her, my dear friend, kiss her. Women like to be kissed."

"You mean on the lips?"

"I suppose there's no harm in being cautious; try kissing her on the cheek first, then you can take it from there. I want to hear all about it when you get home."

"Never!"

"My God! Aren't we the gentleman? I wish I had a sister to introduce you to. I'd never have to worry if she went out with someone like you."

At that point they were interrupted by a secretary coming into the room with a memo, which she gave to Tarık. Tarık handed it to Muhlis, abruptly changing the subject.

"Never mind all that; back to work. This is a coded message from our embassy. Will you decode it, please?"

Muhlis left the room and returned a few minutes later with the decoded message.

"Tarık, here are some instructions that will please you: 'According to the report dated December fifteen, 1942, Turkish Jews whose papers are in order cannot be held in forced labor camps. If such a situation should arise, we will obviously give them our protection. The police authorities should be reminded of this instruction and a detailed report of any such case must be held under the auspices of our competent authorities.' These instructions come from our ambassador."

Tarık heaved a sigh of relief. "Even though I didn't think it possible, there were still doubts in my mind that they might tell us not to interfere," he said. "Now I can relax."

"Well, I suppose you have something to celebrate this evening," Muhlis said, winking at Tarık.

Tarık pretended not to have noticed. He didn't believe in overfamiliarity in the office.

When they sat at one of the white cloth–covered tables at the Brasserie Lipp, Tarık ordered a bottle of Châteauneuf-du-Pape, the wine strongly recommended by Muhlis.

"Your friend said you like red wine," he said to Margot. "To tell the truth, I prefer red too." He didn't know that at the end of the evening he'd be cursing Muhlis for suggesting such an expensive wine.

Tarık needn't have worried; Margot was a talkative girl. They were both homesick, so their countries were the main topic of conversation. They tried to draw parallels between the Hungarians and the Turks. At one point Margot said, "Turkey is the only country in Europe trying to help the Jews. Does this stem from your love of humanity or some tie of love with them?"

"Our offers go back to the fifteenth century, so I suppose you could call it traditional. In 1492, when the Spanish King Ferdinand expelled the Jews from Spain and stripped them of everything they had, the Ottoman sultan offered them refuge in his country, giving them freedom of religion, language, and commerce. He even allocated whole districts to them."

"Really! Why?"

"Probably he was a sultan with an eye to the future. Because of this, the Jews have been the most loyal of Ottoman subjects. They made no attempts to stab their hosts in the back like the other minorities."

"I didn't realize your relationship with the Jews went back that far."

"Way, way back. In fact a few years ago, I was investigating something and I came across a *firman*—an old imperial edict—issued by Constantinople's conqueror, Fatih. According to that edict—it was soon after the conquest in 1453—he invited all Jews living within the borders of his country to settle in what is now Istanbul."

"I wonder why. Could it be because they are an intelligent race and good at commerce?"

"It could well be, Margot. I don't remember who it was that said Jews are like seeds scattered by the wind, cultivating the ground they fall upon. It's possible that Fatih may have had similar thoughts. And there's something else European Christians don't seem to understand. We've never been bothered about different races and religions living among us. We've never felt uncomfortable with that, unlike the Germans who claim to be pure Aryans. For centuries Anatolia has been a mosaic of different colors and creeds.

Our Urfa, for instance, which was called Edessa in the olden days, was a city where both Christianity and Islam flourished!"

"Why do you say *flourished*, in the past tense?"

"Since the declaration of the republic, we've all become more nationalistic. Consequently that mosaic has crumbled in favor of the Turkish Muslims. Like you, we too have had to put our race and religion first."

"I suppose patriotism isn't a bad thing."

"Of course not, but when it flares up, you end up with the sort of problems we have today. Thank God our tolerance of other religions stayed with us even when we became nationalists."

"Do you know, Monsieur Tarık, I've had contact with Turkey before?"

"Really. Is that so?"

"Yes, the company I worked for back home exported pharmaceuticals to Turkey, especially sulfonamide."

Tarık didn't know a lot about this, but he vaguely remembered that when the British stopped exporting many things, including pharmaceuticals, Turkey turned to Hungary for supplies, particularly Atabrin, which was used against malaria.

"You see," said Tarık, "obviously our countries were cooperating long before us."

By now Tarık's anxieties about the evening had gone out the window. When their main courses arrived, Margot couldn't help looking at Tarık's plate condescendingly. Her steak was almost raw, while his was very well done.

"Don't you like rare meat?" asked Margot.

"I'm not a lion," Tarık replied.

That led them to talk about the various food habits in their countries before Tarık admitted that he'd found it very difficult to get used to eating snails. Vegetables in garlic were his favorite food in France, but he still hankered after the dolmas cooked in olive oil back home. Margot complained that she hadn't yet found a restaurant in Paris serving proper goulash, her favorite Hungarian dish.

Toward the end of the evening, Margot leaned forward across the table.

"So what methods are you using to save Jews? Have you managed to smuggle any of them out of France?" she asked.

They had finished the wine some time ago. Tarık hadn't ordered another bottle because he was afraid he wouldn't have enough money to pay for it. Margot posed her question, and he suddenly became upset. It was just as well that he hadn't ordered a second bottle. Who was this woman sitting across the table? Could she be a spy, trying to worm information out of him?

"What are you saying?" said Tarık harshly. "What on earth made you ask that, Margot? We're only issuing passports to those who can prove they are Turkish nationals, that's all! Whether they stay or leave or obtain visas for somewhere else after that is no concern of ours."

"But how is it that some of them ended up without passports, then?"

That's it, thought Tarık to himself. She's been pumping me about the same subject since we've been here. This woman is either from the police or she's a spy!

"There are Turkish Jews who have come and settled here in France. It seems that they haven't bothered to keep their Turkish passports up-to-date. All we do when they apply is extend its validity. That's all!"

"So why do you think they hadn't done it before?"

"Maybe they didn't want to travel abroad. Isn't that possible? Take my family, for example; they've never been abroad, so they didn't need passports."

"How long does it take to get a passport?"

Tarık's mood had changed completely. He waved at the waiter for his bill without even asking his guest if she'd like coffee.

"Every case is different. We have to make inquiries back home, so it depends on how long it takes to get a reply."

He paid the bill and they left the restaurant and got into a taxi. Tarık gave the driver Margot's address. They hardly spoke on the way there and heaviness came over him. When the taxi pulled up at the address, Tarık got out and escorted her to the door.

"Would you like to come in for a coffee?" asked Margot.

"It's rather late, thank you; some other time," Tarık replied as he shook her hand before returning to the taxi.

After she'd gone in, he paid the fare to the driver and started to walk in the cool of the night. He tried to remember every topic they had covered that evening. Damned Muhlis! he thought. He was the one who saddled me with this woman!

Tarık was a bit late waking. When he went into the kitchen, Muhlis was already having breakfast.

"Well, well, how's His Lordship this morning? You appear to have burned the midnight oil last night. I've never seen you wake up this late. Methinks you took my advice."

"What advice?"

"About kissing a girl before saying good-bye."

"If I were in the mood for a fight, I'd punch you right on the nose."

"My, my, aren't we touchy? Have you already started to feel protective toward this Hungarian girl?"

"What do you mean?"

"I only asked you if you kissed the girl and you suddenly took offense."

"Tell me something. How well do you know this girl you saddled me with?"

"I've never *couché d'avec* her, I swear. I never even kissed her, Tarık."

"Don't try to be funny with me!"

"Frankly, I really don't know her. She's Jeanne's friend; they work together. One day when I was meeting Jeanne at that café in Montparnasse, they arrived together and I telephoned you to join us. Do you remember? I've only known her as long as you have. So now will you tell me what happened?"

"I didn't like the questions she kept asking me."

"About what?"

"Things like, are we smuggling Jews out of the country? How do we issue passports? How do we decide who qualifies for them? Loads of questions. I must say I felt most uncomfortable. I didn't like it at all."

"Well, in that case you shouldn't have answered them."

"That's not the point. I'm wondering if she is some sort of spy."

"What!"

"Or a police agent."

"Where did that come from?"

"If you think about it, we have saved so many people from the police and the camps. Would it surprise you if they are keeping tabs on us, possibly having us followed?"

"But we're not the only ones involved, are we? There's also Hikmet, then there's Selahattin in Rhodes and Nazım in Marseilles…"

"So what? They're probably under surveillance too."

"In other words, last evening you dined with Mata Hari, is that it?"

"I'm not sure, but if that's the case, I hold you responsible for involving me."

"Come on!"

"And that's not all. Do you know how much I had to pay for that wine you recommended so highly? Don't expect me to contribute even a bottle of beer to this apartment before the end of the month."

"Every good thing in this world has a high price."

"For those who can afford it."

"Look who's talking. Starting next month, you've been promoted to vice-consul; isn't that enough? As for the girl, leave it to me. I'll try and wheedle some information out of Jeanne when I see her."

"Absolutely not! You mustn't say anything. You'll only make things worse. If my suspicions are right, what's done is done. On the other hand, if I'm wrong we'll look like fools."

As Tarık took his cup of coffee from Muhlis, he looked him straight in the eye.

"Muhlis, this is serious. I'm talking to you as your superior, do you understand? Not a word!"

"Yes, *mein kommandant,*" replied Muhlis. "But tell me the truth. Did you or didn't you kiss the girl?"

MARSEILLES

Samuel and Perla tried to read aloud from their notebooks.

"Winter hash arrived. Today the weatherz wery cold. We fell cold."

"No, no children; that's not correct. Listen carefully. Winter has arrived: *has*, not *hash*. Today the weather is *very* cold: *iz very* cold. We feel cold: feel…*feel*, not *fell.* Come on then, one more time."

The boy with the hazel eyes struggled with all his might: "Winter hass arrived."

"Not *hass*, has…Pronounce the *s* like *z* in *zebra*. I want to hear the *z*."

"Hass…haz…has…"

"Good boy; that's right. You see, you can do it if you try. All you need to learn are about fifty sentences, and I promise to teach you those. Fine. Now, Perla, it is your turn. Sorry, not Perla. What did we say?"

"Peri, like Perry?"

"Good, very good. And what was yours, Samuel?"

"Sami, like Sammy."

Selva looked at the notes in her hand, continuing to teach the children.

"Now, I want you to write down these Turkish words together with their meanings, and I expect you to learn them by heart. *Ekmek*—bread; *peynir*—cheese; *çay*—tea; *kahve*—coffee; *gece*—night; *abla*—older sister; *abi*—older brother; *tuvalet*—toilet; *mutfak*—kitchen; *oda*—room. Right, that's enough for now."

They were all sitting around Selva's table. It had been fifteen days since she'd left the children's identity cards with Nazım Kender. The lessons had begun the day after she went to the consulate. She hadn't telephoned the consulate yet, but she was determined that the children should thank Mr. Kender in Turkish if they should be issued passports.

"They would have phoned you if they decided to issue passports," Rafo had said.

"And they would have phoned me to collect the identity cards if they didn't."

"Oh, Selva! My dear Selva, I don't understand why you poke your nose into other people's business. We are immigrants too; we may need all sorts of help."

"We have our papers, Rafo."

"But we can't leave."

"Because in order to leave we have to travel through hell!"

"Come on, darling, admit it. Having left Istanbul in disgrace, we can't face returning with our tails between our legs, so we're making excuses," Rafo said, laughing. "I wouldn't consider going back, but the way things are, we'll have to swallow our pride for the sake of our son. That is, of course, if this train business materializes…"

"Rafo," Selva said, "there's something I need to confess."

"Who else did you try to save?"

"No one. I'm giving Turkish lessons. So they don't run into trouble on the way—that's if they go at all."

"If you're starting to teach again, you should stick to English."

"You don't understand. I offered to give free lessons."

"I don't know what to say, Selva. You're really amazing. What's the use of teaching Turkish?"

"In case they eventually get on the train and…"

"Selva! Don't tell me you've talked about the train."

"Rafo, I can't believe this is you talking. You've changed so much since we got here. It's all right for you to save your skin, but what about the others? Should they be left to die?"

"Look, Selva, you talk like this because you've never had to look death in the eye. When your life is at stake, you have to think of yourself first, otherwise you don't survive!"

"Oh! I'm sorry, Rafo, maybe there's something I don't know. How many times have you faced death then?"

"I haven't, but the fear of death is in my genes. Death has haunted my race for thousands of years."

"Exactly. That's why I am struggling to save your people, Rafo."

"You shouldn't feel responsible, my darling. It's not your country that's after their lives and possessions."

"I'm not doing this because I feel guilty; I'm doing it for humanitarian reasons. Please don't try to stop me."

The children that Selva had renamed Sami and Peri had finished their lesson, and Selva was getting ready for the next group. They were eleven men and women introduced by Camilla, the grandchildren of Turkish Jews who no longer had ties with Turkey. Ever since Tarık had phoned her from Paris and hinted at the possibility of a train that might be leaving for Edirne in a few months' time, Selva had taken it upon herself to teach those who had Turkish identity papers and might travel on the train enough Turkish to make them plausible. Although they had all asked to be taught Turkish, Selva felt uncomfortable teaching adults the Turkish alphabet and making them repeat sentences taught in primary school.

"Father, buy me a book! Throw me a ball! *Tut*—catch! *Koş*—run! *Git*—go! *Gel*—come! *Söyle*—tell! *Al*—take! *Ver*—give! *Kaça?*—How much? *Nerede?*—Where? *Nasıl?*—How?"

Camilla wouldn't sit with the students; she sat quietly in the corner while Selva got on with her task. Having spent all her energy to help her children, she no longer had the nerve to ask for anything for herself.

"If the children can only make it to Istanbul, they can eventually go to Palestine," she said. "If my husband and I save our children, then we'll simply give up the fight. We'll accept our fate. We've seen and done a lot, through good times and bad. We'll have to be content with that."

"I don't dare telephone the consulate, Camilla," Selva said to her. "I know how frustrating this is for you, but you must be patient. I feel they would have contacted me by now if their response was negative."

"Do whatever you feel is right," Camilla replied.

They had become very close after that first meeting when they witnessed what the Gestapo were doing at the crossroads. After the officers had left, the two of them hugged each other in tears. Selva had then telephoned her husband's pharmacy. "They've gone, Benoit. Rafo can come out of the storeroom now."

Even though she wasn't participating in the lessons, Camilla realized she was picking up a few words here and there. She had learned, for instance, that *çay* meant tea, because every time the students arrived, Selva would ask in Turkish if they wanted tea. She had learned the difference between the letter *ç*, as in *çay*, and the letter *ş*, pronounced "sh." In fact, today she had gone a step further and surprised everybody by saying, "Yes, tea, please" in Turkish, which earned her a round of applause from the class.

Selva ended the lesson a bit early because little Fazıl had a slight temperature, and she had to look after him. The students left in twos and threes at ten-minute intervals, so as not to draw attention to themselves. Camilla was the last to leave after giving Selva a little peck on the cheek.

"Be patient for a little while longer," Selva said.

After closing the door, Selva went to look in the bedroom and saw Fazıl fast asleep. She walked to the window to wave good-bye to Camilla, and as she waited for the woman to walk out the front door, she suddenly noticed a van stopping in front of the pharmacy. Some men with SS armbands were getting out. She ran to the telephone and dialed the pharmacy's number. As soon as Benoit heard her voice, he said, "Wrong number," and slammed the receiver down. Selva rushed back to the window to see the men dragging Rafo outside the pharmacy. She opened the window, and started screaming at the top of her voice.

"Hey there! Monsieurs! Soldiers! Leave him alone! He's Turkish! Turkish. Leave him alone, I said! His papers are right here. Why don't you look at them? Rafooo…"

Her voice was carried away by the wind. She ran to the bedroom and got their identification papers from the drawer in the bedside cabinet. When she got down to the third floor, she met Camilla, who was out of breath climbing the stairs. Camilla gripped Selva's hands.

"Don't go, Selva. Don't. Think of your child!" she pleaded.

Selva pushed the woman aside and rushed down the stairs two and three at a time.

When she reached the front door, she looked back to see Camilla tottering down behind her.

"Please go back to Fazıl. For God's sake, don't leave him alone."

In one quick action, Selva managed to unlock and open the front door; Camilla had locked it from the inside just a few moments earlier. She rushed outside and across the road, without paying any attention to the traffic. A couple of cars screeched to a halt and the drivers hurled abuse at her through their open windows.

The van was about to move as she reached the pharmacy. Selva ran to the driver's window and knocked on the glass; he didn't even bother to look at her. When that didn't work, she pounded with all her might on the closed doors of the van, screaming at the top of her voice.

"Rafooo, can you hear me? Get out! Tell them you're Turkish. Rafooo!"

The van suddenly accelerated away and Selva fell down. Someone tried to help her up.

"Please don't bother, I can manage," she said in French as she scrambled up. She was covered from head to toe in mud. Benoit hugged her tightly, his face as white as a sheet.

"Come into the pharmacy, Selva. Look at the state of you. Don't stand out here in the cold."

Benoit hung up the closed sign as soon as they were inside.

"Look, you grazed your leg when you fell down. Let me clean it and put some iodine on it."

"No, no, Benoit. You must take me to the consul immediately."

"You're covered in mud, Selva. At least wash your hands."

"There's no time to lose."

"What's the point in rushing? They won't be sending anyone anywhere until tomorrow anyway."

"We've got to find out where they have taken him, Benoit. Come on, hurry up. Where's your car?"

"Around the back," Benoit replied, sounding dazed.

"Go get it then."

Benoit switched off the lights and they walked outside together.

"Get a move on, Benoit," Selva pleaded.

"Wait a moment, won't you? Let me lock up first."

As Benoit turned into the side street to fetch his car, Selva leaned against the pharmacy window, covering her face with her hands and sobbing. When she heard the car approaching, she wiped her tears with the back of her hand and looked up to her apartment window and saw Camilla's silhouette behind the net curtain, looking like a sad apparition.

When Selva got out of the car and ran to the steps in front of the consulate gate, there was no one. She rang the bell with one hand and banged on the gate with the other. Suddenly, she heard shuffling footsteps inside. Obviously the kavass had looked through the peephole and recognized Selva. He opened the door and inquired, "What's up? What happened?"

"I must see the consul, Mr. Kender…"

"The office is closed now."

"All the same, I must see him."

"He left about half an hour ago."

"In that case, I must see someone else. The consul general…"

"Nobody's here; they've all gone home."

"Give me Mr. Kender's home address, then."

"I'm afraid I can't do that."

"For God's sake, I implore you. I desperately need to see him."

"Please don't make this difficult for me. I'm not allowed to. What's the matter? What happened?"

"They took my husband away," said Selva. Her voice sounded so desperate. Even though he had only seen her three times, he felt very sorry for her.

"Who took him away? Where to?"

"The Gestapo."

"The Gestapo? It must be a mistake."

"I beg of you, please help me find Mr. Kender, for the sake of those you hold most dear."

"Please don't!" said the kavass.

"I'm begging you."

"Well…as far as I know, Mr. Kender was supposed to meet someone in the café of the Grand Hotel de Louvre. He should be there if he hasn't changed his plans."

Selva grabbed the man's hand and tried to kiss it.

"Please don't, honestly don't," the man said, pulling his hand from Selva's lips.

Selva dashed back to the car. As she got in next to Benoit, she said, "Move, we're going to the Grand Hotel de Louvre et de La Paix. Please hurry."

In the lobby café of the Grand Hotel de Louvre, Nazım Kender was having tea with the Italian commercial attaché and his wife. Because he was sitting with his back to the door, he didn't see the woman rushing in like the wind and heading straight for him. By the time he saw the almost frightened gazes of his guests, he was face-to-face with Selva. It was cold and wet outside, but Selva wasn't wearing a coat; her checked skirt and roll-neck sweater were soaked by the rain. She knelt in front of Nazım Kender and held his hand tightly.

"They took my husband away," she said hoarsely. "The Gestapo dragged him out of the pharmacy by force. They put him in a van and took him away. Please find him. I beg you to save Rafael. Look, I brought all the papers with me…I've got everything here, his passport, his birth certificate, his residence permit…"

The consul stood up. "Selva Hanım, please get up." Selva remained kneeling and put her arms around his legs.

"Please save my husband before they take him away."

"What's happening?" asked the Italian attaché. His wife seemed disgusted at the sight of this disheveled woman grasping on to the consul's knees.

"Please stand up, Selva Hanım."

Selva tried to stand up, but she couldn't. Her strength had drained from her, her knees crumpled, and she collapsed into a heap. At that moment Benoit, who had been parking the car, arrived and anxiously saw Selva on the floor.

"What have you done to her?" he asked the consul.

"She fainted," replied Nazım Kender.

People from other tables started to gather around them.

"I'll attend to her. Please go and see what you can do," begged Benoit. "That's, of course, if you can do anything."

"And who are you?"

"I'm Rafael Alfandari's part—his friend. He works in my pharmacy."

"So when did this happen?"

"A short while ago. We rushed to the consulate and then straight here to you immediately after..."

"Do you know where he was taken?"

"I'm not sure, but I think I heard them talking among themselves about the station."

"What! Are you telling me they're taking him out of Marseilles?"

"I think there are others too. I believe I heard one of those dragging Rafael away telling him not to struggle, and threatening to make him regret it if he delayed."

Nazım Kender bent down and picked up the papers Selva had dropped on the floor.

"I'm leaving Selva Hanım in your capable hands, monsieur," he said. After apologizing to the Italians, he rushed outside.

"Please don't crowd in on us," Benoit told those standing around them. "Madame has fainted; she'll come around in a minute."

"How disgraceful. What's happening?" demanded the Italian woman.

"Please get this person out of here," ordered the headwaiter in a black jacket.

An elderly lady in the crowd suggested calling for a doctor. "I hope she's not pregnant," she muttered.

Benoit carried Selva through the confused onlookers out into the street. The cold air helped bring Selva around.

"What happened?" she asked.

"You passed out. I'm taking you home."

"But what about the consul…Rafo?"

"Don't worry. The consul took the papers and left immediately. I'm sure he'll do whatever's necessary. There's nothing else you can do. All that's left for you now is to go home and wait."

Selva asked Benoit to put her down. Her knees were shaking. Her head was reeling. She linked arms with her friend.

"Benoit, I think I'm going to be sick," she said.

"Please try to hold on until you get home."

Selva walked unsteadily to the car, holding on to Benoit's arm.

WAGON OF FEAR

When Nazım Kender got out of the taxi in front of the consulate, he was surprised to see a crowd of people jostling at the gate of the building. This was strange: it was after office hours, so normally there wouldn't have been anybody there. He hurried toward the gate. Halim the kavass was waving his arms about and trying to explain something to the screaming crowd. When he saw the consul, he rushed up to him and said, "Apparently they've loaded them onto a train, they took them away…"

About fifteen or twenty people rushed to Nazım Kender, clutching at his arms and legs.

"Stop this! What happened?" said the perplexed consul. Because of the women wailing, he couldn't hear those trying to explain things.

"Make way!" the kavass shouted. "You're wasting the consul's time."

The noise stopped immediately.

"They took them away. We told them they were Turkish, but they wouldn't listen…" explained an old man in tears.

"Where to?" asked the consul.

"To the Saint Charles Station."

"Please let me through. I need to get the necessary documents from my room," Nazım Kender said, running into the building. He returned a short while later with a file in his hand. "Is there anyone here with a car?" he asked.

"Yes, I have one," a young man answered.

"Get it immediately!"

"It's over there by the gate. Follow me."

The young man ran ahead and opened the door of his Citroën for the consul. He then ran around to the driver's side and got in, ready to drive away. The crowd of people surrounded the car, some pounding on the windshield and others trying to open the doors. Halim Kavass pushed his way through the crowd to the car.

"Take me with you," he said.

"Get in, then!"

With difficulty, the kavass managed to throw himself into the back seat.

"No time to lose," said the consul. "Drive straight to the Saint Charles Station."

The tiny car shot like an arrow through the assembled crowd.

On the wagon of the train, from which sounds of screaming, wailing, and sobbing could be heard, a notice read: THIS WAGON CAN HOLD 20 HEAD OF CATTLE AND 500 KGS. OF FODDER. Nazım Kender ignored the German officers milling around and ran straight toward the wagon. There were about eighty men and women crammed inside, jostling one another, trying to get to the wooden bars, holding out their papers and screaming for help. Through the noise, the consul tried to make out what they were saying. Then he heard someone who recognized him calling out in Turkish.

"Most of us have Turkish passports, but we are unable to make the Gestapo understand."

Realizing there was no time to lose, Nazım Kender went directly to the main station building, followed closely by the kavass.

"I want to see your superior immediately!" he said to the officer at the door.

A German officer came and stood face-to-face with him. "Are you in a hurry?" he asked.

"Yes, very much so. I believe there's been a mistake. It seems they have rounded up some Turks and loaded them in the wagon. The train is about to leave. You must get them off right away."

"There's been no mistake."

"Look, I've got a list of my citizens' names in this file. We can read through them one by one..."

"Don't bother."

"I promise you, transporting Turks on this train will cost you dearly."

The German officer snatched the file from Nazım Kender's hand and glanced at the list the consul had prepared.

"These are Turks? Alhadef, Jak: Alhadef, Izi; Alfandari, Rafael; Anato, Josef; Franco, Lili; Kalvo, Luna; Menaşe, İsak; Soriano, Moris...If these aren't Jews, I don't know who is." He waved the file in the consul's face. Nazım Kender snatched the file back.

"Yes, they're Turkish. Most of them may be Jewish, but there must be Muslims and Christians among them. According to my country's laws they're Turkish, irrespective of their religion. They're Turkish citizens."

The uniformed officer was about to reply, but changed his mind when he heard the train's shrill whistle. He shrugged his shoulders, turned his back, and walked inside. The train had started to inch forward.

Nazım Kender looked helplessly in the direction of the officer. For a moment he considered following him, but the train was moving faster. Nazım ran alongside the train, pushed the soldier who tried to stop him, and jumped into the wagon. Halim was running just behind him; he was almost out of breath when he grasped the consul's extended hand, stepped onto the running board, and hoisted himself up. For a split second, he almost fell, but those on board lifted him by the shoulders and helped him inside.

The soldier Nazım Kender pushed aside was running, waving his arms, and yelling, trying to attract the attention of the officer walking toward the main building. The officer stopped, turned around, and looked at the moving train, frustrated. There was nothing he could do. The train had picked up steam and was moving faster and faster, shaking the people cramped inside.

Nazım Kender and Halim Kavass looked at each other in disbelief. What had they gotten themselves into? What was going to happen?

There were no answers. Nazım Kender had jumped on board without thinking. Maybe his courage stemmed from a feeling of revolt and anger, from the impetuosity of his youth. As the train accelerated rapidly away from the Saint Charles Station, he began to realize the gravity of the situation and fear the repercussions. But there was only one option now: to finish what he had started. Like any honorable person, he would fight to the end. After all, wasn't he the Marseilles consul for the great Turkish republic? These poor people on the train were expecting him to save them. He couldn't possibly show his fear. There was no going back. He would stay with them until the end.

"Do you know where they're taking us?" asked the kavass.

"For a while you've wanted to go to Paris, haven't you? Well, here you are; that's where we are going—and just think, you are going for free!"

Halim Kavass wanted to laugh but couldn't. Traveling on a train meant for animals, squeezed between people falling over each other, was no laughing matter. The man next to him was rather old, and had obviously wet himself in fear. The smell of urine spread throughout the wagon. Not a sound was heard from the people who had been screaming and yelling before the train pulled away. Apart from the jarring sound of the wheels running over the rails and the wind whistling through the gaps of the wagon, everything was quiet. It seemed everyone had swallowed their tongues.

This must be the sound of fear, thought the consul.

The strange silence was broken by the croaky voice of a woman who must have been a chain-smoker. Her bloodshot eyes exuded fear. "Where are they taking us?" she asked.

"I think they're taking us to Paris, madame," Nazım Kender replied as she struggled to extricate herself from her trapped position. Eventually she managed to stand up by grabbing the hand of a young man reaching out to help her.

"I'm the Turkish consul," he said. "Will those of you who have Turkish nationality raise your hands, please?"

About fifty hands shot up.

"I'll do my best to help the Turkish nationals, but I'm afraid there's nothing I can do for the rest of you. I'm truly sorry."

A girl let out a scream and fainted. Some sobbing sounds were heard again.

"*Monsieur le Consul,* please say we're Turkish as well," shouted a man. "We will take on Turkish nationality and be in your debt until the day we die."

"There are no slaves in Turkey, monsieur, just citizens. You can certainly apply for citizenship when you are released, but I'm afraid I have no authority to declare you Turkish citizens right now."

"Please don't condemn us to death."

"Save us too!"

"Look, let me be clear. I'm not saying I can save even the Turkish nationals. All I am saying is that I'll do my best. That's why I'm here with you, in this wagon. How many of you have your papers with you?"

Halim Kavass counted the raised hands. Most didn't have papers because they had been caught unexpectedly.

"It's easier for those of you who have some form of identification, but as for the rest…"

Suddenly someone screamed from the back of the wagon, "He's dying…My God, my husband's dying!"

"Is there a doctor here? Please, is there a doctor?"

A young man tried to push his way over the seated people. An old man in his seventies was lying on the floor with his head against his wife's bosom and his legs stretched across those nearby. His face was ashen, and he was sweating profusely.

"Please let me through…allow me to get through…"

"Are you a doctor?"

"I'm a chemist…let me…"

The young man loosened the old man's collar and started to check his pulse.

"Give us some space. Would you mind moving back? He needs some air. Please, please, do try to give us a little space…"

"Why don't we carry him to the edge of the wagon, where there's more air?"

"No. No, don't move him, he might be having a heart attack. Does anyone have any med—"

"Move back, move back!" someone shouted.

"How lucky! Isn't he lucky to be dying here, rather than at the hands of the Germans?" said another.

"Move back just a little bit, that's it."

Those around the patient tried their best to move, but it didn't make much difference. There were about eighty people, mostly men, crammed into a space meant for twenty cattle. Rafael Alfandari looked around helplessly. The only thing he could do was try to calm the patient. He wiped the sweat from the man's forehead and his upper lip with his handkerchief, and tried to think what his father would do in such circumstances. He remembered his father saying, "Morale! Boost the morale! That's very important for a patient. A person should feel that his heart is able to fight death."

"This is a panic attack, not a heart attack," he said with conviction. "Please try to remain calm. Relax. Take deep breaths. Come on. You don't have any chest pains, do you? I'm sure you're feeling better already. I can see it from your color. Relax."

A man managed to make his way through, jumping over those around him. There was a pill in his hand. "I always carry one of these because I have a heart condition…You can take it."

"What if you need it yourself?"

"We're going to die anyway," replied the man. "I'm not a Turkish citizen. I'm French."

As night descended, the wagon was plunged into darkness. The passengers had lost all notion of time; they had no idea how long they had been traveling. All that could be heard now were the sounds of prayer. The people continuously prayed, either aloud or to themselves, and an air of doom spread through the wagon. The consul and the kavass continually whispered to each other, trying to work out how and where their dark journey would end. Nazım Kender gave all the change in his pocket to the kavass.

"Here, take this, and if the train should stop at one of the stations, you'd better find a telephone and call our consulate in Paris while I'm arguing with the stationmaster. Explain our situation and ask him to follow it up urgently. They must contact Berlin and Vichy immediately."

"What if we don't stop, sir?"

"Then you will do the same in Paris."

"But the consulate phones aren't answered before nine in the morning."

"Do you know Hikmet Özdoğan's number?"

"I'm afraid I don't. I know the consulate's number, but as I said, they won't be answering at this time of night."

"I did know his number. What was it now…what was it? It might come to me. When I tell you, you must memorize that number, and then you should call him as soon as possible; I'm sure he should be able to do something. My argument with the stationmaster is bound to last for at least half an hour."

"Don't worry; I'll call the consul—that is, of course, if you remember the number."

"Does anyone in Marseilles know we're on this train?"

"I don't think so. Everyone at the consulate was gone."

"I was having tea with the Italian attaché. He realized something awful had happened. Maybe he'll make inquiries."

"You know, sir, something tells me that Turkish lady—you know the one, she came to see you with her child once—that tall young lady, she was the first to come today. I'll bet she'll follow this up."

"Were you the one who told her where I was?"

"Well, sir, I…"

Suddenly there was a terrific jolt. Those standing up fell down, and those on the floor tumbled over one another. The train screeched to a halt. Everyone tried to get near the wooden bars of the wagon to see what had happened.

"Stand back!" shouted an officer in French, but with a German accent.

He jumped inside and stood erect like a bronze statue among the fallen people. The consul too stood upright in front of him. He was a few inches taller than the German. It was rare for a Turk to be so tall. The German officer looked him over from top to bottom. He had probably come to the platform expecting to meet a short, portly, middle-aged diplomat. They must have stopped in a station. There was enough light illuminating this wagon of fear for Nazım Kender to see the surprise in the officer's eyes.

"Are you the Turkish consul?"

"Yes, I am."

A few more German officers boarded the wagon, pushing and stepping over the people inside.

"*Monsieur le Consul*, it seems that the stationmaster in Marseilles made a serious mistake. Apparently the train was ordered to pull out of the station before you got off. I can assure you that those responsible will be severely punished. Please come with me, sir; there is a car waiting for you. You will be driven back to Marseilles."

"Thank you for your concern, but you're mistaken. The stationmaster at Marseilles deserves no punishment. I boarded this train of my own accord."

"All the same, he shouldn't have allowed the train to leave with you on board. Please, this way, sir," said the German officer.

"I must point out that this wagon is full of Turkish citizens. I want to know where you are taking them. What's more, you've loaded them onto a cattle wagon against their wishes. I demand an explanation."

"They're Jews and they're on their way to Paris."

"Even so, they are all Turkish citizens. They have perfectly valid papers."

"I repeat, sir, will you please step down?"

"Step down from this cattle wagon? Please understand that I represent a country that doesn't tolerate such abuse toward human beings because of their faith. I want to make it very clear, too, that my clerk and I are either getting off this train together with these people or we'll continue our journey to Paris."

"*Monsieur le Consul*, you're making things very difficult. The wagon you've boarded is a freight wagon. The two of you must get off. Those with Turkish papers will be dealt with in Paris."

"You leave me no alternative. It seems that we are destined to continue this journey to Paris all together."

"What are you talking about?"

"I mean, I refuse to leave this cattle wagon without my citizens."

"And I repeat, you should get off here and return to Marseilles in the car provided."

"I'm afraid I must repeat too: either we all get off together or we all continue the journey."

"In that case you have made your choice. You prefer to continue the journey with the Jews in these conditions."

"They're our citizens. Either we get off together or we continue together."

The German officer tried to force Nazım Kender by grabbing his arms, but the consul put both his hands firmly against his chest.

"I wouldn't recommend that at all, young man. Don't make an irreparable mistake. I'm a diplomat representing a neutral country. Furthermore, I have diplomatic immunity. Rest assured, raising your hand might lead to a diplomatic scandal."

"You've already caused a scandal," said the German officer, his face flushed with anger.

"Preventing a scandal is in your hands," replied Nazım Kender. "One of the passengers on this disgusting wagon is old. He has suffered a heart attack because he couldn't cope with the stress. Are you prepared to suffer the consequences if he doesn't make it to Paris?"

The German jumped off, muttering something in his own language. The other officers followed—it was obvious the officers didn't know French and hadn't understood a word of what was going on.

Not a peep was heard from anyone.

Finally a timid voice asked, "Where are we?"

"We may be somewhere near Nîmes," replied Halim Kavass. No one had the courage to lean out of the wagon to look, but Nazım Kender leaned over and looked outside. Apart from the fifteen German officers lined up with their rifles, the platform seemed deserted. He couldn't see where they were because the clock obscured the name of the station, but he tried to calculate where they might be by the time on the clock.

"Yes, we're somewhere between Arles and Nîmes," he said, looking at the kavass for confirmation.

The train was at a standstill. There was nobody coming or going, and everyone waited anxiously. Every minute seemed like an hour. All eyes were on the consul, standing erect and ready to argue their cases.

Suddenly the voice of a woman standing in one of the corners of the wagon could be heard. "Come on…Come on," she kept on saying, encouraging the children to do something they were reluctant to do.

"*Monsieur le Consul,*" shouted the woman. "These children have something to tell you."

"Yes," said the consul, "what is it?"

"Me Turkish…Me wants water…tummy hungry…I fell cold… How you are?" The little girl, who was already trembling, burst into tears. It was obvious she had learned all the Turkish sentences by heart.

"Are you Turkish, young lady?" the consul asked in Turkish.

The girl nodded yes.

"What's your name?"

"Pe…Peri."

The consul turned to the boy. "And what's yours?" he asked.

"My name Saami—sorry—Sammy."

It came to him in a flash; he had already seen these two children in a photograph, standing together in a garden.

He called out to the kavass.

"Look who we've got here, Halim. Our Peri and Sami are here."

The kavass looked confused. He was trying to understand what the consul meant when footsteps were heard on the platform. Then he stretched out to look through the gaps in the side of the wagon. The officer the consul had spoken to earlier was returning with the same soldiers. Nazım Kender waited with his hands on the children's shoulders.

The German didn't jump onto the train as quickly as before. This time he pulled himself up by holding on to the iron bolts of the wagon door.

"So, you're saying you won't get off this train. Is that it, *Monsieur le Consul*?"

"Absolutely right. I won't."

The German officer took a deep breath. After a short silence, he said, "Get down; come on then, step down."

"I beg your pardon?"

"If you're not getting out on your own, you'd better all get out."

"Really?"

"Yes, that's the order."

"Let them off first. All of them."

"Are all these Turks?"

"Some of them don't have identification papers, but I'm sure that once we're in Paris—"

"I said get out!" shouted the German. It was clear he was annoyed at having to carry out the order.

"My clerk and I will get out last," said the consul, folding his arms across his chest. The kavass was next to him, standing to attention as if he was his aide-de-camp.

Those in the wagon started jumping out. They carefully lifted down the man who had suffered the heart attack. The two children stayed by the consul, not wanting to be separated from him. The woman who'd urged the children forward seemed happy that they had been able to prove they were Turkish, but didn't want to make eye contact with them for fear of what might happen next.

"Are these children yours, madame?" asked Nazım Kender.

"No, I'm their aunt. We were shopping in the market when they picked us up."

"Come on then, Peri and Sami, it's your turn now," said the consul.

The kavass held the girl under her arms and lowered her to the platform. The boy jumped by himself. The consul was the last to leave, like a captain abandoning his ship. The kavass was beside him.

The German officer approached. "Your car is waiting outside the station," he said.

"Thank you. I'd rather return by taxi. If you don't mind, I'd appreciate it if the car took the old man who's had a heart attack."

A woman interjected before the German officer could speak. "No, no. Thank you very much. I'm sure we can manage on our own. Thank you all the same."

The German officer gave her a look as if to say, "You're mad," then he saluted the consul, turned his back, and marched away, followed by the other soldiers.

When the Germans left, a buzz of excitement erupted. Every one of the eighty people surrounded Nazım Kender, wanting to kiss his hands or cheeks, trying to put their arms around him. Those who couldn't get close stretched their arms just to touch him on the shoulders or back, as though he were some sacred object.

"For God's sake, don't lift me up on your shoulders," the consul shouted. But there was no way he could control the waves of love flowing around him. There were no words to describe the gratitude these people felt.

"I suggest that those of you who don't have Turkish nationality leave and find a safe place. Go back as soon as possible," he said, and then as an afterthought, he said, "Where the hell are we, exactly?"

"In Arles," said the kavass.

"I believe there should be a train to Marseilles in about an hour," someone said, "if it hasn't been canceled."

The consul and the kavass walked out of the station together. The Mercedes-Benz allocated to the consul by the Nazis was parked right outside.

"I wonder if there's a taxi around here—why don't you find out, Halim?" asked Nazım Kender. He sat on a bench outside the station door as the kavass walked away.

In the deep recesses of his mind, he wondered if this experience had been a nightmare, or if it had really happened. A little while later, he was startled by Halim's voice.

"Apparently, there is a wood-powered car, sir. Shall we hire it?"

"Yes, hire it immediately."

Nazım Kender got up, walked slowly by the Mercedes-Benz, and crossed the road with dignity.

PARIS

Ferit watched as his wife crossed the street and walked into the distance. When Evelyn was out of sight, he drew the curtains, checked the lock on the street door, and went into the bedroom. He threw the cover, quilt, and pillows hastily on the floor, feeling the sides of the mattress until he found what he was looking for. It was a tear large enough for a hand to fit through. Ferit put his hand in the hole and extended his arm all the way inside. The communiqués were right there, somewhere in the middle. He grasped hold of them and pulled them out, then carefully remade the bed. He puffed up the pillows, put them in their place, then sat at the kitchen table and scribbled a note for his wife:

Darling, I'm going to see a friend from the university on the other side of the river. Don't worry if I'm late.

He put the communiqués under his vest, left the apartment, and walked toward the Métro.

For some time now, Ferit had been a member of the Resistance, an underground organization whose operations had become more and more important due to the Vichy government's cooperation with Hitler. Ferit might not have been French, but he loved this country like a real Frenchman. What's more, he hated Hitler.

Because he wasn't French, his associates on the committee didn't share sensitive plans relating to nationalist issues with him. They did, however, turn a blind eye to his work with cells that organized the smuggling of Jews and Communists out of France.

Ferit had never mentioned his connection with this organization to Evelyn. She thought that her husband had volunteered to become the assistant of his beloved professor from the lycée, the same professor who had helped him with his thesis. This was the way he could explain his disappearances some mornings, afternoons, and evenings, and very often during the night. The professor was also a member of the same organization, so it seemed there was no way Evelyn could find out.

Ferit had managed to be the go-between for his many Jewish friends and the Organization, issuing passports of neutral countries. Recently, the most sought-after passport was Turkish, because the Turks made a point of protecting their citizens from the Gestapo. Ferit had been able to contact the consulate through his old friend Muhlis. Shortly after, he had met Tarık and, discreetly testing the water, invited him for coffee and raised the subject. He asked whether the Turkish consulate could issue passports to non-Turks. The answer was very clear.

"I wish I had the authority to answer you differently, Ferit," Tarık said. "Every single person we can save from sorrow and death is a source of satisfaction for us. But you know yourself the danger we face every time we visit one of those camps or police stations. After all's said and done, we are an honorable and just nation and, as such, can't get involved with anything illegal."

"Should I give up hope completely?"

"Yes, my friend."

Ferit inhaled deeply from his cigarette and blew smoke rings into the air.

"Fine. In that case, I won't bother you about this again."

"I promise I'll do whatever I can to help you with anything else. I have to admit, I really respect what you are doing. Honestly, I would be on your side if I weren't a government employee."

"I understand."

"I'd like to ask you a question, if you don't mind. How did you get involved in this?"

"Everyone who has a heart is involved, Tarık. It's true the French aren't fighting in the field, but I can assure you, they have an excellent underground organization. As for me, I got involved through a close friend at the university. He used to take me to meetings, and eventually I joined the Resistance too."

"Doesn't it surprise you the French haven't fought bravely?"

"Listen, Tarık, I'm sure you'll agree that Paris is one of the most beautiful cities in the world. In my opinion they didn't want to risk it getting bombed."

"I suppose that's one way of looking at it."

They sipped their coffee for a while in silence. They were sitting in one of the student cafés in the Latin Quarter.

"Shall I tell you a secret, my friend?" Tarık said. "The British and the Americans can't stand de Gaulle. They can't stomach the man at all. Had there been someone else leading the national liberation, you might be able to get more support."

"The British can't stand anything that may damage their interests," said Ferit. "De Gaulle isn't the sort of person to take notice of their interests. He's a stubborn, cantankerous man who regards every attack on himself as an attack on France."

"Strictly between us, I believe that if you changed your man at the top, you'd probably get more support from the British, and even the Americans."

"Another leader was sought, but unfortunately without success. All the Resistance activists are behind de Gaulle," Ferit said. "Just you wait and see. I bet eventually those who don't like de Gaulle will eat their words and support him."

"What makes you so sure?"

"Eventually the Allies will have to invade France to win this war. When that day comes, they will have to recognize both de Gaulle and the National Liberation Committee, because without their support, they'd be unable to carry out the invasion successfully."

"The sooner that day comes the better," Tarık said.

They asked for the bill.

"I hope neither Muhlis nor Evelyn will learn of our meeting today. I can count on you, can't I?" Ferit asked.

"Of course you can…Ferit, I hope you don't mind my saying this, but don't you think it's wrong to keep this from your wife?"

"I do, Tarık, but I don't want to worry her. She's pregnant, you see."

"Oh!" Tarık said. "I had no idea. Congratulations."

"We only found out ourselves recently. We haven't told anyone yet. I'd rather you didn't know either."

"I understand, but do be careful, won't you?" Tarık replied, patting his friend on the back. "Your responsibilities in life are just beginning. Don't get involved in anything dangerous, my friend."

Later that day, while traveling on the Métro, Ferit reflected on his conversation with Tarık. He wished he could have persuaded him to cooperate. As soon as they had met, he'd felt he could trust Tarık. He was an honest, hardworking, brave man who wasn't indiscreet. He had all the virtues of someone who could be a member of the Organization. What a pity that—as was to be expected—Tarık had chosen to stick to his country's laws. However, he had left the door slightly open when he'd said, "I promise I'll do what I can to help you."

Ferit became suspicious when he saw the reflection of a scrawny man watching him in the window of the Métro. He tried to look at him from behind his newspaper. When the man began to fidget, Ferit wondered if he had given himself away. Should I get off at the next stop? he thought. Ferit stood up when the train reached the next station. The man got off, so he sat down again. He had been anxious for no reason at all. "All this worry," he said to himself. "It's not the Gestapo; it's the worry that will eventually kill me."

These worries made him feel that he might try that door Tarık had left open after all. If anything happened to him, Tarık was the only person who might be able to get Evelyn to his family in Istanbul. Neither Muhlis—his friend for the past forty years—nor anyone else would do. There and then, he promised himself if he should accomplish his mission successfully, he would go see Tarık first thing tomorrow. But what would he say? How would he appeal to this man he'd met not more than five times? What could he possibly say to him? "I'm entrusting my wife to you." Surely not. Tarık would probably think he was mad. But then, maybe not. Hadn't he trusted him enough to tell him of his association with the Resistance after only a few meetings? Tarık hadn't batted an eyelid. He wasn't surprised; he hadn't disapproved or tried to give him advice. Yes, Tarık was his man; he could entrust his wife to him. *Inşallah,* he would get through today without any problems, and then first thing tomorrow…

After getting off the train and walking toward the exit, Ferit noticed a long line forming. The women were passing straight through, but the men had to produce identity papers. German officers were loading those who had no identification or had Jewish stamps on their papers straight onto a truck waiting at the Métro's exit.

"This is all I need," he said to himself, anxiously searching in his pockets. Thank goodness he had his papers with him. He gave a sigh of relief, but all the same he was still worried about having to wait in line. Thank God, it was moving quickly. The cursed men were carrying out their job quickly and efficiently. When his turn came, he produced both his birth certificate and his teaching certificate to the soldier with an SS band on his arm.

The scoundrel looked at his papers and said, "Get through."

Ferit grabbed his papers back and stuffed them into his inside pocket. He hurried along for a few kilometers before entering an awful grocer in a back street, with dirty windows and half-empty shelves. There was a very bored looking man sitting behind the counter.

"Give me a *Paris Soir*, will you?" Ferit said.

"Do you want the supplement too?"

"Why not, if it's free."

Ferit put some money on the counter.

"Don't you have change?"

"I don't. Do you?"

"Through that door and down the stairs on the left," the grocer said without looking up. He continued doing his accounts.

Ferit went through the door at the back of the shop, down the stairs, and opened a door. He was now in a garage. Five or six people were gathered around a small table behind some cars.

"Where were you, Turk?" one of them asked.

"Sorry, I've just managed—"

"Sit down, there's something that might concern you. We received some information today."

Ferit took one of the stools nearby and squeezed in between those already at the table.

"What information?"

"The Turks are apparently making preparations to get their Jews to Turkey. Have you heard about this?"

"No."

"*Mon Dieu!* What on earth are you talking about with your friends from the consulate?"

"Well, I'm not about to say, 'Apparently our organization has received some information about getting Turkish Jews out.'"

"You'll ask them now, then."

"Fine, I will. Supposing they are, what then?"

"We'll get those who aren't of Turkish origin to board the train too."

"They won't accept that."

"We're aware of that."

"So what?"

"We will manage it all the same."

"How will you do that?"

"We'll find a way."

"Supposing you do, how many people are you considering?"

"There are twenty-eight so far, but there may be more."

"What! Are you crazy?"

"Tell us, Turk, do you think we'd be doing this if we weren't crazy?"

"You couldn't help us with the passports, so you might as well get on with this," said a man with a hooked nose sitting at the head of the table.

"You must bring us precise details first. Find out if this business about the train is true. If so, when is it going to happen?"

"I'll do my best," said Ferit.

"Now, let's get on to item two on the agenda," said the man at the head of the table. "There's a group we must get over the Swiss border this week…"

Suddenly, the naked bulb hanging from the ceiling flicked off. Everyone around the table got up. Two of them started cleaning the cars. Another got into a car with a screwdriver in his hand. With the other two, Ferit ran toward the door he'd entered. The light went on again.

"OK, gentlemen, the danger's over. Back to the table," said the hooked-nosed man.

Tomorrow, thought Ferit, tomorrow I must speak to Tarık without fail.

PARIS

It hadn't been easy for Tarık to get Selva's message. Had it not been for her insistence and panic on the telephone, the night security guard wouldn't have bothered to send word to Tarık at home, and he wouldn't have known about the developments. News of the eighty people loaded onto a cattle train bound for Paris would have waited until the following day.

The security guard had slammed the telephone down on her twice. Was it possible this woman didn't understand what he had said?

"Listen, the consul isn't here. There's no one here. Neither the second nor the third secretaries are here. Everybody went home. Please call again tomorrow," he had said. But she wouldn't listen. Then he'd gotten a bit scared when she called for the third time. He wondered if she could be someone important, who might have connections with the powers that be. It was then that he decided to call the grocery beneath Tarık Arıca's apartment, as he had been instructed to do in an emergency. He had asked the grocer to let the gentlemen living in apartment five know they should call the consulate urgently. About half an hour passed before the grocer got around to sending his errand boy up with the message.

Tarık had run to the consulate as soon as he received the message. He found out from the security guard that a crazy woman had been persistently phoning from Marseilles. He guessed who it was and phoned Selva straight away. All he learned from her was that a number of Jews had been crammed onto a train leaving the Saint Charles Station for Paris, and Nazım Kender had also been on that train. Selva pleaded with Tarık to meet the train in Paris and save her husband. Tarık immediately called the Turkish embassy in Berlin. Because Paris was under German occupation, the consulate in Paris had to contact the embassy in Berlin for instructions. He had also informed Behiç Erkin, the ambassador in Vichy, of the situation, because he knew he was very sympathetic toward saving the Jews.

Behiç, who had been a close friend of Atatürk, was not a diplomat who had started his profession from the bottom; he had vast experience of state affairs. He was an intelligent and conscientious man with a lot of common sense. It was these qualities that had earned him his post. Maybe that had been a godsend.

"Gentlemen, even though we must be careful not to step on the Gestapo's toes, the necessities of war shouldn't make us forget our humanity," he'd said to his young colleagues. "Even the Urartu who lived in eastern Anatolia in the seventh century BC showed respect to the people whose lands they conquered, giving them freedom of faith. I can't understand what's happening to the Germans, behaving this way in the middle of the twentieth century! Don't get drawn into any confrontations, but of course try to do what you consider is right."

Tarık often wondered if he would have had the courage to visit the camps and police stations had it not been for the support of such a superior.

Within a week of Behiç Erkin renting a suitable building for an embassy, the Germans had settled in the building next door and were using it as their headquarters. The German officers were continuously watching those who came and left the embassy, making them feel uneasy. Eventually, to put a stop to this, Ambassador Erkin employed a huge Frenchman who used to work in the fish market. He gave him a uniform and made him stand in front of the gate as a security guard. His job was to escort the visitors leaving the embassy to the end of the road, thus dissuading the German soldiers from harassing them. Behiç had also given instructions to his staff to issue passports immediately to everyone who had ties with Turkey, no matter how tenuous the connection. If through the years they had forgotten Turkish, or never learned it because they were born in France, it was enough for them to prove their connection simply by learning sentences like "I am Turkish" or "I have relatives in Turkey." The ambassador was convinced that as long as they could compose a couple of sentences, they should be offered the chance to save themselves from the fury of the Germans or the pro-German French.

After notifying his superiors, Tarık had called Selva back.

"Rest assured that our ambassadors have set the wheels in motion. Please go to bed now and try to get some sleep." Not being able to calm her down, he decided, for the sake of Sabiha's sister, that he would spend the night at the consulate. He felt it would reassure her to know that he was at the end of a phone. This way, he would also be able to telephone her as soon as there was any news of Rafael.

Tarık spent two hours making calls all over the place, trying desperately to find some news, when the security guard came in and stood before him.

"There's someone at the door who wants to see you. Says he's a friend of yours."

"What's his name?"

"Ferit…Ferit Say—"

"Saylan?"

"That's it, Saylan."

"Let him in. He's my friend."

Tarık felt anxious when he saw Ferit looking so pale.

"What's up, my friend? What happened?" he asked.

"Actually, I was worried about you," said Ferit. "I popped in to see you at home and Muhlis told me you had rushed over to the consulate in a state. What's the matter, what is it? Is there anything I can do?"

"Thanks, but I don't think so. The Gestapo have rounded up a number of Jews, including the husband of a friend of mine. Apparently they are transporting them to Paris. I've informed our embassies in Berlin and Vichy, so now I am sitting and waiting, as you can see. They will let me know if there are any developments."

"Would you like me to keep you company?"

"Thanks for the offer, Ferit, but there's no point in you sitting here getting miserable too. Besides, Evelyn must be waiting for you at home."

"Evelyn isn't at home. She went to visit a friend who's just had a baby. She's spending the night there."

"Fine, stay, then. What can I offer you? Would you like some tea?"

"At this time of the night?"

"I could ask the guard to get us a bottle of wine, but you never know, it might leave a smell in the room and that wouldn't be appropriate in the consulate."

"Anyone else would, but not you. You're such a stickler for the rules. That's why I like you so much."

Tarık felt embarrassed by his friend's compliment.

"Tell you what, if I receive good news, we can go to the Prolope and have something to eat," he replied.

"OK. Ask for a tea for me, and we can sit and have a chat here. I need to talk to you about something very important. We wouldn't be able to talk freely in the café…"

"What's up? Are you in trouble?"

Ferit didn't answer. Tarık walked out of his office and called out to the guard, "Hasan Efendi. Will you get us two glasses of strong tea, please?"

"Glasses? What glasses?" the guard said. "There aren't proper tea glasses here. We have to drink out of bowls as if we are having soup."

The beautiful, ornate tea glasses brought from Turkey had all been broken; all they had left were huge French china cups. The consul had promised to have someone bring six thin-waisted tea glasses from Turkey. Thank God, he was a man of his word and they'd soon be drinking tea out of proper Turkish glasses—that was, if there were someone mad enough to visit this hell.

Of course, in those days, no one but the persecuted Jews and Hasan Efendi, who was homesick and never went out, believed that Paris was hell. Paris had been declared an open city and was very much alive. Cabarets, cafés, theaters, bars, restaurants, and dance halls were all open until the early hours of the morning. Oddly, Paris had become a city of entertainment.

"Come on then, what's the matter?" Tarık asked. "Are you in trouble, Ferit?"

"I'm not in any trouble, but you know I'm concerned about those who are."

"Yes, I know you're treading on dangerous ground."

"So are you."

"But I have the support of the Turkish government and our embassy. You're dealing with an illegal underground organization. And you're not even French. Who'll save you if you get into trouble?"

"You, I hope!"

"Ferit, I couldn't. How could I help someone involved with the ranks of the Communist Party and who's a member of the Resistance? You're a member of an organization we don't officially recognize. I'll support you with all my heart, but that won't be enough to get you out of trouble."

"I'll settle for that."

"You're being silly. I might not be so against you poking your nose into dangerous situations and acting as a courier if Evelyn wasn't pregnant."

"That's exactly what I wanted to talk to you about, Tarık. If I get into trouble, I'd like you to take care of Evelyn for me, look after her, protect her."

Tarık was shocked.

Ferit continued, "Can you do that for me, my friend?"

"What do you expect me to do?"

"Make sure my wife gets to Istanbul unharmed."

"Doesn't Evelyn have relatives here?"

"Not in Paris, and anyway, we want our child to be born in Turkey. We want my mother to see her grandchild."

"What about Evelyn's parents?"

"They're both dead. She's only got one brother and he's pinning his hopes on going to America. He'll be gone by the time the baby's born."

"Ferit, wouldn't it be better if you washed your hands of all this and concentrated on taking your wife to Turkey yourself?"

"I've got one more mission to accomplish, Tarık, just one last mission. I'm far too involved to back out now. Once it's over, with God's will, I'll get onto this train and go back to Istanbul."

"Train? What train?"

"The one you mentioned…"

"I don't remember mentioning any train."

"But isn't there a train?"

"Has Muhlis been talking?"

"Does it matter where I heard it? Just tell me, when's that train going?"

"You want to get on that train, do you?"

"Isn't it possible?"

"Of course. That is, if it happens at all. We've been trying to work out a way to get the Turkish Jews out of Paris and back to Turkey. We're still working on it. We're trying to figure out how much it would cost to hire a carriage, the safest route, and when… There are still many questions to be answered. We're in the process of discussing it with the countries en route. So yes, we are considering it, but nothing is certain. If you want to get on that train, I'm sure I can fix it for you and your wife."

"You're sure?"

"Of course I'm sure. But for God's sake, don't talk about it all over the place. The Germans would certainly put a stop to it if they heard word of it. We're trying to sort things out very quietly. Muhlis shouldn't have mentioned it at all."

"Please believe me, Muhlis hasn't said a word."

"Then how do you know about it? There are only three of us in the know, apart from the ambassador: Hikmet Özdoğan, Muhlis, and me. You don't know Hikmet, so that leaves Muhlis and me. It must have been Muhlis who let the cat out of the bag."

"I swear on my honor that it wasn't Muhlis. Besides, he doesn't know about my involvement with the Organization."

"So how do you know then?"

"I can't tell you."

"It's imperative that I know."

"A couple of friends of mine on the committee want their close relatives to get on the train."

"How on earth do they know about this?"

"Walls have ears. I do work for an underground organization."

"Frankly, my friend, I don't like this at all. How can such confidential matters leak out?"

"Don't worry, Tarık. Those in the know wouldn't want to jeopardize your plan. They just want to take advantage of it…"

When the guard walked in carrying a tray, they stopped talking. He put the bowls of tea on Tarık's desk and left the room. Just after they had had a couple of sips of tea, the telephone rang. It was the embassy. The ambassador was informing Tarık that the Marseilles consul, Nazım Kender, and those with him had been released.

"Thanks for the good news, sir," said Tarık. "…What?…Oh! The train…Of course, sir, I'll see to it tomorrow…You're right, sir, yes, before these poor people are caught up again. I'm sure the immigration people will be more helpful after tonight's debacle… Pardon?"

Tarık tried to cut his conversation short because he didn't want to say more in front of Ferit, making do with simple answers like "Yes, sir," and "No, sir." Finally he put the phone down and turned to his friend.

"Hooray! The Gestapo released the people being transported from Marseilles to Paris. We've done it again, my friend!" he said in excitement.

"Don't get too carried away, Tarık. They may have released them this time, but I'll bet they'll round them up again pretty soon."

"Maybe…But if you'll excuse me, I must call my friend in Marseilles who's waiting to hear from me. I'll give her the good news, and then we can go out together."

Selva picked up the receiver the moment the phone rang. It was obvious that she was sitting next to it.

"Good news, Selva Hanım. Apparently your husband and all the others have been released in Arles. I presume with so many people looking for transport, they'll have difficulty at this time of night, but I'm sure they'll be home by morning."

There was no sound from the other end of the line.

"Selva Hanım...Selva?"

"I heard you," replied Selva weakly. "You were right, Tarık, we do need to go back...at the earliest opportunity."

"There's the possibility of a train leaving for Edirne. You've got to get yourselves here in case it happens. I'm sure you understand that it can't wait for you to come from Marseilles. You must get to Paris."

"Yes, of course I understand, but where could we stay? If there's no fixed time for the train, it may be a long wait, and as you know we have a child too."

"If push comes to shove, you can always stay with me. You must get ready immediately. You should be here within the next two weeks."

After putting the phone down, Tarık hesitated for a moment. What the hell have I done? he thought. How could he put up three people in his apartment? What would Muhlis have to say about it? He turned to Ferit.

"I might need somewhere to stay," he said. "Would you be able to find me a place? I wonder if there's a little hotel near my apartment."

"For you or for your friends?"

"There are three of them. I'm sure it will be easier to find a place for me; they can stay in my place."

"Till the train departs?"

"Yes."

"Are you telling me there's definitely a train leaving then?"

"Ferit, if that train goes, you're planning to be on it with your wife, right?"

"That may be so."

"In that case, you must promise not to put me in a difficult position. We haven't had this conversation and you have no knowledge of this train! You know absolutely nothing. Is that clear?"

"Didn't I tell you that walls have ears? I would have heard about it even if you hadn't mentioned it. Let me see what I can do about finding somewhere for your friends. What about my place?"

"Your place?"

"Yes, why not? We have a large spare room we hardly use. A friend of mine used to stay there before, but when Evelyn and I got married, he left. Why should you leave your home? They'll be perfectly comfortable staying with us."

"Thank you, Ferit. It goes without saying that whoever stays with you will pay rent."

"That's not important at all. We'll think of something," Ferit said.

Tarık felt like a rat caught in a trap. Ferit might not be asking for rent, but just what would he ask for next?

ANKARA 1943

When it started to snow heavily outside, the bridge party at Dr. Celal's home ended abruptly. The other guests were getting ready to leave, and Dr. Celal's wife, Leyla, tried to persuade Sabiha to stay.

"I really don't want you to go home on your own, Sabiha," she said. "Macit's out of town anyway."

"Thank you, darling. I'd rather go. Hülya is at home, and she'll worry if I stay out," replied Sabiha.

"We could phone."

"It's very kind of you, but I'd rather go home, thank you."

"Macit's doing the right thing, that's for sure," said Dr. Celal, laughing. "He's probably sunbathing in Cairo while we're here freezing in the middle of a snowstorm."

"Give him credit. I'll bet that he's taking quite a roasting, what with Churchill on one side, Roosevelt on the other, and Inönü sitting across the table. Speaking for myself, I wouldn't want to be in his shoes for all the tea in China; I'd rather be here in the snowstorm," said Adnan, one of the guests.

"Inönü's probably getting the roasting, not Macit," said Leyla. "Who knows how Churchill and Roosevelt are cornering him?"

"Actually, it's the Russians who are giving Inönü the headache," said Adnan. "Russia is adamant that Turkey should join the war, at whatever cost."

"Why's that?" asked Dr. Sahir.

"Because when the Germans attack Turkey, the Russians want to send their forces to help us."

"Neither one nor the other, thank you," said Dr. Celal. "I don't want any favors from anybody, thank you very much."

"The old fox Inönü won't be taken in that easily," Ahmet, another of the guests, said. "Who knows what tricks he's got up his sleeve?"

"One has to keep the old devil on his toes," said Ahmet's wife, who was from one of the Aegean provinces and therefore disliked Inönü.

"These good-bye chats at the door can go on forever," said Adnan. "We'll bid you a fond farewell."

"And who did you come with, Sabiha?" asked Dr. Celal.

"The weather was perfectly fine earlier, so I walked here alone," she replied.

"We'll worry about you going back on your own in the snow."

"I'll accompany the lady," said Dr. Sahir.

"There's no need, thank you," Sabiha responded.

"Please allow me the honor," Dr. Sahir insisted.

Everyone left together, walking toward the square at the top of the road before setting off in various directions. Sabiha and Sahir continued walking in the direction of Kızılay. What had started out as sleet had turned into large snowflakes and was now a full-blown blizzard. Sabiha slipped and Dr. Sahir caught her by the arm.

"Here, hold onto my arm, Sabiha Hanım," he said.

"How could one have guessed that it would snow?" she said, taking his arm. "It was sunny this morning. I wouldn't have left home had I known this." They continued walking arm in arm against the blizzard. Sabiha, who wasn't too shy to reveal her hidden, innermost feelings in Dr. Sahir's consulting room, was now silent; she was even too embarrassed to make eye contact with him. She had been rather shaken seeing him at Dr. Celal's house. He was the one she thought of through the dark nights, the man she longed to see, who made her count the days, hours, and minutes between their appointments. The same man whose voice she missed if she hadn't heard it for a few days. Sabiha had been surprised to see him, even though Leyla had mentioned the possibility of his replacing Macit. For some unknown reason, she hadn't imagined that he would be there. When she saw him in Leyla's sitting room, she was taken aback to see this man who knew her inside out. She felt naked—everything she shared with him, her conversations, her confessions, her tears, even feelings she wouldn't admit to herself outside the dimly lit consulting room. Somehow being together in this place wasn't right. She had hoped to God they wouldn't be sitting at the same table.

As they approached Kızılay, Dr. Sahir suggested having something warm to drink.

"It's so cold; you'll feel better with something warm inside you. How about some hot chocolate?"

"That's fine by me."

As soon as she agreed, Sabiha regretted it. They walked into an empty café and sat opposite each other at a small round table by the window. Sabiha removed her gloves and the shawl from around her head. Dr. Sahir called out to the waiter standing behind the glass display counter.

"Two hot chocolates, please."

Sabiha's hands had turned blue with the cold. Dr. Sahir took them in his and started rubbing them. Sabiha blushed, but didn't withdraw them.

"Do you know, I feel strange sitting here with you instead of in your consulting room," she said quietly, so as not to be heard by the waiter.

"Why do you feel strange?"

"I don't know. It's odd."

"Why?"

"I can't think of anything to say…"

"In that case, why don't we talk about the things we discuss in our sessions?"

"Wouldn't that be odd too?"

"Why should it?"

"Well, for a start, in your consulting room, I know I'm paying you for your time."

"Since we're here, why don't you try speaking to me as a friend? Shouldn't we have built up a friendship after all this time?"

"But how can I repay you?"

"The pleasure of your company is payment enough."

"Is being with me a pleasure, Doctor?"

"Absolutely. Just looking at you is a pleasure. You're a very beautiful woman."

"But being with me might not be as pleasurable as looking at me. I'm a very complicated person. I'm always nervous and troubled. Maybe that's why I bore my husband, and come to think of it, even my daughter."

"Is your daughter bored with you?"

"Well, let's just say she doesn't like being with me. You might remember me telling you, she spends all of her time with my parents since they came to stay. She seems to be closer to them."

"Grandparents have a very special place in children's lives. They're a constant source of love and tolerance…"

"No, no, she was distant toward me even before they came. Hülya is an odd child."

"She's your one and only child?"

"Yes."

"In other words she's spoiled, jealous, and stubborn."

"What makes you say that?"

"Because, Sabiha Hanım, you appear to have certain preconceived ideas about first children."

"Really?" said Sabiha, picking up one of the cups. She sprinkled some sugar on it and took a sip. "Ohhh! This is great."

"The chocolate, or recognizing the truth?"

"I have a feeling that you don't have a very good impression of me. You think of me as a capricious and fussy woman, don't you?"

"No, not at all. I regard you as a very emotional and sensitive woman. That's exactly why the sort of mischievousness and jealousy most children feel toward their younger siblings appears to have left such a deep impression on you. In other words, you're neither capricious nor fussy; you're sensitive and delicate."

Sabiha took another sip of the chocolate that she held between her trembling hands.

"You know, Sabiha Hanım, I believe that you're carrying a lot of excess baggage. It's possible at times you feel your daughter could be sharing similar feelings toward you. But in fact, there is no such thing at all. Your past experiences with your sister are all part of life's rich pattern. What you experienced in your childhood is perfectly normal."

"I think I've added too much sugar."

"Sabiha, I hope you don't mind my being so familiar, but don't run away. You don't only have to face the truth in my consulting room, you know…"

"What do you mean?"

"In my opinion, your problem is with your daughter, not your sister."

"If you've finished your chocolate, maybe we should leave," said Sabiha.

Dr. Sahir turned around and called the waiter. He pulled out Sabiha's chair for her, she put on her shawl and gloves, and they left. The blizzard had calmed down.

"I suggest you hold onto my arm again," said Dr. Sahir. "It's very slippery."

"Thank you. I think we should separate at the next corner. From there I can go to my home and you to yours."

"I'd be happier walking you home. Maybe when we get there, you can invite me in for something warm."

"My parents and Hülya are there."

"How nice. In that case I might even meet Hülya too."

They walked silently for a while, and then Sabiha stopped suddenly and, looking straight into Dr. Sahir's eyes, asked, "Do you think I treat my daughter badly?"

"Do you?"

"No, but you give me the impression you think I do."

"I've never seen you with your daughter but I believe I can read what's in your heart. Because you don't like your childhood, you appear to blame your daughter, who represents all little girls, and as a result you're depriving her of your love."

Tears appeared in Sabiha's eyes.

"I don't treat her badly."

"I'm sure."

"Why?"

"Because you..."

"Because I what?"

"Because you're magnificent. You're far too gentle to hurt anyone."

"Do you really mean that? Are you telling me the truth?"

"Yes, Sabiha, I am."

"Tell me, Doctor, will I ever be able to rid myself of all these regrets that torment me so?"

"Of course you will."

"When will I?"

"Sabiha, I want to ask you something. Would you come with me to my consulting room right now?"

"Now?"

"Yes."

"Yes, I will."

"You're sure you want to?"

"Yes, I am."

They retraced their steps as far as Kızılay, where they crossed the road and walked for a while along Kazım Özalp Street, then turned right into Karanfil Street. Not a word was spoken. It was as if they both feared that even a single word would spoil the magic of this moment that held separate meanings for each of them. It had stopped snowing for a while, but now it had started again.

Sahir opened the gate of the building where his consulting room was. He made way for Sabiha to enter. When he couldn't switch on the lights by the stairs, he took out a box of matches, struck one, and held it in front of them.

"It seems the bulb has gone. Give me your hand, Sabiha."

They walked up the stairs hand in hand. Sahir struck another match in front of his flat to open the door. They were now inside. Sahir switched on the light in the hall. In the harsh glare of the light, they both looked rather funny, like figures in a surrealist painting, with their hair and coats covered in snow. Sabiha shook the snow off herself and removed her shawl, coat, and gloves. Sahir went into his consulting room and switched on the lamp on his desk.

"Please come in, Sabiha Hanım." Sabiha walked in. "Please sit down."

Sabiha sat in her usual comfortable chair and stretched out her legs on the footstool.

"Is there no music?"

"Sure. What would you like to listen to?"

"You choose something."

"You like piano, don't you?"

"Yes."

"Give me a minute. I'll find you some Chopin."

Sabiha closed her eyes and stretched out in the armchair. In a few minutes, she could hear a familiar Chopin polonaise.

"You seem to have a great record collection."

"It stems from my years as a student in Vienna."

"Do you play music for all your patients?"

"Yes, if they wish. Music can be very relaxing. What a pity that not too many people in this city like classical music."

They didn't speak for a while, until Sahir said, "So, I'm all ears."

"What do you want me to say?"

"Whatever you wish."

"I'd love to just listen to this music."

"No cheating. If you can't decide what to talk about, let me guide you. We were talking about your daughter earlier. Why don't we take it from there?"

"No, I don't want that."

"Why not?"

"I just don't."

"Why do you always avoid this subject? There's something bothering you about your daughter."

"Who says so?"

"I do, as your doctor, that is. Sabiha, you can tell me everything. I promise not to judge you whatever you say. You know that."

"That's not why I don't want to talk about it."

"I urge you to do so, Sabiha. Didn't you tell me earlier that you wanted to rid yourself of this torment? Here's your chance."

"Please come close to me."

Sahir got up from behind his desk, walked over to Sabiha, and sat on the footstool where she rested her feet.

"Sabiha, let's get this over with tonight. Let's put an end to it, let's confront whatever—"

He couldn't finish his sentence. Sabiha sat upright, leaned toward him, and put her fingers on his lips.

"Please don't speak. Don't say another word. Yes, let's face this tonight."

For a moment they looked into each other's eyes. Sahir pretended not to see the look of desolation in her eyes.

"OK, then, I'm ready."

Suddenly Sabiha sat up, as if she had been scalded.

"No, no, I can't do it. I'm not ready," she said, standing up. "Let's go," she said coldly.

"Why are you so angry?"

When Sabiha didn't answer, Sahir walked to the hall stand to get her coat, putting it around her shoulders. Sabiha slowly turned to face him. Her face was so close that he could smell the chocolate on her breath. They stood silently in the dim light. Sahir suddenly pulled her toward him and kissed her warm lips. For a split second, Sabiha felt as if she might faint. She was shaking at the knees. She let him kiss her face, neck, and lips over and over again. For a while they wrestled together passionately, then Sabiha suddenly pulled herself back.

"No...please, don't. We shouldn't."

"Are you teasing me?"

"I don't understand."

"I don't think you really know what you want, Sabiha!"

"On the contrary, I think you don't know what you want. You sweet-talk me into coming here. You play music for me, and worst of all you do all this when you know very well that I'm a woman neglected by her husband. I'm an unhappy woman and you know I have a soft spot for you. Then…you try to disgrace me by…"

"Sabiha! What are you saying?"

"You…You're trying to degrade me…"

"I always play music for you because it relaxes you. You know that. I can assure you that I felt you were ready to face the facts. There are very special moments when people are ready to come out of their shells. I honestly thought that moment had arrived."

"Surely, though, the way to win my daughter back shouldn't be at the risk of losing my husband."

"There's obviously been a misunderstanding. I'm profoundly sorry."

Sabiha's eyes were full of tears, but her face was expressionless. "I'm an idiot," she said.

"No, not at all. I brought you here because I wanted to help you look inside yourself. Please believe me, I had no ulterior motives—but even a doctor can't always practice self-restraint."

"Are you in love with me?"

"I have no right to be. You're my patient."

Her eyes, cheeks, and the palms of her hands felt as though they were on fire.

"I apologize too," she said softly.

"Sabiha, let's get one thing clear at least. You think you're unhappy because you're neglected by your husband. You're not. Your husband is much more attached to his family than you think."

"What makes you say that?"

"I can't tell you, I'm afraid, but believe me, I know."

"So you think I don't love my husband, is that it?"

"Why should I think that?"

"Because I came here tonight."

"Never!"

"I shouldn't have. I shouldn't have done this."

"You've done nothing."

"But surely you must have known of my weakness for you."

"Maybe, but that's because I can read you like a book, cover to cover. Most patients feel this way about their doctors."

"You mean like students who fall in love with their teachers?"

"Not exactly."

"So what do you mean, Sahir?"

"Sabiha..."

"I trusted you, I was under your influence, because you were good for me."

"It's my job to be good for you."

"I must say you drew out all that stuff inside me very well...I wish this hadn't happened."

The doctor approached her, and then hugged her affectionately.

"Let's forget about our moment of weakness, Sabiha. Please don't forget that I'm your friend as well as your doctor. You're tearing yourself inside out here, and I'm helping you do it. That's all."

"Let's leave, please," said Sabiha. "I want to go home."

"Fine, let's go."

"You don't have to. I can go on my own."

"I won't hear of it. Not at this time of night."

He helped Sabiha on with her coat. He stopped the music, switched off the lamp, and they both went out into the harshly lit hall. When he saw Sabiha's flushed face and ruffled hair, Sahir asked, "Would you like to powder your nose?"

"No, thank you."

They left the apartment. This time Sabiha walked down the stairs without holding on to Sahir's hand.

It was still snowing slightly.

"Please hold on to my arm or else you might slip," said Sahir.

They walked arm in arm again, drifting into their thoughts.

This is so typical of me, Sabiha thought, feeling ashamed. I'm exactly what my father wanted me to be, well educated and open-minded, but underneath it all I'm still a slave to pressures and outdated notions. I'm a coward who wags her tail at the man she's attracted to, but then can't follow through. My father and I are like two peas in a pod. Didn't he banish his daughter simply because she married Rafo, when all the time he boasted he was a civilized, contemporary man?

"What are you thinking?" asked Sahir.

"Nothing," replied Sabiha.

Wouldn't we be happier, she thought, if we could rid ourselves of the old conventions or shrug off the chains binding us to our past? If we could only do that, we'd be happier, more independent.

While Sabiha was treading carefully, crunching the snow under her feet, and holding on to Sahir's arm, she had no doubt that she had made the right decision. She was also aware that she had missed her chance of bliss, and possibly the only opportunity for a fling that she had fantasized about for months. How she had longed to be as naked physically in Sahir's arms as when she bared her soul to him. For months she had longed to offer herself to him, make love with him…but she hadn't. She wasn't as brave as Selva. She kept using the excuse that she shouldn't be hurting those around her. Her mother's famous words came to mind: "Don't throw everyone else's life into disarray." Well, she was certainly as much her mother's daughter as her father's. Not only was she afraid of throwing other people's lives into disarray, she was afraid of other people's judgment.

They walked all the way to Kızılay without speaking. From there they walked up the road alongside Güven Park. At one point Sabiha's foot slipped and Sahir held on to her tightly.

"This way," Sabiha said when they reached her street. When they got nearer to her home, she slipped her arm from Sahir's, walked unsteadily to the gate in front of her building, and waited for Sahir to catch up.

"I'm afraid I won't be able to invite you in."

"I understand."

"I won't be able to make Wednesday's appointment either."

"That's something you shouldn't do. You must be aware of how near we are to successfully concluding our sessions."

"Yes, Doctor, I'm aware of that, but as I said earlier, winning my daughter back shouldn't be at the cost of losing my husband." She extended her hand to him. "Good-bye."

Sahir took Sabiha's hand and removed her glove. He lifted her hand, touching her fingertips to his lips; in the cold night air, they still felt as hot as fire.

"Good-bye, Sabiha."

Suddenly Sabiha held onto his lapels with both hands, stood on tiptoe, and placed a little kiss on the corner of his mouth, then she turned away swiftly and walked in through the gate.

Sahir was once again aware of a faint hint of chocolate on Sabiha's breath. He touched his fingers to the spot where Sabiha had kissed him and, without looking back, walked along the snow-covered street.

Sabiha watched Sahir walk through the steadily falling snow. Just then she felt an intense yearning for her husband.

CAIRO 1943

Macit was taken aback when he saw his reflection in the mirror as he was tying his tie. The big black bags under his eyes were the result of many sleepless nights. He felt deflated.

It was as though he had aged five years in the past five days. Since the fourth of the month, they had been attending meetings without a break. President Inönü, his private secretary, the foreign minister, the general secretary of the foreign ministry, and Macit had been flown to Cairo in two private planes, which had been sent to Adana by American president Roosevelt and British prime minister Churchill. There were many summit meetings and numerous smaller meetings in twos and threes. On top of this, they also had to attend dinners where very important issues were discussed. The whole Turkish delegation—from the president to the most junior member—had to make do with only three hours' sleep a night. Macit couldn't understand how a man of Inönü's advanced years could cope with such pressure and could still be so clear-headed.

Thinking of the day he left Ankara, he couldn't help feeling Sabiha had made a malicious joke remarking that he was lucky to be leaving the bitter cold of Ankara for sunnier climes. All they'd seen of Cairo were long corridors, vast conference rooms, and round tables. Not to mention all the grim-looking men with tired eyes who were each desperately vying for his national interests.

In comparison to Roosevelt, who seemed extremely tall, even though he was in a wheelchair, and Churchill, who was as wide as he was high, Inönü looked like a scrawny fox, struggling to outmaneuver these wolves and come through without a scratch. He was juggling ideas in his mind and trying to avoid stepping on anyone's toes.

"Keep your wits about you," he had said to the members of his delegation. "You must be ready to pick up on any point that might escape me. We will be treading a very fine line. You must all be extremely alert."

Macit had come to Cairo with the foreign minister about a month ago. They had had endless talks to lay the foundations for this political chess game. That had been a tiring trip, but it was nothing compared to this one. Now they were finally reaching the crucial point of the past four days of these intense talks.

Britain was not only forcing Turkey to invade the Aegean Islands without offering support (they were attempting to turn their defeat in the Islands into a triumphant victory), but they also expected to be allowed to have bases in the southern provinces of Turkey. Behind the scenes, Russia was also pulling strings with all her might. She desperately wanted Turkey to declare that she was joining the war and closing the Bosphorus to all German ships, both military and commercial. Russia also insisted that all airports should be used by the Allied Forces immediately; believing that if Turkey took such action, the Germans would invade and Russia would be let off the hook.

This latter condition worried Inönü most. He thought if Germany was to invade Turkey, the Russians, on the pretext of giving support, would be able to send in their troops. Inönü, wearing old patent-leather shoes, was waltzing dangerously on a very slippery floor with three great prima donnas. While Britain put her arms around his waist, trying to make him turn toward her, Germany grabbed his hands, trying to make him sway her way, and Russia was stepping on his toes in her huge combat boots.

Macit had kept a record of the British and Turkish foreign ministers' meeting in Cairo on the fifth of November. Numan Menemencioğlu, the foreign minister, attended the emergency meeting in a well-prepared state, because just before he had left for Cairo, the German ambassador, Von Papen, had visited and warned him that he knew what the British and Russians would be asking.

"Your Excellency, the British are under pressure from the Russians and will be asking you to join the war immediately. That's their sole reason for inviting you to the Cairo summit."

"How can you be so sure, Ambassador?" Menemencioğlu asked. "I haven't even been there yet."

Von Papen laughed; he hadn't told him that a spy called Cicero, who worked in the British embassy, had photographed a coded message from London and sold it to them.

"You don't have to be clairvoyant to know this," Von Papen said. "It will be to your advantage to make sure you refuse the *Allies*' requests. My government expects you to answer them accordingly," he added, without a smile.

Numan Menemencioğlu had kept that in mind at the Cairo meeting with the British foreign minister, Anthony Eden.

We're caught between a rock and a hard place! thought Macit outside the conference room. After everyone entered the room and took their places, Macit watched this verbal duel between the Turkish and British foreign ministers with undisguised admiration. It was like watching a brilliant tennis match. He couldn't help admiring Numan Menemencioğlu's ability to return every volley no matter the speed of delivery.

From the start, Mr. Eden didn't mince his words.

"Your joining the war before the year is out would be a tremendous help to Russia. They are obsessed with the idea that this war should end as soon as possible. Your participation would pave the way to friendly ties with Russia, and that will be to your advantage."

"But wouldn't that mean Russia could invade the Balkans?" Menemencioğlu asked.

"If the Russians had designs on the Balkans, they wouldn't want Turkey to join the war," Eden replied unconvincingly.

"But couldn't you argue that they want Turkey to join the war to wear herself out? That would mean that we would leave ourselves open to a German invasion. We'd have to fight, leading to a second war of liberation. Surely that wouldn't be a wise move."

"It isn't possible any longer for the Germans to invade Turkey. They are left with only fifty bombers. They can't cope with the British fighter planes. They're in no position to deal with yet another front."

"If the Germans are so depleted, why doesn't Britain consider an operation in that area, then?"

"That's a matter concerning our military operations. I'm afraid I can't comment," the British foreign minister replied.

"I fully understand, Your Excellency, but you must try to understand our position. It isn't possible for Turkey to join the war without knowing your plans for the Balkans."

With this, Mr. Eden changed his tune.

"My dear colleague, Turkey could be of help without even joining the war."

"How is that?"

"By allowing Britain to use the airfields in the southern provinces."

"But surely you are aware that if Turkey allowed that, it would be an open invitation for the Germans to attack us."

"I'm afraid I don't agree. When the air bases were used in the Azores, the Germans didn't attack Portugal. Furthermore, during our operations in the Aegean Islands, they turned a blind eye to the facilities you offered us—like storage in your depots and food supplies, not to mention the withdrawal of our troops through Turkey. You know that."

"Of course I do, Your Excellency, but you must know, if you should use our air bases against the Islands, the Germans would instantly attack us."

"Your Excellency, I'm under the impression that you don't want us to use your airfields because you are scared of the Russians and don't want to join the war."

"There is no need to interpret it that way, Your Excellency. We can certainly discuss the subject of Turkey joining the war, but only after having established the guarantees you're willing to give."

"Let's look at it this way. If Turkey joins the war today, it will have a great effect; if she joins in three months' time, that effect will be reduced, and if she should join in six months' time, there will be no effect. And there's another thing to consider. If you don't accept our request—which would be a great help to us—our relationship will change."

"In what way?"

"In a negative one, I am afraid."

"Sir, we're the first country you have approached. You have made no such demands on Russia, America, or even Yugoslavia. Are you telling me that if we refuse, our relationship might reach a breaking point?"

"I'd better clarify: if Turkey doesn't cooperate with the three Allies, our relationship will suffer now and after the war."

Numan Menemencioğlu's face turned gray. Mr. Eden was making threats about their relationship even after the war.

"As I understand it," the Turkish foreign minister said, "the decision made in Moscow was for us to join the war."

"Yes, that's right. The three Allies have come to the conclusion that Turkey's participation in the war will shorten it. The airfield request is a different issue."

"Minister, I am authorized to deal with your request for airfields, and it is with that authority that I am refusing your request right here and now. As for Turkey joining the war, I shall relay that to my government. This decision can only be made by the Assembly in Ankara."

Numan Menemencioğlu finished his sentence, got up, shook Mr. Eden's hand, and left the room.

The Turkish diplomats held countless meetings in their rooms during the following two days. Coded messages were sent back and forth between Cairo and Ankara, cigarettes were chain-smoked, and many cups of coffee were drunk. Various details were scrutinized and evaluated. Three days later, Eden and Menemencioğlu met again.

The Turks were tense. They suspected the British might have been pressured by Russia to stop providing supplies.

"This time I might not be able to abide by diplomatic courtesies, although that could actually be a useful tactic," Numan said to Macit before going in for the meeting.

Even later, thinking about that meeting, Macit's palms couldn't stop sweating.

Eden gave an ultimatum, saying, "You have to join the war!"

Numan replied softly but with hard words. "Honorable colleague, you have tried to influence us twice so far, and had we acted hastily on either of those occasions, we would have both stood to lose."

"For instance?" Eden asked mockingly, with a wry smile.

"Let me remind you," replied Menemencioğlu, "when Italy declared war back in 1940, you asked us to join then. What would have happened to us if we had listened to you? Furthermore, you did the same thing in 1941 in respect to Yugoslavia."

"No, I'm sorry, sir, we didn't ask you to join the war," the British ambassador, Hugessen, interjected.

"So what did you do?"

"We asked you to bluff, in order to encourage the Yugoslav government to resist."

Numan started to laugh. "My dear friend, thank you for confirming what I just said. How else could that bluff be interpreted, with Germany at her strongest and already moving south?"

Mr. Eden couldn't help laughing too. Numan had started laughing, but he ended harshly.

"You tried to get the Germans to attack Turkey before they attacked Russia, without realizing how dearly it would cost you."

Macit and the general secretary looked at each other. Both had a glimmer of pride and anxiety in their eyes. Numan continued on the attack.

"If that wasn't enough, you're about to make the same mistake again today, when you've got the upper hand. Your request is nothing short of sacrificing Turkey. What's more, you're doing it to please the Russians."

Macit watched as the British listened to the Turkish foreign minister with expressionless faces, carefully avoiding eye contact. Numan was like a tenor walking on stage with a croak in his voice, but gradually overcoming it.

"Who on earth can see reason in inducing the Germans to attack us when you know full well our army is in no state to defend ourselves? What good would it do you if the Germans had control of the areas along the Bosphorus? Would we just sit it out and wait for final victory and our liberation? Are we supposed to sit there, hoping the Russians come and defeat the Germans and save Istanbul? Are you telling me the Russians will save Istanbul for our sake?"

Numan stopped and took a deep breath. Eden appeared to want to butt in, but Numan continued.

"All this is so clear; don't you see that threatening to stop supplying aid is pushing us into a vicious situation? If you don't supply us with the necessary equipment, we can't join the war. We can't fight without supplies. Where's the sense in all that?" he asked.

Mr. Eden sat with a blank face, as if wearing a mask. He seemed neither to agree nor disagree. He merely said, "Will you please relate the wishes of the three great powers, Britain, Russia, and America, to your government, Your Excellency?"

After the delegation returned to Turkey, this matter was discussed for a very long time at the ministers' assembly. The final decision was a yes to joining the war, with certain reservations, and no to granting permission to use the airfields.

There had been so much to be discussed during the month between the meetings. Macit was so busy juggling all his duties at the ministry, he simply had no opportunity to spend time at home and deal with Sabiha and Hülya. Husband and wife were drifting farther and farther apart. They hadn't made love for months; for more than a month, they hadn't even exchanged more than a few words. Macit kept postponing dealing with his problems at home. Once this meeting is over...Once we sign this agreement...Once this summit meeting is over...

Now, finally, the five-day marathon in Cairo was over. They would be flying back to Adana in Churchill's plane. His father-in-law would be waiting impatiently for his return; he was sure Fazıl Reşat Paşa would stay up, waiting by the window, no matter how late it was. Once a government official, always a government official. That's the way it was, even if one was over eighty and retired. Having been a minister in the last Ottoman Assembly, he wouldn't be able to sleep without first welcoming his son-in-law back. Macit was sure the paşa would be there in his burgundy dressing gown, his glasses halfway down his nose. He sighed deeply. At least someone would be waiting for his return, even if it was his old father-in-law. Knowing he was the old man's only link with the outside world, Macit started to think about what to tell him.

If he told him that the British foreign minister had fibbed, trying to put Turkey in the firing line, acting on behalf of the Russians and not the Americans, he knew the old man would regale him with stories from history illustrating how untrustworthy the Russians were. He could tell Fazıl Paşa how, when Inönü pointed out that Turkey needed more time before she could join the war and the American president had been supportive, the British foreign minister had said, "Mr. President, you're forgetting our promise to the Russians," so loudly that everyone could hear. Then Fazıl Reşat Paşa would go into a tirade about how it had been the British who stirred up the Kurds and Arabs against Turkey.

After going through the various stages of the meeting in his mind, Macit decided that Fazıl Paşa would really appreciate hearing about Numan's firm response to the insolent Eden. Negotiating the extension of Britain's military supplies, Numan had said, "This aid that you are offering is sufficient for the defense of the British air bases, not the defense of Turkey."

"The aid is for the defense of the British bases in Istanbul, Izmir, and Zonguldak," Eden responded.

Numan replied, "You don't think the Turks are expecting the British to defend their whole country, Your Excellency. What we want is, if necessary, for the Turks to defend our country with your help."

Knowing how happy it would make his father-in-law, Macit would tell him how, at the end of the very tough meeting, the American president had insisted he and Inönü should spend a little more time together before saying good-bye. He particularly wanted to tell the paşa about the warm conversation between the two leaders.

Macit was rather surprised at himself for feeling so affectionate toward his father-in-law. He wondered if he had begun to look upon the paşa as a surrogate father.

If I miss my father's affection that much, maybe I'm desperately lonely, thought Macit.

So as not to be late for the Churchill-Inönü meeting in Churchill's villa early the next morning, Macit had packed his suitcase the night before. All that was left for him to do was to pack his pajamas and toiletries, don his jacket, and gather his files.

After the meeting, they flew back to Adana on Churchill's plane and transferred to a train for Ankara. As soon as Macit was in his compartment, he lay down to rest. He was completely exhausted, but a knock on the door caused him to jump up.

"I'm sorry, sir, the president would like to see you for one last assessment," one of Inönü's staff said, popping his head around the door.

"I'll be right with you," Macit said, yawning. He got up, muttering to himself, and washed his face. What sort of man was this Inönü? Didn't he ever get tired? Didn't he sleep? He promised himself he would sleep the whole weekend as soon as he got home.

But Macit didn't get home when he expected. Heavy snow blocked the line, and they had to wait for hours for it to be cleared. When at last they reached Ankara, they had to go directly to the ministry to show the prime minister the finished version of the report he had to submit to the Assembly the following day. Macit telephoned home to find out how everyone was, and after talking briefly, urged them not to wait up for him. His conversation with Fazıl Reşat Paşa about his Cairo adventure would have to wait.

By the time he got home, Macit was shattered. His eyes were burning, his mouth was dry, and his joints were aching. He paid the fare to the taxi driver, picked up his small suitcase, and walked to the gate. He opened the door with his key and finally entered his dark, silent home. His first thought was for a bath, but he immediately changed his mind. He thought of sleeping on the sofa so as not to waken Sabiha, but then he realized that he would be awakened by the early risers in the morning. The best thing to do was to undress in the sitting room, creep into bed, and collapse. He left his suitcase in a corner, undressed, and in his stocking feet, opened the bedroom door as quietly as possible. He made his way carefully to the bed, slipped between the warm sheets, and lay on his back. His body was numb. Just as he was dropping off to sleep, he was suddenly startled by Sabiha moving near him. Oh no, he thought, I've woken her up. He first felt her slippery silk nightdress on his skin and then suddenly the touch of her warm body. Sabiha pushed her body next to her husband's and put her arms tightly around his neck.

"Welcome back," she said. "I missed you so much, so very much."

PARIS

Ferit walked up the stairs carrying on his back a mattress he'd taken off an old truck.

The truck driver tried to unload another mattress, then shouted after him, "Hey, my friend, you might be as strong as a mule, but I ain't. You'd better find someone to give me a hand down here."

"Wait until I've taken this one up," he answered breathlessly. He deposited the first mattress upstairs, then ran down for the next one.

"Is there a dormitory up there?" asked the driver.

"Something like that."

"Jesus! What the hell are you going to do with all these mattresses? Are you opening a hotel or what?"

"A brothel," said Ferit. "Why don't you pop in sometime?"

"Wow, are the girls beautiful?"

My God! thought Ferit, the idiot believed me. What if he gets drunk one night and comes knocking on the door!

"No, it was a joke. My whole family is coming to stay with me."

"Where from?"

"Come on, be a sport, give me a hand with this one," Ferit answered. He immediately started whistling a popular French tune.

The man decided to call it a day after carrying just one mattress. Ferit paid him, and lifted another mattress that he had rested by the door.

"Come on, man," he said to himself, "if old porters back home can carry three times the weight of these without batting an eyelid, surely you can do it." When he got to the top of the stairs, he nearly collapsed, but hearing the sound of the telephone ring inside, he pulled himself together.

Evelyn sounded cross. "What do you mean you're renting the apartment? What's that all about?"

"Please understand, my darling. You know we need to get some money together for our tickets, and my salary just isn't enough. So I decided to rent out the apartment."

"Without asking me?"

"There was no time for that. In any case, hadn't we agreed that we needed to save some money for our journey and the baby?"

"I thought that we decided that I would get a job."

"I don't want you to work. You're pregnant; you shouldn't tire yourself. Furthermore, the train we want to get on is leaving pretty soon."

"I still say we should have made this decision together. You should have at least asked me first."

"You're forgetting that I'm Turkish, Evelyn. We make our decisions without consulting our wives. What can I do? I can't help behaving like a Turk sometimes."

"Don't try to get around me by turning it into a joke, Ferit."

"Please believe me, honey, there was no time. Not only were you not here, but you were also too far away in the country. I had to make a quick decision and I did!"

"I hope you realize how ridiculous this is. Where are we going to stay? What are we supposed to do now?"

"You'll simply carry on staying with your friend in the country and I'll have to appeal to Muhlis and stay with him. Or I might stay with that teacher friend of mine."

"So we'll have to live separately, is that it?"

"Evelyn, how many more times must I tell you? I couldn't miss this opportunity; we really need the money! We'll be going to Istanbul together within a fortnight or so, and we'll never have to part again. I thought it was a good idea to earn some money from the apartment, that's all."

"I've never heard anything so ridiculous in my whole life, my husband renting out our home without even asking me. He packs me off to a friend and expects me to stay away for God knows how long."

"Weren't you the one not being straight with me because you were scared I'd be angry? Telling me how ill your friend was and how you needed to be with her until she got better? Here you are—you can stay with her now, can't you?"

"You're really something! Why didn't you tell me you knew? You're damned selfish when it suits you!"

"I pretended not to understand only because I knew I'd miss you. I didn't want you to stay away that long."

"So what's changed? Won't you miss me now?"

"Your crafty husband has found an idiot who's willing to pay a good sum of money for the apartment and he grabbed it because he's desperate. All he wants you to do now is be reasonable. It won't be too long. Tell you what, if the local trains are running tomorrow, I'll join you when I finish work, and we can spend the weekend talking this whole thing over again. How's that? I promise to make this up to you, my darling."

Ferit put the receiver down and took a deep breath. "Wow! I never imagined persuading Evelyn would be so much more difficult than carrying mattresses up three flights of stairs!"

He walked through the sitting room that he'd turned into a dormitory, went into the kitchen, and made himself a cup of coffee. He had stocked up with plenty of bread, cheese, and pasta in the pantry. Now he was ready for his guests to arrive. With his cup of coffee, he walked back into the sitting room. He wasn't too happy about the way he'd arranged things: it was no longer a sitting room, for a start. Six mattresses were spread out on the floor, and there was another where the dining table used to be. Another three or four people could possibly sleep on thin mattresses scattered around. He had managed to squeeze a camp bed in his own bedroom, and that meant maybe four people could sleep in there. Selva and her family could use the small bedroom and he could use the settee.

Ferit should go see Evelyn over the weekend at whatever cost. If he didn't, she might take it upon herself to visit him, and then she'd see what he had done. But then, hadn't he told her he would be staying with Muhlis? If she wanted to come to Paris, he could ask her to come straight to Muhlis's home. To prevent her from coming to the apartment, he should take all of Evelyn's belongings to her this weekend. Furthermore, he could arrange for a real estate agent to rent the apartment after they'd left Paris. Maybe he should indeed move to Muhlis's, to leave room for another person on the settee. He realized he should really be speaking to Tarık about all this. Strange, he thought, that he had chosen to confide in Tarık rather than Muhlis, who had been his friend for the past forty years.

Ferit's guests were to arrive from all over occupied France. The Germans were rounding up the Jews and bringing them to Paris before shipping them off to labor camps in Germany. The Resistance was doing much the same thing, except they shipped them off from Paris to friendly neutral countries. Those desperate people who managed to get away from their homes or places of work were gathered in the French supporters' homes or in hotels before going to the neutral countries.

No one knew yet that the German camps were death traps, that people there were being turned into soap or paper or used as guinea pigs.

Meanwhile, there were ninety-seven Turkish Jews waiting in Paris to board the train organized by the Turkish government in Ankara. They waited in fear in various homes and hotels, waiting to continue their journey. Some did not even have any ties with Turkey, which meant they had no Turkish passports or travel documents. All they had—crammed into the accommodations provided for them—was hope. Nevertheless, Ferit didn't doubt that they'd all be saved. He believed he might eventually persuade either Muhlis or Tarık to give in—if only they saw these people's faces, or the yellow badges these poor souls were forced to wear on their chests, symbols of their belief, as though they were the carriers of some dreadful disease; if only they could hear their stories of being separated from their families and children; if only…

When he heard the doorbell, Ferit ran to the window. He couldn't see anyone outside. Maybe the front door had been left open and the person had just come in. He could hear footsteps and voices coming up the stairs. He hastily walked into the hall, opened the door, and was surprised to see Tarık.

"They've arrived sooner than I expected," his friend said quietly. It was then that he saw the small group of people standing behind Tarık in the dark.

"No problem, please come in."

"I'll understand if you aren't…"

"No problem, everything is ready."

Tarık turned around to introduce the newcomers.

"This is Rafael Alfandari, his wife, Selva, little Fazıl…and these are Perla and Samuel."

The tall young woman standing with the little boy in her arms corrected him. "Peri and Sami."

"I thought you had only one son."

"They are my little friends; they aren't my children."

"I didn't know there were five of them either," said Tarık, smiling with embarrassment.

"It doesn't matter at all, please come in," said Ferit.

They came in through the door one by one. Tarık was taken aback by the state of the sitting room.

"What's all this? It looks like a makeshift hospital ward!"

"I'm expecting some other guests too."

"Where are we staying, in this room?" asked Rafael.

"No, you've got a room to yourselves, but I didn't know about your little friends," said Ferit.

"I'm very sorry," said Rafael. "I did try to explain to my wife that it might not be convenient with two extra people, but she wouldn't listen. I can go find a suitable hotel immediately. In fact, I remember seeing a Hotel Bonaparte that might suit us. Do you have a telephone directory so I can find the number?"

"I won't hear of it," said Ferit. "Besides, it's not prudent to be wandering the streets. Unless you need something luxurious, I'm sure that we can manage here."

"The children can stay anywhere," Selva said.

Samuel and Perla were standing by the door trying to understand the conversation, and when they recognized *çocuk*, the word for "child," they looked at each other in fear.

"Do the children speak Turkish?" asked Ferit.

"They're learning."

"Selva's teaching them," Rafael interjected.

"That's great!" said Ferit. "Right, let me show you your room so you can settle in. It's at the end of the hallway and the toilet is immediately opposite." Then, turning to the children, he spoke in French: "As for you two, I'm offering you the settee. I was going to sleep on it myself, but you're welcome to it even though it means sharing. I'll sort something else out for myself. What were your names again?"

"Samu...Saami," said the boy with the chestnut hair, "and she's my sister, Perree."

"Right, Sami and Peri, put your things in the chest of drawers. Leave your valuables and passports in the top drawer."

"We have no valuables," said Perla. She was hiding money given by her mother in a little sachet sewn into her pants and she had no intention of showing it to anyone.

"Ferit, who are these mattresses for?" asked Tarık.

"Those are people we're hoping to bring here to Paris from all over France. I'm expecting three more, but you never know, they might not arrive."

"Why not?"

"There is a possibility they may cross the mountains into Spain."

"What does Evelyn have to say about all this?"

"She doesn't know."

"What do you mean?"

"I'll explain later."

Rafael had joined them while Selva organized things and looked after their son.

"We're very indebted to you, Tarık," he said. "I'm sure you must have had a hand in getting me released."

Tarık was completely taken by Rafael's perfect Turkish that had no trace of an accent.

"Please don't mention it," he said, "I did nothing more than contact our embassies and ask them to intervene."

"You were also the one who told us about the train."

"There will be others on the train in a similar situation to yours," Ferit said. "In fact there are some who are in a worse situation than you. At least you are under the Turkish government's protection. Just think of all those who are French, German, even Italian. Young teenagers, men and women with children, the elderly…Hundreds and thousands of people who have never harmed anyone."

Tarık bowed his head.

"Many poor souls are gathering in Paris with just a thread of hope, a very thin thread. Either someone will have to turn a blind eye to their getting on the train…"

There was complete silence.

"Or?" asked Rafael.

"Someone is bound to turn a blind eye. I'm certain," said Ferit.

"I think so too," said Rafael. "They didn't deprive *them* of passports." Rafael pointed to the two children sitting side by side on the settee. "I'm sure no one could make excuses about saving people in their situation."

"Well, I'd better get back to my office," Tarık said. "I'm behind in my work. Apparently the Russos' son has been missing for days. We might have to check the labor camps until we find him. I won't bother Selva Hanım; she's busy now. Please say good-bye to her for me. I'll come and see you later after work."

Tarık walked out into the hall with Ferit, and Rafael heard them muttering to each other for quite some time.

"Ferit, I need to ask you for a favor," Tarık said, looking somewhat embarrassed.

"By all means, what is it?"

"If those people you mentioned earlier on don't arrive, would you mind if I sent you two people hoping to get on the train?"

"If you're in a spot, of course. I can move to your place, put the children in the kitchen, and offer them the settee. Would your two people be prepared to share the settee?"

"Of course. They're a young couple from Lyon. You might remember me telling you about a woman I saved from the Gestapo. They're her daughter and son-in-law."

"I think I do, but where are we going to put the woman herself?

"I understand she died," Tarık replied.

Ferit returned to the sitting room, and Selva was there.

"Fazıl was very tired, so I put him to bed," she said.

"Selva Hanım," Ferit said, "there's something I'd like to ask you. That's if you don't mind, of course. While you're here, would you—?"

He couldn't finish the question before Selva interrupted. "Yes, Ferit? You've been so kind to us, I'm more than happy to do anything in return. Do you want me to do the cleaning or the cooking, maybe?"

"No, no. As you can tell from the state of this place, I'm expecting more people to stay here."

"Yes, I see. I presume they're like us; they'll be waiting for the train."

"That's right, but they aren't Turkish. They don't speak Turkish, either."

"But I thought only those with Turkish passports could board the train."

"We'll be providing them with passports. But if something should happen en route, they'll have to act as if they are Turkish. They should at least be able to say a few words. You teach Turkish. Would you…?"

"You want me to teach them Turkish, is that it?"

"Would you?"

"Happily. As a matter of fact, I've been doing it in Marseilles for some time. I can help them memorize a few sentences. But I need to ask you a question—what do you mean, 'act as if they are Turkish'? I'm curious to know how one's supposed to act Turkish."

"Hmm…well, for instance, Turks drink a lot of tea and they don't put milk in it. Then there are their special ablutions. Some carry worry beads. They eat cheese and olives for breakfast. We might give some of them copies of the Koran to pretend they're reading it."

Selva laughed. "I could cook some köfte and dolmas, and they could take them on the train."

"That's great. If you cook Turkish dishes, why don't you cook some for us to eat here one evening?"

"Actually, I learned to cook in Paris after Rafo and I were married," said Selva. "I'm not good at it. My parents shouldn't have bothered to make me take piano, violin, and language lessons. They wanted me to find a good husband, but husbands prefer wives who are good cooks. Isn't that right, Rafo?"

"That's not how I look at it. I wanted to find a soul mate."

"And did you succeed?" asked Ferit.

"I was looking for a soul mate, but I ended up with a comrade in arms," said Rafo. "Selva thinks she's a soldier. She's taken it upon herself to save the world single-handedly."

"Let's be partners, Selva," said Ferit. "Why don't we save those around us here in Paris first, then we can try to save the rest of the world?"

"That's the best offer I've had in a long time," said Selva. She wanted to say that it was the best offer she had had since Rafo proposed to her. Then she remembered that Rafo hadn't proposed; it was she who had told him she'd decided to marry him. She turned around and looked at her husband, who was talking to the children. Rafo had lost a lot of weight since the time he was shoved into that cattle wagon. He couldn't sleep at night and had frequent nightmares that caused him to wake up and jump out of his bed.

She wondered if Rafo really loved her, if he considered her a blessing or a pain in the neck. Had he any regrets about marrying her? Did he blame her for being cut off from his family and country? Could it be that he was angry deep inside?

Selva decided then and there that if they eventually got back to Istanbul, she would have a tête-à-tête with her mother-in-law and beg her to forgive her son. She was determined to restore his family to him—his mother, sister, and cousins.

Oh, my dear Rafo, she thought to herself. I wonder if you love me as much as I love you.

DARKNESS AT NOON

David Russo got out of bed feeling great. He stood in front of the window and stretched for a long time. The new year was approaching. Paris! Ah, Paris! This magnificent city of art, music, fun, and feast. What could be more exciting for a young man just turned twenty than to look forward to celebrating the New Year in this city! He had a natural sense of fun, having been born in Beyoğlu, the bustling, colorful quarter of Istanbul.

Young Russo had always considered himself very lucky. He was the son of a wealthy family, and had enjoyed a very privileged upbringing. Soon after he had finished the French Saint Benoit secondary school, he moved to Paris with his family. His father had purchased a beautiful luxury apartment in the Fourteenth *Arrondissement*, one of the most elegant districts of Paris, and David continued his education at the lycée. To tell the truth, it took him rather a long time to finish. As every young man brought up in such circumstances will tell you, there is a lot of fun to be had during one's student years. The best way to avoid military service, or getting married, with the responsibilities that involves, is to prolong one's education as long as possible.

David's time at the lycée had lasted a long time, especially as he had transferred from Istanbul, but he never complained. From the lycée he went on to the Académie des Beaux-Arts. He was a tall, good-looking young man, which together with the melancholic look in his eyes enabled him to have all the fun that went with being an artist. But the war broke out. His dreams of beautiful models lining up to be painted naked would have to wait for a while. He didn't care. His life continued to be full of fun. His father never deprived him of the money he needed, and he didn't keep that from the chorus girls. He and his young friends went out on the town, turning Paris upside down every night. They carried on, visiting the cancan shows, drinking beer in bistros and wine in the street cafés. David made sure to avoid the "in" places frequented by the German officers. He felt safe having a Turkish passport, even if it did have *Juif* ("Jew") stamped on the first page in red.

Both David and his mother were rather apprehensive when his father insisted on taking all their passports and identity cards to the police station to be stamped.

"What's the hurry?" they had demanded.

"Is there something wrong with your eyes and ears?" Mr. Russo replied. "For days now they have been announcing that Jews must have their identification papers stamped. The newspapers are full of warnings!"

"Yes, but how would they know?" his wife had asked. "Vitali hasn't done it."

"I like to have everything in perfect order. I don't want to be in a position to have to explain anything to anyone."

"I just hope you won't regret it, that's all."

"I don't understand why you are arguing with me. For God's sake, it's only a stamp."

And that was how David ended up having a red stamp in his passport.

Now, on this cool, sunny December morning, father and son were sipping their coffee at the breakfast table.

"Are you going to the Champs-Elysées again today?" his father asked.

"Yes, I'm meeting up with my friends."

"This war has turned you all into good-for-nothings. Have you nothing else to do but visit cinemas?"

"What else do you expect us to do?"

"How about coming to work with me?"

"After the new year, Dad! Let's just see out the end of this dreadful year."

"I wonder what year isn't bad for you. I have a feeling you'll go through life just waiting for a good one. As for this war, I don't think it will end very soon. I think you and your friends are looking for an excuse to be idle."

"None of us thinks that it would be wise to start our own business in the present circumstances, Dad."

"But you do feel it's all right to wander around in the bars until the early hours of the morning?"

"We're war kids, Dad," said David. "We're just not a good crop."

"I'm afraid I have to agree. The war appears to have affected you all badly. If you feel inclined to keep gallivanting around because you are a 'war kid,' as you put it, then please at least make sure you have your identity card with you all the time. Apparently the other day our neighbor got into serious trouble because he didn't have it with him."

"Don't worry, Dad. I'll do that."

"In fact, I think it's best if you carry your Turkish passport too."

After breakfast, David read the newspapers and did a few sketches. Today, he and his friends would finally decide where they would be spending New Year's Eve. Here they were, seeing in yet another new year despite the war. For young people like them, life still had a lot of good things to offer. The Champs-Elysées was lit up in all its glory. For some time now, the shops had been decorated for Christmas. Colorful lights were strung up on all the boulevards so they looked just like bridges. It seemed as though the war hadn't touched Paris at all. The rest of Europe was in flames, but Paris was one giant Christmas tree. The streets were full of smart gentlemen in black cashmere coats and white silk scarves. German officers ogled the elegant women drenched in perfume, highly made-up chorus girls, and flirtatious whores wearing bright-red lipstick. David too was having his fair share of fun watching these women parade around.

They decided they would probably spend New Year's Eve at La Coupole or Café de Flore, frequented mainly by artists. David decided he would call Stella and invite her to join him that night. He would kiss her on New Year's Eve. Yes, he would kiss her on the lips. Surely she wouldn't push him away on a night when everyone around them would be kissing each other and celebrating the arrival of the new year! You never know, after walking hand in hand through the crowded streets and kissing each other and going to Les Halles for hot soup, he might even persuade Stella to go to his friend Manuel's bachelor pad. Who knows? Maybe…No, no, there was no need to rush things. Surely the time for that would come later!

David was whistling "Mon légionnaire" while dressing. As usual he put his wallet in the inside pocket of his jacket. Just as he was putting on his overcoat, he remembered his father's advice over breakfast that morning. He went back to his room, took his passport from the drawer, and walked to the front door.

"Will you be late?" his mother called out. "Will you be home for dinner?"

"No, Mum, don't worry about me, I don't think I'll be back before midnight."

"Really, David! It's not the weekend, is it? Give yourself a break for God's sake! You're out every night."

David didn't reply. He was twenty, full of youthful energy, and he was in Paris. He closed the door behind him and ran down the stairs, two and three at a time, out through the main door, where he took a joyful, deep breath. His nagging parents were left behind. Paris, the world's most beautiful, lively, sparkling city was dangling her mysteries before him.

When he got off the Métro at the Marbeuf station, he realized he was a bit late. His friend would be annoyed—this wasn't the first time. So he started to run and push his way through the crowd. But it was rather odd: instead of everyone walking out of the station, they were piling against each other at the exit. He got annoyed, pushing his way past a few people.

Oh dear! These old people taking their time, thinking for an hour before they move! Why don't you stay at home if you can't walk, he thought to himself.

He squeezed between an old couple shuffling in front of him and reached the bottom of the stairs. The congestion continued all the way up the stairs—a long, slow-moving line. He decided that New Year's shopping must have started early this year. The Parisians couldn't care less about the war; life went on, and so did the shopping.

"Why's this crowd not moving? We haven't got all day!" yelled a man in front of him.

David jumped up to try to see what was going on. My, my, my, what's happening? he thought when he saw two rows of German soldiers outside the Métro exit. They seemed to be checking the men's identity papers and asking some to step aside. The women were allowed to pass through without stopping. It was a good thing he had his passport with him. Just as well he had listened to the old man—he obviously knew what he was talking about. David checked his inside pocket; thank God the passport was still there. He followed everybody else as the line inched slowly forward.

Five men showed their identity cards and passed through. They pulled the sixth one aside; seven, eight more people went through… Someone near the front of the line turned back. A shrill whistle was heard, and the man ran a few steps.

"Halt! Halt!"

He stopped, his face turning white as he returned to his place. One of the soldiers beckoned him with his finger; he walked toward him with slumped shoulders. Oh! If only shoulders could talk. For the first time in his life, David realized how much one's shoulders could say. "I'm helpless, help me," they screamed. Then another man was lined up against the wall. Three, four, five more people went through.

David was late, but so what? He certainly had a tale to tell his waiting friends, and what a tale! He'd be the hero of the day. He would be able to tell Stella all about it on New Year's Eve. He wouldn't be bored stiff thinking of what to talk about. "I was almost carried away out of the Métro. If I hadn't had my identity papers with me, I'd be in a labor camp now. Just imagine, Stella!" Great!

"Identity cards!" said a brusque German soldier.

David showed his passport, which he was holding in his hand. Thank God! The ordeal was about to end. The German opened the passport. He looked at the photograph, read the name and surname, the date and place of birth, and saw the red stamp: JEW.

"Stand against the wall."

"But I'm Turkish."

"I said against the wall."

He did as he was told and waited with the others in silence. A soldier came over and separated them into groups of eight.

"Move!"

One of them attempted to say something. "Shut your mouth!" the soldier said.

They were made to get into a gray vehicle. David looked at the young man who was about his age. He sat next to him and was shaking. This young man, who David would later find out was called Lambroso, wrote the word *Jewish* with his fingers on his coat. David nodded yes.

They stopped by a bus. They all got out and were crammed into it. Soon, more vehicles drew up; even more people were shoved into the already packed bus, which then set off on its way. After a while David tried to guess what direction they were going. Everyone was so squashed together, it was difficult to see outside.

After some distance the bus entered a courtyard and stopped. On entering a long building, they realized they were at the École Militaire. They were made to sit on the floor of the corridor. They were afraid to speak to each other. Those who tried to ask the soldiers questions were told off. They sat on the stone floor and waited… and waited…and waited. The light that filtered through the rooms opening onto the corridors faded; then they were surrounded by darkness. It was night.

"Get up! Move!"

Groups of people were herded out of the various buildings, and crammed into five buses that eventually pulled away.

At the Gare du Nord station, they all got off again and were made to walk to the end of the platform. Soldiers swarmed like ants. There, they were made to board a train. After a journey of about two hours, the train stopped and the soldiers made them form columns five deep.

"March, march!"

They marched off in the bitter, cold December rain, hungry and exhausted. There were nearly a thousand males between the ages of twelve and eighty-two. Their sense of fear had gone, replaced by some anonymous feeling. David realized later that it was a feeling of resignation to death.

After an endless march, a very long column entered a camp. Then the men were separated into groups of thirty and allocated huts with floors that were covered in straw. They had been on their feet for so long that they immediately collapsed on the straw, leaning against each other and trying to get warm from each other's breath and body heat. They would be sleeping on the floor like animals for a whole week before their bunks arrived.

At five in the morning, they were awakened and asked to wait in the corridor. There they remained standing for three and a half hours in the freezing cold, waiting to be counted.

"Line up in threes!"

"Line up single file!"

They did. Then they moved toward a soldier sitting behind a table in a large hall.

"Name?"

"David Russo."

"I'll give you four very precious items. Make sure you don't lose them. Here you are! A tin bowl, a spoon, a blanket, and your number. Take them!"

David took them.

"Read your number."

"Three-two-three-three."

"From now on you'll be known as 3233. That's your name. You're better off dead if you lose that number. Understood?"

"Understood."

"Now sign here, here, here, and here."

David signed. He signed for the bowl, the spoon, the blanket, and the number 3233. He was no longer David Russo. Neither his friends at the Café Clossier on the Champs-Elysées nor his mother and father were waiting for him. There was no David Russo. Having signed, David Russo was finished. He was only 3233, a number. A tall, pale-faced tin number with no future.

Someone shouted an order, and he realized it was noon.

"Line up! Single file!"

They walked and stopped in front of a soup cauldron. They were given one ladle of soup each and drank it with their iron spoons. After they finished they put the spoons inside their jackets and pockets so as not to lose them. Then they were gathered outside in the courtyard, in lines of five, and made to walk around. They were forbidden to speak, except to the person next to them. Only two could speak to each other, never three!

"Why are we here? What's our crime?"

"Being Jewish."

"Won't we be saved?"

"I don't think so."

"Surely our families will try to track us down…"

"Hey! You over there! Shut up!"

They continued walking around and around the courtyard, like donkeys on a treadmill. Their hands, feet, and bottoms froze as they walked. Returning to their straw-filled hut, they tried to get warm huddling together. In the evening they again walked in rows to the canteen. This time black bread was added to the menu. A soldier put a loaf of bread on a big wooden table and selected someone to cut the loaf into perfect squares using a template. Then the soldiers started distributing the two-hundred-gram pieces to each of the numbers. Numbers—they were no longer human beings. They ate their slices of stale black bread to the very last crumb, licking and swallowing every bit. Then they lined up in front of the door to the stinking toilet, waiting to relieve themselves, before returning to their hut to collapse into sleep on the straw.

The soldier who locked them in shouted in French with a German accent, "No more talking, you motherfuckers!"

The following morning, after standing for three hours, waiting to be counted, after breakfast, which consisted of coffee in their tin bowls, they were sent out into the courtyard, where bales of barbed wire were stacked against the walls. Now they had a job to do. They were to unravel the barbed wire and carry it to an allocated place. David was pleased that he had something to do instead of pacing around the courtyard. How many days ago was it that he had told his father he wasn't in the mood to work? He didn't know, because he no longer had any notion of time. What would his old man say if he saw him unraveling barbed wire with bleeding hands? Old man! He would never get old. He'd never have children who called him their "old man." He—that is, Robert David Russo—was merely 3233 now, a number who was expected to carry barbed wire. He tried to feel sorry for himself and cry, but he couldn't.

After about a week, the bunk beds with straw-filled mattresses arrived at the huts. One of the guys carrying in the bedding said, "Phew! This place stinks!"

Some of the numbers looked at each other; they hadn't changed their clothes since the day they'd arrived. Sleeping and working in these same clothes, they had lost all sense of smell.

Fifteen days later, a new instruction relieved the monotony of their existence. After the morning coffee, before going out to move barbed wire, they were made to walk in lines of five down a new corridor they hadn't seen before and into another hall.

"Strip down!"

No one moved.

"Strip down, I tell you!"

They were baffled, but looking at each other, they started stripping down to their underpants.

"Take your underwear off too!"

"My God!" said an old man.

"What have you got to hide, you decrepit old man," said a soldier.

They removed their underpants as well, held the bundles of clothes in front of themselves, trying to cover their embarrassment while waiting and waiting. A couple who couldn't cope standing in the cold fainted and fell to the floor.

"Single file!"

They lined up, and the soldier holding a stick in his hand checked them individually for lice. Another threw their clothes into a steam machine, then immediately took them out. Then they were sent into a large room with lines of showers hanging from the ceiling. They showered, shivering under the ice-cold water. When they got out of the shower room, they were given back their damp clothes from the steam machine and sent back to carrying barbed wire.

Time went by, day after day. Some left when their numbers were called, never to be seen again. Some older men became ill and were taken away. They knew which people died when their straw mattresses were rolled up and removed, but they never found out what happened to those young men whose numbers were called and who never came back.

One morning, after the torture of waiting to be counted and having drunk coffee from their tin bowls, the men saw a soldier walk in.

"Three-two-three-three!" he shouted. No one moved.

"I said 3233, you fuckers."

That's me, thought David. I'm 3233. What should I do now? He took one step forward.

"So you're 3233, are you?"

"Yes."

"Go to your hut; collect your bowl, spoon, blanket, and number; and come back here."

David walked to his hut, picked up his blanket from his bunk, and his bowl and spoon. His number was in his pocket anyway. Then he returned.

"Have you got everything?"

"I have."

"Move!"

David looked at his fellow prisoners still standing in line. Some bowed their heads and others winked good-bye.

"They'll probably shoot him," someone whispered.

David heard him but wasn't sorry. He was glad to be saved from this brown liquid called coffee, the soup worse than mud, the solid piece of brown bread, and shifting the barbed wire. No more missing home while lying on his straw mattress, feeling desperate that he would dic without kissing Stella, being stripped of his dignity and relegated to just a number. He followed the soldier. They walked into a small office. The civilian man sitting at the head of the table had a huge book that looked like a tax registry in front of him.

"Your number?" asked the man.

"Three-two-three-three."

The man opened the book. "Look for your name on this page!"

His name! David remembered he had a name. But what was it?

He bent forward, looking at the book. Everything was blurred. The letters were dancing all over the page. He rubbed his eyes and looked again, carefully. First he saw his number, 3233. His name was written beside it. He pointed at it.

"Did you find it?"

"Yes."

"Read it!"

"Robert David Russo."

"Leave your things behind."

David looked at him blankly.

"Why are you looking like that? Put everything—your bowl, spoon, blanket, and number—on the table."

David carefully placed his bowl, spoon, and blanket on the table, then he put his number on the blanket. The man checked the items as if they were precious jewels, then he asked David to sign for each one.

"Where am I going?" asked David.

"To hell!" the man answered.

"May I speak to my family one last time before I die?"

The man smiled.

"Or would it be possible to send them a message?"

"What about?"

"That I'll be put before a firing squad."

"Is that what you think?"

"If I'm not allowed to speak to them, if I give you a telephone number, would you kindly tell them what's happened? I'm sure they'd rather know than just be wondering."

"Know what?"

"That I'm dead."

The man smiled mockingly. Nasty dog, thought David.

The soldier who'd escorted David ordered him to move again, and David followed him outside the building. They crossed the courtyard and entered the gate of another building with the German flag and a swastika hanging outside. Inside, they walked up some stairs, and along a corridor.

"You wait here," the soldier said before entering a room. David collapsed on a bench by the door. He even thought of stretching out on it. He presumed he could do anything now that he was going to his death. For instance, he could spit in the face of his escort or the officer passing by. He could swear at them or even unbutton his trousers and pee all over the place. What difference would it make? He thought all this, but did nothing; the fresh air was making him feel extremely lethargic. It was as though he had no energy for anything except unraveling and carrying barbed wire, as though this were the duty given to him at the gates of hell, the only thing he would ever be able to do.

The soldier returned with a file in his hand. "Move!" he said again. David tried to get up from the bench but realized that he didn't have the strength.

"Move!"

He tried again, dragging his feet, and managed to follow the soldier. Had he not been ashamed, he would have crawled. They went back down the stairs, out of the courtyard, and into the street, finally entering a garden full of chrysanthemums. David saw an elegant villa in front of him.

David, he thought, you're a dead man, you're just not aware of it! That street…this beautiful garden…these flowers…this villa… surely it can't be true…I must be dead. I am dead. Thank God. I didn't feel a thing. I'm saved. Finally, I'm saved. Hooray, death!

A guard saluted the soldier as he passed. David saluted back, bowing almost to the ground. The guard looked in amazement, waving back. The soldier led David up the steps to the villa and into a marble hall with fantastic paintings on the walls. David kept expecting a houri to appear from one of the rooms. He wished her eyes would be like Stella's and her voice would be like his mother's. True, there were no houris or angels waiting for Jews in heaven, but he had heard that Muslim men were supposed to be greeted by pretty young virgins called houris. He had died carrying a Turkish passport…He smiled to himself. He wasn't in the mood for pretty girls right now, but he desperately needed to see someone he knew, a friendly face, someone to remind him of his past. That's why he wished the houri would look like Stella. As for his mother's voice, it had never occurred to him, even in his wildest dreams, that he would miss his mother's voice. All he wanted was to hear his mother saying, "My son, my lovely son," and to be able to respond, "Mother, I missed you so, Mother!"

"Take this and go into that room. I'll be waiting here," the soldier said, handing over the file. David took it and went into the room, which was furnished with expensive furniture. A man was sitting behind a Louis XIV desk.

"Can you find your name in this notebook?" asked the man.

Can you! Yes, he was dead all right; he was going to heaven. David approached and looked at the notebook. His vision didn't blur this time and he found his name.

"Here…my name's here."

"Sign next to your name."

He signed.

"Here you are, this is for Auschwitz, and this is your ticket to Paris."

"Pardon?"

"Your exit certificate and your train ticket. You're free to go. Good-bye."

"Where am I going to? Do you mean I'm going home?"

"What sort of imbecile are you?" The man saluted like a soldier and pointed to the door. "Straight to Paris," he said with a bad French accent, "and when you get there, make sure you get down on your knees and kiss the hand of the Turkish consul!"

David left the room and followed the soldier who had been waiting outside down the stairs, out of the villa, through the chrysanthemums, to the gate. No, he wasn't dead; he was being set free. What is freedom? he wondered. The soldier went into the guards' hut, said something to them, and one of the guards opened the gate.

David walked out.

He had weighed sixty-five kilos when he arrived at the camp two months earlier. Now he only weighed forty-seven. He looked like a skeleton or a ghost walking between the bare chestnut trees. He felt nothing, neither happy nor hungry. He wasn't excited; he had no expectations. It was as though he was just drifting toward the station where the train would take him home. Who was he? What of his heart…what of his whole being? All he was now was a wretched number and old, very old, even older than his father, whom he referred to as "the old man." He was now 3,233 years old.

PARIS

Selva had begun to like some of the people she taught very much, and Margot was one of them. She and Selva had become very close. Maybe because Margot was Hungarian, she had been able to pick up the Turkish language more easily than the others.

One day she said in Turkish, "I have Turkish friend."

"Yes, of course you're my friend," Selva responded sincerely, putting her arms around her. Margot smiled, a little startled.

After Margot had been dismissed from her job, she'd started to visit Ferit's apartment very often, trying to help Selva. While Selva was teaching, she'd look after Fazıl. She'd take him out for fresh air and also help with the shopping.

When Selva asked, "Didn't you at least ask why they sacked you so suddenly?" Margot had replied, "I thought it better not to ask too many questions. What could I have said if they told me it was because I'm Jewish?"

She was one of those people who had decided if they couldn't take refuge in Paris, it was better to go to Palestine via Turkey.

"You never know, you might like Istanbul enough to settle there for good," Selva had said. "We might even find you a handsome Turk."

"Turks don't fancy me."

"I don't believe that, Margot! Turks are mad about blondes."

She contented herself with just a smile, murmuring, "If only..."

Because of the close friendship that had developed between them, Selva had asked Margot to help her. They were to stick photographs in passports brought home by Ferit, write Turkish names inside, and have them ready by lunchtime.

Selva and Ferit had tried to think of new names that were as similar as possible to their own. Roxanne had become Rüksan, Constance became Kezban, David, Davut, Lillian, Leyla and Marie, Meryem. But Selva had difficulty finding a name for Margot.

When Margot arrived that morning, Selva asked her in French, "Margot, would you like to be Meral?"

"Aren't there other names beginning with *M*?"

"Let me see now, there's Makbule, Madelet, Mergube, Mehire..."

"Why don't you choose one for me?"

"I think Meral's the best. It's a young person's name."

"What do you mean?"

"Well, it's modern."

"I've heard of names being fashionable, but modern?" Margot said.

"I assure you, Margot, there'll be many more surprises in store for you once you've reached Turkey," Selva replied. "I promise you, you'll be surprised by things every day. My country is very different."

"Oh!" Margot said with a sigh. How wonderful it would be, she thought, to be able to return to my own country as easily as this woman can.

They spread the passports out over the work surfaces in the kitchen. Selva was sticking the photographs on and Margot was pressing them hard with a heavy iron. Most of the passports had been issued by the Turkish government to students. They were now removing the original photos and replacing them with those of the Jews. Those over a certain age had to use other passports provided by the Organization.

Ferit had asked them to have them ready by his lunch break so he could collect them and have them stamped. When the doorbell rang, Margot ran to open it, thinking Ferit had arrived. The voice Selva heard from the kitchen was familiar.

"What on earth are you doing here?"

"Excuse me, I should be asking you the same question!"

"I need an explanation immediately."

"How dare you speak to me in that tone of voice."

Selva rushed to the hallway when she realized that the voices were getting harsher. Both Tarık and Margot were looking daggers at each other. They were baffled and taken aback.

"Tarık! I thought it was Ferit at the door. Please come in."

Tarık held Selva by the arm and dragged her into the kitchen. He closed the door and spoke in Turkish.

"Selva, do you know this woman? Who on earth asked her to come here?"

"Tarık, she's Margot…my friend."

"I know who she is, but where did you meet her?"

"Here."

"What do you mean here?"

"Ferit brought her here so she could learn Turkish along with the others. She'll be getting on the same train."

"My God! Do you realize what you are doing?"

"Of course I do."

"Listen to me, Selva. That woman could easily be a spy."

"You must be joking. She's Jewish, a Hungarian Jew."

They heard the kitchen-door handle move. Margot was knocking on the door, and Tarık stopped talking. The door opened.

"Monsieur Tarık," Margot said in a soft voice, "you're very wrong about me. Admittedly I'm to blame because I misled you. I owe you an apology. I hope you understand that we all live in fear. How could I have told you that I am Jewish?"

"You should have told me outright, Margot. You know that we're doing our best to be helpful."

"I tried to wheedle it out of you. I tried every way I could to find out if you would give me a passport, but you slammed every door in my face. I ended up thinking that you must have realized I was Jewish and simply wanted to wash your hands of me."

"You couldn't have been more wrong."

"But you never called me again."

"I thought totally different things. I've only just found out that you are Jewish. Muhlis said nothing to me."

"Muhlis doesn't know. Nobody does. All of us are obliged to hide even our identity cards so we can keep our jobs."

"How did you find this place?" Tarık asked.

"Monsieur Ferit brought me here."

"Where did you meet him?"

"He's a friend of my cousin's."

"Tarık, have you and Margot already met?" asked Selva.

"Yes, but I have to admit I was totally surprised to see her here," Tarık replied, and then in Turkish he asked if the passports were ready.

"Yes, they're ready."

"I've brought you some christening certificates. I thought you might be able to put them to good use too."

"Excuse me, I don't quite understand," said Selva.

"Monsignor Angelo Roncalli, who's the Vatican representative in Istanbul, sent us some fake christening certificates. If you don't have enough passports, maybe we can use these, especially for the children."

"Where did they come from?"

"I just told you, from Istanbul."

Margot and Selva looked baffled.

"You mean a man of the cloth is trying to help the Jews?" Margot asked.

"He's a truly God-fearing man; why not? Aren't we all God's children?" Selva remarked.

"I'll leave these with you," said Tarık, handing over the certificates. "Let me have the passports that are ready."

"But Ferit was supposed to collect them."

"Selva, we need to stamp them anyway. Let me have them so I can get going. Apparently, Ferit can't come until this evening," said Tarık.

So, Selva thought, obviously Ferit's endless talks with Tarık have come to fruition. Hasn't Ferit said Tarık is the most kindhearted man in the world?

Margot put the passports in a cotton bag with a stale loaf of bread sticking out a bit.

When Tarık saw what she was doing, he said, "Don't worry, I have diplomatic immunity."

"Yes, of course. Don't forget, I owe you a coffee," said Margot. "You bought me a bottle of wonderful wine, Monsieur Tarık. The least I can do before leaving Paris is to offer you a cup of coffee."

"We'll do that, at the first opportunity," said Tarık, feeling rather awkward. As he rushed down the stairs with the bag in his hand, a group of about eight or ten boys and girls were climbing up.

Later, Selva looked at the youngsters one by one. They were sitting on the beds, the chairs, and the floor. She had eventually gotten to know them rather well and started calling them by their new names. The students, who were of different ages, had learned their names by now. The girls had their initials stitched on the front of their sweaters and the boys had done the same on their shirt pockets.

They had been coming to Ferit's apartment in groups of fifteen, at fixed times. Selva had been able to teach them all the numbers up to a thousand, the days and months, and some basic conversation. In case background information should be needed, she had taken great pains to make up stories that would suit them. For instance, if any strangers sat with them in the same train compartment, some young ones would say they had been studying, others would say they'd been undergoing medical treatment, a few older people would say they had been visiting their children, and others would simply pretend not to understand. All of them, whether old, young, or middle-aged, were afraid.

On one occasion, Selva tried to reassure them. "Why are you so scared? The Germans don't understand Turkish anyway; how would they be able to spot your mistakes? If necessary, just carry on making Turkish sounds and you'll be OK."

"But what if someone among them speaks Turkish?"

"Even if that happens, they won't be able to speak as much as you. They might know just a few words. You'll just have to do your best to learn as many sentences as you can."

Selva knew that the countdown to the day of the train's departure had started, even though Tarık hadn't given precise details yet. He had just said, "The carriage is on its way."

"Where's it coming from?"

"From Ankara."

"You mean the train."

"No, the carriage. It is a big car that they've linked on to a train leaving for Europe…"

"When will it get here?"

"Is it possible to say during the war? With a bit of luck, and if there are no problems, it should be here within a fortnight."

"In that case, we should tell everybody."

"No, for God's sake, no! We should only tell them the day before. If the information falls on the wrong ears, all our efforts could go down the drain," Tarık warned.

"What? But how will they manage to get ready?"

"Come on, Selva, they've been ready for ages. All they'll need to do when the carriage arrives is pick up their bags," Rafael said.

Tarık had started coming to the apartment more often. Sometimes, after everyone squeezed in the apartment was fed, Ferit would go out with Selva or Rafael and meet up with Tarık at a nearby café. The Alfandaris took turns staying behind to babysit. One of the new residents, Constance, renamed Kezban by Selva, had said time and time again that she was willing to look after Fazıl so the couple could go out together. Selva had declined the offers. She wasn't comfortable leaving Fazıl with someone she hardly knew. She felt Fazıl should always be with a person with whom he felt safe. But most of those coming and going to the apartment had become close friends by now, and they would soon be leaving Paris, so they decided to make the best of it. Even if they didn't go to the cinema or theater, they would sit in a café people watching. With Tarık and Margot, they enjoyed looking at the elegant women in their colorful clothes and fur stoles, swaying their hips, arm in arm with high-ranking German officers, or the young middle-class girls cycling, their ankle socks and high-heeled shoes going round and round. They had fun trying to imagine which woman was a spy, or which man in a leather jacket was a member of the Organization. They enjoyed making up scripts to suit the characters they picked out. When Margot joined them, Tarık stopped being his usual serious self, shook off his dullness, and managed to have fun.

One evening it was Rafael's turn to babysit, and Selva went out with Ferit and Tarık. While they were waiting for Margot to arrive at the Café des Artistes, Ferit took the opportunity to thank Tarık for the passports.

"I'm sure God will reward you for all your efforts," he said.

"Don't give me all the credit," Tarık replied. "I wouldn't have been able to have the passports stamped without the approval of my superiors."

"But I'm sure you're the one who persuaded them to do it. My sister wrote me so much about you. She told me what an exceptional man you are," Selva responded.

Tarık felt himself blushing. "I can assure you, Selva Hanım, that both our government and our foreign ministry are being extremely cooperative. I wouldn't have been able to do anything on my own."

Selva turned to Ferit. "As for you, Ferit, I must say no one can deny that what you're doing is incredible too. Would you mind if I asked you something?"

"Of course not."

"Why exactly *are* you doing all this? Especially when, as far as I know, your wife isn't even Jewish."

"What can I say, Selva? Perhaps I want to prove to myself that in the midst of all this horror, I'm still a human being."

"By risking your life?"

"After all is said and done, what is life anyway? Aren't we all going to die in the end? I believe life is only worth living if, while we are on this earth, we can do honorable things."

"I take my hat off to you, Ferit," Selva said with obvious admiration in her innocent wide eyes.

Margot was a little later than expected. Tarık took out his pocket watch to check the time. "Are you getting worried?" Selva asked mischievously.

"No…not really. I mean, yes, a bit. No one is completely safe these days."

"Do you know that I am trying to persuade Margot to stay in Istanbul?"

"Why's that?"

"Come on, Tarık, don't pretend you don't know why. I can see through you, I know what's going on in your heart. I understand matters of the heart very well."

"Maybe so, Selva, but you're forgetting that I'm a member of the Ministry of Foreign Affairs. I cannot marry a foreigner."

"I can't believe that. Why?"

"We're simply forbidden to marry foreigners."

"Even if that foreigner is prepared to adopt Turkish nationality?"

"Even then, unfortunately."

Selva bit her lip. "I didn't know that," she said sadly. "I find this incredible; it seems our country is finding excuses for separating people. They are kept apart, not only because of their religion, but also because of their nationality."

"Not only in our country, Selva," Tarık responded. "Discrimination is rife throughout the world. Just look at what's happening to Europe, despite her long history!"

Margot appeared from around the corner, walking hurriedly. She was wearing her red coat. Her blonde curls were bouncing from side to side. Selva bowed her head when she saw the spark light up in Tarık's eyes; her heart went out to him.

At the end of the evening, Ferit and Selva got up to return to Ferit's apartment. Tarık turned to Margot and said, "May I take you home?"

"Would you mind if we walked for a while? I'd like to get some fresh air."

"Why not? Certainly."

"And when we get home, you might like to come up for that cup of coffee you refused last time."

"I feel awful about that, Margot. How can you ever forgive me? I'm so sorry, but you must admit you did ask a hell of a lot of questions. I wish you had been more straightforward."

"That's all water under the bridge now."

"But we've wasted so much time," said Tarık. "Especially since time is so precious for both of us."

He squeezed Margot's hand and she snuggled up to him, like a kitten. They walked hand in hand along the brightly lit street.

The following morning, Tarık got annoyed when he saw Muhlis staring at him.

"What's up? Why are you looking at me like that?"

"You were late last night."

"True."

"In fact, very late. You got back in the early hours of the morning."

"So what?"

"Is there something you want to tell me?"

"Like what?"

"I don't know, but there must be something."

"All right then. I kissed her."

"Anything else?"

"Enough, Muhlis, you're going too far now. What's more, I know you've got tickets for the theater this evening. If you don't watch your step, you won't be leaving the office before seven…and I mean it!"

Tarık rose and picked up his jacket and his shirt with the lipstick on the collar, which he had thrown hastily on the sofa when he got home, and took them into his own room.

COUNTDOWN

"We need to choose a route for this carriage. With such a group of people on board, it needs to be a route that won't arouse any suspicions," Ferit said.

"For instance, there are a lot of identity checks being carried out, particularly on those passing through Switzerland because of her neutrality."

"In that case, the train should not go through Switzerland."

"I wonder if it would be safer to have the train go all the way down to Lyon and through Italy."

"Are you crazy? They'll be sitting ducks in Fascist Italy. They'll knock them off one by one. Mussolini's men are worse than the Nazis."

"Well, the train has to go through somewhere, doesn't it? It has to go through Switzerland, Italy, or Germany. There's no alternative!"

"Checks are being carried out everywhere, gentlemen. Some clerks arrived from Turkey only a week or so ago and they had to go through thorough checks at every border."

"On the other hand, apparently when Galip went to Istanbul, nobody bothered him."

"Which Galip? You mean our consul in Hamburg?"

"That's right."

"Yes, I hear there are no strict checks on trains within Germany, or even those leaving the country," Tarık said.

"I hope that you're not suggesting that we let those professors and scientists who are being particularly sought by the Germans take that route!"

"You're forgetting that these people are being hunted down in France, not in Germany!"

"For heaven's sake, give me a cigarette, Ferit. I've run out," said Tarık.

"Here you are." Hikmet Özdoğan passed a silver cigarette case across the table.

They had gathered in the apartment of Hikmet Özdoğan, the consul in Paris. Finally the countdown had begun. The train was on its way. It would have to be serviced in Paris, and would set off on its journey back immediately. It was possible that the Germans could commandeer any train at a moment's notice to transport their troops, so they shouldn't take the risk of the train staying in Paris for more than a day.

This group of diplomats had gathered together to decide on a route for the train's return journey. Hikmet Özdoğan felt uneasy about Ferit's presence, as he was a total stranger to him. It was Tarık who had insisted that Ferit should come to the meeting because of his association with the Organization. He had very good connections that could be useful to them.

The train would be carrying 176 passengers considered *personae non gratae* by the Germans. Half of the passengers would have Turkish passports even though they might not be Turkish citizens; they had Turkish connections, but didn't necessarily speak Turkish fluently. It was therefore decided that a Turkish national for whom Turkish was his mother tongue, and who could speak other languages too, should be on board. This person would be the leader of the group and could communicate with German officers, police, or inspectors en route if necessary.

After Ferit was thoroughly investigated in Turkey and the results vetted by the Turkish ambassadors in Berlin and Vichy, it was agreed he would join the group as leader.

Suddenly, Ferit exploded, "Eureka! Eureka! I've found the answer!" He jumped out of his seat and was giving Tarık, who was about to light a cigarette, sloppy kisses all over his cheeks.

"What have you found? What's happening? Are you crazy?"

"Yes, yes, I'm crazy. But it's thanks to you, Tarık, that I've come up with the solution to our problem. Eureka, my friends! The train must go through Germany."

"That's out of the question," said Hikmet Özdoğan. "We simply can't take that risk. If they're caught, don't forget that the carriage belongs to our government."

"Trust me, they won't be. They won't because even the devil himself wouldn't dare think of sending a carriage full of wanted Jews through the heart of Germany."

"Absolutely not!"

"But Hikmet, it's a brilliant idea! Only a genius could come up with such a scheme. Just think about it."

"What do you think, Tarık?" Hikmet Özdoğan asked, expecting support from his colleague. Tarık remained silent. "You see, Tarık disagrees too."

"Why not think about it, Hikmet? Let's sleep on it."

"We have no time to sleep on anything, gentlemen. We have to make a decision and act immediately. Don't forget that we also have to get permission from the countries on the way."

"Give me that map," said Ferit.

The map leaning on the sideboard was huge, not the sort one could pass around. They took a picture off the wall and hung the map in its place.

"Have you got something I could use as a pointer?"

Hikmet went into the kitchen and returned with a wooden spoon. Ferit took the spoon and started pointing at the routes.

"If we go to the south, we have to pass through Switzerland and then either Italy or Austria. The Germans will be carrying out their thorough checks either way. Alternatively, if we go all the way up to Berlin and have our documents stamped there, the route may be longer but once our passports have been stamped no one will bother to waste time checking us again. That's most important, isn't it?"

"So how are we supposed to go through Berlin?" asked Özdoğan.

"We can ask the Turkish embassy in Berlin to help. Our embassy official can come and meet us, collect the passports, have them stamped, and return them."

"And why would an embassy official take the trouble to do all this?"

"Because he'll receive instructions to do so; I'm sure our ambassador, Saffet, will be more than happy to do that," said Tarık.

"I wonder if we could get someone on the inside to help us," Ferit said.

"What do you mean? I don't follow."

"A German soldier, for instance, some decent, fair guy who might be willing to help. I don't really think all those Nazis are as devoted to the cause as everyone thinks."

"I'm sure some of them hate this Jewish animosity, but it might be too risky to try to find someone like that."

"If we know the exact day and time that the train is passing through, I might be able to fix something," said Ferit.

"I don't get it. Do you mean to tell me that you even have friends among the German soldiers?" Hikmet Özdoğan asked, looking at Ferit in amazement.

Tarık looked at his friend angrily. "Please don't meddle so dangerously. The only people of authority we can rely on are officials from our own embassy or consulate. We shouldn't seek cooperation from anybody else," he said.

"I totally agree with my colleague," said Hikmet.

Ferit had considered asking the Organization to assist, using its own people who were planted all over the place, but he decided not to persist with this line of argument. He was content simply to say, "I can see you're warming to the idea of traveling through Berlin and down from there."

Hikmet Özdoğan responded, "Ferit, my friend, we're not the ones in danger. If the real identities of some of the passengers are discovered, they'll be given hell. We have to be careful not to jeopardize their lives. Say we do manage to convince the authorities that the youngsters on board are Turkish students; what about the professors, doctors, and scientists that the Germans are really after? How are you going to get them through Berlin? Will they wear some sort of disguise or what?"

"Of course!" replied Ferit. "Do you think that it's hard to change people's identities? Those who are bald will be given wigs. Those with curly hair and mustaches will shave them off. Others can wear glasses, or dye their hair, and others might even pluck their eyebrows."

"This is turning into a circus carriage," said Hikmet Özdoğan.

"Hikmet, as we said before, let's sleep on it; we might see things more clearly in the morning," Tarık said in his calmest voice.

"Fine, but let's not dither. We've got to make the final decision tomorrow. The train should be arriving in a few days, and remember, we can't keep it waiting for more than one night."

"So, here again tomorrow after work?" asked Ferit.

"Unfortunately not," replied Hikmet. "My wife and daughter will be here tomorrow morning."

"My apartment is full to the brim," said Ferit. "There's no room to stand, let alone sit."

"And Muhlis will be in my apartment. He's got a general idea of what's going on, but since we're trying to keep this on a need-to-know basis, the fewer people that know any details, the better."

"What about meeting at the consulate then?"

"There'll be the night guard and the duty clerk."

"I know," said Tarık. "There's a friend of mine who's traveling on the train. She lives on her own. We can go to her apartment. She doesn't speak much Turkish anyway. I can ask her to go to the cinema or something."

"Is this friend Margot, by any chance?" Ferit whispered, leaning toward Tarık's ear.

"Yes."

"Killing two birds with one stone, eh?"

"I thought you were my friend!"

"I certainly am," said Ferit, "but I love teasing you."

"All the same, there are limits."

"What on earth are you whispering about?" asked Hikmet Özdoğan. "Is there something you're keeping from us?"

"No, not at all, Hikmet, we're just talking about our meeting place for tomorrow. I'll get in touch with my friend and let you all know," said Tarık. He took the map off the wall and rolled it up.

"I still say it will be dangerous for the train to pass through Berlin," Hikmet Özdoğan repeated.

"Something tells me the opposite. Mark my words, and don't forget my pregnant wife will be on board too. Would I want to put my wife and unborn child in danger?" replied Ferit.

"In any case, our ambassadors in Berlin and Vichy have the final word."

"Not necessarily. They're expecting us to weigh all the pros and cons and reach our own decision."

"Hikmet, the final decision carries a lot of responsibility. By the way, it's not prudent to discuss this over the telephone. I'm seriously thinking of going to Vichy early tomorrow morning. Why don't you come too?" asked Tarık.

"It's not right for both of us to be out of the consulate. You'd better go alone. I'll send a coded message to Saffet Arıkan in Berlin," Hikmet Özdoğan replied.

As they walked toward Tarık's car, Ferit asked, "Your colleague seems very apprehensive, doesn't he?"

"Not particularly. He's a very cautious man who wants to carry out his duties to the best of his abilities," replied Tarık. "Working for the government involves a lot of responsibility. You can't act on instinct or your own preference. One has to consider every minute detail carefully."

"God save me from any governmental job that might stifle my creativity!" said Ferit.

FAREWELL EVENING

When Margot returned from the cinema, the meeting in her apartment was over. Tarık was in the sitting room, sipping his wine. When he heard Margot's key in the door, he rushed to the kitchen and returned with another glass.

"So, how was the film? I hope you enjoyed it," he said, offering her a glass of wine.

"I saw two films, one after the other, so that I wouldn't disturb your meeting."

"Here's your reward for being such a good, understanding girl. I remember that you liked this wine very much when we first went out to dinner." He made a toast, raising his glass: "Bon voyage; may you have a comfortable journey, without any problems."

Margot took a sip, placed her glass on the table, and put her arms around Tarık. "Did you reach a decision?"

"Yes, we did. Do you want me to tell you or should it be a surprise?"

"I'm petrified, Tarık. Please don't tell me we're going through Berlin."

"I'd better not tell you then."

"No! Are you telling me the truth?"

"What do you mean by that?"

"That we're going through Berlin?"

"Come here," he said, sitting her on his lap. He cradled her in his arms like a baby. "Trust me, Margot, the safest way is through Berlin. We've debated the whole thing. We've asked others. We've even communicated with Turkey. Finally even Hikmet Özdoğan agreed that it's the best way."

"Just thinking about it makes my hair stand on end."

"That's why it's the safest way. If even thinking about it gives you the creeps, who on earth would think that a train carrying so many Jews would dare to pass through Germany. Can't you see? This very thought is your security."

"No one could imagine such a thing."

"Exactly, that's what we're counting on. We're doing something even the devil himself wouldn't think of. Once they see that your passports have been stamped in Berlin, no German, Italian, or Austrian will bother you. From there it will be plain sailing all the way to Köstence."

"Weren't we going to Istanbul?"

"Most of the passengers will board a boat in Köstence. Those continuing to Istanbul will be transferred to another train. The Alfandaris are going to Istanbul; you'd better stick with them."

"How long will this adventure last?"

"It's indeed an adventure. Nobody can tell. You'll have to take this one day at a time. Some tracks may have been bombed, others may be disconnected. If that happens, you'll be diverted. Then, of course, you may be delayed in places where soldiers get on board to be transported."

"Could it take a year?"

Tarık laughed. "One can go around the world in eighty days. How could your journey take a year?"

"But there's a war on."

"Don't worry, Margot. I'm sure it will take between ten and twenty days. You must send me a wire as soon as you arrive. Do you promise?"

Margot started to cry quietly in Tarık's arms.

"Please don't cry, my baby. Don't forget you're not alone. You'll have your friends with you. The Alfandaris promised they will take care of you in Istanbul. Then of course there's Ferit and Evelyn. Can you imagine that Ferit would let his pregnant wife board a train if it was that dangerous?"

"Tarık, that's not why I'm crying. It's strange that I don't feel like going now when I was so desperate before. I—I don't want to leave you. Can't you see?"

Tarık kissed Margot all over her face and neck. "I wish I could ask you to stay, my darling."

"Why don't you then?"

"I can't, Margot. I have no right to ask you to waste the best years of your life. You're young and beautiful, and like all young women you'll want to get married and have a family."

"I know you can't marry me unless you resign, Tarık."

"It hasn't been easy for me to get where I am. My father worked very hard to give me a good education. I can't tell you what he went through so that I could study in Istanbul. It wasn't just a matter of getting the money together for the school and boarding; there were also the books and my clothes; he took into account that I shouldn't look worse than my peers. Eventually his heart couldn't take the strain. I'm where he wanted me to be, Margot. I couldn't possibly resign. To do that would be to disrespect his efforts and his memory."

"I wouldn't expect you to resign, Tarık. As for having children, well, what will be will be."

"Oh, my darling! You really don't realize. Having a child out of wedlock, or not being able to give your son your family name, is considered a fate worse than death in Anatolia. You may not necessarily feel that way now, but believe me, in a few years' time, you'll want what every young woman does and then you'll blame me. No, Margot. We shouldn't do this to each other."

"In that case, let's make the best of tonight."

"Yes, let's. Let's make tonight our very own, our own special night, beautiful, precious, and emotional, the night I'll remember as long as I live…"

Tarık lifted her from his lap and gently put her down on the carpet. He started kissing and undressing her tenderly. He removed her clothes piece by piece, breathing in the scent of her body, gazing in awe at her slender pale form on the dark-blue carpet as though she were a Goya masterpiece. He wanted this picture, this image of this beautiful, blonde woman eagerly and lovingly abandoning herself to him, to settle in his mind forever, erasing the image of the other blonde woman imprinted there.

ANKARA

Macit was so surprised by the telephone call he had just received, he was still holding the receiver and looking around the room for his colleague. He was alone. Only his secretary was in the adjoining office, and he preferred not to discuss the news with her until it had been confirmed. He put the receiver down and walked into her office.

"Mediha Hanım, I'm going to Hüsnü's office. Let me know immediately if there are any calls."

Just as he turned to leave, he came face-to-face with Hüsnü. They went back into Macit's office and he closed the door.

"Is this true?" asked Hüsnü.

"I just heard it myself. I was on my way to your office to ask the same question."

"When did it happen?"

"Von Papen, the German ambassador, asked for an appointment to see our foreign minister, Numan, at eleven o'clock this morning. He arrived right on time and went straight up to see him. Their meeting lasted about twenty minutes. I didn't see Von Papen leave, but those who did said he had a very long face. At about one o'clock, the prime minister telephoned Numan and asked to see him before the lunch break ended. I realized something strange was happening, but I never thought that it would end in a resignation."

"Obviously it did."

"Hüsnü, I suggest we keep this under our hats for a while. Maybe President Inönü will persuade Numan to—"

"The Numan I know will never change his mind if he has decided to resign."

"I wonder if resigning was his idea, or if he was pushed," said Macit.

"We'll find out soon enough. In the meantime, I will be at the chancellery."

"Be careful, Hüsnü. Don't discuss this with anyone. Everything might change."

"Don't fret, Macit. Of course I understand that as the minister's pet you don't want him to leave."

"That's not true at all! I can't believe you said that. I'm a bureaucrat at heart. I got to where I am through years of hard work, not by favors," Macit said angrily.

"Don't be so touchy. I was only joking."

"I was only telling you to hang fire for a while. There's no point aggravating a situation that might change. After all, no one knows if the resignation will be withdrawn or not. That's all. Do as you wish!"

"I said I'm sorry, didn't I? No need to prolong this any further. I'll be careful; I promise. I'm just as aware as you that it would be unwise to change horses midstream, especially when the stream is so turbulent. *Inşallah*, we have been misinformed. I'll find out the details."

"I've got to deal with two separate delegations today, so I'm stuck here. If you do hear anything, let me know," Macit said coldly.

Macit was upset at both the foreign minister's resignation and his friend's insinuation. He sat at his desk trying to analyze some files, but he was unable to concentrate. The telephone rang continuously. Everyone wanted to discuss the same subject and offer their personal opinions.

Macit asked his secretary not to interrupt his meetings with the delegations unless a call was urgent. The second meeting lasted much longer than expected, and when Macit left the room to go to the toilet, the secretary told him that Hüsnü had called several times. It was only toward the end of the day that Macit got around to going to Hüsnü's office.

As soon as Macit saw the expression on Hüsnü's face, he knew the news he had received that morning was true.

About an hour later, Macit was deep in thought as he walked home through the drizzling rain. Why couldn't things go well for him? Just as things were beginning to improve at home, now this problem at the ministry. If his dear mother were alive, she would certainly say, "Let me lift the curse of the evil eye from you, my son."

Having almost reached the breaking point, his relationship with Sabiha had suddenly improved. He didn't know exactly what had caused this sudden change of heart, just as he never found out why she'd become so distant in the first place. But one thing was certain, that night when he returned home from Cairo, she had cuddled up to him in bed.

Even though he didn't like to admit it, Macit felt that that know-it-all doctor had been good for his wife. Sabiha's relationship with Hülya was better too; at least she was making more of an effort to show an interest in her daughter. Macit couldn't believe his ears when Hülya told him that she had been to the cinema with her mother.

"Is that true?" he had asked Sabiha.

"Of course it's true," Hülya interrupted. "Auntie Hümeyra and Pelin came with us. We saw an Esther Williams film. Doesn't she swim beautifully, Daddy? I'd like to learn to swim like her."

"In the summer, my darling, when we go to Istanbul. You can practice when we are on the island."

"Won't I need a teacher?"

"What for? Your mother is an excellent swimmer—I'm sure she could teach you."

"Actually, I wish your aunt Selva were here. She was much better than me, she could teach you really well," Sabiha said.

Macit noticed his father-in-law, sitting opposite him at the table, looked quizzically when he heard Selva's name. At least it was a look of sadness now rather than the anger of the past. They were able to talk about Selva quite comfortably now in his presence.

When Macit reached Kızılay, he turned toward Sakarya Street. He stopped at the florist on the corner and bought some white carnations for his wife. When they got engaged, he'd promised to always buy her white flowers, saying, "Because you're pure and delicate like a white flower."

That objectionable psychiatrist had certainly helped improve things at home. Since Dr. Sahir had accused him of neglecting his wife in favor of his heavy work schedule, Macit had realized that there were ways he could make things up that would mean a lot to her.

On the way home with the flowers, Macit wondered why he had taken such a dislike to that doctor. The poor man hadn't really done anything wrong. On the contrary, he had tried to be helpful by insinuating that Sabiha's attitude might in fact be due to Macit's own negligence. Was it possible, then, that he might have been jealous because Sabiha spent so much time being "naked" in front of this man? Not *really* naked, of course. Nonetheless, Sabiha had told him, "I feel naked in front of this doctor. He somehow manages to strip me of my inhibitions and look deep into my soul!" Macit suddenly felt uncomfortable thinking that he might have been jealous of his wife. Who knew how angry Sabiha would be if she knew his thoughts? She'd certainly say, "What the hell do you take me for?"

Macit quickened his step as his thoughts started racing. What was Sabiha doing all the time that she was on her own? Who was she seeing? Was there someone else in her life causing her to be distant? He stumbled and looked around. Had anyone noticed that he nearly fell just then? No, Ankara was full of tired people immersed in their own thoughts, going over their own problems while rushing home. Where had all these doubts suddenly come from? Why was he having these strange fantasies concerning his wife after so many years?

Suddenly his mood changed and he felt warm inside despite the drizzling rain and the cold weather. He remembered how his wife had snuggled up to him the night he had returned from Cairo. The way she had rekindled the fire in his body when he felt her naked breasts rubbing against his chest. Her hot lips had filled him with desire, making him feel a passion he hadn't felt for ages. He'd been taken aback by the emotional intensity between them that night. Could it be that he had fallen in love all over again with this capricious and coy wife of his?

When Macit got home, Fazıl Reşat Paşa opened the door for him.

"You shouldn't have troubled yourself. Isn't Hacer at home?" he asked.

"No trouble at all. It's Hacer's day off today," his father-in-law answered. "I was standing by the window waiting for Leman Hanım to come home, and I saw you arriving."

"Is Hülya with her?"

"No, Hülya went next door to play with her friend. I think Sabiha is in her room. What lovely flowers! Are you going out this evening?"

"No, I just got them for us. I'd better get out of these wet clothes," Macit said, walking to his room.

Sabiha was in her dressing gown with a towel wrapped around her head. She was sitting on her bed applying polish to her toenails and was surprised to see him.

"Good Lord, Macit, you're early! I didn't expect you yet."

Macit put the flowers on her lap.

"What's all this about?"

"They're for you."

Macit took the bottle of nail polish from his wife's hand and placed it on the bedside table. He then pulled her dressing gown off and pushed her down onto the pillows. Sabiha tried to resist. He pulled down her green knickers with one hand while trying to unbutton his trousers with the other.

"Macit! What are you doing? Mind my nail polish. You'll get it everywhere. Macit, what's come over you all of a sudden? My father's next door. You're crushing the flowers!"

Macit took Sabiha by force. He kissed her lips passionately so that she wouldn't be able to speak. As she whimpered under him, he looked at this jasmine-scented woman and wondered if she had indeed been unfaithful with that doctor.

"Ohhh!"…Or someone else?…"Ohhh!" He thrust himself, again and again, deep inside her before finally rolling over.

"Oh, Sabiha!" he said.

Macit left the room feeling a bit embarrassed. He walked into the sitting room where Fazıl Reşat Paşa was still looking out of the window, waiting for his wife.

"You look a bit tired, Macit," he said, looking over his glasses.

"Yes, it's been a tiring day," Macit replied. "We've had some upsetting developments."

"I'm sorry to hear it. What happened?"

"Our prime minister asked for the foreign minister's resignation."

"Really! Why's that?"

"Numan was never in favor of siding with the Germans. On the contrary, he always believed, if we eventually had to take sides, it should be with the Allies. But apparently he's done exactly the opposite."

"What's that?"

"He's apparently come down on the side of the Germans."

"You mean he changed sides?"

"Frankly, I don't believe Numan would do that. But you see, when the German army pressed against the Bulgarian border, we signed an agreement with them not to intervene. Furthermore, as you know, there's also the question of our chrome…"

"What about it? Weren't we supposed to be selling it to the Allies?"

"The agreement we signed with the Allies has expired. Not only have the Germans asked to buy it, but they've also agreed to sign a contract committing themselves to continue buying it until the end of the war. We desperately needed such a contract. Numan was against the Germans, but he wasn't against an agreement that would be to our advantage. He believes that nations have no friends or foes; they only have their interests."

"So what happened?"

"Apparently, low-tonnage German ships are being allowed to pass through the Bosphorus without being searched. The Montreux Agreement forbids the searching of commercials vessels. Despite that agreement, the British sent us notes urging us to stop their passage. But Numan was against the decision."

"When did all this happen?"

"Today. Apparently the British sent another note threatening that they wouldn't sign our economic agreement unless we stopped and searched the ships. Our foreign minister pointed out that his hands were tied by the Montreux Agreement; however, the prime minister disagreed and forced him to call the German ambassador, informing him that, from now on, all German ships passing through would be searched. Afterward, he delivered a very harsh speech at the Ministers' Assembly. The ministers were completely taken aback, and when he'd finished his speech, he called for Numan's resignation, which Numan offered there and then."

"Strange, I've been listening to the radio all day and I've heard nothing of this."

"I suppose it will all come out this evening. Our foreign minister was strict about sticking to international rules and regulations, and there's also the other side of the coin—our economic interests, money…especially these days, when our country is in such dire straits. Anyway, I'm still very sorry about Numan. I've gained most of my experience under his wing and I'll always be grateful to him."

"These economic agreements are two-edged swords," Fazıl Reşat Paşa said. "Nations like ours accept loans like life support, forgetting that when they have to be repaid it can bring a country to its knees. Wasn't that just what happened to the mighty Ottoman? That aside, who's taking over the foreign ministry?"

"Nobody has been named as a successor. The prime minister will be running the foreign ministry himself for a while."

"I hope it will be someone you approve of," said the paşa.

"No one cares what I think. I'll simply have to carry on with my duties, serving whoever steps in."

The old man got up, switched on the radio, and went back to the window.

Sabiha appeared at the end of the hallway carrying the white carnations. She walked into the dining room and picked up a crystal vase from the sideboard. She looked flushed and rather sheepishly avoided looking at her father, saying only, "Look, Father, Macit bought us some flowers." She walked to the kitchen to fill the vase with water. Fazıl Reşat Paşa didn't even hear his daughter; he was concentrating on the road outside, waiting for his wife.

"Where the hell is that woman? It's getting dark already," he grumbled.

"Mother's gone to her dressmaker Fazıla Hanım," Sabiha shouted from the kitchen. "I don't think she'll finish early. I bet she's going through every fashion magazine there."

"Why does it have to take so long? It's so dark outside."

"Don't worry, Father, Hacer is with her," Sabiha said, walking back into the sitting room with the flowers. Suddenly the telephone rang and she rushed into the hall with the vase in her hand. Macit tried to eavesdrop when he heard her gasping, but he couldn't hear what she was saying because of the radio.

A while later, Sabiha appeared at the sitting room door. Her cheeks, previously flushed, were as white as the flowers in the vase. She could hardly speak.

"Macit, Tarık's on the phone. Tarık Arıca. He'd like to speak to you. Apparently the Gestapo took Rafo from the pharmacy and put him on a train with some others. They let him go later, as far as I can understand. My poor darling sister, what she must have gone through."

"What's that? What happened?" Fazıl Reşat Paşa asked as Macit jumped forward to catch the vase about to slip from Sabiha's hands.

Husband and wife looked at each other but didn't answer.

"What are you hiding from me?" asked the old man. "Don't tell me something's happened to Selva." This was the first time he had mentioned his daughter's name in years.

"Don't you worry about Selva; she knows how to take care of herself," Macit replied.

"Tarık wants to speak to you," said Sabiha. Macit ran to the phone.

"Who's that, Sabiha? Who's on the phone?"

"It's a friend of ours from Paris, Father. He's the consul there, he's got some news."

"What news?"

"I don't know exactly. I'm sure Macit will give us the details..."

"What happened to Selva, then?"

"As Macit said, she knows how to take care of herself. She'll be all right; don't worry. It seems the Germans got hold of Rafo, but then set him free."

"What about the child?"

"You mean Fazıl?"

The old man didn't reply.

"Fazıl's all right. Everyone's all right. Father! Your hands are shaking, please calm down. Mother should be back shortly; don't let her see you this way. Please relax—do it for me, please."

When Macit returned, he found Sabiha on her knees next to her father.

"Tarık says that the Alfandaris will probably be returning home soon."

"The Alfandaris? You mean Selva?"

"All three of them."

"Who persuaded them to do that?"

"I imagine this latest episode was the last straw."

"When are they coming?"

"That's not certain yet. Tarık said probably within a month."

"We've got to find them somewhere to live, haven't we?" said Sabiha.

"For whom?" asked Fazıl Reşat Paşa.

"For Selva, Father. It seems they are coming back."

There was complete silence. Fazıl Reşat Paşa turned away to hide the tears in his eyes. He looked outside into the darkness.

ON THE TRAIN

The Gare de l'Est was chaotic. People rushed every which way, changing platforms. There were women dragging children, men trying to catch their trains, porters carrying baggage, confused foreigners—obviously tourists—and, most of all, soldiers. Young, innocent-faced men with squeaky boots moved in groups. They were all over the station, going to kill or be killed. People called to each other, some reunited, screaming with joy, others being separated and screaming with anguish. There were the sounds of bells ringing, whistles blowing, train wheels screeching on the rails, and soldiers marching monotonously. And different smells: that distinct, smoky smell of wet steam that fills one's nostrils; the whiff of perfume from women passing by; the stench of sweat and garlic permeating the coarse clothes of peasants; and the acrid smell oozing from the bodies of the young soldiers. Hope and grief coexisted in this station.

Ferit was running toward the fifth carriage of a very long train, holding his wife's hand tightly with one hand and carrying a rather large suitcase in the other. Two bags hung over his shoulders.

"Monsieur, please. Monsieur, have a look at this ticket."

The conductor, whose cap came down to his eyebrows, looked at the ticket and grumbled, "What are you doing here, monsieur? Your platform is on the other side. Go down those stairs and across."

Ferit turned around, dragging his wife by the hand.

"Wait, Ferit. Let go of my hand; you'll make me fall," complained Evelyn.

"I can't do that, darling; can't you see how crowded this place is? If I let go of your hand and lose you, I'll never be able to find you again. Please try to keep up."

They ran down the stairs hand in hand, across and up the next flight of stairs, and along the platform of another long train with steam coming out of the engine. Ferit noticed someone tall in the crowd who he thought looked like Rafael. He heaved a sigh of relief and slowed down. Ferit showed his ticket to another official standing by the door of a carriage.

"That one, farther along," he said, pointing. They carried on walking. The difficult moment was approaching. It was Ferit's duty to sort out the seating arrangements for the passengers, and he needed to get to the carriage quickly.

Ferit had been at the station overnight and met up with Evelyn early in the morning. Hikmet Özdoğan and Tarık had come to the station to take over the carriage and deal with the necessary formalities. The carriage had been connected to the very end of a train leaving for Berlin at nine o'clock in the morning. After completing the formalities, Hikmet Özdoğan left to go home. Ferit and Tarık decided to go into one of the all-night cafés and order coffee and cognac. Tarık was deep in thought.

"Don't forget, Ferit," he had said, "it's very important that the garrison at the Turkish border is notified of your arrival in advance. Our officials in Bulgaria are supposed to let them know that you are on your way. I just hope that nothing goes wrong."

"Everything will be fine, my friend. Don't worry. I don't see your problem."

"The timing is very important. While you're crossing the border, the garrison there will be having a soccer match with a neighboring garrison."

"Oh my goodness!"

"Exactly. Such are the sensitive intricacies of diplomacy. It's absolutely vital that the soldiers at the border have no knowledge of your crossing. God forbid, someone could spot something wrong with those passports, but if they are busy playing soccer, no one will notice anything."

"Whew. Why all these precautions?"

"The Germans, of course; do you think it's easy to flirt with the British and protect the Jews while making sure the Germans don't turn against us?"

"Of course not. I do understand, my friend. May Allah be with you," Ferit said. "Is there anything I can do to alert our garrison at the border?"

"I don't think so. Your calling our embassy might be risky. We'll try and sort it out with our colleagues in Bulgaria."

They sat side by side drinking coffee and cognac, one after another, without talking much. Their friendship was relatively new, but they felt comfortable with each other, sharing their anxiety about the adventure ahead. Eventually, Tarık left Ferit alone with his thoughts. He saw his colorful and exciting early life flash before his eyes like the cascades of a waterfall.

Ferit had earned the nickname Smartass while studying at the Galatasaray lycée in Istanbul. Memories flashing through his mind revealed why he had earned the name. His life was full of successes and obsessions. He could turn his mind to anything—theater, music, law, mathematics. As well as academic success, he had turned his attention to fighting for causes that he believed in. All this came to his mind now in this dirty café in Paris. He'd been studying in Paris in 1940 when Hitler invaded France and the Turkish government ordered all Turks to return. Because the war was waged by this lunatic, he had joined the secret Resistance organization to fight for humanity. No one knew how much longer all this would go on. The only sure thing was that he would be on the train bound for Berlin tomorrow. He had reached the point of no return, and everything crowded in on him at once.

As if this wasn't enough, he stood waiting at the station for Evelyn to arrive, worrying how he was going to explain to her that they would be traveling in separate carriages.

When they reached carriage number five, Ferit helped Evelyn on board before lifting up the suitcase. Then he got on board himself. Inching their way along the narrow corridor, they looked at the compartment numbers.

"Here it is!" said Ferit. "Look. You've got a window seat. Isn't that nice?" The rest of the compartment was still empty.

"I still don't understand why we have to go to Istanbul through Berlin," Evelyn said.

"How many times do I have to tell you? Beggars can't be choosers," Ferit replied, putting the suitcase on the luggage rack and the shoulder bag on the seat beside his wife.

"Are you sitting next to me? It would be more comfortable if you sat opposite and we could stretch our legs out."

Ferit pretended to check his ticket. "Actually, it seems I'm not sitting in this compartment."

"What!"

"Unbelievably, I've been allocated a seat in a different compartment."

"Why?"

"You're right to get angry, Evelyn. I'm angry too, but there is nothing we can do."

"I bet you already knew this."

"Well, you see my sweetheart, when I went to pick up the tickets, the train was almost full. They could only offer me seats in separate carriages. I promise you I tried my best to get seats together, I even explained that my wife is pregnant. They promised to do all they could, but obviously that wasn't possible."

Evelyn raised her voice. "I can't believe this! I'm to travel all the way to Istanbul on my own, and you've accepted it. Is that it?"

"Shh. Please don't shout, darling. People are looking at us."

"I couldn't care less. Get that suitcase down." Evelyn got up from her seat and tried to reach the suitcase.

"Stop it, Evelyn! Are you going mad?"

"Either we travel together or not at all—that's final!"

"Darling, please sit down. If you insist on leaving your seat, someone else may take it, and you'll lose the window seat. Look at all these people…Look!" Ferit lowered the window and pulled his wife over. "Just look at these thousands of people all struggling to get seats on trains. Can you imagine how many of them will have to travel standing up in the corridors? I managed to get you a seat, and by the window, and yet all you can do is moan. There's gratitude for you! So what if we can't sit next to each other!"

"I only don't understand why we're traveling all the way separately when you supposedly reserved these seats so long ago."

"OK. You just sit there like the good girl I know you are and I'll go and find my seat. You never know, maybe we can swap seats with someone."

"What if we can't?"

"In that case, we'll just have to make do with what we've got. If we can't sit together, I promise to come and see you every time we stop."

Evelyn was going to object again, but then some people came into the compartment. She looked like she was close to tears.

"Please, Evelyn, be reasonable. Darling! Just let me go and find my carriage. I promise to do all I can. For God's sake, don't leave your seat. I'll be back as soon as possible."

Ferit left the compartment, got out of the carriage with his bag on his shoulder, and started walking toward the end of the train. Evelyn got up and leaned out of the open window and watched her husband. He stopped beside a carriage some distance away. Evelyn saw him talking to a tall man.

"Would you mind closing the window, madame, it's getting rather cold," said an elderly lady who had settled opposite her. Evelyn pulled away from the window and looked at the woman with tearful eyes.

"Allow me," said a young man who had just come into the compartment. He closed the window.

Evelyn pressed her head against the windowpane. She could no longer see where Ferit was. She took a newspaper out of her bag to try to alleviate her stress. The compartment gradually filled up. Ferit was right. Seats were scarce. The family sitting opposite had three children, but they only had two seats; obviously they intended to sit the children on their laps. Ferit returned while Evelyn was doing the crossword. He no longer had his shoulder bag with him.

"What happened, are we swapping seats?" she asked.

"Very difficult. I'm in a second-class carriage. It isn't as comfortable as yours."

Evelyn looked around as if to say, *You call this comfortable?*

"No one from here would agree to swap places with me."

"I will," replied Evelyn. "We could ask someone in your carriage to exchange his seat for mine by the window."

"You think I hadn't thought of that? But there are no single people in my compartment. They are all couples or families."

"So what are we to do?" Evelyn asked with tears in her eyes.

"We will have to put up with the situation, my sweetheart. You never know, someone may get off; we'll just have to wait and see. Would you like me to get you something? Another newspaper, a magazine, cigarettes, sweets?"

"No, thanks."

"Water?"

"Don't try to get around me."

"Evelyn, please don't give me that sad look. I promise I'll come see you at every stop." Ferit bent down to kiss his wife. As he was leaving, he turned to an elderly gentleman sitting beside her and asked him to keep an eye on his wife.

"Is there really a difference of class in this mayhem?" said the man, indicating the crowded compartment. "Rest assured, young man, I'll take care of your wife."

Ferit pushed his way through the packed corridor with difficulty and jumped out, running all the way to the last carriage. They had filled the compartments of this special carriage brought over from Turkey with people holding Turkish passports. Ferit found his way to the compartment where he had left his passport in his bag. Selva had seated Samuel and Perla side by side next to the window. Fazıl was sitting on Perla's lap, looking out. When he saw Ferit, he clapped his hands with joy.

"Hi, little man," said Ferit. "Did you look after my bag?"

"Where's your wife?" asked Selva. "Where is she sitting?"

"She's in another carriage."

"How come?"

"She doesn't know about this carriage. All she knows is that we are going to Istanbul via Berlin, that's all."

"I don't understand."

"Selva, Evelyn is expecting a baby. She had a hemorrhage when she was only two months on. I didn't tell her anything because I didn't want to cause her any more anxiety than necessary. She has no idea about this carriage."

"But is she to travel such a long way on her own?"

"There are some nice people in her compartment and she has a perfectly valid passport. She might get bored, but that's nothing compared to other possibilities…"

"You mean that we might not reach our destination?"

"You know we are all taking a gamble. I told you so many times, didn't I? In fact, I insisted that you and Fazıl should travel with regular passengers, just like Evelyn. Both your husband and Tarık begged you, but you wouldn't listen. You're very stubborn, you know."

"I realize that."

"In that case, please don't ask me questions I can't answer! Where's Rafael?"

"He went to the pharmacy next to the station to buy a few things we seem to have forgotten."

"I'm going to check who's sitting in which compartment. Don't forget that you, Rafael, and I have to split up the way we discussed."

"I know. How many people should sit here?"

"Well, in normal circumstances, only three on each side, but there are nine even in Evelyn's compartment. When I'm organizing the seats, I'll try not to crowd you in."

"No, no, that's not the reason. Don't think about it," Selva said.

All those staying in Ferit's apartment had become very close friends, especially during their last night together. When Ferit announced to them that they would be leaving the following morning, no one seemed very pleased despite having waited for the news for some time. They must have been embarking on the longest and most difficult journey of their lives. Either they would make it to their destination or not. Each of them had been quiet, eating their cheese and lettuce baguettes and drinking their wine. Undoubtedly, they all had the same apprehension in their hearts. They might be traveling into the unknown, but they had each other for support.

Outside, Tarık was moving along the compartments, carrying a paper bag and peering through each window, one by one. When he saw Evelyn's profile, he stopped and tapped on the window. Startled, she turned around and looked out. Her eyes lit up when she saw Tarık. Because of the station noises, she couldn't hear him say, "I'm coming in," but she read his lips. She got up and met him in the corridor, and they put their arms around each other.

"Is your seat comfortable?" asked Tarık.

"Yes, but do you know what that crafty husband of mine did?"

"Yes, Evelyn, but I can assure you it wasn't his fault. He's upset about it too. I spoke to the conductor myself earlier, and he promised he'd let us know if there should be an available seat. Don't worry too much. The important thing is to have a safe journey," Tarık said, avoiding her eyes. "At least you're safe in here. There's no way of knowing where Ferit's carriage will end up."

"I'm so worried, Tarık," she said. "I don't understand why this train is going through Berlin."

"Apparently some of the other lines have been bombed. This sort of thing happens in wartime. Anyway, look what I got for you!" Tarık took some chocolates and biscuits out of the bag and gave them to Evelyn.

"Oh, Tarık! You're such a good friend! Thank you for coming to see us off."

"I couldn't let you go without saying good-bye."

"We could have seen each other earlier, but Ferit wouldn't allow me to come to Paris until the last moment. I'm sure you know that rascal let our apartment, don't you?"

"I do, but wasn't that great? At least you'll have some money coming in each month." Tarık insisted on helping her back to her seat. "Don't tire yourself, relax, and have a safe journey," he said, leaving her.

Tarık walked all the way back to the carriage with the star-and-crescent emblem on the windows and found Margot in the same compartment as Selva.

"You're traveling in this compartment?" he asked.

"Yes, Selva and I will be together. Rafael's in another compartment," Margot replied. She seemed much calmer than she had been a few hours earlier.

After Tarık had left Ferit at the station café, he had rushed home to have a shave and change his clothes before seeing Margot off. Margot already had her suitcase packed and was ready by the door. She was wearing a gray two-piece suit and her favorite hat. Tarık had been surprised to find her sitting bolt upright on a chair that she had pulled next to the window.

"What on earth are you doing all dressed and ready to go at this time of the morning?"

"I've been ready since midnight. I waited for a while in case you came over, but when you didn't, I decided to get myself ready for the journey. There was no way I was going to sleep anyway."

"Margot, there were some very important things I had to discuss with Ferit."

"I know, I know, my darling. Thank you for coming."

"Why don't you make us a cup of coffee?"

The coffee smelled so good. They wrapped themselves in each other's arms and drank their coffee without speaking. Later, Margot put her red coat around her shoulders. They went to the station together in Tarık's car, and after Tarık saw her to her carriage, he left to get a few things for her journey.

"Margot, I haven't been able to get you what I really wanted; some of the stores aren't even open yet. But I did get loads of magazines and newspapers for you to read on the way. I also picked up a few things for you in case you get hungry—just what was available, of course." He emptied most of the contents of the paper bag onto the seat next to Margot.

"You shouldn't have gone to all this trouble," said Selva. "I've got enough to feed the world and his wife."

Finally Tarık took out a package from the bottom of the bag and gave it to little Fazıl.

"And this is for you to play with, my little friend."

Fazıl immediately tore open the package; it was a wooden train.

"Goodness me, Tarık! How did you manage to find a toy store open at the crack of dawn?"

"That was a present I bought earlier, same as this one," he said, taking another parcel from the bag and offering it to Margot. Margot unwrapped her gift very carefully. It was a framed photograph of the two of them Rafael had taken with her camera one sunny morning at La Closerie des Lilas. She looked at it, remembering how happy they had been that day. Tarık had his arms around her and their eyes were sparkling with joy. Margot pressed the frame to her heart.

Suddenly, Ferit appeared at the door with a tall, well-dressed man. "This is Monsieur Brodd," he said. "He used to be the general manager of the German bank in Turkey. He is now working for the immigration department and has spent a lot of time and effort to make this journey possible. He traveled all the way here to deliver this carriage personally, and he wants to wish you a pleasant journey—particularly you, Selva."

Selva was surprised. She stood up and shook the man's hand; then Ferit introduced him to the others.

"This is Margot Palley, and Samuel and Perla Afnaim—in other words, Sami and Peri Naim."

The man shook everyone's hands and wished them a pleasant journey. Then he turned to Selva again. "Young lady, I had the honor of meeting your father in Istanbul."

"Really! When?"

"Just before traveling here; he was very concerned about you and he came to see me. I promised him I would make sure to see you if you were on this train."

Selva couldn't believe her ears. Her heart beat crazily, and her ears began to buzz.

"This is incredible. You mean you actually met my father?"

"That's right, just before coming here. He visited me at the immigration department's office in Karaköy. He inquired specifically about this train. You probably know that our department depends entirely on public support. Your father made a very generous donation to us, for which we are extremely grateful."

Selva heard nothing but the buzzing in her ears. She wanted to cry, but she bit her lip and averted her eyes, trying to stop the tears from running down her cheeks.

Ferit and Monsieur Brodd left, and an elderly man walked in, trying to squeeze a rather large suitcase and briefcase onto the luggage rack.

"I'm sorry, monsieur, the suitcase will have to go in the baggage compartment," said a conductor passing by. "Why didn't you leave it there before getting on?"

The man didn't argue. He left his briefcase on his seat and walked out with the suitcase.

"I think I know that man. Where did I see him before?" muttered Margot. Selva, who was watching her husband return with some parcels, said, "Search me. I don't know him."

Rafael walked in and Tarık stood up.

"It's time for me to say good-bye; if I don't get off now, I might end up having to travel with you," he said.

The noise of the engine getting up steam could be heard, but there were so many trains and whistles it was difficult to separate one from another. While Tarık stood, another group of people gathered in the doorway: Constance and Marcel, who'd been taught by Selva in Paris; a tall, young man; and another elderly man walked into the compartment.

Selva and Tarık hugged each other. Tarık kissed Fazıl on the forehead as he played with his train on the floor, and he wished Samuel and Perla a pleasant journey. He nodded good-bye to the others and stepped into the corridor. Margot followed him. She hugged Tarık tightly as the train slowly began to move.

"I'll always remember you, Margot," Tarık said, jumping off the train. He bumped into Ferit, who was running back after visiting his wife. He was out of breath, and just managed to shake Tarık's hand firmly before stepping on the train.

"Take care of yourself, and thanks for everything," he shouted as the train pulled away.

As the train gathered speed, Margot lowered the window and leaned out, waving good-bye to Tarık with her handkerchief. Selva, Rafo, Perla, and Samuel crushed her against the window, trying to do the same. Ferit, who was still standing on the running board, waved. The tall young man was also waving to someone. Tarık caught a brief glimpse of Margot's sad face as the train passed by him. He stood there, his hand held high, as the train moved farther and farther away, becoming smaller and smaller in the distance, until it finally disappeared in a cloud of engine smoke.

THE TRAIN

Margot could no longer see Tarık's silhouette in the distance, so she sat down, closed her eyes, and pretended to sleep to avoid talking to anyone. Just as the train approached Reims, she opened her eyes and again noticed the elderly man sitting opposite her. She certainly knew that face. She was sure she'd seen him before. He hadn't removed his cap like the other elderly gentleman in the compartment. He was wearing glasses and reading a book. Perla and Samuel were playing a game of battleships together. Because she had been up the whole night, Selva had fallen asleep with her son on her lap. The compartment was quiet. Margot hoped this peace and quiet would continue. She felt like she had no expectations anymore. She couldn't return to her own country because it was run by the Nazis. Her whole family was scattered; she had been forced to leave her job and the man she had begun to love. She wished she could go on traveling on this train as long as the world turned. *Clickety-clack, clickety-clack…*

"Would you like a cigarette, mademoiselle?"

Margot almost jumped out of her seat. "No, thank you."

"Do you mind if I do?"

"No, not at all," she said. The young man was sitting right beside her. He was well-groomed, clean, but extremely thin. The skin under his eyes was purple. Margot hoped he didn't have tuberculosis.

"Are you going to Berlin?"

He was a chatterbox, and all Margot wanted was to be left in peace. She wished this bag of bones would talk to someone else.

"No, I'm going farther," she replied.

"To Prague?"

She didn't reply, and pulled out a Hungarian book to read.

"What language is that?"

"Hungarian."

"So you must be Hungarian."

"Yes," Margot replied, burying herself in her book.

"I'm sorry to disturb you. It's just that I miss talking."

It was Margot's turn to feel sorry. She wondered what had happened to him.

"There's nothing to forgive," she said. "It's just that I'm rather unhappy about having to leave Paris; on top of that, I'm tired. Where are you going?"

"To Istanbul. That's, of course, if we get there."

"Really?"

"Why are you surprised? Is that such a long way to be going?"

"That's where I'm going too," replied Margot.

"So we'll be together for some time. I'm David, by the way," the skinny young man said. "David Russo."

The train was passing through pretty green valleys, past the gardens of suburban houses with children playing and dogs jumping around; women were hanging out their wash and men were mowing the lawns. They traveled through towns and cities too, where one could see the domes of churches in the distance. Looking at all this, one had the impression that all was well with the world.

If an alien visiting the Earth for the first time were on this train, he'd have the same impression. Europe's hell wasn't visible from the train's windows.

The passengers in the compartment, apart from the children playing, were either reading, looking at the passing view, or having a nap. They weren't talking. Their hearts were heavy. The children were busy asking each other history and geography questions, one after the other. Selva woke up, but she didn't dare move in case she disturbed Fazıl, who was still sleeping on her lap. Rafael had come and gone twice to check on his wife and son while they were asleep, and Margot had made signs to him that everything was fine.

"How high is Mount Everest?" Perla asked.

"Seven thousand, five hundred meters."

"Right. What separates Europe from Asia?"

As Samuel was about to answer, the man in the cap spoke for the first time since he had gotten on the train. "Your previous answer was incorrect, young man."

"Which?" asked Samuel.

"The height of Mount Everest is 8,848 meters not 7,500."

"How do you know that?"

"I just do."

Margot moved uneasily in her seat. Not only did she know the face, but she recognized the voice too. She had definitely heard that voice before. She couldn't resist asking him, "Excuse me, monsieur. I think we have met before, but I just can't remember where."

"These things happen, mademoiselle. One can remind one of someone else. I've never seen you before."

"Allow me to introduce myself, then. I'm Margot Palley. I'm Hungarian."

"Pleased to meet you."

When the man didn't respond with his name, Margot looked at Selva quizzically. Constance got up to go to the toilet. She turned to Selva and said in Turkish, "I need to piss," so the men in the compartment couldn't understand. Selva couldn't help laughing at how Constance expressed herself.

"Well done, Constance," Selva said. "My efforts have not been in vain."

David Russo turned red. He wondered if he should tell them he understood Turkish, so as not to embarrass them later if they spoke about private things. As the cathedrals with their domes and spires got nearer, they realized they were arriving at a large city. The train huffed and puffed, slowed down, and finally came to a halt with a big moan. Selva read the sign: REIMS.

"Are we stopping here?" asked Marcel.

"Ferit and Rafael know all the details; we should ask them," Selva answered.

Rafo appeared at the door. The man wearing his cap put on his glasses and started reading again, hiding himself behind his newspaper.

"We're stopping here for a little while," said Rafo. "Are you hungry?"

"Can we get off?" asked Constance.

"There's no need to. We've got plenty to eat here," said Marcel.

Selva saw Ferit from the window, rushing toward the front carriages. Fazıl had woken up and was fidgeting on her lap. "The poor thing has been sitting for hours. Do you think I should take him out for a breath of fresh air?"

"We've only got about twenty minutes here. Please don't go far, Selva," Rafo warned. "If you're getting off, perhaps you should get a few things to eat?"

"I've got a basket full of food."

"But the next stop might be over the German border. If you want to get off, you'd better do it here."

The old man sighed. "What difference does it make, monsieur? We may be in France, but we are under German occupation. It doesn't seem to make much difference. Germany, France; France, Germany—the Nazis are everywhere."

"Yes, but at least French is spoken here. We can understand the language," said Rafael.

Selva got up and put Fazıl's jacket on. "Rafo, will you come with me?"

"I have to check the passengers Ferit put me in charge of. There might be an identity check. You'd better go on your own."

"Is there anything I can get for anyone?" asked Selva.

"I'll come with you," said Constance. When she got up, Margot, Marcel, and David Russo left too. No one except the two elderly men and the kids remained in the compartment. The children's aunt, Camilla, had made them swear again and again that they wouldn't leave the compartment.

Outside, Margot and Marcel changed platforms looking for cigarettes, and Selva looked for a toilet for her son—the toilet on the train had started to smell bad after the few hours' journey. When she saw Ferit returning from Evelyn's carriage, she asked if he wanted any cigarettes.

"Thanks, but no thanks," he replied. "I've got plenty of extras. But I wouldn't recommend you wander too far. If the train starts moving, it'll be difficult to get back on with the child."

"I'll come back as soon as we've found the toilet," Selva said.

Ferit got on the train and was walking along the corridor when he saw an SS official going into Selva's compartment. His hair stood on end like a cat's when it has seen a dog. He prepared himself for the possible danger ahead. He walked slowly and waited beside the door.

"Tickets, please. And your identity cards!" said the SS official.

Suddenly Perla felt a pain in her joints. Her face turned yellow. Samuel reached for his bag and pulled out the passports.

"What's your name?"

"Sami."

"Are you Turkish?"

"Yes."

"Really?"

Samuel repeated his answer in Turkish and handed over the passports. The man checked them.

"And this is your sister?"

"Yes."

"I'm Turkish," said Perla in Turkish. Her voice was trembling.

"You don't look Turkish to me. Did your mother sleep with a carrot?"

Samuel imagined clearing his throat and spitting all over the man's face. When the official finished with the kids, he turned to the old man, who was sitting quietly.

"Ticket. Identity!"

The old man took his passport and identity card from his pocket. The official glanced at them and returned them. When the other old man's turn came, Ferit stepped in.

"Monsieur, I'm the group leader," he said. "Please don't trouble yourself. I can gather all the passports and identity cards and bring them to you if you like."

"Is this a tourist carriage? Are you their guide?"

"As you know, it isn't possible to organize tourist travel these days. This carriage was sent from Turkey to pick up Turkish citizens stranded in Europe. All the stations en route have been informed. Haven't you?"

"I haven't been told anything about it."

"That's strange. Our embassy was assured that every station was informed before the train departed."

"If these people are returning to Turkey, what are they doing on a train bound for Frankfurt and Berlin? These tickets are only for Berlin."

"I have the tickets for the remainder of their journey. I took the precaution of safekeeping them, because there are a considerable number of elderly people and children in the group. I didn't want them to be confused or lose their tickets. There are also passengers boarding the train in Germany. The Turkish government can't afford to provide different carriages for each place. We thank God that at least they sent this one."

"Fine, bring me all the tickets and passports. You'll find me in the first carriage right at the front. I won't let you go without seeing all of them."

"Don't worry, I'll find you."

"I hope there isn't anyone on the wanted list."

"You think I'd go through Germany with a wanted person in my group?"

The official left the compartment, and Ferit and the man in the cap looked at each other for a split second. The man wiped his forehead with his handkerchief. Rafael stood by the door, pale faced.

"Rafael, you'd better collect up the passports and tickets from everyone in the carriage," said Ferit. "I'll go and find those still outside."

Some who had gotten off were walking back slowly. Ferit stood by the carriage door, waving at them to hurry back, then he got off and ran toward the toilets to warn those who were there. About thirty people were waiting on the platform to board the train. They were getting agitated and jostling one another to get on.

When Selva saw the man with the SS band in the carriage, she broke out into a sweat. She was exhausted, both from fear and from carrying Fazıl. Immediately, she got their tickets and passport ready for collection. Rafael collected everything from those who had gotten back on board. Everyone was back in their places except Perla, who was sitting upright in the seat by the door with an odd look on her face.

"You should really be sitting in your own seat, Peri. That's Marcel's seat," Selva said, but Perla didn't move. "What's wrong with you? Were you very scared?"

The girl didn't reply.

"Perla, Peri, my darling, are you all right? Why don't you sit in your own seat?"

Perla stood up, and Selva saw the bloodstain spreading across her blue-checked skirt.

"My God! What happened? Don't tell me you're…Don't be afraid, Perla; you'll be OK, my pet. I'll help you," she said.

Perla stood there, mortified.

The train continued its journey…*Clickety-clack, clickety-clack, clickety-clack*…lulling them all into a daze or even to sleep. Their nerves were drained, but they felt more relaxed than when they first boarded the train. They had gotten past one episode. They realized that such events could be dealt with. Perla had settled down with the help of Margot and Selva, and she had changed her skirt. She still felt a twinge of pain in her groin, but more than anything, she felt embarrassed. She sat quietly by the window, avoiding eye contact with her fellow passengers.

They were speeding through land covered with woods of dark trees, and cows and sheep grazing the hills. The houses they passed had red-tiled roofs, window boxes, and magnificent gardens separated by well-groomed hedges. Only a sensitive eye would notice they were passing through a country that had been invaded.

"If we don't have something to eat, we'll starve to death," Selva said, taking her food basket down from the luggage rack. The sadness they felt leaving Paris and their fear leaving Reims had made them lose their appetites. Now there was solidarity among the passengers, who shared the same destiny, and that had made them feel more relaxed.

Margot and Constance followed suit and got their food down too. They offered the men, who appeared to only have dry cakes and apples, some of theirs. David Russo was the only one of the three men with a bagful of things to eat; everyone's mood rose when he pulled out two bottles of very good red wine to go with the food.

"I'll find Rafo," Selva said to Margot. "I bet he'd like something to eat too."

Rafo appeared to be quite happy, sharing all the goodies on the table in his compartment.

"If you fancy some wine, pop in to see us," Selva said to her husband.

"If you fancy some cognac, you'd better pop in to see us," Rafo said in Turkish. "There's a young man in here who has a bag full of bottles. I wouldn't be surprised if he's an alcoholic."

"He probably needs it to relax his nerves," said Selva.

Seeing that Rafo was happy, she returned to her compartment feeling better.

Passengers who had started the journey feeling suspicious were now more relaxed and at ease with each other. They were mingling together and asking all sorts of questions. Everyone was talking except Perla, who still felt embarrassed and just looked out the window, and the man Margot thought she knew. It was gradually getting dark. The lights of the distant cities started twinkling, like stars in the sky.

Suddenly the train screeched to a halt, causing the passengers to jolt sharply. Shots were heard in the distance. Everybody looked at each other with fear in their eyes. Fazıl started to cry. David Russo got up, lowered the window, and leaned out. The whole compartment was filled with the smell of coal.

"We're not in a station. We seem to be in the middle of nowhere," David said.

Others jostled him to look outside. It was very dark, and there was nothing much to be seen, but it was obvious that the pretty places they had passed through during the afternoon were long gone.

"I must find Rafo. I wonder what's going on," Selva said, leaving the compartment. When her son saw her leaving, he started to cry.

"Come on then," she said. Fazıl toddled toward her, held her hand, and together they tried to walk down the corridor. It was full of people who'd rushed out of their compartments to see what was going on. Selva picked up Fazıl and held him in her arms to prevent him from getting crushed. She looked into each compartment as she passed by. She saw neither her husband nor Ferit. Her heart felt heavy. She walked back to the carriage exit. Marcel was standing by the door. They tried to force the door open and eventually succeeded. Marcel stepped out onto the running board and looked toward the front of the train.

"Madame Selva, there are some armed men standing by the side of the train."

Selva leaned out to have a look too. There were some soldiers holding lamps gathered around the engine at the front of the train.

"My God, maybe they've taken Rafo away. I can't find him anywhere!" she said.

"I'm sure he must have gone to find out what's happening. Why should they pick on him among all these people?" said Marcel. "Besides, hasn't he got a Turkish passport?"

"You're probably right. I'm just so on edge. All the same, I'd better walk up to the front just to see."

"Are you out of your mind?" Marcel said. "Go back inside."

Selva felt embarrassed and decided to return to her compartment. As she turned around, she bumped into David Russo, who was right behind her. Although it was dark, she could see the terror in his eyes; they were jutting out like organ stops.

"Did you say there are armed soldiers up front?" he asked.

"Yes, somewhere near the engine."

"Step aside. Please step aside," he said to Selva and Marcel. "I want to get off."

"To go where?"

"Wherever. Where I go isn't important. I must get off immediately."

Selva and Marcel looked at each other.

"But we are not in a station. Where on earth will you go?" Marcel asked.

"It doesn't matter. I'm going to get off and walk toward those lights in the distance."

"But you don't know where we are, David. You're bound to get lost."

"I can follow the railway lines."

David Russo jumped down without using the steps. Marcel and Selva, holding her child, followed him off the train. Marcel tried to hold on to David's arm, and the two began pushing each other.

"You're putting all of us in danger. Get back on the train immediately!"

"I can't bear being put back into a camp," said David. "Never again, never!"

"Hold on. No one's taking you to a camp."

David freed himself from Marcel. He started running toward the back of the train. Selva and Marcel ran after him. Fazıl, who appeared to be enjoying the chase, began screaming with joy. Suddenly they heard the sound of footsteps running after them. David started running faster, then a shot was heard! Suddenly, he stopped, Selva and Marcel ran into him, and they all fell over. The footsteps got nearer and nearer and then came to halt beside them. Two armed soldiers were pointing their guns at them.

"What's going on here?" asked one of the soldiers.

"We fell," replied Marcel.

"Were you running away?"

"What for?" said Selva.

"Where were you going then? On a picnic?"

"My son wanted to pee," explained Selva. "These gentlemen wanted to do the same and needless to say, they felt they had to distance themselves from me."

"Aren't there toilets on the train?"

"Of course there are, but they stink. What's more, there's a line. The carriage is very crowded."

"So why the hell were you running after these men who wanted to take a leak? Why were you running with your child in your arms? How come you fell?"

"I was trying to help my son do his business by the side of the train door. I heard a shot and I panicked and grabbed my son. I was running away trying to prevent him from being shot, when I ran into them."

"What shot? What are you talking about?"

"There was a shot," said Marcel. "Didn't you hear it?"

"Oh, that! That's the peasants trying to scare wild boar from their fields," one of the soldiers said. "Get up!"

They looked funny trying to disentangle themselves before they stood up. Selva saw Rafo and Ferit looking openmouthed and petrified behind the soldiers. She couldn't help laughing.

"I don't see what's so funny," Rafo said, reprimanding her.

Selva just couldn't stop laughing. Tears were streaming down her cheeks. Ferit held out his hand to help her get up, and Rafo picked up his son, who seemed to be having a whale of a time. He was trying to say something to his father while clapping his hands. Ferit also helped Marcel and David get up.

"Return to your carriage at once," said the soldier. "I'll also want to see your identity cards. We'll see how much of all this is true."

"What do you want from my wife?" asked Rafo.

"She was running away."

"What? Don't make me laugh," he said.

"We'll find out soon," the soldier replied.

Back in the carriage, the other passengers were all hanging out of the windows trying to see what was happening. When Selva returned to the compartment with the soldier, the other occupants started panicking. The man in the cap was totally unaware of what was going on; he was sleeping with his cap pulled down to his nose.

"Right! I want to see all three tickets and your identity cards. I want to see the child's as well," said the soldier.

"The child is registered in my passport," Selva said, then she turned to her son and pretended to scold him. "All this is because of you," she said to Fazıl, who looked surprised. "Just because you couldn't hang on for a little while."

Rafo took out his passport too. Ferit rambled on with an explanation of what *they* were doing outside while the soldier scrutinized Selva's, David's, Marcel's, and Rafo's passports and tickets.

"Hmm…You've bothered us for nothing," one of them said. "You'd better use the toilets on board next time you want to relieve yourself!" Then they turned their backs and marched away. As soon as they left, the man in the cap pushed it back and sat upright. David was sitting in his seat as if in a trance.

"What the hell were you doing outside?" Rafo asked furiously.

Selva couldn't reply, because she was scared of bursting into laughter again.

Marcel explained what happened and turned to David. "Didn't I tell you you'd get us all into trouble!" he shouted. Tears started running from David's empty eyes.

"Why are you so scared?" Selva asked, approaching him.

David didn't answer.

"You mentioned a camp. Did they take you to a camp before?"

"Yes, I just came out of one."

Selva sat beside him and put her arms around him. She gently stroked his hair. Everyone in the compartment was totally silent. Eventually, Marcel broke the silence.

"So, why did we stop? What did the armed soldiers want?"

"Apparently we are waiting for some soldiers to board this train. They are being transported somewhere."

"I wonder how long it will take?" asked Margot.

"It seems that we may be spending one or two nights here," said Ferit.

A murmur of discontent spread through the compartment.

"I'd like to have a word with you outside," Rafo said to his wife. Fazıl, who was sitting on Perla's lap, started to make a fuss when he saw his parents leaving the compartment, but one look from his father put a stop to that. Rafo and Selva stood in the corridor face-to-face.

"Listen to me, Selva. I'm warning you for the last time: if you bite off more than you can chew trying to help others again, I promise I'll divorce you the minute we get to Istanbul!"

Selva turned her back on him and returned to the compartment, slamming the door in his face.

The next morning, even though the sun was low, the rays disturbed David and woke him up. The sedative the old man had given him last night had sent him into such a deep sleep that he woke up totally rejuvenated and happy. When he was wide-awake, he remembered the previous night's incident and blushed. He had behaved like an idiot. Even though his traveling companions had treated him with compassion after hearing his story, he couldn't help feeling ashamed.

I wish I'd listened to those back home when I was released from the camp and seen a doctor, he thought. If I'd done that, it's possible we might not have had that incident last night. He realized that if Marcel and Selva hadn't run after him, he might have been shot by the soldiers trying to stop him from running away! He decided he was indeed a lucky soul: this was the second time his life had been spared by God.

A new day was dawning, a sunny, quiet, run-of-the-mill day. David, who couldn't bear being cooped up in small places since his time in the camp, felt stifled by the thought of spending the whole day in the compartment. He tried to relax.

Your life has been spared yet again, he thought. You're among friends. You're heading toward freedom. Come on, man, pull yourself together!

Margot was opposite him, sleeping. He smiled to himself. She was a beautiful girl. He wished she had been the one who showed him the care Selva had; maybe then this boring journey would be a little more interesting.

Selva, Perla, and Fazıl weren't in the compartment. They had probably gone to the toilet. The rest were still sleeping, their heads leaning on the shoulders of those next to them. Samuel's head was on the knees of the man in the cap. David went outside to go to the toilet and saw Selva talking to Perla.

"For God's sake, David, don't get off again, even if you really need to relieve yourself. They might recognize you and cause you trouble."

"I promise I won't. Please don't worry," David assured her.

"How did you sleep?"

"Extremely well. Madame Alfandari, I want to apologize sincerely for last night. Had it not been for you and Marcel, I would have been in big trouble. I'm deeply sorry for putting you in danger. Please forgive me."

"Don't mention it, and let's not talk about it again. There's nothing more natural than being scared of armed soldiers, after what you've been through. I can assure you that there is no need to apologize. Now then, I want to ask you a favor. First of all, please call me Selva, and second, throughout this journey, I want you to feel free to talk to me about anything, anytime, whatever it is that bothers you."

"I promise you it won't happen again."

"I know, David. This sort of thing doesn't often recur anyway. If it does, we'll *all* get locked up."

Just then David saw Rafael coming out of another compartment. "Here comes your husband," he said, trying to cheer her up, but she wasn't amused.

Rafo hugged and kissed his son. "Did you sleep well?" he asked his wife. Selva didn't reply, and David felt obliged to answer.

"Extremely," he said. "How about you?"

"Thanks to you, I've been having nightmares all night," Rafo replied.

David bent his head down as his face turned crimson. Selva held Fazıl by the hand and walked him back to the compartment. Margot had woken up and was staring at the man in the corner.

"Haven't you figured out who he is yet?" Selva asked.

"No, I just can't place him."

The man's cap had slid back while he was sleeping, and despite the stubble on his face, Margot could see him more clearly now.

"Oh dear!" she said suddenly. "Selva, I've got it. I know who he is."

"So who is he?"

"Come outside with me." Margot pulled herself together and they went out.

"I'm dying to know—for God's sake, who is he? Is he someone important?"

"You bet. He's only one of the world's leading scientists. He's a force to reckon with in the world of physics. Two years ago he won many awards for some discovery or other. Don't you remember? I remember seeing his photograph all over the medical magazines at work. He was being interviewed on the radio all the time. He's Meyer…Siegfried Meyer. That's it! The famous Siegfried Meyer."

"Oh yes! I remember. Oh, Margot!" said Selva, choking with excitement. "The Germans must be looking for him everywhere. They'd take him away the moment they spotted him."

She wanted to share this exciting discovery with her husband. What a pity that she was still annoyed with him. They returned to the compartment. Now Selva started scrutinizing the man's face herself. Yes, of course it was him. She was absolutely sure. In spite of his shaven head and having no beard, it was definitely him.

The sun had finally brightened up the whole compartment. Everyone had woken up. When Samuel opened his eyes and realized he had his head on a stranger's lap, he immediately sat up.

"Where's Perla?" he asked Margot, who was smiling at him. "Let me go and find her."

"Go if you wish, but don't worry about your sister. She's fine now. There's nothing to worry about."

All the same, Samuel got up and walked out. When Selva heard him greeting Ferit outside, she jumped from her seat and rushed out to see him.

"Ferit, I need to tell you something," she said, holding him by the arm.

"What? Has something gone wrong again?"

"Ferit, do you know who's traveling with us in our compartment?"

"Who?"

"Siegfried Meyer, the—"

Ferit covered her mouth with his hand. "Yes, I know."

"Why didn't you tell us?"

"No one knows. Is there anyone else who does?"

"Margot. She's the one who recognized him."

"Please keep this to yourselves," he said.

"Does Rafael know?"

"Yes, he's the only one apart from me."

"What name is he traveling under?" She tried to hide the fact that she was disappointed her husband hadn't shared his knowledge with her.

"Kohen."

"Has he got a Turkish passport?" she asked.

"Yes, he does."

"But he doesn't speak Turkish, does he?"

"That's why I sat him in the same compartment as you and David, and those who, thanks to you, can manage a few Turkish words. The Nazis don't generally speak Turkish, but you never know. An officer who spent time in Turkey might come along and want to show off. I know how quick and capable you are in such situations. I thought I'd better put him with you."

"How would I have known that? I should have been warned."

"I have faith in you, Selva. You don't miss a thing."

Samuel interrupted their conversation. "How much longer do you think we're going to wait here?" he asked.

"That's what I was just going to find out," replied Ferit. "I'm just going to see my wife, and then find out if anyone knows when we're supposed to continue."

"Give my regards to Evelyn, even though I've never met her. Ask her if she needs anything to eat or drink," Selva offered.

"Thank you, but I'm afraid that I can't do that. She isn't aware we are all traveling on the same train."

That Thursday by the German border was a rather long day. It was boring being cooped up in the train. Time passed more easily when the train moved through ever-changing scenery. Stopping away from a town or village, in the middle of nowhere, waiting from morning until night, was stifling, even though they were allowed out of the train to stretch their legs. Most of the passengers took advantage of a stroll along the track to get a breath of fresh air.

Ferit spent most of his time with his wife. In spite of her brother's insistence, Perla decided not to go out, but rather to lie down and read her book in the nearly empty compartment. The only other person who stayed was the man in the cap. He would be solving puzzles until the early hours of the morning.

At one point, David and Marcel played backgammon on a board Marcel had brought with him. Passengers in different compartments, even in different carriages, now had had a chance to mingle and talk with one another. Those in the same carriage somehow felt bound together. Realizing they shared the same fate, they had begun to feel more and more like a family. Even Selva, who had avoided eye contact with her husband all day long, had begun to relax a little. But at about five o'clock, as the evening sky turned from blue to purple, people started feeling restless again. The weather turned cooler and everyone returned to their seats, cramming into the small compartments. How much longer would this tiring journey last?

Marcel was able to coax a very uncooperative conductor who hadn't deigned to answer any questions all day to give them some sort of indication as to when they'd continue their journey.

"Don't hold me to it, but I don't think for one moment we'll be leaving before midnight," he said, grinning through his teeth.

Having eaten dinner in their compartments, the passengers decided to call it a day. They began to settle down to sleep early. Selva had had to take Fazıl to the toilet frequently the previous night, so she swapped seats and sat by the door, next to Siegfried. When the lights were turned off, just a few switched on their reading lights. Selva turned to the man whose identity she finally knew.

"Excuse me, monsieur. Would you mind terribly if I read for a little while, or would you prefer me to switch off my reading light?" she asked softly.

"Read to your heart's content, madame. I don't mind at all."

"Thank you very much. By the way, I'm Selva, Selva Alfandari. We haven't had the opportunity to meet yet."

"Let me introduce myself too. My name is Kohen," said the man.

"I'm pleased to meet you, Monsieur Kohen. I hope my son isn't disturbing you too much with his fidgeting."

"He's a bright lad, and very lovable," the man replied.

They had spent so much time together even he was beginning to relax a bit now. When he took off his cap in the dim light of the compartment, Margot winked at Selva.

A new night was beginning. Who knew what the following day had in store? Feeling a bit more optimistic, the passengers in the Star and Crescent carriage went to sleep.

Selva was dreaming that they had reached Istanbul. Her father had come to meet her. She wasn't on a train; she was on a ship. As the ship approached the deep-blue harbor with its background of minarets and domes, she jumped into the sea, swimming toward her father, who was waiting. Father and daughter were diving hand in hand into the depths of the sea. How she missed being together with him. They were swimming and swimming, down among the fish and the green seaweed.

Selva was woken up by a sudden shudder.

"What's happening?" Constance whispered.

"I think we're moving."

No one knew what time it was. Outside, it was still pitch-dark. While the train began to creak into motion, Fazıl grumbled, turning in Selva's arms. David Russo walked into the corridor, making sure not to disturb anyone. It was impossible for him to remain in the same place for more than a few hours. He lit a cigarette. Far away in the distance, lights could be seen. Would his life ever brighten again? As he paced up and down the corridor, the dark-blue sky was gradually making way for the crimson-red colors of dawn.

The train crossed the German frontier while they were having breakfast. Selva's heart nearly broke in fear when she saw Ferit and Rafo walking toward customs. "Please, God, protect us; don't let anything go wrong," she prayed aloud. She had woken up so happy after her dream, and she didn't want anything to spoil it.

"I wonder if we could go out for some fresh air?" asked Constance.

"Stay right where you are!" replied her husband.

Margot boiled some water on the hot plate at the end of the corridor. Their bread had become stale, but they were managing with biscuits and cakes. Selva offered some to the old man, who never wanted to eat anything.

"You didn't eat anything last night either. I know it's all a bit dry, but please let me slice you a piece of cake at least."

"Thank you, my dear," he said. "I just can't."

"I guess dry cake isn't very appetizing. How about a slice of salami?"

"I'll just have some tea, thank you."

Selva was suddenly aware of a bad smell coming from the salami she'd taken from her basket. I'd better throw this away in the station later, she thought to herself.

She left the basket on her seat to go to the toilet. Stepping out of the compartment, she found several German soldiers in the corridor checking the compartments. Selva joined the line at the toilet and when she'd come out, the Germans had gone.

Rafo had returned and asked Margot where his wife was. When he saw Selva, he asked, "Am I still getting the silent treatment?"

"Weren't *you* the one divorcing me?"

"Don't be silly, for God's sake."

Selva passed by her husband without saying anything, and Rafo grabbed her by the arm. "Can't you see that I worry about you? You keep putting yourself in dangerous situations. One of these days, you'll get into serious trouble."

Back in the compartment, Selva lifted her basket to put it away, but the salami was no longer there. She looked around. Fazıl was sitting on Samuel's lap, munching away. She immediately rushed and took the remaining piece from him.

"Did you eat all of it?" she asked.

Fazıl looked at her with pleasure in his eyes, nodding his head.

"What have you done? This salami is rotten!"

She became extremely anxious. What would she do if Fazıl became sick on the train?

"He ate this rotten salami while I was in the toilet," she said, turning to Margot. "What are we going to do?"

"Was it really rotten? He seemed to be enjoying it immensely."

"He loves salami."

"Don't worry. The worst that can happen is that he gets the runs."

The train rocked again and they were on their way. Ferit came into the compartment.

"I hope we're safe," he said. "We managed to cross the German border without any bother."

"Didn't they ask you anything?"

"What's to ask?" said the old man. "We're coming from a country they're occupying! There's no such thing as a border anymore."

Their entry into Germany went without a hitch, and the carriage was filled with joy. Everyone was talking, laughing, and joking together.

Siegfried and the old man, whose name, they found out, was Asseo, were having a deep conversation in German. The rays of the autumn sun filled the compartment. First the train passed through peaceful villages with small mud-roofed houses and neat vegetable gardens and fields of grazing cows; then there were small towns with stone houses under red-tiled roofs, and swimming pools and churches; finally, they moved through cities with baroque buildings. The train was going full steam, as if it were racing against time.

"Ahhh, look at that; we've just passed Karlsruhe station!" announced Marcel.

"Karlsruhe is in the south," the old man said anxiously. "I wonder where they are taking us."

A cloud came over Siegfried's face too.

"Would you like a cigarette, Monsieur Kohen?" asked Margot.

"Thank you, but I'd rather smoke my own brand," he replied, walking out into the corridor. Asseo followed him. Margot watched Siegfried take an elegant cigarette case from his pocket and offer a cigarette to Asseo. The two men started smoking, and once again, anxiety spread through the compartment. Everyone, except the children, was disturbed.

"I'm going to find Ferit," Marcel said, leaving the compartment.

When he came back, he reported, "Apparently we're unable to follow our route. Some of the tracks have been bombed and others have been closed. It seems we have to continue our journey weaving our way north and south like this. What else can they do? The journey will be longer, but it seems there's nothing to worry about."

After leaving Karlsruhe, the train turned north toward Mannheim and they relaxed again.

"If this anxiety continues, Selva, it will be the death of us, I'm sure," Margot said.

"If this is as bad as it gets, I can put up with it," Selva replied.

The train reached Frankfurt around lunchtime. Despite the fact that the station was inundated with soldiers, it was nice to be in a crowded station, bustling with people, after spending so much time in the middle of nowhere. But the presence of soldiers and SS guards became more and more pervasive. The worst they'd experienced was the wait at the border, so they felt confident enough to get off the train for the half-hour stop. They hoped they would have sufficient time to replenish their food, buy newspapers, or have coffee in the station café.

Selva didn't leave her seat. She didn't want to disturb Fazıl, who had had a stomachache for over an hour. He had managed to relax after having a cup of tea and falling asleep on her lap. Asseo and Siegfried were the only others remaining in the compartment. Asseo's face was very pale.

"Why don't you go out for some fresh air, Monsieur Asseo?" Selva asked.

"I don't feel well enough to cope with the crowds," he replied.

"Of course you're not well enough. You've hardly eaten a thing. I'll give you some cake when Fazıl wakes up."

"I must say I find you Turks extremely generous," replied Asseo. "I hope my health will allow me to reach your country."

"Don't say things like that, Monsieur Asseo. You'll be all right. You'll see. We only have another few days before we get to Turkey."

"Provided, of course, we don't have to go too slowly and we're not kept hanging around. If we continue at this rate, the journey could even take a month."

"That's wartime for you," said Selva.

Rafo didn't see his wife among the crowd on the platform, so he went back to the train.

"What's wrong, Selva? Why didn't you and Fazıl get off?"

"Fazıl has a bad stomachache. He ate a huge piece of rotten salami this morning." Her anxiety over her son had made her forget about their fight.

"Where did he get the salami?"

"From my food basket."

"Why on earth did you let him eat it?"

"He took it when I went to the toilet."

Suddenly she realized that she had offered some salami to the old man.

"Monsieur Asseo, I assure you I didn't know it was bad. It's good you didn't accept it."

The old man smiled. "Believe me, madame, I've had to eat far worse things than that. The important thing is not to go hungry."

"Rafo," Selva said, "will you go and find a pharmacy in the station and get something for Fazıl's tummy immediately?"

Rafo took Siegfried's cigarette order and left. Asseo and Siegfried sat with Marcel's backgammon set between them and started playing. Selva waited anxiously. Rafo took a long time to come back, but eventually he did, laden with all sorts of things.

"What took you so long? I was worried," said Selva.

"Really, young lady, now you know what it means to worry."

"You think I don't know, Rafo?"

She reminded him of the anxiety she had gone through when he was taken away by the Gestapo. Rafo kissed Selva affectionately on the cheek.

"I couldn't find a pharmacy, Selva. I couldn't risk leaving the station to look for one. I asked a nurse who's in another carriage, and she told me to either make him be sick, or give him something diarrhetic to eat. She assured me he would be OK after that."

"Where on earth will I find something diarrhetic here? Are you suggesting that I cook him vegetables on the train?"

"She suggested salty water to make him vomit."

Selva screwed up her face.

"He's relaxed now. Let's see how he is when he wakes up." Rafo looked at the men playing backgammon.

"Who's winning, gentlemen?"

"Is it possible to win playing him?" said Asseo.

"Don't tell me Monsieur Kohen is a backgammon champion."

"I win whenever we play," replied Siegfried.

Selva decided then that the two men must be old friends. She hadn't realized it before, because they had hardly spoken to each other. She thought they had just met on the train.

"I'm a good player too," said Rafo.

"In that case, you should play the winner," said Siegfried.

When, at last, those who had got off started returning to their seats, Selva gave a sigh of relief. She wanted to continue the journey without stopping at all. Although she had no one to meet her there, she wanted to return to her country as soon as possible. Her father had met the director of the immigration department. He obviously knew of their imminent journey. Would her mother be there to meet her? If her mother knew the date of her return, she would probably come in spite of her father. Her heart felt heavy just thinking about it. Now she couldn't bear to think of parents and children not communicating with each other. How would she explain all this to Fazıl one day? Thank God he was only a child now, but she was sure that he would be asking questions one day.

Margot, Constance, Marcel, David, and the children came back to the compartment loaded with food, drinks, and newspapers.

Siegfried and Asseo immediately fell upon the newspapers.

"Russia and Czechoslovakia have signed an agreement," Siegfried said after scanning his paper, and everyone was all ears. "The Russians have agreed to train the Czechs on their own soil in order to fight the Germans."

"They did the same with Poland," said Asseo. "The Germans were prepared to let the Poles train for their own purposes, but then in 1939, they invaded. The Russians don't want to give up Poland."

"It's all up to the British," said Siegfried. "Churchill claims he can't force his new allies to give up vital territories. However, if he insisted, the question of the border between Russia and Poland could be solved."

"Look what it says here."

"What? I haven't read anything good yet."

"There's a statement saying that the 1939 agreement is no longer valid. In other words, Poland can redraw her borders," said Asseo.

"You're very optimistic. This is just a ploy to delay things. If it were up to me, I'd be against both the Czechs and Poles training in Russia."

"There's a saying in Turkish, Monsieur Kohen," said Rafo. "He who falls into the sea will cling even to a serpent."

"That's very appropriate," said Siegfried. "It certainly explains this situation."

"Are the two of you Polish?" asked Marcel.

"We aren't," answered the old man with a sad smile. "We have Turkish passports."

Asseo and Siegfried closed the backgammon board.

"Who won?" asked Rafo.

"The outcome was obvious right from the start," Siegfried answered, smiling cheerfully.

Margot and Selva looked at each other happily. They realized he'd finally managed to overcome his tension.

Then the train pulled away. The skinny conductor had been replaced by a more robust one.

"Where are we stopping on the way to Berlin?" asked Marcel.

This new conductor was more forthcoming. "We have an eight- to ten-hour journey ahead of us. If there are no problems and no instructions to the contrary, we should stop at Kassel and Magdeburg on the way."

It started to rain as they passed through woods full of tall trees with their leaves turning red, and then the suburban towns again. The pouring rain made it impossible to see through the windows. The passengers in the various compartments felt secure together in their own little worlds. The men played backgammon, and the women were exchanging recipes. The pain in Fazıl's stomach disturbed him from time to time, but then he'd calm down. The passengers seemed to have lost all notion of time.

It was dark all around, and a strong wind had started to blow. Food appeared all over again; Fazıl saw the food and wanted to eat in spite of his tummy ache.

"You haven't eaten a thing all day, Monsieur Asseo," Selva said. "Why don't you have some cheese and biscuits?"

The old man took some, thanking her.

"I'm opening my last bottle of wine," said David. "Now we have to stock up every time we stop."

He poured wine into everyone's tin mugs.

"Here's to the exquisite taste of our last French bottle."

They made a toast for a safe rest of the journey, lifting their mugs as if they were glasses.

"There's just a little drop more in the bottle," David whispered into Margot's ear. "I've saved it for you. Who knows if we'll ever drink such good wine again?"

"Why me?"

"Beautiful women like you deserve it."

"I can see you're feeling much better, David."

"Let's just say I'm resigned to my destiny…But I still can't bear being cooped up in narrow spaces."

"I'm sure you'll get over it soon. Try not to worry. God has given us the power to deal with anything."

"Look! We've just passed Magdeburg," Selva suddenly shouted. "Weren't we supposed to stop there?"

"That's not possible, surely. Are you sure?" asked Marcel.

"Of course I am. The sign was huge, but we passed through at full speed."

"In that case, we didn't stop at Kassel either," said Asseo. "Strange! I didn't notice because I was concentrating on the game."

"I wonder why," said David.

Rafo, who was playing backgammon with Siegfried, became alarmed.

"I'd better go and find Ferit and see why we didn't stop. He may have spoken to the conductor."

The train was plowing through the night at full speed. They hadn't traveled so fast since they boarded the train, and their efforts to see outside were in vain. The station Selva claimed to have seen was left far behind. The soft, relaxed atmosphere of just a few minutes before now became tense. Fazıl started to be a killjoy again.

Rafo and Ferit returned to the compartment.

"I spoke to the conductor," Ferit said. "Selva was right; we didn't stop at either of the stations. We're heading for Berlin."

"Why didn't we stop?"

"Apparently the train has to be in Berlin before midnight."

"In that case, we might be able to make up some lost time," said Constance.

"I was supposed to get more wine at Mannheim," said David.

"You can get it in Berlin."

"At this time of night?"

"I don't know about wine, but I'm sure you can get beer, young man," the old man said. "Beer runs out of the taps in this country."

Realizing that there was no chance of stopping and getting off for fresh air, Rafo returned to his own compartment. Some of the others took out their books to read, or prepared to sleep.

The lights in the compartments had been turned off. Apart from Siegfried, who sat gazing at the dark window, everyone else was sleeping. Suddenly Fazıl started to scream and cry.

"My tummy…my tummy hurts."

"Shush, Fazıl, please don't cry; everyone's asleep. Show me where it hurts," Selva said.

The child pointed at his tummy with his tiny fingers. Selva removed his pants so they weren't too tight around his waist. She cradled him on her lap, but the child wouldn't stop crying. Everyone switched on their reading lights, one by one. Selva looked around desperately.

"Shall I call Rafo?" asked Margot.

"What can he do about a stomachache?"

"You remember he said there was a nurse on board."

"Surely we can't wake the woman up at this time of night."

"If it's an emergency, why not?"

"Wait, Margot," she said. "Let me try some salty water first. If he throws up, he might feel better. If he doesn't, then we can call this lady."

Everyone started making suggestions at the same time, but no one could really help. While they prepared the salty water, the train came to an abrupt halt, just as it had done before. Selva, who was standing up, nearly fell down.

Margot looked outside.

"We seem to have stopped at a small station," she said, "but I can't see a sign. I wonder where we are."

"I just hope to God that we don't stop *here* for hours."

As Selva gave Fazıl the water, she heard the crunch of soldiers' boots outside. Every time she'd heard that sound over the past few years, she got goose pimples. The others heard the familiar sound as well and they got up from their seats, jostling one another at the window. A squad of soldiers was outside. Agitated passengers could be heard in the corridor. Selva stood with the glass of salty water in her hand. Fazıl was frightened, and he stopped crying. Siegfried picked up his cap from his knees and put it on, pulling it well down to his nose. Rafo appeared at the door, looking very pale.

"I hear there's going to be a search."

"What kind of search?"

"I think it's to do with a fugitive or something like that."

The soldiers could be heard getting onto the train. They started from the first compartment, asking for identity cards. The faces of those in the compartment were ashen. Rafo stood upright by the door, not knowing exactly what he should do.

A soldier saluted and walked in. "Passports, please!"

Ferit came running with the passports.

"I'm responsible for this carriage. Here are all the passports."

"Let everyone hold their own passports."

Ferit handed them out.

"Kezban Mitel, Yakup Mitel, Peri Naim, Sami Naim, Monsieur Russo, Monsieur Kohen, Monsieur Asseo…"

While the passports were being distributed, Selva was trying to make Fazıl drink the salty water.

"Drink all of it, all of it…that's my boy…what a good boy!"

The child struggled, but his mother managed to coax him into finishing the whole glass. The soldier started to scrutinize the passports. He looked carefully at the face first, and then checked the photograph in the passport. There wasn't a sound from anyone. One of the old man's eyes started twitching badly. While the soldier checked the passports of Siegfried and those sitting opposite Selva, she pushed her finger down Fazıl's throat. The child dry heaved, then dry heaved again as if he were drowning. He was sitting sideways on his mother's lap, facing Siegfried. Suddenly he began to struggle, his eyes full of tears, and he retched and vomited all over the man. Apart from the smell of vomit, another disgusting smell spread throughout the compartment. Selva was agitated. She lifted Fazıl from her lap onto his feet, and tried to remove his badly soiled pants. Mother and son were struggling when he kicked his feet, and his pants flew off and landed on Siegfried's lap. Siegfried didn't utter a word. He just sat upright with his cap on, his lap covered in excrement and vomit and a tearful expression in his eyes.

"*Pardon*, Monsieur Kohen, *mille pardon*; you know the child was ill."

David intervened, saying, "Give me your passport. I'll give it to him."

He took the soiled passport from Siegfried, who remained frozen to the spot and gave it to the soldier.

The smell was unbearable and Fazıl was screaming at the top of his lungs. He too was covered in excrement and vomit.

"Damned kids!" said the soldier. He looked at the passport David offered him from a distance, as if it were some disgusting insect, and beat a hasty retreat into the corridor. Before getting off the train, he shouted to a dumbstruck Rafo, "Quick, open the window in the corridor."

Even after the soldier had gone, no one moved from their seat. Only Rafo moved, first to open the window in the corridor, then the compartment window. Then he rushed out, as he couldn't stand the foul odor. Nobody uttered a word until the train moved again. The only sound was of Fazıl screaming at the top of his lungs.

As the train slowly picked up speed, Selva turned to Siegfried. "Please don't move, Monsieur Kohen. I'll clean up my son and then see to you."

"Thank you, madame. I thank both you and your son."

After Siegfried finished cleaning himself up, fresh air, smelling of rain, wafted through the window. After the air in the compartment had cleared, they closed the window. Fazıl had fallen into a deep sleep in his mother's arms. Asseo stood up and reached for something on the rack, and when he couldn't find it, he turned to David. "Can you help me, young man? There's a box I can't reach behind my suitcase."

David pulled a violin case from the rack. The old man opened it, took the violin out, and turned to his fellow passengers, who all looked surprised.

"I'd like to play some music for all of you. I hope it will relax you. At the same time, I think we ought to celebrate young Alfandari's magnificent recovery." Asseo placed the violin under his chin and started to play with all the power left in his body.

The notes of the Paganini violin concerto flowed through the compartment like a stream rippling down snow-covered mountains. The music touched the souls and hearts of those in the compartment, carrying them far away. Siegfried found himself transported to the shade of the pine trees back home. Marcel and Constance were taken back to Lyon, where they had first met, fallen in love, and married. Margot, on the other hand, was reliving that last night before she boarded the train, the night she hadn't wanted to end. The music was transporting them all far beyond the clouds hanging over them.

The adagio…It was as though the bow was playing the notes on their heartstrings, not the violin. As the bow wandered through the chords of the violin, it seemed to relate the sad stories of those on board. It was expressing their fear, degradation, exclusion, separation, longing, and pain.

Other people from the carriage started gathering around the compartment door. They crammed into the corridor and listened in awe, almost afraid to breathe in case they broke the magic spell of the music that seemed to describe their grief.

The *allegro spiritoso*...The old violinist turned into a young man, transporting the listeners through love and hope to bright sunny days in a different country. He was promising them peace of mind and a happy life ahead in a fruitful land. The exuberant music excited them, lifted them to heaven's most beautiful corners. They seemed to be quickly climbing a ladder leading to hope. Life was beautiful. It was worth living, even in a cramped, narrow corridor. Just one note, a single note, was enough to symbolize the power of humanity.

It was about midnight when they arrived at the Berlin station. The engine screeched on the tracks as usual, waking some of those who were sleeping.

Evelyn, who had been sleeping uneasily, clutching her bag firmly on her lap, woke up. She relaxed a little when she saw that her bag was safe.

She wasn't feeling secure in her compartment. She was sitting with people she didn't know at all. Just as she would get used to passengers beside or opposite her, they would get off and new passengers would take their place. Her fellow passengers changed each time the train stopped. Ferit came to see her too at each stop. He had shopped for whatever she wanted at the stations, but she still couldn't help being angry with him. There were some unanswered questions in her mind about her husband. Why had he almost forbidden her to come to Paris? Why had he suddenly decided to rent their apartment? Why did he insist that they meet at the station? Why had he emptied the cupboards and drawers of their apartment, and why had he packed her bag for her? Was there another woman? Could there be another woman?

Evelyn had been in love with her husband ever since they had met. She had found the young Turk handsome and intriguing. He was a mysterious man from another world, molded by a different culture. She had been a bit apprehensive at the beginning of their relationship. She was worried that he might behave like a Turk—whatever that meant. There was a French saying, for instance, that was a little condescending and alarming: "*tête de Turc*." Ferit, however, was the most civilized and courteous man she'd ever met, and that included her father. He was an excellent combination of Eastern and Western cultures: brave, trustworthy, affectionate, sensitive, and very knowledgeable. Surely a man with such qualities wouldn't betray his wife when she was pregnant. He couldn't have. And yet why did she feel this way? Every time she felt suspicious, she felt an ache in her heart.

The train had stopped. Evelyn looked out the window. They were some way outside the station. There were junctions outside most big stations where trains met and separated in all directions, and this was just such a place. Although it was very quiet, one could hear the noise of the station in the distance. She felt sure that Ferit would be along to see her, and she walked out into the corridor. There were some others there, either smoking cigarettes or just curious to know why they had stopped. She lowered the window in the corridor and breathed in the damp air. She could smell coal—coal yet again! She looked forward to the moment she would no longer smell it. She was looking forward to breathing the fresh air of a sunny day, filling her lungs with air from the sea and the meadows. Ferit had promised her this. He had assured her that the sun in his country was just as bright as in France, that the sea was deep blue, sometimes dark blue, and the air definitely cleaner. His relations in Istanbul would come to greet her fondly at the station. He claimed that the loneliness felt even among a crowd in Paris didn't exist in Istanbul. Even in the most unlikely places, one could feel the warmth of the slightest contact. That was how Ferit had described it all to her.

Several workers in overalls were bustling to and fro over the maze of railway lines. A man from a neighboring compartment was leaning out the window and calling to them. They spoke for some time. At one point she thought she heard Istanbul mentioned.

"Excuse me, do you speak French?" she asked.

"A little."

"What did he just say? Did he mention how much longer we are supposed to wait here?"

"Apparently we're leaving shortly."

"Oh, good. I was wondering why we had stopped out here so far from the station."

"It seems they're switching the points."

"Why?"

"It's to do with the carriage at the end. It's to be connected to another train that won't be stopping in Berlin."

"Why's that?"

"I didn't understand the details. It's taking a different route to Istanbul or something."

The train suddenly jolted as if moving away.

Evelyn was terrified. "What about us?" she asked.

"We're pulling into the station now."

Evelyn ran to the door and tried to open it but couldn't manage it. She called out to the man, "Please help me, monsieur, I beg of you…"

The man ran toward Evelyn, whose pregnancy wasn't very obvious.

"How can I help you? Is there something the matter?"

"Please help me open this door."

"Why do you need to open it? We've started to move."

"I beg you," Evelyn said, struggling with the door.

"If it's fresh air you want, the window is open."

"I need to get off. I must get off."

"Life is worth living, madame. Please don't do that!"

Finally the door opened. Evelyn stepped down onto the running board. The train had gradually started moving forward. She jumped in the opposite direction. Her bag went one way, and she the other. She stumbled a bit and then fell to her knees. Two of the workers who were changing the points ran to her aid. She couldn't understand what they were saying, but she understood from the way they were moving their hands that they thought she was crazy.

"French?" she asked. The man nodded to say no. "English?"

"*Nein, nein.*"

One of the men held Evelyn's arms and helped her get up. The other retrieved her bag. Evelyn tidied herself up and looked at the train pulling away.

"My God, what have I done!" she said. "What have I done?"

The workers were as shocked as she was. Evelyn started walking back along the line. There was a carriage waiting in the dark, far away in the distance. That must be the carriage Ferit was in. She knew Ferit was in that carriage because she remembered him saying to her, "Unfortunately, my darling, no one's getting off on the way because all the passengers are going to Istanbul." On the other hand, if that wasn't Ferit's carriage in the distance, it could be the end of everything. When it was eventually connected to another train and entered the station, her husband would go to see her, but he wouldn't be able to find her. She started to cry. She was walking and crying at the same time. If she couldn't find Ferit in that distant carriage, she would walk back to the station. Surely her husband wouldn't leave without her. She was certain that he would hear of the crazy woman who had jumped off the train and realize that it must be her. Or would he simply think some woman had attempted to commit suicide? She remembered that man in the corridor who had told her that life was worth living. Silly man, she thought. He must have thought I wanted to kill myself. Suddenly she heard someone running after her. Evelyn started running too. Some men started shouting and blowing whistles. When she heard dogs barking, she got scared and stopped. Uniformed men were approaching her. One of them was a policeman. The others were obviously stationmasters.

They started yelling and saying something in German. Evelyn pointed to the carriage in the distance, trying to explain that she wanted to reach it. The men held her by the arms, trying to take her back, and she tried to resist, but when they started dragging her, she shouted at the top of her voice, "Feriiiiit, Feriiiiit!" She yelled and yelled, but her voice was drowned out by the sound of train whistles.

"Let go of me," she screamed, but eventually she realized they would drag her back anyway, so she gave up struggling and decided to walk with them obediently.

Some footsteps were heard behind them. A man was running fast and out of breath. "Stop!" he shouted in German.

The men stopped and turned around. When she saw her husband, looking all disheveled and obviously in distress, she collapsed.

"What are you doing with my wife?" asked Ferit. "Where are you taking her?"

"Frankly, we ought to be taking her to a lunatic asylum, but we are only taking her to the stationmaster's office. She jumped off the train."

"What?"

"Look here, who are you? What the hell are you doing out here in the dark? You'd better come with us too; we'll need a statement!"

Ferit knelt down beside his wife. "What did you do? Did you really jump off the train?"

"It hadn't accelerated yet."

"You're not hurt, are you?"

"I'm fine," Evelyn said as she got up with Ferit's help. "You weren't going to leave me behind on my own in Berlin, were you?"

"I only realized that we had been disconnected from the train a few minutes ago. I was running to the station to find you. I panicked thinking about what I would do if the train had already left…" He couldn't finish his sentence.

Ferit put his arms around his wife, feeling very guilty. The two of them walked back to the station buildings with the Germans.

❧

After listening to Ferit's explanation, the stationmaster asked, "So why were you and your wife traveling in different carriages?"

"My wife is expecting. I wanted her to travel first class."

"There are first-class compartments on every carriage."

"But I just explained to you. Our carriage is special. It's carrying Turks who want to return to Turkey from France. It's very crowded."

"I don't know why all these Turks are so keen to go home in these crowded conditions, especially when they've been living in Paris," he said sarcastically.

"They're running away from the war."

"But there's no fighting in France."

"Don't you think we're going through war?"

"Of course, but France is not at war."

"This is wartime, *Mein Herr*. It can spread anywhere at any moment."

"It can also spread to your country."

"We're neutral, and we're doing our utmost to keep it that way, despite the Allies' insistence that we change our attitude."

"You don't say."

"Yes. For instance, we're selling chrome to Germany, even though Britain is not at all happy about it."

"Don't try to change the subject. You said you wanted your wife to travel first class, yet her compartment was just as crowded."

"How could I have known in advance that that would be the case?"

"So who exactly are these passengers traveling in this special carriage of yours? Are they Jews?"

"Most of them are Muslim Turks. There are some who are Jewish or Christian. But they're Turkish citizens, born and bred in Turkey."

"Is that so?" the German said with a provocative smile.

"Surely, *Mein Herr*, you don't think for a moment that at a time when Turkey is struggling so hard to remain neutral she would provide a carriage for the transportation of Jews? There's a saying we use in Turkish: 'Even the crows would laugh.'"

The German burst into laughter. He seemed to appreciate the joke. Because Evelyn couldn't speak German, she sat by her husband listening, but not understanding one word.

"In that case, if I were to off-load those few Jews, Turkey surely wouldn't mind."

"I'm afraid that's where you're totally wrong. Turkey fought for the right to have her citizens returned from the camps, even in France. If you did such a thing, that would be your decision, but I'd have to report your actions to our embassy in Berlin. The embassy would have to make all sorts of inquiries and then send officials here to deal with the matter. We could all be stranded here for days. Not only that, but we'd delay one of your lines as well. All this for the sake of a few people. Is it worth it, I ask you? If it were up to me, frankly, you could take them all."

"Didn't you say earlier that Turkey wouldn't jeopardize her position providing a carriage for Jews? Would she now go to all that trouble for a handful of them?"

"It's a question of prestige, *Mein Herr*. Because we are a secular nation, we have to be seen by the world to be abiding by the rules of our constitution. As for providing a carriage for the Jews, surely no one can accuse Turkey for helping its stranded citizens. You understand this is just a token gesture, don't you?"

"You certainly have a gift for bullshitting. I'm letting you go, because your documents are in perfect order and your wife is pregnant. Make sure you're not a nuisance to your fellow passengers or the station personnel inside our borders. Is that clear?"

"Yes, of course, *Mein Herr,* rest assured."

"Now take your wife and make sure she sits next to you for the rest of the journey."

Ferit and Evelyn left the stationmaster's office hand in hand, walking toward the Star and Crescent carriage waiting at the far end of the station.

"Why didn't you tell me the truth, Ferit?" asked Evelyn.

"I didn't want to put you in any danger."

"Why would it be dangerous for me to travel in a carriage sent by Turkey to pick up Turks?"

"That's not the whole story. There are people on board who have Turkish passports but who aren't Turkish. If they're found out, I didn't want you to be traveling in the same carriage."

"You made a big mistake," Evelyn said. She was surprised to be feeling mixed emotions, both relieved and frightened at the same time.

At the end of the asphalt platform, passage became difficult. Stumbling over the railway lines, they held onto each other and walked toward the distant, dim yellow light.

People were leaning over one another, trying to look out of the windows. When they saw Ferit and Evelyn, they all applauded enthusiastically. Evelyn was taken aback. The conductor standing by the carriage door asked to see her ticket. Ferit wanted to tell him to mind his own business, because this carriage was the property of his country, but he put on his most courteous manner and presented it.

"Here you are. Paid for all the way through to Istanbul."

"Is there room inside?"

"She'll sit on my lap," Ferit said, winking at the man.

As they passed Selva's compartment, Ferit turned to Asseo and said, "I want it to be known, Monsieur Asseo—I expect a concert to celebrate our return."

It wasn't until the following morning that the carriage was on its way. The Star and Crescent carriage was hitched to a freight train destined for Bucharest. They would be traveling at a slower speed, but there were no scheduled stops on the way, which was a great relief to them all. Even if they were stopped randomly by the SS, the checks would be less stringent now. They would travel via Leipzig, Prague, Bratislava, Budapest, and finally Bucharest. Once they reached Bucharest, those going to Köstence would disembark, and those going on to Istanbul would wait to be connected to another engine.

Waiting, escaping, hiding, and waiting again for another departure, another way out; going, going, without resting; scattered to the four corners of the world, seeking refuge in every corner, struggling for survival. Uprooting, having to go somewhere else again. Was this the price to pay for not having a motherland?

Old Asseo's eyes were closed. Those in the compartment thought he was sleeping, but he was only thinking. The train was going through countries neighboring his motherland, the motherland he hadn't been able to return to since he was twelve.

Lech was born in Poland. His father had died when he was ten. Then his mother had met a German engineer while she was working as a secretary. They'd married and moved to Germany, taking Lech with them. Lech's stepfather had been kind to him. He had sent his stepson to the Salzburg Music Academy when he realized Lech had a talent for music. Lech studied diligently so as not to let his stepfather down. His greatest ambition was to join the Vienna Philharmonic as a violinist.

When his mother gave birth to his brother, Lech was fifteen. Lech was never jealous of his brother, and when his brother started school, they found out he was a genius. At this time, his stepfather died of a heart attack quite suddenly, much like his own father. After the funeral, when they returned home, his mother held his head between her hands.

"From now on, Lech, you must be your brother's father. I'm entrusting him to you. I want you to protect him the way your stepfather protected you."

From that day on, Lech abandoned his dream of becoming a famous violinist. He played anywhere where he'd be paid so that his brother could study. He played for his brother to continue his education in the best intermediate schools; he played to pay for summer schools, for special tuition, to see his brother through university. He kept playing and playing the violin, and never married. He had no children, but he never regretted anything. From the age of twenty, he had felt that his brother was his son. His brother's success was his own success; his happiness was Lech's happiness.

His brother managed to get his master's in America through scholarships, and everyone expected that he would settle there, but instead he returned to Germany because he wanted to give back to his own country. He got married and started a family, and from that time on he and his family enjoyed happy days full of hope. Lech's brother had reached the peak of his career. He had become famous, successful, and very wealthy. Lech's sacrifices hadn't been in vain. It was too late by then to follow his own dreams, but he had no regrets.

In Germany the brother lived happily and comfortably until Hitler came on the scene. Then all hell broke loose. The family first ran away to Belgium. When the brother lost one of his sons in a street skirmish, the family escaped to France, where he was offered an important teaching post at a university in Paris. They settled in well and got used to living there, until Hitler arrived. Then they fled south, farther and farther south. His wife, who had been ill since the loss of her son, finally lost the will to live during one of these flights and died.

This was just another example of the Jews' endless flight, a flight that had lasted for five thousand years! The Germans were everywhere. They seemed to permeate Europe like smoke: Holland, Belgium, Poland, France, Czechoslovakia, Austria, and Hungary. There was no getting away. The Germans seemed to be working like a malignant cancer, spreading through the organs of a body. People were continuously on the run, running away under assumed names and holding false passports. Lech had reached the point where he only wanted to rest his tired, miserable body, to find peace pushing up the daisies. He wanted to rest somewhere in the Promised Land, away from German soldiers, SS officers, the Gestapo, and the collaborators.

Asseo became so tired of thinking that he eventually fell asleep. Four SS officers boarded the train. He didn't hear Rafo and Ferit arguing with them.

"This is a private carriage; as you can see, it is totally full," Ferit insisted, but eventually had to give in and make room for them in one of the compartments. The soldiers were guarding some war equipment that had been loaded onto the freight train. Obviously they had decided to enjoy the comfort of a luxurious carriage. They thought they'd be able to stretch their legs on the opposite seat and sleep for a while.

It was morning when Monsieur Asseo opened his eyes. He was glad to be with his fellow passengers, who had become like a family to him. It soothed him to feel the warmth of being together. He was going to Istanbul and would find out how to get to Palestine from there—to die in the Promised Land. But now, having met these people, he began to feel different. He wished it was possible to continue this journey forever, as though he were snuggled up in some long black cradle... *Clickety-clack... clickety-clack.*

They were traveling again through gorgeous countryside: pretty villages with houses made of sun-dried bricks, vegetable gardens, green fields with cows happily chewing their cud, towns with little domed churches, streams cascading down mountains, lush green valleys. The view from the windows was ever changing, all reminiscent of postcards people send with affectionate notes scribbled on the back.

Fazıl, playing with Samuel, was gurgling away happily. The women got down their food baskets and were offering everyone cheese, jam, pickles, cold meat, and fruit. Siegfried played backgammon with Marcel. The train continued its journey, rattling through scenery that was like a kaleidoscope. Not only was the train carrying its passengers through different geographical features, but it was exposing them to life itself, transporting them through different countries and different cultures.

Through conversations in the compartment, fellow passengers had learned that Monsieur Asseo and Samuel and his sister would be continuing their journey to Palestine. Margot would try her luck in Istanbul, hoping that if this turmoil in Europe ever ended, she could return to her own country. Marcel and Constance would stay in Istanbul until they could arrange their passage to America. They had a friend working in the American consulate whom they were counting on to help them. David's journey would also end in Istanbul, just like Rafo's, Selva's, and Fazıl's.

What about Monsieur Kohen? Siegfried had said nothing about his plans. Whenever anyone asked his destination, he gave a vague answer such as, "I'm happy as long as we keep on the move." He was fully aware, always frightened, that if the Gestapo should board the train and recognize him, they would take him back to Germany.

If the Germans should get hold of him, they might use his God-given genius to carry out projects that would exterminate his people. Like thousands of other Jews, he had had to give up his job, his fortune, his family, and finally his name. He was running away with a passport bearing a false name, a name he hadn't been able to get used to. He couldn't even answer the question, "What's your destination?" Perhaps he avoided it because he didn't know if he was going to his death. He had decided to terminate his life if he was caught and had already taken the necessary precautions. But what if he should be saved? He would first of all have to keep the promise he had given to someone dear, a promise he considered sacred. And after keeping that promise, he might eventually be able to devote his knowledge, his experience, and his findings to the benefit of humanity.

The train rattled on through forests of oak and beech, rumbling over narrow bridges connecting high slopes, curving around hills and through deep valleys.

The evening set in. The occupants of the compartment brought down their food baskets, and since supplies were diminishing, they shared what was left. They opened one of David's bottles of Rhine wine.

"Isn't there any red wine left?" asked Marcel.

"I'm afraid not. We've only got white. If there are many more delays, we'll have to do without wine with our dinner," replied David.

"Dinner? You call this just dinner? For someone who had to hide away crouched in the rafters of a house for twelve days, this is a banquet," Monsieur Asseo said.

Marcel felt embarrassed. True, he and Constance had had to keep on the move from place to place, from one house to another, but they certainly hadn't had to hide in a cramped loft. He realized they had been lucky. At least they had leftover dry cake, a bit of cheese, and stale bread to eat.

They had been eating dry food, and Fazıl, like everyone else, had become constipated. He kept crying from the discomfort.

"If we do stop in a town or village, we should get some fresh vegetables and fruit," Selva said to her husband.

"Don't tell me you're planning to cook spinach!"

"Don't make fun of me, Rafo. I'm serious. We should get some salad, fresh eggs, and some tomatoes at least."

"I don't know that the soldiers on this train would let us do that."

"Why not? We can offer them some as well."

"I'll see what I can do. I'll talk to one of them. The dark one appears to be in charge."

The passengers were getting tired and bored as the train continued its journey, shaking them around. The clouds were rather low in the sky.

"I think it's going to rain," said Margot. "It's getting darker."

"It's getting dark because it's late, not because it's going to rain," said David.

"How lovely! Another day over," said Selva.

They had been traveling for nine days. Sometimes, they had to wait for hours; sometimes they stopped overnight. They'd changed route: south, north, then south again. They'd even had to change engines. Sometimes, they didn't know where or when the next stop would be. One thing was certain: slowly but surely, at the pace of a tortoise, they were heading toward their destination.

"This is just like playing blind man's bluff," David said. "It's as if they're blindfolding us: we move on, and then we remove the blindfolds, and presto! We're in an unexpected town or city."

"Well, it's time for me to say good night," Asseo said, closing the backgammon board. "Let's see where we'll be in the morning."

"We must be very near Bucharest now. If there are no diversions, we should be crossing the Bulgarian frontier by the morning," said Margot.

"Thank God. This torment is coming to an end!"

"Don't be too optimistic," Margot said. "Don't you remember that night when we thought we'd wake up in Leipzig and found ourselves God knows where?"

"Yes, and I also remember that night when we went to sleep thinking we would wake up in Romania. You were so happy when you woke up and realized that we were still in Hungary. You burst into tears of joy."

"Since there's no possibility of going back to Hungary, let's hope all this is over pretty soon. Aaagh…" moaned Monsieur Asseo. He was clutching at his left side.

Siegfried jumped out of his seat, got his bag down from the rack, and took out some medicine.

"What's that?" asked Margot.

"I have the same problem sometimes. Can I have some water, please?" He added a few drops of medicine to half a glass of water, and offered it to his friend.

"Why don't you lie down, Monsieur Asseo?" proposed Selva. "I'll sit the children somewhere else."

"Please don't. I'm fine. It's just wind, I suppose, right here, that's all."

"I just hope to God the wind inside me doesn't come out. If it does it'll stink like hell," David whispered in Marcel's ear.

"The toilet stinks as well. We've all had enough of this," Marcel said.

On Selva's insistence, they stretched Asseo out on the seat with his head in his friend's lap and his legs on Perla and Samuel.

"Please don't worry about anything. Try to get some sleep. I've got the medicine in my pocket in case you have more pain," said Siegfried.

The rest of the passengers were finally lulled to sleep as the train continued through the night.

Constance was woken in the middle of the night by the sound of snoring. All her fellow passengers seemed to be in a deep sleep induced by the *clickety-clack*'s lullaby. She quietly jumped over her husband's feet and crept outside. She decided to use the toilet while everyone was asleep and there was no line. She entered it and held her head briefly under the dripping tap water that smelled of rust. When she came out, her hands and face were still wet. The corridor was dark, and she could see the yellow, melon-colored moon in the sky. It looked like a loaf of bread that had been bitten into. Oh, how she longed to bite into a fresh loaf of bread. She opened the window for a breath of fresh air, but when she realized how icy cold it was, she closed it again. She pressed her forehead against the window and looked at the pointed, flat silhouettes of the mountains. Backlit by the moon, they formed dark-blue shadows. How lovely, she thought to herself. I'm just standing here as nature is parading herself outside.

The heat in the carriage seemed to envelop her whole body: the palms of her hands were burning, and she lifted her arms, resting them on the window to feel the cold dampness. She remained in that position for a while until she felt someone breathing on the back of her neck. A pair of hands held her hips tightly and a body pressed against her.

"Marcel," she said. "Oh, Marcel…"

She tried to turn her head, but Marcel held her head with one hand and held her arms up with the other against the window. Constance had missed her husband very much; she loved him kissing the back of her neck, his tongue caressing her neck, feeling his breathing all over her hair. She resisted when he tried to go further.

"Marcel, don't. Not here. Please don't—someone might want to go to the toilet."

Marcel forcefully lifted her skirt with his knee. Constance wanted her husband both to stop and to continue. What if someone should come out into the corridor?

"Don't, I said!"

But deep inside, she wanted him to continue, not to stop at all. When her husband let go of her hands to pull her underwear down, she tried to turn her head toward him, but she was pushed violently against the window. My God! she thought. My God! This isn't Marcel. This isn't my husband!

They struggled madly in front of the window; while holding her head tightly with one hand, the stranger put his other hand over her mouth to stifle her screams. She tried to bite the hand over her mouth without success. Her panties were around her knees, and the buttons of his pants were already undone. She realized that he must have followed her, fully prepared…

"My God!" she screamed with all her might—"Aaagh!"—but the muffled sound disappeared in the noise of the train. She moved her hips from side to side trying to escape his clutches, but she was getting weaker.

David, meanwhile, was in a cell, asleep on the straw among smelly feet. It was pitch-dark. Everywhere was covered in a blanket of darkness. He was just like an animal in a pen. The straw smelled of dampness and dried dung.

David opened his eyes; the darkness around him was like a wall. He jumped from his seat, tripped on Fazıl's toy train, and fell on Selva.

"Oops!"

"Shush, Fazıl's asleep. Everyone's asleep. It's all right, you can get through."

David felt his way to the door and stepped into the corridor. He was breathing heavily and went to open the window. He needed the cold air to wake him up and bring him back to his senses, to save him from the nightmare he had just had.

He walked toward the window. What was that? A voice. Was someone groaning? He smiled to himself. Obviously basic instincts overcame these circumstances. Then, as he started to walk back to his compartment, he realized that the groaning had an edge to it.

"Help, please help me..."

The muffled sound obviously came from a woman. He moved toward it. In the moonlit corridor, he could see a heavily built man running away. He began to run after him, but he tripped over something. A woman was lying on the floor. He knelt down.

"My God! Constance!"

She was trembling under the window, her knees to her chest and her arms around her legs.

"What happened?"

Constance tried to explain, but she was sobbing. David couldn't understand what she said.

"Did that man do something to you?"

Constance nodded yes.

"Who was it? Did you recognize him?"

Constance shook her head no.

She was now pitifully sobbing her heart out. David put his arms around her and stroked her hair. "Now, now, it's over, it's all over. Please calm down. Let's wash your face. Please don't cry."

They heard a noise and both looked up. Marcel was standing right there, looking at them, dumbfounded.

The train continued its journey. All the passengers in the compartment except Constance woke up one by one to a new day. Constance slept by the window with her knees pulled up to her chest and her raincoat over her. Asseo felt fine this morning, but not Marcel. He couldn't settle at all. He went back and forth to the toilet, up and down the corridor, smoking. Siegfried was quiet as usual, and so was David.

Selva and Margot got the food baskets down again and prepared a breakfast of bitter coffee that had been left at the bottom of the thermos, boiled eggs, bread, and some honey they'd purchased from local peasants the previous day.

"Monsieur Asseo, you mustn't miss breakfast today," Selva said. "The honey is delicious and has a beautiful scent of flowers."

"So do you, madame, you're as sweet as honey."

Selva blushed even though the man was nearly eighty. Who knew? Maybe he wasn't that old. Sometimes difficult circumstances added years to a person's appearance.

Ferit and Evelyn came for a visit. Had it not been for that incident in Berlin, Ferit would have given his wife a seat with Selva and Margot so they could keep each other company, but since that night Evelyn hadn't wanted to be separated from Ferit at all.

"Please take my seat, madame," said David, getting up and offering it to Evelyn. "I'll go sit in your place. You stay here as long as you like."

"Just a moment, David. I need to talk to you all," said Ferit. "We're approaching Bucharest. We'll be disconnected from this freight train when we get there. Apparently we're to be connected to another passenger train from there. I want to tell those of you who want to get off that we'll have just about half an hour in the station."

"Fine," said David. "I'll try to get some wine. I can do with a drink."

"I've noticed you're not quite yourself today," said Margot. "I guess you've had it, like all of us."

"And how!"

As David walked to Evelyn's compartment, he bumped into Marcel.

"Do you have a second?" Marcel asked.

"Yes, of course. What's the matter?"

"I just don't understand how you weren't able to see the guy, David."

"I've told you a hundred times. I just saw him from the back as he was running away."

"What color were his clothes? Was he wearing a uniform?"

"I told you, it was very dark. He must have been wearing dark clothes. He was well built. That's all I noticed, he was big."

"There are exactly forty-nine well-built guys in this carriage."

"Don't tell me you've been checking all the compartments. Have you gone crazy?"

"I just have to find the bastard."

"Look, Marcel, he must have been one of the soldiers. Who else would do such a thing unless he was a sex maniac? What the hell can you do? Are you going to ask the soldiers who raped your wife?"

"Why not?"

"Marcel, I beg you, control yourself. Otherwise you'll get us all into trouble. We've only got a couple of days left on this train. Be reasonable, for God's sake. Suppose for just one moment that one of them admits to the crime. What will you do then? You can't beat him up."

"Who says I can't?"

"If you do, you'll put us all into a situation; all that we have gone through the past nine days will go for nothing, and we'll all rot in some Romanian prison. If you attack an SS officer, we might even be sent back to a prison camp in Germany. Would you like me to remind you just what that's like?"

"Maybe I should punch you in the face," said Marcel.

"You've gone crazy," said David, pushing Marcel aside and walking away.

Why the hell do I bring on all this aggravation, he thought. Is it because I don't pray on the Sabbath?

When the train stopped in Bucharest, everyone started rushing out of their compartments. The German SS officers were standing in the corridor and tried to stop them from getting off.

"Halt! Halt!" they yelled.

"What do they want now?" asked one of the women.

"It seems they have to get off first," Ferit explained. "They need to disconnect the carriage, and we'll get off later. After it's been disconnected, they'll shunt this carriage to a different platform."

"Hey there, Marcel! Didn't you hear them? Where are you going?"

"To the toilet."

Marcel stopped in front of the exit door. The soldiers walked toward the door laughing, joking among themselves.

One of them made signs toward Marcel and spoke in German, "Don't get off now! Later, later," he said. He was a handsome young man.

Marcel nodded with his head to show that he understood. He spotted the tallest and biggest among them. The handsome soldier got off first, then another one followed him, and then the big man. Marcel put his foot out to trip him and he fell onto his head. The following man bumped into him as he fell over as well. Marcel saw the second soldier's rifle stab into the big guy's neck. He quickly ran into the toilet and locked the door.

They arrived in Bulgaria somewhat depleted. Forty-seven passengers had disembarked in Bucharest to continue their journey to Köstence. Ferit had gotten off the train to try to speed up the disconnecting of their carriage. He couldn't understand why the soldiers, who seemed to be in a huff, were taking their time. Eventually he had to sacrifice their last jar of coffee as a bribe to get them to get a move on.

This endless journey was coming to an end. The Bulgarian frontier had been notified of their arrival. This time, they weren't thoroughly searched. Ferit as usual had collected half the passports, Rafo the other half, and the passports were stamped.

The policeman told them, "You are not allowed to stop within the Bulgarian borders; you have to travel straight through."

Who the hell would want to stop here, Ferit thought; mischievously, he said, "Not even if there's an emergency?"

"What, is there someone ill on board?"

"No, there's not."

"There aren't any contagious diseases?"

"Of course not. What on earth made you ask that?"

"So why did you ask that question?"

I wish I'd kept it to myself, he thought.

"It was just a joke," he replied.

"It's no joke. These days wounded soldiers can die on board and spread diseases. If that happens, you must definitely inform the authorities. You should pull the emergency cord."

Ferit interrupted, "We have no soldiers in our carriage. There are only men, women, and children, all looking forward to getting back to their homeland as soon as possible. You can have a look if you like. I was only joking." Ferit was suddenly covered in sweat.

The man looked thoughtful; he was obviously a stickler for rules and regulations. "Fine, take your passports back."

Ferit ran all the way back to the carriage. On board, he stood in the middle of the corridor and called out, "Right then, there's no stopping until we reach Edirne. No getting off, and no dying. Is that clear?"

All the passengers applauded heartily. Until Edirne…Edirne…EDIRNE…No city in the whole world sounded better to their ears. Edirne meant liberation. It meant reaching their goal. It meant peace. A new beginning, a rebirth!

The train pulled away. The passengers were full of joy. Only Constance was still sad. She hadn't gotten off the train in Bucharest and had had nothing to eat all day.

"You don't look at all well. I wonder if you have a fever," said Margot, putting her hand on Constance's forehead. "Anyway, we're almost there. I'm sure you'll feel much better once we get to Edirne tonight."

"What's the matter?" asked Selva.

Constance didn't reply. She closed her eyes and pretended to be asleep.

Margot and Selva left the compartment to pay Evelyn a visit.

"I think there's something going on between Marcel and his wife," Margot said. "They haven't spoken a word to each other all day."

"I don't think so," said Selva. "If they'd had an argument or something, surely we would have heard it. You can't even sneeze in there without everybody knowing."

David was smoking by the window.

"David, you're smoking like a chimney today," said Margot. "I hope you'll be opening that wine you got in Bucharest."

"I didn't get any."

"What! Why not? Weren't they selling any at the station?"

"I didn't ask."

This journey seems to have got to everyone, thought Margot. How strange. One would have thought that the nearer we got to our destination the happier everyone would be, but it seems to be just the opposite.

Everyone had settled back in their own compartments now, the euphoria felt by all when they had entered Bulgaria having disappeared.

Marcel didn't want to play backgammon, David was sour faced, and Constance kept dozing off in her corner. The atmosphere was heavy.

"Monsieur Asseo," said Selva, "would you do me a favor?"

"Anything for you, madame."

"It seems to me the atmosphere in here needs lifting. What would you say if David got your violin down from the rack and you played something for us?"

"With pleasure," said the old man.

David reached up and got the violin down. Asseo stood up in the middle of the compartment and nodded to everyone.

"Beethoven's Concerto in D Major," he said, resting the violin under his chin. He started to play.

There was something magical in Asseo's performance. The moment he started playing, he captivated his audience, transporting them to their own worlds. Maybe each note took them back to themselves, helping them solve questions about their new lives. Constance turned her head away again, looking outside. Tears started running down her cheeks. Marcel ran his hands tenderly through her hair, stroking her head gently. David sighed deeply.

The train was traveling at speed. Asseo played the violin as he had done all his life, with love and passion. Suddenly he remembered the time when he performed as a soloist at the Vienna Opera House on New Year's Day. He was playing the same concerto, to a full house. The place was packed with aristocrats, elegant ladies, and young music lovers. They were all in awe. He had begun the *allegro ma non troppo* with enthusiasm, then playing more slowly and deeply, evoking fairies cavorting in deep forests...His violin was resting on a pristine white handkerchief, his bow in his right hand, his fingers caressing the strings, and his body swaying to the rhythm of the music. He dabbed sweat from his brow during a moment's rest, then continued again with the larghetto, slow, quiet, relaxing, as if he were swimming in the warm sea with long, slow strokes; he didn't even look at the notes, playing, playing...the rondo, now faster, more enthusiastically; now he was a large white bird with white wings, flying, forming big white circles against the blue sky, among the clouds, round and round...The last note! The grand finale! The whole house is on its feet, the whole of Vienna; the applause is endless, and the conductor congratulates him to more applause..."Bravo, maestro! Bravo, maestro!" they call. He's bowing to the audience, again and again, as the applause grows distant, quieter...

Siegfried jumped up suddenly from his seat; "My God! My God!"

David and Marcel also jumped up, then the women stood. Asseo's head was bent forward as if bowing to them at first, then his head bent further and further until he finally collapsed to the floor. They tried to lift him up to the seat, but when they couldn't manage, they let him lie where he was. Siegfried kneeled next to his friend and touched two fingers to his temple. Selva screamed, "Monsieur Kohen!"

Siegfried was sitting on the floor. He nodded, tears streaming down his face. He lifted his friend's body carefully, resting the balding head on his chest, and cradled Asseo in his arms like a baby, rocking him gently.

"We must stop the train immediately," said Ferit. "I must report this."

"Wait. Please don't stop the train."

"But we have to, Monsieur Kohen."

Siegfried rested Asseo's head on the floor as if settling an infant in its crib; he stood up and took Ferit's hands in his own. Everyone around them held their breath.

"Monsieur Ferit, I beg you not to stop the train. I don't want to abandon his body on Bulgarian soil. I don't want a Bulgarian hand laid on him. We've only got a few hours to go. We can report this after we've crossed the border in Edirne. It's just a few hours. Please don't let the Fascists touch him, strip him, and take possession of his belongings. I beg of you."

Ferit stopped. As if one, all eyes were upon him. Constance, Selva, Margot, David, the children, everyone's pleading eyes.

"Fine, Monsieur Kohen, but nobody should know about this, otherwise we will all be in trouble. It's a crime not to report a death," he said, staring back at the eyes one by one.

"He was sleeping," said Margot. "How are we to know that he died in his sleep?"

They picked up Asseo carefully and rested his body on the seat.

"Put his head on my lap," said Siegfried, sitting back in his place. Siegfried closed Asseo's eyes, as if he was stroking them, then he lifted the hand hanging down, kissed it affectionately, and left it to rest on his chest.

Margot took her red coat from around her shoulders and covered Asseo. The others sitting on the seat where Asseo lay sat perched on its edge or squeezed onto the opposite seat.

The train continued its journey. The notes of Asseo's concert still flowed inside the compartment. They were all sitting together, still listening to the music he had played to them, letting it warm them deeply in their hearts. They were Asseo's last friends.

A uniformed Bulgarian official walked into the compartment and saluted. "We're approaching the border. I want you all to line up with your passports and tickets when we stop," he said.

They were all dumbstruck. "Our passports are with a friend in another compartment," Marcel said politely.

"Why is that?"

"He's in charge of our group. I'll go get him if you don't mind." Marcel walked shakily to Ferit's compartment.

"Is he asleep?" asked the official, nodding toward Asseo.

"Yes, he's sleeping."

"Wake him up."

"He's only just dropped off," said Margot. "He didn't sleep at all last night."

"He can sleep again later."

Ferit and Rafo came in together; they both looked shattered.

"Here are the passports," said Ferit.

"Fine. I want you all to get off the train once it stops. We're almost there; we're slowing down now."

"No one has asked us to do that since we left Paris," said Ferit. "We even passed through Berlin."

"That may be so, gentlemen, but you have been traveling through occupied countries—France, Czechoslovakia, Hungary—these days they're all considered Germany. Now you're entering a different country. This is what one calls a real border."

"I understand. Why don't you carry on your work in the other carriages while I sort things out here," Ferit said, playing for time but not really knowing why. Was he to jeopardize everyone's safety just to keep Asseo on board for another ten minutes?

David got up and whispered in Ferit's ear, "Let's offer him a bribe." Ferit nervously lit a cigarette by the window.

"How? Do you mean money?"

"Why not? Money, wine. I'll even sacrifice my Moselle."

"Let me see," said Ferit.

"Monsieur Kohen said he could offer money."

"Fine. We'll see."

Ferit threw the butt of his cigarette out of the window and looked out. Already there were some passengers from the other carriages standing by the train. Ferit reluctantly returned to the door of the compartment.

"Right then, everybody off!" he announced.

No one moved.

"Do you want that inspector to force you to get off?"

Ferit turned to Siegfried and pleaded, "Monsieur Kohen, will you please leave Monsieur Asseo where he is and get off the train."

Marcel, Constance, Selva with her son in her arms, Margot, Samuel, and Perla left the compartment.

"Would you like me to stay, Monsieur Ferit?" asked David. "I mean, can I be of any help?"

"No, thank you, David. You go ahead. Monsieur Kohen, come with me."

David left the compartment too. Ferit got frustrated when he realized Siegfried wasn't about to move. "Believe me, I do sympathize with you, but surely you can understand my situation too."

"You think you understand, monsieur, but you don't. I know that you intend to bribe the inspector and you need to be alone with him, but I wish to remain behind so I can raise the amount if necessary. I can raise it until he can't refuse!"

The inspector was approaching the compartment just as Margot was about to get off. Suddenly she decided to return, bumping into the inspector in the doorway. She took his hands in hers.

"Will you please help me," she pleaded. "The old man lying on the seat is my father. He's extremely ill. He was in pain, so we gave him a sleeping pill to help him sleep. I beg of you, don't wake him up now. We've only got a couple of hours' journey left. If you force him to get up, he might not make it. Please allow him to stay where he is. Even if he shouldn't last the journey, let him at least die in his own country."

The inspector looked at Asseo from where he stood in the doorway and walked toward him. Weak at the knees, Margot could hardly breathe. For a split second she and Ferit made eye contact. All the color had drained from Ferit's face. Suddenly, the inspector stretched out his hand and lightly stroked the red coat covering Asseo.

"Beautiful coat," he said. "It's so soft. Is this what they call cashmere?"

Margot moved between the inspector and Asseo. "I'd love to make a present of it to you in gratitude for not disturbing my father." She removed the coat from the corpse. "Please take it; you can give it to your wife or daughter, perhaps, maybe your girlfriend. I know I can't give it to you here in front of everyone, but I will forget it in the customs area." She put the coat around her shoulders. "Now, please be kind enough to take me to customs."

When Margot left with the inspector, Siegfried rested Asseo's head on the seat, got his raincoat from the rack above, covered Asseo with it, and left the compartment. Ferit followed him, shutting the compartment door firmly.

The train pulled out of the station as soon as the formalities were completed. It wasn't long before Selva screamed with joy, "*Kapikule!*" The train moved very slowly, and then stopped.

Ferit stepped out into the corridor and shouted, "Welcome to Turkey!" as loudly as he could. Everyone applauded, hugging and kissing each other, their eyes filled with tears. Some shook hands, congratulating each other, others screamed with joy. Selva's compartment was the only one where there was no sign of enthusiasm. Not even the radiant Turkish sun shining through the window was enough to disperse the melancholy.

Ferit greeted the policeman and the customs officer at the door as they boarded the train.

"I'm afraid we have some sad news," he said. "One of our fellow travelers has passed away."

"Our condolences," said the customs officer.

"Should we inform the frontier garrison?"

"No," said the policeman, "this has nothing to do with them. They are not here anyway; they are off playing soccer right now. We'll do whatever's necessary. Don't you worry."

After carefully supervising Asseo's removal on a stretcher, Siegfried took down Asseo's violin case and suitcase, and then his own belongings.

"My friends," he said, "what a pity that I've got to bid you farewell now. I hope to God that our paths cross again. I thank you with all my heart." He hugged each and every person in the compartment. Then he offered Margot Asseo's violin. "Please accept this from me, mademoiselle," he said. "It's a precious violin. Even if you can't play it yourself, maybe one day in the future your children might."

Margot was taken aback. "You shouldn't do this, Monsieur Kohen," she said. "Really you shouldn't. This is far more precious than my coat, I couldn't..."

"You'd make me very happy if you did. It has nothing to do with your coat...It's simply a humble token of my gratitude."

"But this is a Stradivarius! Surely Monsieur must have some relatives, maybe..."

"He does," said Siegfried. "Only one brother—and that's me."

The train set off on its journey from Edirne to Istanbul with two fewer passengers. Selva handed over her son to his father, rolled her jacket up like a pillow, lay down, and closed her eyes. Why couldn't she feel happy? She didn't want to cry, as if there mightn't be anyone to meet them at the station. It was as though she were empty inside, as though her nerves had gone and she could feel nothing. All she knew was that she was tired, very tired. Not physically tired, but tired of having chosen to live in exile...

The train was finishing its journey through its homeland. The *clickety-clack, clickety-clack* was like a lullaby and sent Selva to sleep.

"Look, Selva, isn't that the ancient Sinan bridge?" asked Constance.

"Selva is sleeping," said Margot. "She's been talking in her sleep."

❧

Selva was now on one of the Princes' Islands in the Sea of Marmara. She seemed to have been transported back to her youth and was following Sabiha through some pine trees.

Just as Selva was catching up, Sabiha kept dodging behind the trees. The skirt of Sabiha's dress was billowing like froth in the wind.

Each time Selva got near enough to reach out for the hem, her hands clutched at nothing but thin air.

"Selva can't catch me! Selva can't catch me!" Sabiha taunted, disappearing in and out of the trees. Sabiha's dress suddenly turned to pomegranate red. Selva almost caught up to her, but just then her sister turned into a pomegranate-colored butterfly. Selva still ran after the butterfly as it flew away.

She fell over a cliff, down and down into a bottomless abyss. Finally, when she reached the bottom, her father was standing there with his arms wide open. Selva was screaming, "Father, catch me… Catch me, Father!"

"Selva, my love, wake up. Wake up, we're almost there."

"Almost where?" she said, looking at Rafo with startled eyes.

"Istanbul, Sirkeci Station, of course."

"What?"

She sat up straight and blinked her eyes. She could see the iron columns of the station, and there was that familiar smell, that blend of sea and seaweed, the smell of Istanbul. The train was approaching the station slowly, almost like a coquettish bride dragging her veil.

The lines and colors of the city that Selva had missed so much; the outlines that reflected the Selcuk style; the crowds at the station with its colorful stained-glass windows typifying the mystic atmosphere one associates with the East; the porters almost crushed by the heavy loads secured on their backs by ropes. There were gentlemen in fedora hats and double-breasted jackets, men in breeches, ladies wearing hats and scarves, cheeky children being spoiled by their mothers, and of course the *simit* sellers. When she spotted those *simit* sellers, tears started streaming down her cheeks.

The platform was extremely crowded. It was like thousands of hands swaying together. Selva scanned the crowd anxiously…

No, he'd never come. Wasn't he, after all, the one who had remonstrated with her in front of the big mirror in the sitting room, saying, "You've not only disappointed me. You have also turned six centuries of tradition upside down!" Surely he wouldn't come! Some children were yelling at each other, a few pigeons fluttered their wings, a grandmother was greeting her grandchildren, two lovers hugged each other…Suddenly, in the distance, she spotted Sabiha in her fuchsia two-piece suit. Her mother was standing next to her. They were waving their white handkerchiefs to attract her attention. Leon, Rafo's brother, was standing behind them; he didn't seem to know what to do with his hands, and placed them firmly in his pockets. He stood stiffly with a cigarette in his mouth. Selva searched the platform: he hadn't come.

She lowered her head so that no one would see her disappointment. Extinguishing that spark of hope in her heart was painful. Why had she hoped anyway? Didn't she know how similar she and her father were, both with that strong-willed character that never went back on a decision? Had she not had endless arguments with her father over his opposition to the formation of the republic, despite his secretly offering money for the troops during the war of independence in Anatolia? He was in awe of Atatürk, but his loyalty lay with the sultan. Sabiha used to tell them off: "Don't tell me that you're back on that same old subject again! Don't you ever get tired of arguing and not coming to any conclusion?" They never tired. Selva continuously pointed out that their father's progressive ideas about freedom suited the republic's ideals, while Fazıl Reşat Paşa never stopped insisting that it was wrong to end the sultanate. They had argued for hours.

When Selva pleaded for her father's blessing to marry Rafo, she used the same logic she had learned from him. But deep inside, she knew he would never give his consent. When she sat at his bedside after his humiliating attempt at suicide, she knew he would never forgive her. She could never forget how, when he had recovered, he'd opened his eyes and looked at his family gathered around the bed, but closed his eyes when he saw her. He'd not only closed his eyes, but closed his heart, forever. Selva wondered if her decision to leave the country had been encouraged by this attitude. Could it be that she had decided to leave because she couldn't bear to be ignored by her father? God knew how often she had thought this through. Before falling asleep in her husband's arms, she had thought about it hundreds—no, thousands—of times. Once Rafo's passionate thrusting was over and he held her affectionately, she forgot her passion for him and opened the window of longing for her father. Sometimes she'd think about him until the early hours of the morning. Missing him, longing for his love and care, her heart breaking into pieces.

She'd paid a high price for offending her father, but she was never able to talk about her bitterness with Rafo or anybody else. What was the name of that stout German man, the one working for the immigration department in Istanbul? Until the day he had informed her of her father's concern, she hadn't hoped for forgiveness, even though, from time to time, she'd said to Rafo, "It may all settle down one day." But now she began to realize that forgiveness and concern were two entirely different things. Fazıl Reşat Paşa would do all he could to carry out his fatherly duties, but that was all. She had hoped in vain. She could still vividly remember that awful echoing sound, the shattering of the gigantic mirror and the china vases in the living room. That sound, similar to the shrill sound of a soprano, still echoed in her ears. Surely her father, who had broken those rare objects as if breaking the ties that held them together, wouldn't meet her at the station. No, he wouldn't.

Rafo passed Fazıl to Selva so that she could show him to her mother, who was standing behind the glass partition by the exit.

She tried to pull herself together and lifted her son high up for her mother to see. It was just then that she noticed a gray-haired gentleman, holding a cane, waiting farther away from the crowd. He was leaning against one of the cast-iron columns in the distance, without moving a muscle.

ACKNOWLEDGMENTS

Last Train to Istanbul is not based on the lives of real characters. It is based on the experiences related by a number of Turkish diplomats who were posted to Europe during the Second World War. They succeeded in saving many Turkish and non-Turkish Jews from Hitler's grasp. There were also the experiences related by a young Turkish man who was a member of the French Resistance.

I cannot fully express my gratitude to the now deceased Ambassadors Namık Yolga and Necdet Kent, may they rest in peace. They devoted so much of their precious time to recalling their experiences, which enabled me to write this novel. I sincerely hope that their honorable careers may be seen as an example to all young diplomats.

Special thanks are also due to Mr. Robert Lazare Rousso and his wife for recounting both their experiences and hardships in a labor camp and their train journey. My gratitude also goes to Mrs. Luiz Behar for telling me about her experiences aboard a Star and Crescent carriage during her journey back to Istanbul.

For his general assistance in my research, I would like to acknowledge the counselor of the 500 Year Trust, Mr. Harry Ojalvo, who provided me with various rare documents. Thanks are also due to Naim Guleryüz and my dear friends Rahmi Aktaş and Jak deLeon, who helped me greatly in contacting a number of people who provided me with documents and photographs. I'd also like to thank Ambassador Taylan İzmirli, who related valuable facts over the telephone. And I'd be remiss if I didn't mention Meyzi Barın, Ayda Köseoğlu, and Engin, who read the book chapter by chapter and enthusiastically encouraged me to continue.

And finally, in a novel drawing so heavily on the struggle of the Turkish diplomats to save innocent people from the Gestapo, I have to express my special thanks to Lale Akkoyunlu Bulak, whose assistance in drawing my attention to the events of the time was instrumental in the writing of this book, as well as to the unsung hero Faruk Sayar and the trains sent by the Turkish government.

Below is a list of books I have used as references for the political and social aspects of my novel, including the discussions that took place between the leading politicians during those years:

Kâmuran Gürün, and Tekin Yayınevi, *Savaşan Dünya ve Türkiye 1939–1945*.

Kâmuran Gürün, *Selim ile Celiné*

Altan Öymen, *Bir Dönem Bir Çocuk*

Moris Karako, *Kalderon Ailesi*

Jak DeLeon, *Eski Istanbul'un Yaşayan Tadı*

Gülseren Engin, *Cehennemde Bir Ada*

Various booklets, documents, and newspaper clippings provided by the 500 Year Trust.

For this English edition, I would like to thank my translator, John W. Baker, who, with his unsurpassed knowledge of Turkish, has enabled my book to come alive in English. My thanks too to Tony Readwin, who skillfully helped John W. Baker edit this edition.

ABOUT THE AUTHOR

One of Turkey's bestselling and most beloved authors, with more than ten million copies of her books sold, Ayşe Kulin is known for captivating stories about human endurance. In 2011, *Forbes Turkey* declared her the country's top-earning author. In addition to penning internationally bestselling novels, she has also worked as a producer, cinematographer, and screenwriter for numerous television shows and films. A mother to four sons, she lives in Istanbul. *Last Train to Istanbul,* winner of the European Council Jewish Community Best Novel Award, has been translated into 23 languages and is the author's second publication in English, following *Farewell.*

ABOUT THE TRANSLATOR

John W. Baker spent his formative years living in Istanbul due to his father's posting and was educated at the English High School for Boys there. Following in his father's footsteps, he had a career with the Foreign and Commonwealth Office in London until he took early retirement to live in Turkey again. He is honored to have been the first British writer to have written a play in Turkish, *Ihtiras (Passion)* which was produced in 2003 by Gencay Gurun and was voted as one of the best five new plays that year. The success of *Ihtiras* led to favorable publicity resulting in Baker being asked by Ayşe Kulin to translate two of her novels, *Last Train to Istanbul* and *Bir Gun (Face to Face)*.

Other translations followed, including *Theodora* by Radi Dikici, about the Byzantine Empress, and most recently, *Unfulfilled Promises* by Leyla Yildirim, a love story set during the Gallipoli War.

Baker returned to live in England in 2010 and is now happy to be back living in London again and doing the occasional translation.